BROOMTAIL BASIN

The front window bellied in but did not break. Plates danced on the shelves. The Chinaman hollered, "Holy Sloke! Somebody shoot off cannon!"

They hit the street, Judge Lemanuel Bates in the lead, Tobacco Jones ahead of the Chinese cook. Dirt and debris filled the air. A wild-flying two-by-four, strips of siding still clinging to it, landed in the street not more than thirty feet away. Tarpaper floated in the air.

"Cannon, nothin'!" Tobacco growled. "That was dynamite."

TRAIL TO GUNSMOKE

Doc Buck hurled into hard and fast action. He hit Ron Powers below the knees with a flying tackle. His lunging drive sent Powers reeling. The rancher lost his footing and Doc Buck let him fall.

Hatchet John said: "Be careful, Doc. He's packin' a gun and he knows how to use it."

Doc Buck's fingers were taloned over the black grip of his dead father's Colt. For one moment, all hell hesitated, ready to break loose in roaring, flaming death.

LEE FLOREN

BROOMTAIL BASIN/ TRAIL TO GUNSMOKE

LEISURE BOOKS **L** NEW YORK CITY

A LEISURE BOOK®

April 1992

Published by

Dorchester Publishing Co., Inc.
276 Fifth Avenue
New York, NY 10001

The name "Leisure Books" and the stylized "L" with design are trademarks of Dorchester Publishing Co., Inc.

Printed in the United States of America.

BROOMTAIL BASIN

CHAPTER 1

Horses were running somewhere in the moonlight. And the measured rhythm of their hoofs against the parched Wyoming soil told Judge Lemanuel Bates that riders bestrode them.

For a range cayuse, running without a rider, does not seek a measured stride.

"Riders, to the north."

"Swingin' wide of us," Tobacco Jones stated.

The heavy-set jurist stood on stirrups, right hand braced on the surface of his whiskey-jug strapped to his kak's fork. Stretched like this, he could see over the tall sagebrush. Moonlight slanted in to glisten on the hammered-silver buckle that laced together the tie-thongs of his Stetson.

Tobacco Jones had also risen against his oxbows.

"Yonder they head, Bates." The postmaster jabbed a finger northeast. "Three of 'em, ain't they?"

"Four."

"Blast my buttons! You always argue with me. I still say *three* riders!"

The horsemen swept across the floor of Broomtail Basin, riding through the tall sagebrush, hitting across alkali flats marked by grotesque greasewood. They were about two hundred yards away.

They had come out of the moonlight-dappled hills that flanked the northen rim of Broomtail Basin. They seemed intent on putting plenty of sod between themselves and those northern hills.

One rider pulled ahead, a dark shadow separating from the darker bulk, and suddenly the riders broke apart, disappearing into the moonlight and the distance. The pound of their hoofs ran out and died.

Tobacco grunted. "You're right again, Bates. Four riders. An' did you mind how they fanned out like mebbe they aimed to break up an' ditch any pursuit?"

"I don't savvy this, Tobacco. Must be close to midnight, too."

A sudden roar jerked their gazes north. From the foothills flame lashed upward, ripping apart the still moonlight. The ground trembled under their broncs' hoofs. The flame lanced upward—a quick, ripping red—and then died.

"Dynamite," Judge Bates said.

Tobacco Jones' mule had reared. The postmaster put the beast's hoofs again on sod. "Them riders has set that powder. Used a long fuse an' got to Hades outa the country before the powder worked. Now who would blow up a hill?"

"Seems to me I saw lumber in that flame."

Tobacco speared a look at his companion. "Seems to me I saw the same. That means a cabin went up, huh?"

Judge Bates figured that if they'd wanted to blow up a cabin, they'd never have used so much powder. "Let's ride over and take a look, partner. It isn't more than a half-mile off, I'd say."

But Tobacco Jones did not consent. He pointed out that they had ridden into Broomtail Basin so that Judge Bates could sit on the bench of Judge Hostetler Mackenzie, who was injured and in bed They had not come in to find out who had dynamited what, and why.

"Had I figgered you'd gone huntin' trouble, Bates I'd've stayed home an' minded my post office. I come along with you to get in some fishin' an' to see some new country."

The postmaster's argument held logic, the jurist conceded. They turned their mules east again in the general direction of Wild Horse Town, the county seat of Broomtail County. That noon they had left

the railroad town of Diamond Willow and had intended to bed down at a ranch when night came.
But they had not run across a ranch, so they had
kept on riding.

"Wild Horse must be about fifteen miles yet,"
the judge said. "According to what that sheepherder
told us back in the hills, we'd hit a road along now.
All we have to do is follow it into Wild Horse, he
said."

Tobacco bit off a chew. "Sheepherders are crazy,
an' you know it. Otherwise, if'n they weren't loco,
they'd never herd sheep." This logic dispensed—
along with a brown squirt of tobacco-juice—the postmaster settled deep between horn and cantle, fitting
his lanky body to the sway and walk of his mule.

A quarter mile further, they found the wagon-
trail. It lay under the moonlight, dusty and pale,
twisting like a tired snake through the sagebrush
and greasewood. Cattle were bedded down around
springs and waterholes marked by boxelders and
chokecherry trees.

"I still wonder about that powder—" Judge Bates
pulled in his mule. "Are my ears right, friend?
Seems as if I hear riders."

Tobacco had also pulled rein. "I hear them.
Comin' this way—yonder, they hit the road, headin'
this direction."

Judge Bates counted six riders. He frowned, for he was puzzled; he was also sure this was a new bunch of riders. It had to be, for the other four he had seen would by this time be far across the basin.

"They're over there!" a man hollered.

The six riders, looking like puppets pulled by one string, swerved and converged down on them. A rifle-ball whistled over the pair's heads.

"Hold fire, you blamed idiots!" Judge Bates' voice held anger.

"Stay where you are," a man rasped. "We got our rifles on you men."

They had slowed to a walk. Now about a hundred yards away, they came up cautiously, spreading out as they approached. Judge Bates, his first anger gone, watched in puzzlement.

"I don't savvy it," Tobacco grumbled. "But them buttons better watch their rifle fire or they will get in trouble."

Now Judge Bates could see the six riders clearly. They were astride work-horses, some bearing collar-marks, and four were bareback. Each man carried a rifle and each had a pistol at his hip. And each rifle was on himself and his partner.

"Who threw that shot at us?" Judge Bates asked.

"I did!" The man was rawboned, and wore overalls and a faded shirt. "No man's blowin' up the

Great Western reservoir and' ridin free!"

Judge Bates glanced at Tobacco. The postmaster scowled and spat. The riders halted, still fanned-out, holding rifles.

"We heard the explosion," the judge said, "but we didn't blow up this reservoir, or whatever was blown up."

"We figger you did. You two look like cowmen. An' the cowboys don't want Great Western to run tracks in here."

Tobacco chewed. "I don't get the run of this," he finally said.

The judge was in a similar quandary. Only one thing was certain—these men meant business. He wasn't armed and neither was Tobacco.

Patiently he pointed out this fact. He admitted hearing the explosion and that he and his partner had seen four riders heading across Broomtail Basin. Those riders had been so far away and riding so fast they had not made out their faces. And, of course, they were strangers here.

"What's your handles? The rawboned man snapped the words.

"I'm Judge Lemanuel Bates, and this man is Tobacco Jones."

The rawboned man studied them.

"I've heard of Judge Bates," a man said. "But

this ain't him. I heard tell he was a long shoebutton, an' this runt is short an' heavy-set."

"Lots of gents travel under a 'judge' handle," the rawboned man claimed. "I knowed a gent onct they called Judge Lonnigan, an' he weren't no judge. What you got in that jug, fella?"

"Hard liquor."

"That settles it," the man stated. "A real judge wouldn't drink. We still figure you two was in on that dynamitin'."

The judge pointed out that that assumption was illogical. If he and Tobacco had helped put the dynamite, would they ride so slowly? And wouldn't they put up a fight when cornered?

"He's right," a rider conceded.

But the rawboned man was tenacious. "You two is ridin' mules. Mules can't run as fast as hosses. You might've figgered we'd catch you if'n you tried to escape—seein' our hosses, even if plow-hosses— can outrun a mule. These cowmen are hirin' some purty slick characters. I figger you saw you couldn't get away, so you stowed your weapons into your saddle-bags an' decided to play dumb."

"You possess a sterling imagination, sir."

"That could be so," a man grumbled.

Tobacco sat askew in saddle, hand on his open saddle-bag. Judge Bates said, "Don't fight them, friend." Tobacco drew his hand back. "Don't like to be shoved aroun' by these runts, Judge."

"Get movin'," the rawboned man ordered.

"Which direction?" Judge Bates asked.

"Straight down the trail. We're takin' you into Wild Horse to the sheriff. If'n your story is straight, an' you can prove it, then he'll turn you loose, of course. All right, hike them jassaxes along."

The rawboned man gave quick orders. Two men would ride between the judge and his partner. The other four—including himself—would trail them.

"You two men—ride atween these hellions. Let us boys have your rifles. Can't tell but they might grab a rifle outa your grip an' put up a fight. Us men who trail behind'll hold guns on them."

"We were heading for Wild Horse," the jurist said.

Tobacco smiled. "Never figgered the town would see us come in with a parade, though. This is kinda Egyptian to me, men. I wish you'd do some explainin'."

"You know enough. We don't need no explainin'."

The postmaster shrugged.

Judge Bates said, "Make no move toward weapons, Tobacco. Just humor the boys; they have to have their fun, you know. Anyway, they'll take us where we want to go, an' Judge Hoss Mackenzie will recognize us."

"You know Judge Mackenzie?"

"Friend of mine, Lantern Jaw."

"Maybe the gent is a judge," a man said, worried. "Maybe he'll put us all in the clink, Jocky."

"I still think they're lyin'."

"Me, I'm worried, Jocky. What that fat geezer said is right—cowboys who set off that powder wouldn't ride mules, either. They'd straddle fast broncs that could get them to hell an' gone in a hurry——"

"Shut up, Slim!"

"I still don't cotton——"

"We gotta play our cards, Slim."

Slim fell silent. They rode at a walk down the road. Tobacco started to reach in hs coat pocket. A man grabbed his arm.

"What're you diggin' for?"

"My eatin' terbaccker."

"Keep your hand outa that pocket. You might have a short-gun in there. I'll get your tobaccer for you."

The hand went in and came out with the plug.

"Service, Judge." Tobacco glared at his partner. "Now why don't you hold it for me, pal, while I bites off a chaw?"

The man held out the Horseshoe. Tobacco bit,

and his teeth ground down on the thumb. The man hollered. He jerked his hand back, leaving the plug in Tobacco's teeth. He pulled his arm back, fist balled.

Judge Bates grabbed his elbow. He almost unhorsed the man. "Go careful," he warned.

The men behind were laughing.

Tobacco bit off his chew and restored the plug to his pocket. They went on for a few miles with only the sounds of hoofs on the dust. Neither of the partners asked any more questions. That was useless. This would be cleared when they reached town.

Finally ahead of them reared the black bulk of buildings, evidently Wild Horse town. Jocky rode his horse even with that of Judge Bates.

"You was stuffin' about that iicker in that jug, huh? You got drinkin' water in that, h'ain't you?"

The judge assured him the jug held whiskey.

Jocky ran his tongue around his lips. "I'd admire a slug of it. We bin through a rough night. But don't you untie it, fella. Your hand'll be too close to your belt, an' you might have a gun cached there."

"You're trusting, sir."

Jocky leaned on one stirrup and attempted to untie the jug. But Judge Bates had pulled the strap tight to keep the jug from bouncing. The buckle was under the jug's handle, too.

Jocky leaned back, "You unstrap it, fella. But no monkey bizness, savvy?"

Judge Bates unstrapped the jug. He held it up. "What's that? Up ahead?"

Jocky swivelled his head. The jug came down and Jocky left his bronc. He sprawled in the dust, knocked cold.

Judge Bates drank. He lowered the jug with, "Now I feel better, Tobacco."

CHAPTER 2

Judge Lemanuel Bates, district judge of Cowtrail County, Territory of Wyoming, lay flat on his broad back, covers pulled over his protruding belly, and snored as if each snore were destined to save him from the gallows. But there was no sleep for Cowtrail's postmaster, one Tobacco Jones.

Lanky Tobacco Jones, chewing tobacco methodically, sat on the edge of his bunk, dressed only in his red underwear. He could stand it no longer. He got one of his socks and put it over the jurist's vibrating lips.

The snores ceased.

Judge Bates sat up, snatching at the sock, which had already fallen.

"Too bad I changed socks last week," Tobacco said soberly.

"I dreamt some button was choking me. What's

the matter?"

"Those snores. They woke me up."

"Why didn't you turn me on my side? You know I don't snore then."

"Like tryin' to turn a dead bull."

The judge lay down. He put his chubby hands behind his head and laced the fingers. "In jail. . . . Here I come to be judge and I land in jail."

Tobacco looked mournfully at the floor. "Don't mention it. It'll make my head ache again."

The whole proceedings had been mournful. After they had gotten Jocky back into leather, they'd headed into town, with the other members of Jocky's party muttering dire threats toward the partners. Jocky had sworn he was going to kill Judge Bates, but they had unloaded his rifle.

Because of the late hour, Wild Horse town had been in bed; the irate riflemen had unearthed Sheriff Will Brown out of his soogans. He had turned out to be a lanky, beanpole individual, with thin unshaven face made prominent by a beak-like nose, and his Adam's apple danced up and down his skinny neck.

"Who be you two customers?"

The judge stated their identity.

"Hell, I locked Judge Bates up in the calaboose, not more'n three nights ago. He was a short gent, too."

"Judge Bates is tall," a man said.

Judge Bates said, "Probably somebody impersonating me, Sheriff."

"Don't know if'n he was impersonatin'——" the sheriff stumbled over the word "——you, but he weren't Judge Bates. I run him outa the burg on a floater."

"He ain't Judge Bates," the man assured him.

"I can run my own bizness, Whitey." Sheriff Will Brown looked angrily at the partners. "Judge Bates —the *real* Judge Bates—is hailing into town sometime next week. Judge Hostetler Mackenzie done told me the real Judge Bates was takin' over his fall term of court. We'll throw you two jugheads into the clink an' when the real Judge Bates comes, then you face him, Fat Man, an' tell him you're Judge Bates. He'll give you twenty years for lyin'."

Tobacco said, "But——"

"No use, partner," Judge Bates said.

Sheriff Will Brown turned and called, "Jailer, come out!"

The sheriff's office was about fifty feet distant from the jail. Both buildings rested in the shadow of Wild Horse's courthouse—a rambling stone affair seemingly put up without a building plan, the way it ambled all over the block.

A head stuck through the pail door. "What is it, Sheriff?"

"Coupla customers here say they are Judge Bates. Throw them into the tank an' make it snappy."

The judge threatened to sue for false arrest.

"That's an ol' one," Sheriff Will Brown said.

The jailer—an old, bent-over ex-waddy, escorted them to a cell, and locked the door. Outside, Judge Bates heard, "Now tell me about this dynamitin', Jocky. You're a man of responsibility here an' your story will naturally be straight. . . ."

The voices trailed off as the men went into Sherff Brown's office.

Judge Bates, grinning, undressed and turned in, grumbling at the hard steel cot. Now, hands laced behind his head, he was almost smiling.

"Come morning, Tobacco, Judge Hoss Mackenzie will identify us. Then watch the fur fly."

"But the judge is sick in bed."

"We'll get to him, someway."

Tobacco started pacing the floor. "Bates, this is the last time I go any place with you. What starts out to be a peaceful trip turns into a riot. We went fishin' up north a while back, an' smack-dab we run into ol' Jed Lipp. We gets in trouble there. Then we goes up to Post Hole Valley to side—"

But the judge was snoring again.

Next morning the skinny jailer took in their breakfasts. Toast burned dry and black, coffee you couldn't dent with a spoon, eggs fried to crystal hardness. Sheriff Will Brown came in later.

"We demand an attorney," Judge Bates said.

"Went through your packs," Sheriff Brown said. "Couldn't find no credentials sayin' you was a judge, Fat Man. Rode out to that explosion, too. That dynamite just plumb blew that dam skyhigh. Blew up the guard's shack, too. That guard got slugged hard, but he come to."

"Greek to me," Tobacco said.

The judge said, "We demand an attorney."

"Only one shyster in this burg. He's County Attorney Delton Myers. You can't hire him, 'cause it's his duty to persecute you. You gotta be your own law-talker, fella."

Two cells down, the jail's only other occupant watched them, dirty hands braced on the bars. He and the partners had had a brief conversation about daylight. He was One-Step Connors, he had said; called One-Step because he had a game leg. He was in jail for mooching drinks.

"No bail?" the judge had asked.

"Don't want none," One-Step had assured him.

Now Judge Bates said, "Go tell Del Myers I want to see him."

For a moment indecision showed in Sheriff Will Brown's dog-like eyes. "You talk like you know Attorney Myers."

"Tell him to come down here."

Brown chewed thoughtfully on a dirty thumb-nail. "Maybe I bit off more'n I can chaw," he said reflectively. "Maybe I put too much accent on what Jocky Smith told me."

"I think you did," Tobacco growled.

Brown turned. "When Del Myers gets in his office, I'll send him over to see you."

The lawman left.

Tobacco sat down. The judge glanced at One-Step Connors.

"Now you see, sir, what justice is, in Broomtail Basin."

The judge queried with, "But Judge Hoss Mac-kenzie, sir, is noted for his fairness, his great judicial decisions. His verdicts, sir, have gone down into case record, and are studied in various universities. Take his brief on the great case, Worthington ver-sus MacCarty—"

"You know about that?" One-Step studied the jurist. "Did you ever go to law school?"

Judge Bates sat down, back to the prisoner. "Oh, hell."

Silence, except for the wind.

Finally One-Step said, "You look like a man of great abilities. Your face is jovial, your lips are those of a smiling man, and I would say you would be a connoisseur of liquor, an epicurean in taste. Your manner has that appearance. Myself being a graduate of a great eastern university—I shall not cast reflection upon that university by stating its name—"

Tobacco groaned. "Another educated drunk, Bates."

Judge Bates glared. "You imply, partner, I am a drunk!"

"Don't kick over your tugs, Bates."

"Bates? Then you are truly the great Judge Bates." One-Step was beaming, homely face lighted. "Long have I heard of you sir. It is a pleasure indeed. Were I closer, I'd shake your hand."

Silence.

"You would welcome a drink, Judge Bates?"

The judge got to his feet. "How would you get whiskey in jail?"

"My secret, sir."

One-Step had a flask. He slid it across the concrete in front of their cells. Judge Bates drank deeply.

"Wonderful whiskey, sir. Bottled in bond?"

"Bottled without bail." One-Step giggled. "Keep the bottle, sir, for I have another. Give a drop to your partner with my compliments?"

Tobacco growled, "He couldn't give me a drop if he got me down an' tried to get an eye-dropper atwixt my lips!"

One-Step's brows rose. "A teetotaler, I understand."

The judge asked questions.

The set-up according to One-Step Connors, was simple. The Great Western had built as far west as Rawhide, a town across the mountains. From Rawhide, rails would either go straight west, crossing Broomtail Basin, or they would swing northwest, going into Sagebrush Flats, and then across the Rockies on Bridger Pass.

"So far," Judge Bates said, "it is understandable."

"Broomtail Basin and Broomtail Divide is the shorter route, and the lower route—less grade would have to be made and therefore there would be fewer fills. But Broomtail Basin, because of the drought has no water."

"Who does this gent Jocky work for?" Tobacco asked. "The railroad, I figgered."

One-Step assured him his guess had been correct. "Jocky is head muleskinner and, being a well-digger by trade—or so he says—he is head of the well-diggers in this locality. He spudded down a well and built a reservoir to hold storage water—"

The partners nodded.

"The rest," said One-Step Connors, "should be apparent."

The judge agreed with him. He judged that the

neighboring cowmen did not want a railroad across their range. For, if the railroad came, then the farmers would flock in wth their women, kids, chickens, cows, and farming equipment.

"Precisely, sir."

Tobacco Jones took on from there. The cowmen had blown up the reservoir. Those four riders, fleeing from the explosion—they were cowmen.

One-Step took another drink. "I presume they were cowmen. The intelligence of Jock Smith, sirs, is a minus quality. But I myself have had no truck with this combat. Years ago I divorced myself from all earthly logic. I wanted, sirs, to retain my sanity."

"Maybe you're right," Judge Bates grunted.

"I am, sirs, of the cult that lives for the moment, not for tomorrow, for this afternoon, nor for yesterday. What man does on this foolish block of granite is irrelevant to the man called One-Step Connors."

One-Step sat on his bed and recited,

"A loaf of bread, a jug of wine,
And thou beside me, singing in the Wilderness,
Ah, Wilderness, were Paradise enow."

Judge Bates said, "Omar Khayyam."

"Correct. The Persian Bard."

Tobacco got to his feet. "This ain't gettin' us outa this flee-trap. This ain't—"

The door opened. Sheriff Will Brown came in with a nattily dressed, slender man of about forty.

"Here's County Attorney Del Myers," Sheriff Brown said.

Del Myers stared. Finally he croaked, "You idiot —you fool, Brown! This man—this is Judge Lemanuel Bates!"

CHAPTER 3

Judge Hostetler Mackenzie's thin head rested on a white pillow, the lips thin and bloodless, the nose Roman and pale. Beside his bed at his right was a tray that held nicely browned toast, a cup of coffee, and a dish of oatmeal covered with thick cream.

A squaw, evidently the cook, watched from the opposite doorway.

"Glad you got here, Judge Bates. And happy morning to you, Mr. Jones."

Tobacco Jones grunted something. Yeah, happy morning. In jail, burned toast, rock-hard coffee, and a drunk in an opposite cell. His eyes rested on the toast and he swallowed.

He had tried to get Judge Bates to stop into the Cinchring Restaurant for breakfast, but the judge had been determined to see Judge Mackenzie.

"Mr. Myers just left, gentlemen. He—er—he told me about your misfortune. You must not hold this against Sheriff Brown. An honest man, a hard worker, nevertheless—well, I do not like to talk degradingly against my other county servants."

"Myers must've run," Tobacco said.

"Will you sit down, gentlemen?"

Judge Bates said they had just a few minutes. He spread the old line about it being nice to see Judge Mackenzie again and said that he would be delighted to sit on the jurist's bench during his illness.

"Somebody shoot you?" Tobacco asked.

Judge Mackenzie peered at him. "Why do you ask such an absurd question, Mr. Jones?"

"Somebody almost shot us. There's hell about to rip loose here in Broomtail Basin."

Judge Hoss Mackenzie said that Attorney Del Myers had told him about the run-in they had had with Jocky Smith and his well-diggers. He was indeed sorry this had happened. He himself had been hurt lifting one corner of the piano, for he and his wife had recently moved into this new home. He had sprained his back.

"The judge sprained his back onct," Tobacco volunteered. His eyes held a mischievous gleam. "He lifted a barrel of whiskey on its end to send down the tap."

Judge Bates glared at him.

Judge Mackenzie seemed to disregard the post-

master's remark. He went on to say that Broomtail
Basin—so named because it had once been the graz-
ing-grounds of big herds of wild horses—was run
by two big cattle outfits. Cy Montana ran the southern outfit—the Cross H—and the northern spread
was owned by one Ross Frazier, who ran the Bar
S iron.

"Neither of them at first owned the land they
ran cattle on. But when talk came about the Great
Western running rails into Broomtail Basin, both
cowmen spotted cowboys on homesteads and then
bought the rights to those homesteads from their
riders. The railroad right-of-way has only one logical course—that through the bottom-lands of the
basin. And, to get this right-of-way, the railroad will
have to purchase land from either Cy Montana or
Ross Frazier."

"Who would profit the most?" Judge Bates asked.
"In other words, who owns the most land to be
bought for right-of-way?"

Judge Mackenzie nibbled his toast, mouse-like.
"I'd say that Cy Montana and his Cross H own
most of the right-of-way survey. At least three-
quarters of it, I'd say."

"How much will the railroad pay for right-of-
way?" the judge asked.

"A fair price."

"Fair to them, maybe." Judge Lemanuel Bates stared absently out of the window. I know these big corporations. Backed by Eastern capital, they try to buy everything west of the Mississippi at lowest possible rates. They think we're still all Indians out here."

"You sound like—er—you are against our capitalistic system?"

"Not against it," Judge Bates grunted. "I'd just like to see more honesty injected into its muddy veins."

"Our system," Judge Mackenzie said stoutly, "is perfect, I maintain."

Judge Bates decided to steer clear of politics. He had heard Judge Mackenzie's stubborn logic too many times at judicial conventions. Although usually fair-minded, Judge Mackenzie, like every other human, had particular spots where he went temporarily blind, and Judge Bates, knowing this, turned the conversation to other subjects.

"When is fall term of court to open, Judge Mackenzie?"

"Next week. September 10, sir." More toast was nibbled on. "I understand, Judge Bates, you ran your fall term early?"

The judge, smiling a little, told him that assumption was correct; he and his partner had wanted to get in some fishing before winter came. At this, Judge Mackenzie frowned deeply.

Judge Bates knew what bothered the ailing jurist. By territorial law, fall court should never start before the first day of September, and Judge Bates had run through his calendar a few days before court was legally supposed to convene.

Tobacco saw Judge Mackenzie's frown and, unnoticed by the ailing jurist, grinned at Judge Bates, all the while jerking his head toward the door in a gesture which said, "Let's get out of this joint, an' leave this ol' fossil rest."

"One more question, Judge Mackenzie. How many cases on your calendar?"

"One."

"Only one. Hardly worth wasting the taxpayers' hard earned money over. Who is the vic—er, who is the accused?"

The accused turned out to be one Wilbur Connors, commonly known as One-Step Connors, charged with drunkenness, vagrancy, subsisting with no visible means of support, panhandling, and being a general community nuisance.

"They sure threw a book at him," Tobacco grunted.

They took their farewell of Judge Mackenzie. They were in the hall when a human gusher gushed out of a room. "Oh, Mr. Bates! Judge Bates! How good it is to see you again! How kind of you to preside over my ailing husband's court!"

Mrs. Mackenzie was a fat, beaming woman who talked continuously. Judge Bates introduced Tobacco, who shook her hand and nodded silently. She and Mr. Mackenzie wanted them over for dinner soon. Would they stay at their home during their sojourn in Wild Horse?

The judge, lying masterfully, expressed regrets, saying they had already secured lodging at the Wild Horse House, and had paid two weeks rent in advance. Yes, they would be glad to come over for dinner when the good woman named the date. Finally he and Tobacco were out in the open air.

"What a mouth," Tobacco said. "An' damn' fools still look for perpetual motion. Reckon none of them inventors know about Wild Horse town, though. She ain't goin' have me for dinner. I don't crave her to cook me."

"An old joke," the judge said.

"That ol' Hoss Mackenzie. He ain't got a drop of human sympathy in him. He might make a good judge, as you say, but I'd hate to stand up in front of his Bench. Unloading a ton of coal on that ol' drunk One-Step."

"An educated man, One-Step."

"An educated drunk, as I said before." Tobacco spat. "Hospitality, hades! You noticed they didn't ask us for breakfast, didn't you? Not that I'd crave to eat there with that river running outa that woman's big mouth."

"An ol' pessimist," Judge Bates said.

"I may be a pessimist, like you say." Tobacco's scrawny fingers tightened on the sleeve of Judge Bates' buckskin jacket. "But you cain't dodge this— we're in for a mess of trouble, Bates. You're actin' judge here now, an' that pulls you into this trouble, an' you know it."

"You can stay out."

"Sure I could stay outa trouble. Yeah, an' bring you back to Cowtrail in a pine box, Bates! We've been pards too long for me to set by an' watch you run into a stray slug."

"You don't sound broken-hearted."

By this time they were on Wild Horse's main street. This stem was about two blocks long and the plank walks were lined by false-fronted buildings, some painted and some unpainted. Pine-pole hitch-racks were in front of the single store—the general store—and in front of the two saloons and various other business enterprises. A few ponies stood and switched flies.

One saloon bore the legend, Bridle Bit, and the

other, across the street, was called The Last Shot.
Two horses stood by the Bridle Bit's hitchrack, and
the partners saw the Cross H iron on their right
shoulders. Across the street stood three broncs that
packed the Bar S on their left flanks.

"Reckon Cy Montana must patronize the Bridle
Bit an' Ross Frazier an' his cowdogs spend their
dinero at the saloon, The Last Shot."

"That don't look good, either," Judge Bates
opined.

Tobacco turned into the Cinchring Restaurant.
"Good or not, I'm aimin' to chaw my breakfast."

Only two of the stools in the Cinchring were taken.
A slender man about forty-five sat on the closer
stool, and he swung gray, unreadable eyes around
to them. Those eyes darted over the partners in
quick inspection, then returned to their owner's ham
and eggs. The stool beyond the slender cowman was
occupied by a wide-shouldered cowboy earnestly engaged at the present moment in destroying the pro-
ducts of about four hens. This cowboy glanced over
his upraised fork and then continued his morning
chore.

A Chinaman slid out of the kitchen and started
rattling off the menu. Judge Bates said, "Ham and
coffee." Tobacco nodded. "Same here."

The Chinese stopped in front of the two cowmen. "Somethling else, Cy? You, Shorty Betton?"

"More coffee," Cy said. He was the slender man.

Judge Bates reasoned that the older man would be Cy Montana and the younger would be one of Montana's Cross H punchers.

Montana finished eating before the partners had their breakfasts. He put two silver dollars on the counter and speared a toothpick. His cowboy went outside. Cy Montana looked at the partners.

"Nice mornin'," he said.

"Might turn out bad," the judge said.

Montana dug into a molar. "Might at that," he said. He went outside.

Judge Bates chuckled. "He's busting his cinch, wondering who we are. He's a tough apple."

The Chinaman skated in with their orders. He slid the plates on the counter, speared the two bucks, dug under his apron. Judge Bates heard a clink as the two silver dollars joined other silver somewhere under the Chinaman's belt.

Tobacco jabbed an egg with his fork. He wondered if the egg were not so hard it would bend the tines. He was sure now that his first breakfast, served in the local jail, had come from this same cafe.

The Chinese poured coffee. "You men new here?"

"Yeah," Judge Bates grunted.

"Where you ride from?"

"We just broke out of jail. Slept there last night."

The Chinese doubled with mock laughter. He slapped his skinny thigh. "Good joke, fella man." He skated back into his kitchen.

Judge Bates said, "What a cook! We eat here once, and that's all. Somebody told me there was an eating place in the Wild Horse House. We'll have to try it."

For the second time that morning, the partners tried to eat a bum breakfast.

They were at the front of the restaurant, paying for their chuck, when the explosion occurred.

CHAPTER 4

The front window bellied in but did not break. Plates danced on the shelves. The Chinaman hollered, "Holy Sloke! Somebody shoot off cannon!"

The hit the street, Judge Bates in the lead, Tobacco Jones ahead of the jabbering Chinese. Dirt and debris filled the air. A wild-flying two-by-four, strips of siding still clinging to it, landed in the street dust, not more than thirty feet away. Tarpaper floated in the air.

"Cannon, nothin'!" Tobacco growled. "That was dynamite."

"Dynamited a house," Judge Bates grunted.

The Chinaman skidded to a halt. "Holy Clannon! Someblody, she blow up Great Western office. Me, no likeum trouble." He skated back into his cafe and slammed the door.

Heads peered out of windows. Townspeople broke out into the street. Stores and business establishments debouched customers, owners, and clerks. A Cross H horse broke his hackamore rope, and a cowboy ran out and caught him by his bridle-reins.

The Great Western Railway's office had been set apart from other buildings. A frame building, the powder had blasted it apart, leaving only the concrete floor. Had it been flanked closely by other buildings, they would have gone down too, The place was a complete loss.

"Maybe they had powder stored in it," a man said.

By this time Sheriff Will Brown had arrived. He surveyed the wreckage, Adam's apple bobbing. County Attorney Del Myers came running out of the courthouse. He stood beside the sheriff, both speechless.

"Anybody in it?" somebody asked.

"If they was somebody," Sheriff Brown said, "he sure ain't in it now." His humor was grisly.

A man said that Jocky Smith and his men had spent the night in the office, but he'd seen the well-digger and his crew head out of town at daylight. Yes, Smith had locked the door behind him, the man told Sheriff Brown.

Brown was in a grumpy mood. He'd ridden out to the dynamited reservoir, he said; the thing was a total wreck. Somebody had slammed the guard out there over the head and then blasted that to a wreck too. He'd been catching a little nap in his office when this explosion had sounded.

"Too much trouble around here," the lawman muttered. "Some fine day I'll land on somebody's neck, spurs an' all."

Cy Montana and his rider stood a few paces away from Judge Bates and Tobacco Jones. Both of the partners caught the sly wink Cy Montana sent his cowboy, who grinned a little.

The sheriff asked questions. Had anybody seen anybody snooping around the Great Western office? He put the question directly to a short, heavy-set man, evidently a cowman.

"Don't look at me," the cowman warned. "I never blasted this joint down. I was in the saloon, drinking. I was in The Last Shot, an' I got witnesses. Why don't you question Cy Montana? A rider of mine just seen him an' Shorty Betton walk down the alley behind this joint. They come out of the Cinchring eatin' house an' walked down this alley."

Eyes turned toward Cy Montana and his man.

Cy Montana's thin face was the color of gray clay. "I've stood enough of your lip, Ross Frazier. Yeah, me an' Shorty did go down that alley, but we went to the livery-barn to look at a hoss of Mack

West's I bought."

"That all you did?" asked Ross Frazier.

Judge Bates caught the impression that Ross Frazier was deliberately egging Cy Montana into trouble with him. Frazier, the jurist noted, was big and tough, while Montana was slim, and somewhat older than Frazier. If it came to fists, Frazier would probably kick the stuffing out of Montana.

"No fightin'," pleaded Sheriff Brown. "Let's settle this as peaceful citizens, men."

"No man's accusin' me of usin' dynamite," Cy Montana growled. "Me, I fights in the open—guns or fists." He started toward Ross Frazier, who stood wide-legged, a crooked grin on his thick lips.

County Attorney Del Myers grabbed Montana by the shoulder, and Montana's cowboy pushed the lawyer with the palm of his hand, knocking Myers back. When Montana went in front of Judge Lemanuel Bates, the jurist's boot shot out.

Montana fell sitting-down. Hand on his gun, he glared up at Judge Bates. "Who in tarnation are you to butt into this, stranger?"

"He's the new judge!" Sheriff Brown spoke quickly. "He's Judge Bates, Montana, an' he come to set on Judge Hoss Mackenzie's bench."

Cy Montana got to his feet, brushing off his pants. Ross Frazier and his men walked toward the Last

Shot Saloon. Montana said, "Judge or no judge, he ain't trippin me," and he swung.

Judge Bates ducked the wild blow. He wished he had his jug along and he'd've buffaloed Cy Montana. He had a gun on his hip now, but he hesitated using it unless he were forced.

Rage rode Montana. He hit again, and then Tobacco's knuckles came in. The postmaster hit the cowman on the jaw and knocked him down. By this time Sheriff Brown had his gun on Shorty Betton.

"Watch yourself, Shorty."

Shorty pulled back his right hand.

Cy Montana spat blood. County Attorney Del Myers leaned down and speared Montana's six-shooter from holster.

Judge Bates glanced at Tobacco. "Thanks."

"Hurt my knuckle."

People watched, silent.

Finally Montana got to his feet. "Reckon I was wrong, Bates," he said. "Maybe it was best you kept me from tanglin' with Ross Frazier. He might've cleaned me with his fists. When I come at him, I'll have a gun in my hand."

"No ill feelings?"

"Don't ask me that," Cy Montana growled. He beckoned to Shorty Betton, "Let's get outa here."

Shorty asked, "My gun, shyster?"

Sheriff Will Brown said the pair could get their guns from his office inside of half an hour, if they had cooled down by then. The pair went into the Bridle Bit Saloon, which had suffered a broken front window in the blast.

"Thanks, Bates," Brown said.

The judge and Tobacco and Attorney Myers and the sheriff stood talking for some minutes. Sheriff Brown was sure either Cy Montana or Ross Frazier —or some of their men—had blasted down the Great Western's headquarters. An old fellow, who claimed to be a miner, said he thought the blast had come from inside the building.

"Must've come from the outside," Sheriff Brown maintained. "Jocky Smith always kept the building locked. He only used it now and then, mostly as a pay-office when he paid off his well-diggers."

The old miner got mad. "If you know so danged much, you tin-star, why ask anybody's opinion?" He stomped off, a banty rooster.

Sheriff Brown complained, "See, that's what I'm up against, Judges Bates. Not a bit of co-operation outa anybody. Here I ride to that danged reservoir, look at where it used to be, an' try to cut tracks— can't find none, though. Then I get in trouble over you for juggin' you. Judge Hoss Mackenzie called me over to his place right after you two was over there. He's got a tongue like a drunk squaw. He cut me to the quick, gentlemen."

Judge Bates felt sympathy for the skinny lawman. "Don't reckon we hold anything against you, Sheriff. Had you found my credentials and then held us—that'd have been different. But I left my credentials home, seeing that Judge Mackenzie knew me so well."

"Now I got another unsolved case. . . ."

Judge Bates and Tobacco Jones left the sheriff moaning to himself. Tobacco muttered. "You shouldn't've tripped Cy Montana. You ought've kept your big boot—an' your big mouth—outa that mess, Bates."

Judge Lemanuel Bates reminded the postmaster that, above all, he was a public servant, a hireling of the taxpayers, and thus, in that role, he was commissioned by his office to stop trouble before it began, even at own personal danger. Tobacco listened and spat and remarked, "I don't think public duty called you, Bates. I figure you was just hankerin' for trouble."

"An unworthy thought, sir."

Ahead of them walked an elderly woman and a young girl of about twenty. Tobacco gazed at their backs and decided without seeing her face the girl must have been a beauty. When the women turned into the Wild Horse House, the partners got the first look at their faces.

The first woman was not elderly; she was just middle-aged. She had a hatchet-face with a trace of whiskers over her upper lip. Both partners noticed those lips were thin and cold.

The girl, though, had a full face, reflecting happiness and a good disposition. She was very pretty. Brown hair showed from under her small pushed-back Stetson, giving beauty and color to the tanned, clear face with its stubby nose and dark brown eyes.

"Holy smoke," Tobacco grunted.

Judge Bates glanced at the postmaster. "That older woman is a striking beauty, sir."

Tobacco snorted. "That ol' mud fence! Bates, don't devil me! That young girl, though—she makes me wish I was twenty."

"Don't go back ninety years."

The older woman looked at them. Her eyes ran over the judge's corpulent frame, then dwelled on Tobacco's weatherbeaten features. The judge noticed that she gave the postmaster a careful scrutiny.

"Come on, Mother," the girl said.

"Just a minute." The older woman walked over to them. "Aren't you the new judge, sir?" And, without giving Judge Bates a chance to reply, she spoke to Tobacco. "And you are Cowtrail's postmaster,

Mr. Jones?"

"That's us," Tobacco said.

The woman introduced herself as Minnie Jacobson, commonly called "Ma" Jacobson. Her daughter was Trudy. Together they operated the Wild Horse House.

"We have rooms, gentlemen—clean, comfortable, quiet rooms. Our dining-room puts out splendid food, cooked by my daughter and myself. We do hope you make our hotel your home during your stay in our beautiful village."

"Too late for breakfast?" Tobacco asked.

Trudy smiled. "Not too late, Mr. Jones."

Tobacco said, "We had a bite to eat at the Chink's, but it tasted like latigo straps. I'm hungry for some hotcakes."

Trudy and her mother turned into the hotel. Tobacco Jones and Judge Bates followed. Judge Bates muttered, "You're not hungry, you idiot. And she called this a 'beautiful village!' Humph. . . ."

CHAPTER 5

"Wilber Connors, stand before the Bar."

"Aye, aye, sir."

"You stand before a tribunal of justice. Take off your hat."

A claw went up and its talons grabbed the old hat.

"Stand erect, sir."

One-Step Connors said, "I'm standing straight up and down, Your Honor."

Judge Bates almost smiled. But his office demanded an official mien, so he kept a straight face. One-Step had imbibed rather deeply from the bottom of his flask, and his breath did not smell of roses and perfume. One-Step's bum leg was very unreliable and his other seemed also to lean strongly toward that same trait.

Judge Bates looked down at the Mackenzie docket.

He had decided to hold One-Step's trial immediately. Never one for too much pomp, always with an eye to reduction of the cost of courts, he had come from the Wild Horse Hotel, the inner man satisfied. He and Tobacco had carried a small table into the bull pen, and then Tobacco had summoned Sheriff Will Brown and County Attorney Del Myers.

"This h'ain't legal, be she?" Brown asked.

"The legality of this procedure," assured Judge Bates, "is a matter for me to dwell upon as acting judge of this county, Sheriff. Your official capacity only requires that you arrest law breakers."

"I'm one of them," One-Step assured him.

"Judge Hostetler Mackenzie's docket, prisoner, states that you are accused of the following misdemeanors: to wit, drunkenness on the public streets and in public buildings; vagrancy without visible means of support; begging on the public streets and in public buildings; also it had you charged as a public nuisance."

"That's right, Judge Bates."

"Have you an attorney?"

"Don't need none. I aim to plead guilty. They's another charge against me too, Your Honor. I spit deliberately in the sheriff's face when he arrested me."

Sheriff Will Brown scowled and nodded.

"We'll forgit that charge," Brown said.

Judge Bates looked at Attorney Del Myers. "I guess, sir, the case is finished, then." He appealed to One-Step Connors. "Sir, had you denied the charges, I would have freed you. You are an expense and burden to the taxpayers who gain nothing by your continued incarceration. Do you want to go free, or what is your plan?"

"I want at least ninety days in jail."

"Why, pray, such a long sentence?"

One-Step swayed precariously and Sheriff Brown reached out to steady him. "Your Honor, I like it here. I have three square meals a day. Outside, my eating habits are uncertain. I also want to keep away from alcohol for a length of time to attempt, if possible, to acquire my former equilibrium."

Judge Bates looked at Sheriff Brown. "Where does this man get his alcohol?"

"I don't know, Judge Bates. Neither of the saloons will sell whiskey to anybody unless they drink it on the spot. I made them promise to do that; I figgered somebody was smugglin' him licker. That was a week or so ago and he still has whiskey. I've staked out a deputy to watch his cell window from the alley, and the deputy h'ain't seen nobody smuggle a bottle through the bars. It's beyond me."

"Drag him to the door and throw him out," the

judge said.

With One-Step screaming and protesting, the lawman pulled the skinny inebriate to the door and tossed him out into the street.

"I'll get back in," One-Step hollered.

"You get outa town," Sheriff Brown ordered. He slammed shut the door and stomped back into the bull-pen, fluttered and puffing. "Me, I cain't understand it, men. Most hombres don't cotton to go in jail, an' you can't keep him out. I've searched this jail lookin' for his whiskey-cache, but if it's here, I sure can't find it."

Tobacco had been watching out a barred window. "Look," he cried.

One-Step stood in front of the store, about five feet beyond the edge of the sidewalk. He swung a rock in his right hand. His skinny arm flew back and the rock slid out and glass crashed in the store.

"He's busted that big window!" Sheriff Brown jumped for the door.

Soon the lawman came back. But One-Step had already passed right outside the door, streaking for the jail. He ran in ahead of Brown, smiling and clowning. He ran into his cell and slammed shut the door.

"Back again, men."

An irate storekeeper, still wearing his white

apron, stormed in immediately. "I'll kill that drunk — I'll bust his neck!"

"I'm safe," One-Step panted. "You can't get me in this cell!"

The storekeeper appealed to Judge Bates. "Let me in there, sir. I'll drag him behind my establishment and tar and feather him an' ride him outa Wild Horse on a string of barbwire!" He quieted a little. "That window cost me twenty-three dollars and fifty-eight cents, not including freight charges. Seriously, what'll we do with this drunk? Judge Mackenzie couldn't cope with him at all."

Judge Bates assured the man the county would pay for the broken window. He also stated that One-Step was a problem that needed further study.

"He's an educated man," the storekeeper reminded him. One minute he talks worse English than a bum, and the next minute his English is polished. There must be some twist in his so-called brain, eh?"

Judge Bates told the storekeeper to bring his bill into Attorney Myers' office, where it would be honored. The storekeeper left to make out his list of damages.

Judge Bates looked at One-Step. "I'm ashamed of you."

"I'm not."

The jurist rapped with his jug on the table. In

solemn tones he intoned that the fall term of the county court had cleared up its official matters and would now dissolve to take up its duties the following September. Attorney Myers went to his office, and the judge and sheriff and Tobacco went to the sheriff's office.

"I got a sack of beans for One-Step," the sheriff said. "He's doin' his own cookin' now; don't cotton to the Chink's grub. He cooks on that little wood stove in that back cell."

"That saves the county money," the judge acknowledged.

Sheriff Brown hoisted the sack across one skinny shoulder and started for the cell-block. Tobacco and the judge went out on the main street.

"That ol' Hoss Mackenzie is a first class liar," the postmaster said. "Hades, he ain't laid up, the four-flusher. He's just got too much here to fight against, so he took an imaginary ailment to bed an' hollered Uncle to Judge Lem Bates."

"Don't speak of a professional colleague of mine in such degrading terms, my friend."

"Humph. . . ."

The partners stood and looked at the wreckage of the Great Western office. The storekeeper hurried by and nodded. The horses of the Cross H men and the Bar S riders were gone from the hitchracks in front of the two saloons.

Tobacco chewed. "One thing is certain, Bates. Cy Montana an' Ross Frazier pack no love for each other. Looks to me like they're fittin' against each other an' the Great Western, too."

"On the surface, yes, it appears that way."

"What'd you mean . . . on the surface?"

"Still water cuts a deep channel. According to Hoss Mackenzie, Cy Montana stands the most to lose. Montana owns most of the right-of-way. Judging from that angle, Montana would have blown up the dam and reservoir. And Montana would have dynamited the office here."

"Well, Ross Frazier is in on this, too."

"Hard to tell, friend. There are still lots of things we don't know."

"The court term is over, Bates." Tobacco grinned and spat. "Lasted all of ten minutes. Your duty is done; now let's ride out an' get some fishin', workin' our way slow-like back to Cowtrail."

"I don't think you mean that, Tobacco."

Tobacco allowed that he didn't. He was just as anxious as Judge Bates to solve this riddle.

"Just figgered I'd egg you on to get your reactions, Bates. Now this county attorney—is he aboveboard?"

Judge Bates spoke very softly. "Del Myers—right

after he got out of law school—got in some trouble in his native state of Indiana. He almost drew a prison term. He was disbarred from practice. About ten years ago he came to Wyoming. He went before my court—I was sitting as a judge in Cheyenne—you weren't along. He told about his trouble, took an oath to be honest, and I restored his right to practice."

"Oh."

"Since then, he has been honest, and an asset to the legal profession."

"We'd best watch him, huh?"

Yes, they would watch Attorney Myers. In fact, many people here on this Broomtail range could be carefully watched. They would have to play their cards close.

"We got shot at," Tobacco grumbled. "I don't cotton to that. We landed in the calaboose. That hurt, too. But I don't carry no love for no railroad an' its big-bellied bosses."

"Neither do I."

"Still, this railroad come through here, an' this basin'll prosper. Turn into fields of wheat an' flax an' oats, an' there'll be happy farmin' families with their barns and homes. Had a nephew who had a hard time back East. He settled down on the Hunt-ley project. Irrigates an' makes money. This land—

'cept for them alkali spots—will raise good crops, if'n it has water.".

"Deep wells will furnish it. I've seen the geological tables for this area. There is much under-surface water."

"Looks like we settle for a while," Tobacco said.

The storekeeper hurried by. "Thanks, gentlemen," he said. He had a check in one hand.

"Let's get Del Myers," Tobacco said, "an' ride out to that reservoir of Jocky Smith's."

"Here comes Myers now."

Myers was coming out of the courthouse. The partners walked up to meet him by the jail. "We're riding out to the reservoir," Judge Bates said. "We'd like to have you ride along, Mr. Myers."

"Sure thing, Judge Bates. An honor, I assure you."

A voice said, *"Hasta la vista, señores."*

The partners looked up. They were beneath a jail-window. They could make out the homely features of One-Step Connors behind the bars.

"Bonjour," One-Step said.

CHAPTER 6

The harsh voice came from the buckbrush ahead. "Just you hellions rein in your broncs an' wait until I look you over! Remember I've got a .30-30 rifle on you, an' make no funny moves with your paws!"

The trio pulled in reins.

Del Myers said, "You know me, you fool, even if you don't know Judge Bates and Tobacco Jones! Come out of that buckbrush and act civilized!"

The brush stirred and a man came out carrying a rifle. "Couldn't see you very well, Mr. Myers. That sun was right in my eyes." He studied Judge Lemanuel Bates and Tobacco Jones. "I thought them two hellions was behin' bars."

"You thought wrong," Myers clipped.

"Ride ahead," the sentry said.

Soon they came to the marks of water that had gushed down a small coulee, washing it wider and rolling rocks and debris before it. Keeping on the rim of its muddy bank, they rode ahead a few rods and came to a clearing. Beyond them, blocking partially the mouth of a gulch, were the remains of the dam.

Evidently the dynamite had lifted the center of it skyward. Mad water rushing through had torn deep into the banks that were toed into the sides of the gully. Rocks and brush lay around, gray with mud.

"That powder sure fixed it," Attorney Myers murmured.

"Where was the guard's shack?" Judge Bates asked.

Myers pointed out the former location of the shack. The guard was in bad shape, down in Wild Horse, so the local doctor had told him. He'd been slugged and knocked out, but whoever had blown up the dam had dragged the guard out of danger of falling rocks and tons of mud.

The camping quarters of Jocky Smith's crew was further back in the hills about a half-mile. After looking over the dam, the trio headed in that direction.

"That water washed out all hoofprints," Tobacco grumbled. "Mind them riders we saw, Bates? They come outa this draw, remember? They rid down it so's the water, when the dam busted, would wash out all their tracks."

"You didn't identify those riders?" Attorney Myers spoke quietly.

Tobacco shot the lawyer a quick glance.

"Too far away," Judge Bates said. "And the
night was too dark."

Del Myers was silent. Then, "That's too bad.
This would have been solved, had you seen them
closer."

There was another guard around the camp. Again
Myers got them through. Teams of mules stood at
long log mangers and chewed hay. Men lounged in
front of tents, loafing or playing cards. Judge Bates
judged the camp contained about twenty some men.
Jocky Smith saw them and left a card game.

"What're you doin' out here with these two
skunks?" he demanded of Del Myers.

The attorney pointed out that "these two skunks"
were none other than Judge Lemanuel Bates and one
Tobacco Jones.

Jocky Smith rubbed his heavy jaw with its thick
reddish stubble. "Well, shoot me for a poison duck.
You mean—they really were Judge Bates an' Jones!
Lord, I'd sure cottoned to seein' ol' Hoss Mackenzie bawl out that string-bean sheriff. I'll bet he sure
et his head off."

The well-diggers had heard the conversation. A
few crowded forward, hardly believing their ears.

"How's your head feel?" Judge Bates asked.

Jocky Smith's grimy fingers went to the base of his skull. "Still got a sore spot, Judge Bates." He stuck out his right hand, grinning. "You sure out-foxed Jocky Smith. Well, I was wrong, men. I offer you my hand an' my apologies!"

They all shook hands.

"Your men aren't working?" Judge Bates asked.

Jocky Smith said that he had sent word to Raw-hide, at the end of the rails, and asked for a rail-road official to come out to verify the damage done by the blasting. When that official came, then he would know whether he should go ahead on the dam, or drop the project.

"These two local cowmen boosted our dam sky high," he maintained. "I know one of 'em—or both of 'em—were in on it. But what can I prove?" He spread his hands, dirty palms out.

"Nothing you can prove in court," the judge said.

"Maybe it won't get to court, Judge Bates."

Tobacco knew the construction boss had said the wrong thing there. And Judge Bates' clipped words substantiated his partner's guess.

"Remember, Mr. Smith, that I am judge here now. Judge Hoss Mackenzie is not on the bench. Every move in this trouble will hark back on me, for I have jurisdiction over the sheriff and Mr. Myers.

My viewpoint is wholly impartial, you may be assured, but only lawfulness will be in the saddle—not mob rule."

Jocky Smith seemed to take no offense at Judge Bates' warning. He said, "I'll work with you, Judge. Be proud to. But I would like to know who done blasted this dam all to smithereens."

"So would I, sir," Judge Bates assured him.

The partners and Lawyer Myers rode off. Tobacco Jones said, "That Jocky Smith seems like a nice gent, Bates. Reckon he was hot under the collar last night, or else he'd never have taken us to the jug."

"He seems co-operative," Myers said.

They went to where some of Smith's crew was digging a well, down on the bottom land. It was a drilled well, and the cable was raised and lowered by a noisy steam engine. Here a guard was out also.

Judge Bates realized that this Broomtail Basin was, in all reality, an armed camp, with railroad workers pitted against cowmen. The seriousness of this predicament drew lines deeper into the jurist's heavy face.

They watched the workers pull up the bit and clean it and jam down another length of casing. Lawyer Myers remarked that they should be heading back toward town, for soon night would be with them. They would follow Beaver Creek, now a dry creek bottom, down into the basin proper, and then hit the trail into Wild Horse.

A herd of wild broncs—about ten of them—jumped out of the brush, where they had been grazing around a water-hole. A stallion, a beautiful pinto horse, led them, his mares and colts running behind. They went fast and hit the foothills and became lost from sight.

"Some broomtails the cowmen evidently haven't been able to corral," Lawyer Myers remarked. "Ross Frazier and Cy Montana have cleaned most of the wild horses out of here, but some are too wild to corral."

Judge Bates admired the pinto stud. "Egad, Tobacco, how I would like to have my saddle on that beast, and be in that saddle."

"You wouldn't be in it long," Tobacco grunted. "That hoss could buck until fire spouted out his ears. You sure ain't no bronc-stomper, Bates."

The judge assured him that, in his youth, he had climbed on board many a wild one, and ridden him to a standstill. And if called upon today, he could still put up a fair bronc ride.

"You'd best stick with your old Betsy mule. A mule is better'n a hoss anyway. Easier-gaited and more sure-footed, although a mite slower on a run."

"Tougher, too, for a long ride," Del Myers stated.

They were in the brush along Beaver Creek. Once Myers pointed to the east, and there the partners saw two wagons coming along the rim of the hills. Although about three miles away, Judge Bates could see that the wagons were loaded, and their four-horse teams, strung out two abreast, were pulling hard.

"Railroad wagons," Del Myers explained. "Freighting in supplies for the well-diggers. They also freight in oats and hay for the horses that worked on the reservoir. Cy Montana and Ross Frazier are losing money by not selling those camps beef. As it is, the railroad has to freight in beef, and by the time it gets here it costs about ten times as much as Montana and Frazier could sell it on the hoof—if they wanted to sell, which they don't."

"They can't break the railroad by the high price of beef," Tobacco grunted.

The judge was unstrapping his jug. He uncorked it and offered it to Del Myers, who shook his head. When the judge was raising the jug, the rifle spat out its ugly, whining message.

Judge Bates heard the high whine of the bullet. Evidently the rifleman was hidden in the thick brush somewhere ahead. There was only one shot. Del

Myers and Tobacco Jones left their broncs, with Tobacco dragging his rifle out of boots as he hit the sod.

"Git down, Bates, yuh idiot!"

Judge Bates, jug forgotten, whirled his rearing mule, and rode into deeper brush. Tobacco and Del Myers were flat on the ground. Somewhere ahead sounded the pound of running hoofs—retreating hoofs.

Tobacco said, "I'm lookin' up ahead," and ran into the brush. Del Myers was still flat.

By this time, Judge Lemanuel Bates was spurring his mule up a side-hill, hoping to gain altitude enough to catch sight of the bushwhacker. But the hill was steep, and despite the panting and laboring of his mule, the ambusher was almost out of sight when he finally reached the summit.

He glimpsed the rider heading into the dusk, riding fast, riding low over his fork. He figured the rider was heading in the general direction of the Cross H. He was too far away to throw a shot at. The bullet would only have been wasted.

Judge Bates finished his drink, restrapped his jug, and rode down to where Del Myers, grinning crookedly, was climbing back into saddle.

Myers growled, "So now it's ambush, huh?"

Judge Bates nodded.

Tobacco came back, jammed his Winchester into the saddle scabbard. "He got too good à start, Bates. I never even caught sight of him. You see him?"

Judge Bates told about seeing the fleeing ambusher, but that he could not recognize him. "He rode toward the Cross H."

Del Myers was still shaken. "Cy Montana must mean business, Bates. Would that be grounds enough to swear out a warrant for his arrest?"

"We oughta throw both Montana an' Frazier into the calaboose," Tobacco grumbled. "Learn the bigwigs they ain't bigger'n the law."

Judges Bates smiled. "Whoa up, partner. That isn't justice. Besides, just because an ambusher rides toward Cy Montana's Cross H, is that any sign he is working for Montana?"

"Well . . . no."

"Wonder he didn't kill one of us," Del Myers stated.

Judge Bates shrugged. "I don't reckon he shot to kill. Mind how high that bullet sounded? Way overhead it was."

"Then what was the idea?" Tobacco growled.

"He only wanted to scare us. That ambusher never shot to kill; he shot to scare—to warn us we were in a range full of trouble." Judge Bates rubbed his heavy hand over his polished jug. "Had he wanted to, at his range, he could have knocked any of us out of saddle."

"Who t'Hades was he?" Tobacco wondered.

CHAPTER 7

Ma Jacobson stood in front of the mirror, humming as she worked on her hair. Trudy, her afternoon nap over, sat on the edge of the bed. Ma Jacobson, her hair fixed right, straightened her new gingham dress, humming softly.

"You sound happy," her daughter said.

"I am happy."

Trudy yawned. "I was dreaming of a nice young man." She kept watching her mother. "You're too happy, Mother. Are you in love again?"

"Hush up, now, and get downstairs, and get to work. We should have those buns in the oven by now."

"Buns. All my life it's been *buns!*"

"Daughter!"

"Wish I could meet some good young man and marry him so I could get out of this darned hotel and eating-joint."

"This is not a *joint!*"

Trudy smoothed her hair, slipped into her apron, and decided to skip this quarrel. She went downstairs into the kitchen and started to work. Ten minutes later her mother came down, singing a soft song.

Customers started coming in. Once Ma Jacobson looked over the swinging doors that led to the dining-room. "I guess Mr. Jones hasn't come in yet."

Oh-oh, Trudy thought. She knew why her mother was so happy, now. . . . She decided to play dumb. "Mr. Jones?"

"Yes, Mr. Jones. Judge Lemanuel Bates' partner."

"Oh, that is his name, isn't it?"

Ma Jacobson sent an angry glance at her daughter, who apparently was busy filling a steak order. The dining-room had almost run out of customers when Tobacco Jones and Judge Bates entered.

"I'll get their orders," Ma Jacobson said.

So far, Ma hadn't waited on a customer. Trudy smiled and cleaned a skillet. Her mother came back, cooked the orders of the judge and his partner, and Trudy noticed that more generous helpings went on one plate. Unnoticed by her mother, Trudy watched to see who would get that plate, and it went to Tobacco Jones.

Judge Bates also noticed the plate.

"I haven't eaten yet," Ma Jacobson said.

"There are two extra chairs at this table," Judge Bates assured her.

"Thank you, sir."

Ma went back into the kitchen for her plate. Tobacco glared at her back, then said quietly, "Judge, what's the matter with you, you simpleton? Why invite that ox to eat with us?"

"Courtesy, Tobacco."

"Courtesy, Hades! Notice how much more chuck I got than you? All these old women—they go after me."

"You're a bachelor."

"So are you. But they don't chase you."

"Maybe you got something I haven't got."

Tobacco shovelled in some spuds. "Yeah, I have. Brains."

Ma came back and sat beside Tobacco. Trudy came out of the kitchen. "I've cleaned up everything but the dishes you folks have."

Tobacco invited her to sit down and talk with them. She declined, saying she had an engagement for the evening.

"Going over to see Sid Potter?" Ma asked.

"To see Nancy Potter," Trudy corrected her.

"Yeah, but Sid'll be there."

Trudy tossed her brown hair and stuck out her tongue. She went into the lobby and they heard the outer door close.

"Some local swain is indeed lucky," Judge Bates said.

"A daughter is a problem," Ma Jacobson said. "In this small town there are no young men of promise. I suppose she'll marry some worthless cowpuncher."

After eating, Tobacco bit off a chew. Ma Jacobson said, "Would you like me to escort you around our fair village, Mr. Jones? Possibly you have not seen all the dwelling section yet?"

"Saw it when we rode out to the dam."

"Oh, that is right; you two did ride out there. Did you find any—er—clues?"

"Just mud and dirt," Judge Bates said.

Tobacco pushed back his plate. "I'm tired an' I'm trottin' upstairs to my bed." He said goodnight and left. Judge Bates tried to keep up a conversation with Ma Jacobson. But, with Tobacco gone, the woman had little response. The jurist was glad when she carried their soiled utensils back into the kitchen.

Sheriff Will Brown slouched in, hooked a chair, and sank into it. Judge Bates offered him a drink, but the lawman turned him down. He asked if the partners and Del Myers had found any conclusive evidence pointing to who had blasted the reservoir into Kingdom Come.

"Not a sign, Sheriff."

The judge did not tell that an ambusher had shot at them. He had Sheriff Will Brown catalogued as a befuddled individual who had been elected sheriff because it was an easy job and because nobody else had wanted the post. Now, with sudden trouble on Broomtail Basin, the judge had a hunch that Brown wished he hadn't been re-elected the fall before.

"I don't get it," Brown said slowly. "First, that reservoir got lifted with black powder—you saw them four riders. Four cowboys, that's all they could be. Then this railroad office got blasted. No clues there, either. Now just what do you think, Your Honor?"

"I'd like your opinion, sir."

"Well, I'm always reluctant to say something I cannot back by evidence, but it looks like Cy Montana or Ross Frazier—and Montana, more than Frazier. 'Cause if this railroad does come through, Montana will stand to lose the most."

"Keep your eyes open. Something will point toward the guilty parties soon. It always does."

"I'm sure glad you rode over, Your Honor. Judge Mackenzie is all right, but it needs a strong character to cope with somethin' like this."

"Hoss Mackenzie wouldn't be much in a hand-to-hand struggle," the judge admitted. "But cheer up, friend. Have a drink?"

"Then I got that scissorbill One-Step Connors makin' my jail his home. I tried to throw him out again. He kicked an' bit an' scratched me on the face, see. Heck, reckon I will sample your licker."

"Strange character, One-Step."

Judge Bates drank. He noticed the jug was getting empty.

Ma Jacobson, her work over, came out of the kitchen.

Judge Lemanuel Bates said, "Madam, it would please me if you walked with me. I must apologize for my partner, for he was dreadfully tired. It would honor me greatly if you accompanied me on a short stroll through your village."

"Thank you, Judge. I'll get my coat."

Ma Jacobson hurried into the lobby. Sheriff Will Brown said, "Bates, I don't want to give the impression I'm buttin' into your business, but that ol' girl has been married four times. I figured you as a family man."

"Never been married, sir."

The judge left his jug behind the desk in the lobby and got his coat from the corner hanger. Then he grandly gave Ma Jacobson his arm and they went down the steps. Lights from various stores and establishments cut yellow squares in the soft night.

"Where to, madam?" the judge asked gallantly.

"Just for a stroll."

They met a few townspeople. Once the judge glanced back and a man and his wife had stopped, staring at them. The judge smiled.

"Why the smile, Your Honor?"

"The name," the jurist corrected, "is Lem, Minnie."

"Well . . . Lem."

The judge put his hand over Ma Jacobson's. She did not withdraw her hand. They left the business section and its plank walks and followed a gravel sidewalk that went past homes.

She kept up a running chatter. Judge Lemanuel Bates listened with one ear and let it run out the other. She hoped, in a way, the railroad would build through Broomtail Basin. It would bring much trade to her hotel and to the town in general. There was talk of putting the division point in Wild Horse. That would bring in a roundhouse and many men as workers. The whole town and country would boom. But she hoped, in a way, they would run rails from Rawhide up Sagebrush Flats. For she had a daughter—an unmarried daughter.

"And with those boomers coming in—wild men—Well, it's hard to tell about a girl, although I did try to bring Trudy up correctly, giving her a good Christian home."

The judge assured her that her daughter was a level-headed and lovely girl. "But not nearly as lovely as her mother," he fibbed.

"Lem . . ."

You could stand in the center of Wild Horse and walk two blocks in any direction, and you'd be out on the prairie. South of town a few rods was a bunch of black rocks. They sat in the shadows of these.

"Your partner, he seemed rather shy," the widow Jacobson said.

"He is bashful, Minnie. But after a while, that wears off. Underneath, he's a devil."

Judge Bates was glad Tobacco wasn't around to hear.

"I like him."

Judge Bates put his arm around her ample shoulders. Her head came down and rested on his broad shoulder.

"You have never been married, Lem?"

Judge Bates told her a cock-and-bull story about

once being married, then divorced. "My wife is somewhere back East now. I have tried to locate her and the child. By this time, my son will be a man."

"And you want to see him?"

"Naturally."

"A man—or woman—shouldn't stay single," Ma Jacobson said. "I myself have been married twice. Both husbands died." The judge almost shuddered but caught himself in time. Sheriff Will Brown had said *four* times; now it was *two*. He found himself thinking that none of the four husbands had died; they had taken it on the run after seeing what they'd gotten into.

"Very unfortunate, madam. I myself have considered re-marriage, but my wife still gets alimony, and my salary cannot support two families."

Ma Jacobson took her head from his shoulder.

"We'd best get back to town."

She was quieter on the walk back, and the judge, grinning in the dark, knew why.

They came back into the town. By this time, most of the lights were out, and the judge glanced at the ruins of the Great Western office, wishing the ruins could talk.

"Trudy is home," Ma Jacobson said. "I can see the light in her room. I guess Mr. Jones has gone to sleep, for his room is dark."

"A wonderful man," the judge said.

"I like him."

They said goodnight in the lobby—a rather stiff goodnight on the part of Ma Jacobson—and the judge climbed the stairs wearily to his room. He lit the lamp and Tobacco rolled over and regarded him sleepily.

"Where you bin, Judge? Almost midnight."

The jurist, pulling off a boot, informed him he had taken Ma Jacobson for a walk, and that they had just gotten back. He also told his partner that Ma Jacobson was very interested in him.

"Why ain't she more interested in you, Bates? You own as much property as I do, get a bigger salary each month, and you're much better-lookin' an' you got a greater gift of gab."

"But I, Tobacco, have been married. I pay alimony."

"You big liar."

"A white lie," the jurist corrected him. He unbuckled his belt. "You have never been married. You want to marry, too."

"You told her that?"

"She pumped it out of me, sir."

Tobacco reached down for his boot. He couldn't

find it. "I oughta brain you, Bates." He rolled over, face to the wall. "Whenever I get hitched, it'll be an awful cold day."

"Gets cold up here in northern Wyoming," the judge said.

CHAPTER 8

The girl was eighteen or thereabouts, and pretty as a daguerrotype. Judge Lemanuel Bates doffed his hat and said, "Pretty lady, I am looking for Mr. Cy Montana. This is his ranch, I presume."

"Cy is my dad."

"And a lucky man he is, young lady."

"Who you talkin' to, Cynthie?" The voice was feminine and shrill.

"Talkin' to a fat gink, Ma. He's got a lanky guy with him."

Mrs. Montana came out, rubbing her hands on her dirty apron. "Thought mebbe my daughter was spoonin' with some iggnerant cowboy again. Cy's in the corral, right aroun' the bend of the hill. Though if'n you're lookin' for jobs, they ain't none on the Cross H. With all this trouble, we'll be lucky if'n we come out alive."

"Thank you, madam," Judge Bates said.

He and Tobacco rode away. They were astraddle
horses they had rented at the Wild Horse livery-
stable; their mules were getting a well-earned rest.
They found the corral and found Cy Montana and a
cowboy shoeing some saddle horses. The cowman
saw them and came over and climbed the corral.

They exchanged greetings, and the judge asked,
"Tell us your side of this case, Mr. Montana."

Cy Montana talked readily. He didn't want the
Great Western to lay rails across his land. He
didn't want farmers in Broomtail Basin. His cowpunchers had settled on homesteads, proved up on
them, then sold him their rights. Now the Great
Western wanted to lay rails across his land and pay
him the ungodly price of one hundred dollars per
five miles of right-of-way.

"Not much pay," the judge conceded.

"I worked for years to build up my spread," the
cowman said. "I ain't kowtowin' to no mess of New
York capitalists. I won't sell. Of course, they could
finally get acrost my land—seein' Judge Hoss Mackenzie's court is so blamed crooked—but they'd pay,
men."

"I'm running Mackenzie's court," Judge Bates reminded him.

"I don't like judges," Cy Montana said hotly. "I
don't like shyster lawyers. And no railroad is going

acrost my land!"

The judge reminded him that he, not being connected with the Great Western, knew nothing, of course, of the railroad's plans. He pointed out that if the railroad did build through Broomtail Basin, and did put a round-house in Wild Horse, there would be a big market for Cross H beef, and cattle would have to be driven to Diamond Willow, down on the Mountain Empire railroad, to be shipped east to market.

"Let that blasted pirate Ross Frazier feed the crews," Cy Montana growled.

Cy Montana, the judge guessed, was a pretty tough customer.

"What's the trouble between you and Mr. Frazier, if I may ask?"

"Any of your business?"

Anger flushed the judge's jowls. "Don't get huffy with me, my friend. Don't forget I am now the presiding judge of this county. Down in Wild Horse is a man who has been slugged over the head and is critically ill. My bench is always impartial. But it might be that some sign would point to you and your men as having blown up that Great Western reservoir." He raised a hand and shut off Cy Montana's intended words. "As judge, I can swear out a warrant for your arrest, any time I care to. And I could have you taken into jail in town and question you."

Cy Montana's eyes pulled down. Slowly a grin creased his weather-seamed features. "Now that's the way I like to hear a judge talk, Your Honor. Well, I bin in this Broomtail Basin for over twenty years. I even killed buffalo so my cows could have some grass. Even salted down a Cheyenne or two. About ten years back, Frazier moves in on my grass."

"Enough range for both of you."

"But I was here first——"

"Don't get into trouble while I'm here," Judge Bates warned. He studied the cowman. "Can you tell me, honestly, you have had no part in blowing up this reservoir and dynamiting the office in town?"

Cy Montana raised his right hand. "On my name and my honor, sir, I had no piece of either."

"I thank you," Judge Bates intoned.

The judge and Tobacco rode away. Out of hearing Tobacco said, "Anybody can raise his hand and swear, but does it mean anything?"

The jurist admitted that some people fabricated, even under oath.

"What'd we get outa this, Bates?" Tobacco answered his own question. "Just a ride that raised a few more old saddleboils."

"We saw a pretty girl."

Tobacco spat on a sagebrush. "She was purty, at that. But her mother weren't no beauty. I wonder if'n that girl will grow up an' be as homely as Mrs. Montana? Funny how a purty girl can grow up to be so homely."

"Wonder if Trudy will get to look like Ma Jacobson."

Tobacco spat again. "Jus' forget ol' Ma, will you?"

The day was a typical fall day in Wyoming—clear and with a touch of coolness that would increase with the fall of night. They met Sheriff Will Brown down in the thick sagebrush on the floor of Broomtail Basin.

"Was out lookin' over that reservoir again," the lawman said. "Still couldn't find no tracks, what with all that water washin' them away. Hit tracks of some barefooted broncs, but them four riders you saw would use shod hosses, a man would figure eh?"

"Just keep looking," Judge Bates said. "We'll find a clue soon."

"You're optimistic."

The afternoon—and their broncs—were far gone when they reached the mighty Bar S spread of Ross Frazier. Frazier had evidently just ridden in from the range, and the cowman was unsaddling a sweat-marked bay gelding when the partners rode in.

"Long ways from home, men."

"Too far," Tobacco grunted.

Frazier said, "Light an' rest your saddles an' tackle some chuck, huh?"

Frazier's wife was a slender woman, who seemed very timid. She put on two extra plates and served a fine meal. After eating and a drink, Judge Bates got down to business.

Frazier also objected to the railroad coming through. But he also had much land under patented deeds, as did Cy Montana. Judge Bates got the impression that, if the railroad did build through, there would be little open land for nesters to homestead. The Cross H and the Bar S had the basin sewed up, and sewed up legally.

"The logical way for this railroad to go," Ross Frazier said, puffing a cigar the judge had given him, "is up through Sagebrush Flats—that's about fifty miles northwest of here—and then across the Rockies on Bridger Pass. I was hoping their engineers would give up this idea of crossing Broomtail, but it's hard to tell what an engineer will do. They're as unpredictable as a woman."

"Ross," his wife chided.

"Who owns this Sagebrush Flats country?" Tobacco asked.

Frazier shrugged. "Danged if I'd know. Been up in that country onct or twice—good cow country, if it rains, and it hasn't rained much now for about ten years. Not much water here, but enough for our stock without diggin' wells."

"Would you fight the railroad?" Judge Bates asked.

Ross Frazier looked at him. "Yes, if they start rails this way, I'll fight. But first, I'll do it through court; if they whip me then—that's another matter. I guess you're hintin' at: Have I been in on this dynamiting of this dam an' that buildin' down in Wild Horse? My answer is no."

"And a truthful answer," Mrs. Frazier added.

Judge Bates scowled. He believed the man. He believed Cy Montana, too. But when it was all added the digits didn't come out correctly.

Every time Mrs. Frazier went into the kitchen Ross Frazier took a nip from Judge Bates' jug. The cowman was pretty garrulous when the partners left. Frazier rode to the gate with them.

"If it ain't Cy Montana that's blowin' up these things," Frazier said, "then who in Hades it is? It sure ain't me or my hands."

"What makes you and Montana enemies?" Judge Bates asked.

"Well, we ain't what a man would call real enemies. Up till last year we always run out one wagon
for roundups an' worked our crews together. But
last year I got his Cross H iron on one of my spring-
calves that was still suckin' a Bar S cow. Of course,
Cy claimed it was an accident and wanted to brand
one of his calves with my iron."

"Maybe it was an accident," Tobacco Jones sug-
gested. "Maybe the caller called out the wrong
iron to the brandin' hand."

Frazier shook his head stubbornly. "Me, I don't
figure so. . . . Well, this year we run out our own
wagons. We might run a drift-fence up to keep our
cows from mixin'."

"Then your troubles would boom," the judge said.

The night was dark and the wind was chilly. By
this time the jurist's jug was almost empty and he
killed it. He wondered where he could get some
good whiskey to refill it.

He had sampled the best in both the Bridle Bit
and The Last Shot. Neither had a taste of whiskey
worth hollering about unless the drinker hollered because of the poor quality. He had only had one real
good drink, outside of his jug, in the town of Wild
Horse.

That had come from One-Step Connors' flask
there in the jail.

Many thoughts were running through the jurist's
agile brain. He was trying to get the numbers into
rows, to align them, to add them up. He would
have liked to believe both Cy Montana and Ross
Frazier. But at this stage of the game, with as little
evidence as he possessed, he had to be suspicious of
both the cowmen.

The memory of that bullet, coming out of ambush, burned in his memory, a red-hot coal that
would not be dimmed or turn cold. Plainly he and
Tobacco Jones were not wanted in Broomtail Basin.

No wonder Judge Hostetler Mackenzie had taken
to his bed, nursing an illness. For Judge Mackenzie
was no horseman, no gunman. Neither, for that matter, were he or his postmaster-partner gunmen in
the strict sense of the word.

"We oughta pull out," Tobacco grumbled. "This
Hoss Mackenzie pulled a dirty trick on us, Bates.
Hades, he ain't sick. He's hit his sogans to get out
of trouble. The term of court you come for is done
with—lasted all of five minutes . . . too."

"Somebody shot at us, from ambush."

Tobacco spat. "Yeah, that's right." They rode
a quarter-mile in silence. "Naw, we ain't runnin'
Bates. We're stickin' till the last coyote is roped an'
cut down, friend. Even Ma Jacobson can't run me
out now."

"Stout and good talk, *compadre.*"

"We're ridin' nowhere in a heck of a rush," the postmaster said slowly. "Two cowmen, both buckin' the railroad, an' both innercent . . . so they say. Could there be a third party out somewhere who'd try to keep the railroad out?"

The judge admitted he had thought of this angle. But for the life of him he couldn't reason out who this party would be, and what would be his reason. He had boiled it down to its single element.

This element was land. At the present time, this land was owned by Cy Montana and Ross Frazier. Nobody else, to the best of his knowledge, owned any land in Broomtail Basin.

"It's got me," Tobacco admitted.

"Every case has to break," the judge said.

By the time they reached Wild Horse the night had progressed so far the only light was in the hotel lobby. Sure enough, Ma Jacobson was behind the desk.

"Would you care for a bit of warm tea, gentlemen?"

The judge assured her that he only desired to go to bed. Then he added that Tobacco would surely like some tea—back home he drank tea each night before going to his sogans. At this the widow beamed.

Tobacco turned wicked eyes on his partner. Judge Bates had made up the whole tale, for Tobacco always was fussy about going to bed with an empty stomach.

"Come into the kitchen, Mr. Jones?"

Tobacco was trapped. He glared again at the judge, but that worthy was already climbing the stairs to their room.

Unnoticed by the widow, the postmaster spat viciously on the floor.

CHAPTER 9

The doctor said, "He is still in a weakened condition, Judge Bates. His skull is fractured. Evidently he has been slugged by the barrel of a heavy gun."

"Do you figure he will pull through?"

The doctor, a small, well-dressed man, frowned and drummed his fingers on his desk. He had turned his dwelling-house into a two-bed hospital, having the rooms on the back of the house. Judge Lemanuel Bates, his ears ever pinned back for information, had learned that the medico had contracted tuberculosis back East, and had come to Wild Horse four years before—not so much as to practice medicine as to regain his health.

The medico rattled off some medical terms that the judge understood clearly, but that the doctor figured were just terms to the jurist. The guard had suffered a fractured skull and there was therefore some pressure against his brain.

"He has a fifty-fifty chance, Your Honor."

"I'd like to see him."

The doctor took the judge through a hall that smelled of chloroform and the other various smells that inhabited doctors' offices and hospitals. The room was darkened, and the medico raised the blind a little.

Judge Bates stood beside the bed. The guard was evidently either unconscious or asleep.

The doctor took his wrist and said, "His pulse is fast, sir."

Pity struck the corpulent jurist. This guard, so he had heard, had a girl back in St. Louis—a girl still in grammar school. His wife had died the year before, and he had gone West because he needed work and with the hope he could find land and locate and then send for his motherless daughter.

He had stood there, guarding the reservoir, and somebody had sneaked in behind him, smashed a pistol barrel across his head, dragged him to one side out of danger, and then had blasted the dam to bits.

But the judge was not worrying about the dam. It could be rebuilt. But a human life was valuable; no price could be set on it.

The eyes opened. They looked up at Judge Bates and the medico, but they did not see them. Slowly they closed.

Judge Bates shook his head and silently left the room. The doctor slowly closed the door.

"Maybe he could tell me something, if he could talk." Judge Bates spoke quietly. "And maybe he couldn't. The night was dark and his attack was sudden, I understand."

"Now and then he babbles. I'll listen carefully, Your Honor. So far, he has just discussed his girl."

"Have you notified her?"

"We don't know her address. And then, she's just a little girl, and it would strike her hard. So we are sending out no telegrams just now unless he suddenly takes a turn for the worse." The medico spread his hands. "And she'd come after he had passed on, anyway."

"No use notifying her, Doctor."

Tobacco was coming toward the medico's office, and the jurist met him on the corner. "I finally got away from the widow's breakfast table," the postmaster said. "Bates, do me a favor, huh? I know you like to horse-play and joke, but don't encourage that woman any more, huh?"

Judge Bates noticed the desperate note in his partner's voice. He promised, in all sincerity, he would not drop another hint to Ma Jacobson. "But how about her daughter?"

"You can sure encourage Trudy," Tobacco assured him.

"You're just like a Cheyenne buck. The old bucks always want young squaws so they can get more work out of them."

"What about this guard?"

The judge told him.

"I spent half the night tryin' to think this out," Tobacco grumbled. "I still am ridin' a hoss on a merry-go-round, Bates."

"You've got company," the jurist said. "I'm on that same merry-go-round, only I'm ridin' the lover's tub, not a painted horse."

"What'll we do, Len?"

The judge reminded him they hadn't talked to any railroad officials yet. He'd get his jug filled and they'd saddle their mules and head for Rawhide, the end of the rails. By this time, their mules would be rested.

"But I'm not rested, Bates."

"I reckon," Judge Bates said, "I've heard that for thirty years, Tobacco."

Tobacco sighed. "Thirty years only? You make me feel like a spring chicken, Bates."

Tobacco went to the livery-barn to saddle their mules. Judge Bates went into the Bridle Bit and asked to sample the finest of that emporium's whiskey. He sipped, then shook his head, and crossed the street to The Last Shot Saloon.

"What's wrong with him?" the bartender wondered.

The Last Shot's whiskey—its top grade—turned out as awful as that in the Bridle Bit. "That your best, bartender?"

"Twenty years old, aged in oak."

"Not distilled down finely enough."

"Sorry, Your Honor."

The judge went to the jail. Sheriff Will Brown was out in the country, the jailer said, and was evidently still searching for some clue as to who had blasted out the reservoir.

His Honor went back and found One-Step sitting in the bull-pen, feet on the desk, a warm fire in the stove. Opposite One-Step sat another old fellow, who evidently had been jugged the night before for drunkenness, and was still sourly nursing a hangover.

"I have company, sir," One-Step said. "Stand up and shake hands with Judge Bates, Juanita."

"Juanita?" the judge asked.

"A feminine name, of course, Your Honor. A name conjured by my mind on some idiotic whim not accountable to my personality or to scientific advancement. Really his given name is George, his surname Hannibal."

"Looks like he just crossed the Alps on his head," the judge said.

Juanita George Hannibal did not shake hands. "I can't joke this mornin'," he said. "You goin' give me a floater outa this burg, Jedge?"

"If you want one, sir."

"I think it would be best for me," Juanita said. "Then I'd escape this rascal's ill-famed company."

"That, Juanita, is an insult!"

One-Step Connors' voice held-a hurt dignity. But the drunk winked at Judge Bates. Juanita glared at him for a moment and then again lowered his head into his arms on the table.

The judge took a chair and became sociable. He praised One-Step on his education and great fund of knowledge. He praised him as a student, a scholar, and a gentleman, adding that sometimes, though, the gentleman in him was submerged under the influence of one John Barleycorn. Juanita's snores came thin and distant, for his nose was pushed against a grimy sleeve of his coat.

"You crave a boon, Judge Lemanuel Bates?"

Judge Bates smiled. "You're too darned smart, One-Step. Yes, I crave a boon, as you say. The best whiskey in this town is that which you had in your flask. Is it possible to get a gallon of it?"

One-Step watched him, eyes twinkling.

The judge waited.

One-Step said, "You are a sterling man, Judge Bates. You are a great judge of mankind and his strengths, his frailties. You are a judge—a competent judge—of good whiskey and undoubtedly a judge of fine women. Am I right?"

"Much as I hate to admit it, I believe you are right."

Juanita snored louder.

"If I take you into my confidence, Judge Bates, do you swear to keep my secret to yourself and not act in your legal capacity and therefore prosecute me further?"

"I do."

"Then, sir, the gallon is yours." One-Step held up his hand. "No, no awful money is involved, sir. This is gratis, a gift from my welcome heart to yours."

"You mean *throat*, not heart." The judge sighed. "And I shall pay you, sir, whether you like it or not!"

Juanita looked up. "Hit him again." He put his head down and snored again.

One-Step glanced toward the sheriff's office, but the door was closed. He pointed at a big copper kettle on the stove. "That kettle, sir, is supposed to cook my mulligan. Now come with me, please?"

They went to the rear of the bull-pen. There was an eye-latch on the floor, bolted down, with a lock in it, and One-Step opened this lock easily, using a key made of a piece of metal. He lifted the hatch-door, and Judge Bates knelt and looked into a cellar, barely making out sacks stacked in a neat row and a wooden barrel in the far dim corner.

"It is only by oath, Your Honor, that I show you these implements."

The sacks, One-Step elaborated, held chicken-feed for Sheriff Brown's flock. It seemed that thieves had once looted the sheriff's feed-house and stolen some sacks of chicken-feed, and the feed was hard to get, being hauled in by freighter wagons. So the sheriff had stored his chicken-feed in this cellar.

"He figured, Your Honor, that it would be safe here, under lock and key, with only himself having the key. Those sacks contain wheat and corn, sir."

One-Step Connors lit a match and let it drop to the earth floor below them. "Now look good at yonder barrel, sir."

The judge did, and whistled softly.

One-Step dropped nimbly, despite his game leg, into the cellar, taking Judge Bates' jug. While he was in the cavern, the jurist inspected the copper kettle on the stove. The copper tubing ran into the. wall, a few inches behind the stove, then evidently took a bend down dripping its contents into the barrel in the cellar.

One-Step stuck out his scraggly head, looking like a gopher with whiskers. "Here is your vessel, sir; filled to the brim."

Judge Bates slapped a heavy hand against his thigh. "Making whiskey in jail! Right under Sheriff Brown's nose, too! And he thinks you are cooking mulligan for chuck!" He sobered suddenly and regained his judicial mien. "But this, sir, is a direct violation of Federal Laws, for you pay no tax on your whiskey."

"I swore you to secrecy, my friend."

"And that you have, sir, and that you shall receive. I owe you, sir, for this fine brew?"

"Two bucks."

The judge dug. "Not enough, sir. Too cheap." He gave One-Step three silver dollars. The prisoner dropped two into his pocket and the jurist heard it join other coins. He then returned the single dollar to the jurist, putting it himself in Judge Bates' pocket.

"To you, my friend, the price is two bucks."

"May I ask one question: Are you selling this whiskey outside?"

A frown crossed One-Step's dirty forehead. "I must confess—alas—that my outside man here—"

a thumb jerked toward the snoring Juanita "—in one of his drunken moments, sold a quart to an equally drunken Cross H cowboy. I have issued orders to him not to sell another drop or I shall shut off his supply. He was deliberately jailed—he deliberately picked trouble with Sheriff Brown last night. He wanted to come in and have a long rest on the county's expense."

"Sheriff Brown," said the jurist, "is an ignorant fool."

"An unlettered man, Judge Bates. Unskilled in conversation, in legal enforcement, in the proper use of his pronouns. But do not bother him, please. Were an intelligent man to take his place, our game would be over. See how quickly I can disconnect this copper tubing leading into the wall?"

A snap, and the tube was loose, under the stove. And to a casual observer such as Sheriff Brown, it would appear only a harmless copper kettle was simmering on the stove.

"I hope to spend the rest of my life here, Judge Bates."

Judge Lemanuel Bates was blinking a little when he came out on the sidewalk. Part of the blinking, though, was caused by the slant of the sharp Wyoming sun. Then that blinking suddenly passed.

Two men were fighting in front of the Bridle Bit

Saloon. They had just broken out of the bar, the door still swinging behind them.

One was Shorty Betton, range-boss for Cy Montana's Cross H iron. And the other, Judge Bates noticed hurriedly, was Tobacco Jones.

CHAPTER 10

Shorty Betton, head down, was digging in, fighting hard. And Tobacco Jones, tobacco juice running down his chin, was moving backwards, dodging and ducking. Judge Bates stopped beside the bartender, who had come out to see the fight.

"What're they fighting about, White Aprons?"

"Shorty gets mean when he's drunk. He came into town this morning and started to drink. Jones came into my establishment lookin' for you. Shorty glared at him an' told him to stop walkin' on his boots."

"Deliberately picked a fight, huh?"

"He sure did. 'Cause Mr. Jones, wasn't at any time within twenty feet of him. But when Shorty gets drunk—the first thing he wants to do is fight— an' Jones was handy— That was a tough one Jones just stopped!"

The blow had sent Tobacco Jones back a foot or so. And Shorty Betton, using his advantage, pulled in fast, aiming to knock Tobacco Jones down. But

Shorty was too drunk, and his wind had run out on him. Tobacco, although older, had more wind. He straightened Shorty with a hard right fist.

Shorty stopped, pain and surprise across his thick face. He hit and missed, and Tobacco Jones knocked him down again. A man reached down and took the Cross H range-boss' gun out of his holster. This time, Shorty stayed down.

"Never knowed that ol' pelican had that much fight in him," a townsman grunted.

Tobacco breathed heavily, catching his wind. Shorty sat, head down, rubbing his jaw slowly. One of Sheriff Brown's deputies, a pot-bellied man, pushed through the crowd. "What's the matter here?"

"You're only about ten minutes late, as usual," a man grumbled.

The judge got Tobacco up on the sidewalk and away from the crowd. He asked what had happened to bring on the fight. Tobacco's story was the same as the bartender's. Shorty Betton had accused him of stepping on his foot.

"An' I weren't within twenty feet of the critter, Bates. I just went in lookin' for you to tell you the mules is saddled. He just wanted a fight, that was all, an' I reckon he got it—an' plenty of it."

"Just troublesome."

Tobacco Jones flared up with, "An' I'll bet Cy Montana sicked him on me, Bates. I tell you, that Montana gent is the cur behind all this. I can feel it in my bones. I'm sure he is. We oughta jug him, just for the devil of it."

The doctor looked at the cut over Tobacco's left eye. "Doesn't need any stitches," he said. "You intend to press charges, sir?"

"I oughta."

Judge Bates walked back to where Shorty Betton still sat on the ground. He said roughly, "Stand up, prisoner!"

"I'm no prisoner."

"That's what you think. Deputy, get him on his feet, and get him up pronto." Anger rimmed Judge Bates' voice. "You are now standing before a court of justice, sir."

The deputy got Shorty Betton on his wobbly boots, Shorty had what would soon be a black eye, and his nose didn't track right.

"Fat Man—"

Shorty Betton's words were choked short as Judge Bates' beefy hand contracted around his neck. The judge shook him as a terrier shakes a muskrat. "Address me, sir, as Your Honor."

Fear lit the Cross H foreman's eyes. "Your Honor."

"That's better."

"This town needs a lot of your treatment, Judge Bates," a grocer said soberly. "Throw the lib'ary at him."

"I'll work you over, Bat Crawford!" Shorty Betton glared at the grocer.

"You touch Mr. Crawford," Judge Bates intoned, "and I'll see you land in the territorial pen, prisoner. You are found guilty of inciting a fight, of brawling on the public streets, endangering the lives of women and children by your antics, and of violating the community peace."

"I'm not guilty."

"You are guilty. Deputy, how much money has he on him?"

The deputy searched Betton. He said, "This much, sir," and held out a mixture of paper money and silver coins.

"You are hereby fined that sum, prisoner. Deputy, turn the money into my office at a later date. Do you own the horse you ride, sir?"

Shorty studied him. He said, "No, Cy Montana owns him," and Judge Bates knew he was lying.

"That bronc, prisoner, is now the property of this county. As an additional fine, I fine you two month's wages, as yet unearned. Tell Mr. Montana to report to me when next he is in town and to bring in the money."

"Your Honor—"

"Case is dismissed," the jurist clipped. "Now Deputy, take him to the outskirts of town, head him for home, and kick him hard in the seat of his trousers. You hear me?"

"A pleasure, Your Honor."

"This court, by my order, is recessed," Judge Bates intoned.

The deputy, holding Shorty Betton by the arm, started him down the street. A few townspeople crowded around Judge Bates with congratulations. One openly said he hoped the judge would fix things so the railroad could cross Broomtail Basin. "It would bring much dinero into this burg. Your Honor."

"That is not for me to decide. My position requires that peace be maintained. The decision to cross this basin depends upon the railroad and its settlement with Mr. Montana and Mr. Frazier."

The judge and Tobacco went to the livery-barn Tobacco was washing his face in the watering-trough when a man came in, chuckling. "Deputy Peterson sure booted him, Bates. Kicked him right in the rump. Shorty almost fell down. He's hikin' for the Cross H now. Them boots of his'n sure raise blisters."

The judge nodded.

They got astraddle their mules. Tobacco wiped

his face with his bandana. His upper lip was swelling rapidly. "One good thing'll come out of this, Bates. With my mug beat up like this, the Widow Jacobson can see how homely I am, and switch her lovin' attentions to you."

"Heaven forbid."

They put their mules to a lope, heading east. A day's rest had put new life into the wiry mules. Tobacco said, "He opened up that cut over my eye—that one I got busted open in that Post Hole Valley fracas."

"Not a bad cut, though."

They met Cy Montana on Willow Creek. The cowman glanced at Tobacco's face but made no comment. He was out hunting a stray bull, he said. Judge Bates told him about the fight and the way he had handled Cy Montana's range-boss.

The jurist loaded his words with implication.

Cy Montana's leathery face grew hot with anger. "I never sicked Shorty onto your partner, Bates! Shorty has the rep of being mean when he's drinkin'! Besides, he wasn't supposed to be in Wild Horse town—he rode out this mornin' for Beaver Dam line-camp, aimin' to look for a cougar over there. But he's done sneaked into town, the runt."

"You owe his next two months' wages to the county."

"What if I don't pay?"

The judge shrugged. "That's up to you. But I can assure you this, Mr. Cowman, if you don't pay you'll sit out sixty days in the local jail, and in the next cell will be your foreman, one Shorty Betton."

"Bates, you can't run this country."

"I am running it. And if Sheriff Brown and his deputies can't jail you two, then the territorial militia from Fort Cheyenne can jail you—or bury you. And when you refer to me, I'm not 'Bates'—I'm Your Honor, sir."

Their gaze met. Montana was the first to look away.

"The money will be delivered, B—Your Honor. I'll pay you the next time I get into town, which should be tomorrow."

"That is good, sir."

The partners turned to ride on. Cy Montana said, "And make sure the money is turned over to the county treasurer!"

Judge Bates held his mule by severe reining. He asked quietly, "How much does your foreman make a month?"

"Thirty dollars."

"Then, for that remark, I am fining you—personally—two months of Mr. Betton's salary. That means, sir, you turn over not sixty dollars to the

county, but the sum of one hundred and twenty. And
if you make another remark, sir, reflecting upon
my honesty, I shall double that fine, and require you
to pay all of it from your own pocket, charging
none against Mr. Betton."

The knuckles of Cy Montana's right hand, resting on his saddle-fork, were strained and white. He
looked at Tobacco Jones. The postmaster had his
hand on his pouched .45.

"You're not gettin' popular, Your Honor."

"With you no."

Montana nodded. "I'll pay it. I owe the county
one hundred and twenty bucks." He roweled his
pinto savagely and loped away.

The partners rode on. Tobacco chuckled suddenly. "We sure know how to lose friendships in a
hurry, Bates." He winked. "I mean, Your Honor."

Judge Bates showed a small smile. He agreed
that when the time came to be tough, a judge had to
be tough. He judged that Cy Montana had ridden a
tall saddle for too long on this grass and it was due
time that somebody jerked him out of that kak. Ross
Frazier was due to take a fall, too.

For His Honor was in an angry mood. For
three days he and his partner had been bucking a
stacked deck and they didn't know yet who was
dealing the cards. He had a few plans in his head,

though, and he did not reveal these to Tobacco. Later on, if nothing constructive was found—either through chance or guesswork—he would act on one of those plans.

About five miles further on, a rider came down off the foothills on a sorrel, and they saw he was Ross Frazier. Frazier informed them that he was also looking for one of his bulls that had strayed.

"Must be a habit," Tobacco grunted.

"What d'you mean by that?"

The judge told about Tobacco's fight, his treatment of Shorty Betton, and their run-in with Cy Montana. Frazier leaned back in a saddle and slapped his bronc on the wethers.

"That's good medicine," he said. "Your Honor, you should have been on the bench here a long time ago."

"Nothing to laugh at, Mr. Frazier."

Ross Frazier stopped laughing. He studied Judge Lemanuel Bates. Suddenly he got a new—and true —insight into the jurist's character. Up to now, Judge Bates had seemed an easy going, good-natured heavy-set man. Now he was grim and thick with authority.

Ross Frazier suddenly remembered tales he had heard: How Judge Bates, aided by Tobacco Jones, had turned the tide against old Jed Lipp, up on Bon-

anza Creek, when Lipp was hard-pressed by desper-
adoes; how the partners had brought peace—by
shotgun and bench—into Post Hole Valley.

"I guess it ain't funny," he said lamely.

"Legality shall hold this range," Judge Bates assured him.

"That's right, Your Honor. Well, I gotta get
goin'. Glad to have met you men again."

Frazier loped toward the west. The partners continued toward Rawhide and Tobacco Jones suddenly chuckled.

"You sure hatched that hen's aigs in a hurry,
Bates."

Judge Bates had no answer.

Their trail led them past the reservoir. Jocky
Smith and his crew were refilling the blasted area
with dirt, pulling it in with fresnos that had four
horses hooked to them.

According to Smith, the railroad official had arrived, and told them to go ahead and refill and rebuild the dam. Then he had ridden into Wild Horse
to see Sheriff Will Brown.

"He demands pertection the law is supposed to
give citizens," Jocky Smith said, smiling.

"And with me on the bench," Judge Bates said,
"he'll sure get it."

CHAPTER 11

The partners spent the night at the railroad camp. The district superintendent and another official were in the dirt camp. Word had got back to them that the reservoir had been blown up. The superintendent had sent his assistant out to look at the scene.

"We might not go through Broomtail Basin," he told the judge and Tobacco Jones. "Each day is precious, and we can't have our men stand around and mark time. As it is, the fill and rails will reach this point in a few days—they're at Goose Bend now."

So far, the partners had been under the impression that the rails had been laid to Rawhide. They talked and then went in for chuck. After chuck, the superintendent got out a deck of cards and some chips, and started a poker game, dealer's choice.

By midnight, Judge Bates had won almost a hundred dollars. The superintendent, who had lost to both Tobacco and the jurist, was getting grouchy. He kept taking deep pulls at the judge's jug.

"Fine whiskey, Your Honor. Where did you procure such an excellent brand, and what is its trade-name?"

"Old Fence Post," the judge fibbed. "I got it in a Wild Horse saloon. I raise you five, sir."

"I'm staying," Tobacco said.

The judge raked in another pot. "Then you figure perhaps, you'll lay rails up into Sagebrush Flats, huh?"

"Yes. We can buy right-of-way there. The price, though, is rather high, but even at that, with fall coming down on us, we can still save a little money. We'll wait for Mr. Straw's report."

Mr. Straw, the partners knew, was the official who had ridden into Wild Horse, looking for them and Sheriff Brown.

The sound of the cook's bell awakened them. The superintendent was still snoring, and they dressed without awakening him. They ate breakfast, eyed by the crew, and went outside. Teams and fresnos and skinners were heading for Goose Bend, and they could hear the distant puff of the steam engine, getting ready to lay rails.

They could not see the locomotive, for the toe of the hills hid it.

A team went by, the driver trotting behind his four horses. Tug chains rattled and dust rose in a fine cloud. The cook's flunky threw out a pan of dish-water, almost hitting a skinner who was coming in the door.

For a while, it looked like a fight.

The cook came out with a long breadknife, and the skinner, seeing it, hastily went to the mangers built of logs in the middle of the camp of tents and lean-tos. The cook glared at the partners.

"You two bums get your bellies full? If yuh have, hit the dust outa here. I'm not cookin' for range-bums."

"We'll go," the judge assured him.

Their mules had eaten good hay all night. They watered them in the spring and rode toward Wild Horse. The sun was up but the wind was chilly. Luckily, it came from the east, and was behind.

"That super got purty well pickled," Tobacco said. "Well, what did this ride accomplish; Bates, besides renewin' old friendships with old onfriendly saddle-boils?"

"We have the name of the attorney back in Kansas City who is handling the transaction for the land in Sagebrush Flats, if the road does build that way."

"What good will that do us?"

"Never can tell."

Tobacco started to rub his jaw, then remembered it was still plenty sore. "Wonder who does own that Sagebrush Flats country. How could a man find out, Bates?"

They could wire to the territorial land office in Cheyenne, the jurist said. That office would know who owned that particular territory. Tobacco frowned at that idea. To get a wire into Cheyenne would call for a ride to Diamond Willow the town to the south twenty-five miles. A wire from the telegraph line, back beyond the Rawhide junction, would not make contact with the Mountain Empire line to Diamond Willow, for no cross-line went to the Mountain Empire Railroad.

"One of us might have to ride into Diamond Willow," the jurist said, "and send off a wire. Somewhere it seems to me that maybe this Sagebrush Flats deal ties into this trouble in Broomtail Basin."

Tobacco snorted. "How could it, Bates? Has your brain pulled its picket pin? Fifty long miles from Wild Horse to Sagebrush Flats, they tell me."

The jurist had no answer to that. They met a rider about ten miles out of the railroad camp. The jurist introduced himself and Tobacco and asked if the rider were Mr. Straw, and his assumptions turned out correct—this man was the railroad superintendent's assistant.

"Glad to know you, Judge Bates, I heard talk of you down in Wild Horse."

The judge shook his head in feigned sadness. "Bad talk, I suppose."

Mr. Straw did not catch the joke. "No, Your Honor, I heard high and praising talk. With you in the saddle, I am sure the railroad company can put through its lines." He winked at the judge.

Play with the railroad, that wink said. Play hand in glove with us and get our lines through and we'll see a nice fat bonus gets into your mail. And it won't be a check; it will be in hard cash or in good United States paper money. It has been done before, Your Honor.

But Judge Lemanuel Bates only felt anger. "Sir, I will have you understand that my office and my decisions are impartial. I can fully see the side of Mr. Montana and Mr. Frazier and I appreciate their backbone and determination, for these are valuable assets to any man."

Mr. Straw's weak jaw showed a little slack. Up to now, the railroad had bought its way across Nebraska and Missouri and money had shoved any obstacle out of its path. He could hardly believe this.

"I did not mean it that way, Judge Bates."

"I am glad I misunderstood you, sir."

The railroad man said, "It points up this way,

gentlemen. Within a few days our rails will meet Rawhide. The next decision is this: Will we push on into Broomtail Basin, or will we go northwest into Sagebrush Flats? Our present decision is to go through Broomtail Basin."

Judge Bates warned, "You will have a stiff legal fight, sir. I understand the deeds of Mr. Montana and Mr. Frazier to the right-of-way you seek are registered and recorded and otherwise in legal, tip-top shape."

"We can seek condemnation proceedings."

"They will be aired in my court, sir. I will abide by the strict letter of the law. I can see no chance of you winning this case?"

"There are other ways, then."

"And these, sir?"

Straw's jaw tightened. "Means we have used before, Judge Bates. We have Irishmen and Poles and Italians, and they'll fight for their eats. They'll get clubs, and we'll put in goons and ginks to beat those cowmen. If we cannot whip them in court, we'll beat them outside of court."

"You try that," the judge warned, "and the territorial militia will be in here, and this area will be under martial law, and I'll head that martial law. Think a long time before you do that sir."

Straw said, hotly, "You've turned against your

class, Judge Bates!"

"There, sir, you are wrong. My class is the working class, for I came out of the hills of Tennessee. But I do not let my past obstruct justice and human rights in my courts. Now turn your horse and go immediately before I lose my temper."

"To hell with you!"

Nevertheless Straw loped away, and loped fast.

"An arrogant son," the judge mumbled. "How I would like to have him stand before my bench, Tobacco."

"You might get him there, Bates."

The anger left Judge Lemanuel Bates as he unstrapped his jug and again tasted the savory smoothness of One-Step Connors' brew.

"A man should never ponder on the unsolved riddles of the past, Tobacco. He should keep eyes to the future and the present, for the past is dead beyond recall, but still I cannot help remembering."

"And that, Bates?"

"Mind those four riders we saw, the night friend Jocky Smith bestowed us in the Wild Horse calaboose? Had we been close enough to see them clearly, we would have had definite clues either pointing to Cy Montana or Ross Fraizer, or completely eliminating those two worthies."

Tobacco was realistic. "But we weren't close

enough, Bates."

"A regrettable fact, sir. A trick of subtle fate."

They stopped at Jocky Smith's dirt camp for dinner. The cook was growling about running low on supplies and Smith told him rather angrily to stop bellyaching, for a wagon-load or two of supplies would come in that night from Rawhide.

Smith also said that Straw had told him to go ahead with the reservoir and refill it from the well, pumping up the water with a small steam engine that was stoked by cordwood. Straw had also ordered them to continue sinking down the dug-well they were drilling down in the basin.

"The big push back at Rawhide hinted the rails might go through Sagebrush Flats," Tobacco said, speaking around a forkful of antelope steak.

Jock Smith studied the postmaster. "Straw sure never told me that, Mr. Jones. What did you find out, Your Honor."

The judge said he had understood approximately what Tobacco Jones had stated. "Perhaps an overlap of authority, Mr. Smith. Sometimes that happens with big companies, you know."

"Reckon I'll just keep crews working, then." Jocky Smith speared another slice of antelope steak. "But 'pears to me the logical step would be to drive rails up into Sagebrush and acrost Bridger Pass."

The judge and Tobacco got their mules and

headed toward Wild Horse. By this time, with two days consecutive travel under the saddles, the mules were getting leg-weary. The pair kept them at a fast walk.

"Yonder," Tobacco said.

A rider had come down off the hills about a mile away. He was heading toward them. "Looks like our friend Shorty Betton," Judge Bates said.

Evidently the rider suddenly recognized them, for he turned his pony and rode east, deliberately avoiding meeting them.

"That *is* Shorty!" Tobacco chuckled. "He sure don't cotton to meetin' us, either. He swung east in a whale of a hurry."

They left their mules in the livery-barn and went to the courthouse. Sheriff Will Brown sat with his feet on his desk and his brows pulled down. "Reckon you had quite a mess yesterday, Mr. Jones, while I was out in the country?"

"Interestin'," Tobacco murmured.

The judge asked if Cy Montana had been in to pay off his one hundred and twenty dollars. Sheriff Brown said he had been in that same morning. He opened a drawer, and the judge counted one hundred and twenty dollars and five cents.

"Cy said the five cents was your commission, Your Honor."

Judge Bates smiled. Evidently the cowman had a

wry sense of humor. He gave Sheriff Brown a receipt for the money—adding the nickel to the receipt—and he turned it over to the county-treasurer, getting a receipt from him.

The treasurer put the money in his safe. "Biggest fine levied in the county for years. We need you here more often, Judge Bates. That more than pays my salary for a month. This county needs higher fines, and more fines, coming in."

They went outside.

Tobacco said angrily, "Pay his wages for a month. . . . That's all he thought about, the idiot. And him a county official, with the trust of the voters in him. . . . County parasite, Bates."

Judge Bates smiled.

CHAPTER 12

Judge Bates was riding a bronc, a high-pitching, stiff-legged, bucking bronc. Somebody was hollering encouragement. Probably the rest of the cowdogs gathered around the corral, the judge thought.

Suddenly the bronc threw him. He was awake. But still he was shaking, or being shook. Then he realized Tobacco Jones was shaking him by the shoulder.

"Wake up, Bates, an' quit your jerkin'."

"What is it, Tobacco?"

For the first time, His Honor noticed that the pot-bellied deputy was also in the room. The moonlight, thin through the open window, showed on the deputy's shiny badge.

"You sure sleep sound," Tobacco growled. "Here this deputy almost knocks the door down gettin' me awake, an' I have to shake you to make you come to."

"Somebody done blasted up that wagon-load of chuck," the deputy said shortly.

The jurist remembered the wagon-load of grub that Jocky Smith had said would be delivered that night in the dirt-camp at the reservoir. He was wide awake now, pulling on his trousers.

"What time is it?"

"Right after midnight."

By now the judge was fully dressed, even to his jug and his .45. The deputy told him what little he knew.

"The driver came stumblin' into the Cross H Ranch. Cy Montana an' Shorty Betton hauled him into town with a rig. He claims a man must've caught his wagon by the end-gate, sneaked up behind him, an' slugged him to sleep."

"Yes."

"Then this feller—or fellers, whichever it was—drug him to one side an' put dyneemite under his load, after unhookin' his four mules. They sure lifted it, he said."

"I see."

"Well, this driver headed out on foot, forgettin' to unhitch a mule an' ride him, an' he staggered into the Cross H camp, an' that's the story, Your Honor."

"Another dynamitin'," Tobacco growled.

Ma Jacobson, wearing a robe, stood in the lobby, big as a young colt. Beside her, slim and pretty, a robe over her nightgown, stood Trudy. When they hurried out, Tobacco glanced quickly at Trudy, but completely ignored Ma.

"What's the matter?" Ma demanded.

"Horse kicked the ol' hostler an' busted his leg," Tobacco growled. Outside, he said, "Nosy ol' battle-hatchet, Bates. Always jabberin' questions."

"A woman's right, Tobacco."

"My wife is the same pattern," the deputy said.

The old hostler was asleep in the barn. The deputy threw a bucket of water over him after they had saddled horses. Then he hit his stirrup and galloped out the back door, following Judge Bates and Tobacco Jones.

Behind them, the hostler was hollering curses.

Neither the jurist or his partner had seen this bit of horseplay, for they had already been out of the stable. Judge Bates asked, "What's the matter with him?" and the deputy said, "I scooped a bucket of water outa the hoss trough an' woke him up. He prob'ly figures a Cheyenne buck has slapped him in the mug with a wet scalp."

"Poor old man."

Tobacco eyed his partner. "Poor ol' man, Hades. He's a crabby ol' sucker. He needed it."

According to the deputy, Sheriff Will Brown, accompanied by Cy Montana and Shorty Betton and the teamster, had ridden ahead, and Sheriff Brown had sent him to awaken Judge Bates and Tobacco Jones.

They rode fast, but they never caught Sheriff Brown and his party. The judge and Tobacco had slung their saddles on the first broncs they had seen, back there in the barn. They had, by luck, picked out fresh broncs, tough broncs.

They ate up the miles, dust sifting in the moonlight behind them. They hit the toe of the hills, about four miles out of town, and the deputy said, "There she be, men. The wagon is still smokin'."

Ahead, on a sidehill, was a small fire.

When they got closer, they could make out the identities of the men grouped around the fire. Sheriff Brown, Shorty Betton, Cy Montana. Also there were the slugged mule skinner and two other men, one of whom turned out to be Jocky Smith, the other his cook.

The men heard their horses and turned, and Judge Bates caught the glint of a rifle barrel.

"Coming in," the jurist hollered. "Bates, Jones, and the deputy."

The rifle slanted downward again.

The mules were tied in a grove of bullberry

bushes. Judge Bates went down, bridle-reins ground-tying his borrowed horse.

"Whole thing a loss," Sheriff Will Brown said sourly.

Jocky Smith said he had been up late, playing poker, and, while going to his tent, he had noticed the fire, and he and his cook had ridden over to investigate, fearing the worst.

"Lemme fin' out who's doin' this, Your Honor, an' I'll bust his neck with me bare hands!"

The dirt-boss, Judge Bates noticed, sounded sort of angry.

Cy Montana said, "Somebody sure used the right amount of powder. Not too much; just enough. Must be a good judge of powder. That tells us it's somebody who has worked around powder a lot."

"An' that's just about all it does tell us," Sheriff Brown mumbled.

The driver was shivering. Although Judge Bates hated to question the man because of his nervous state, nevertheless the jurist plied him with questions. Had he any clue as to who had slugged him? Had he heard any names called? Had it been one man, or two—or possibly more—that had blasted his wagon?

The man spoke slowly. "Now that you do mention it, sir, I believe there was more than one man, at that. I heered somethin' behin' in the wagon, savvy.

I started to turn an' somethin' beaned me, but right afore I passed out I'd swear I heard a man holler, 'Sock him again, Shorty.' "

"What was that name?"

"Shorty. I swear to it."

There was a silence broken occasionally by the snap of a burning ember. Judge Bates did not look at Shorty Betton who, so far, had completely ignored him and Tobacco Jones.

But the implication was there. It lay between the men, although nobody mentioned it until Shorty Betton spoke.

"I know what you're all a-thinkin'. But I can say this, they's more'n one gent roamin' the hills who's named Shorty."

Cy Montana spoke for the first time. Shorty had been at the Cross H; he had witnesses to that. Shorty had been home when the guard had staggered in, hadn't he? That should be evidence enough.

"You are right, Mr. Montana," Judge Bates hurriedly conceded. "All evidence, I am sure, will point out that Mr. Betton was at your ranch, as you say. And, as Mr. Betton said so stoutly, there are many other cowpunchers named Shorty. The name, as well as we know, is a nickname tied to many men."

"That's right, Your Honor," Shorty Betton stated.

Sheriff Brown growled, "Let's quit the snarlin' an' look for tracks."

They got remains of the tarp that had been spread across the load, wrapped these around sticks of dried wood, and lit them. By their feeble, uncertain lights, they circled, looking for tracks. But the torches were too weak and they had to stop, for they were just wasting their time.

"Have to wait until mornin'," Sheriff Will Brown said. He was grumbling, for he did not like to stay until dawn. Toward sunrise it would be pretty cold. They threw more driftwood on the fire and squatted around it to keep warm.

Cy Montana said, "Well, no use me an' Shorty staying here any longer. We've done all we can do."

Montana and Betton got their horses and rode toward the Cross H.

"Wish I knew what they knew," Tobacco murmured.

"I don't figure you'd know much," Judge Bates said. "I don't think they were in on this."

"I do."

The partners were squatting in the brush, apart from the sheriff and deputy and the mule skinner and Jocky Smith and the cook. The rest of them therefore could not hear their low voices.

"Explain yourself, Tobacco?"

"Well, the way I understand it, Shorty Betton has a cabin alone on the Cross H. That's beside the point, though. Him an' his boss could've rid out here, dynamited this rig, then high-tailed back to the Cross H, an' waited for the driver to stagger in."

"That's logical."

"Sure it's logical. Then, to make it look good, they've brought the driver into town an' Sheriff Brown, an' even rid out here to listen to what was said. An' Montana might've made a slip an' hollered Shorty's name."

Judge Bates nodded.

"Cy Montana might've got excited, an' made that mistake."

Judge Bates took a long nip out of his jug. He had to fortify himself against the night's chill. The plan was logical . . . to a degree. There seemed only one thing wrong with it. He doubted if either Cy Montana or Shorty Betton would have brains enough to think up such a devious undertaking.

"When a man's pressed, Bates, he can think up lotsa things."

Jocky Smith came over. He and his cook were riding back to the dirt-camp. They were of no use here. He was going to send a messenger to Rawhide and tell the railroad officials what had happened.

"Men, I'm beginnin' to fear for my life, an' the

lives of my workers. Judge, I wish you could convince the big-wigs not to run rails through Broomtail Basin. This might end in serious gunplay an' death."

Judge Bates reminded him that he sat on Judge Hostetler Mackenzie's bench, and his job was impartially to deal out decisions, not to persuade a bunch of lug-headed railroad big-wigs their rails should run through Sagebrush Flats, and not through Broomtail Basin.

"I have met them, Mr. Smith, and tasted of their arrogance. I will have no further word with them unless they come to me."

"They sure are bull-headed," Smith agreed.

The cook came up, leading Smith's bronc. The cook was grumbling about having to go out and shoot jackrabbits to feed the dirt-crew and saying that they could have eaten wild onions, but wild onions grew only in the spring, and here it was fall with snow soon to hit them in their pants. He was still bellyaching as the pair rode away toward the dirt-camp beside the reservoir.

"Nothin' we can do here, either," Tobacco grumbled.

The judge walked over to Sheriff Brown. "You can handle things here," he said. "Report on your findings tomorrow, Sheriff. As for you, mule skinner, you'd best head back to town with us, where the doctor can put you under his care. A blow on the head sometimes has unfavorable aspects later on."

"You go with them," Sheriff Brown grunted.

Brown's deputy squatted beside the low fire. He had unsaddled his horse and draped the crusty saddle-blanket around his shoulders. The jurist could see that he did not relish the long wait for daylight out here in the cold foothills. But the deputy was silent.

"See you in the mornin'," Sheriff Brown said.

CHAPTER 13

Judge Hostetler Mackenzie sat in a soft chair with pillows behind his back. A red dressing robe hung to his bony shoulders and leather slippers graced his bony feet.

"I am indeed sorry, Judge Bates, as I said before, that I am an invalid during these stirring times. From reports, you and your partner though, seem to be doing well. How I wish I could be in saddle with you."

The judge almost smiled at that, but managed to keep a straight face. He got a quick vision of Judge Hostetler Mackenzie approaching a snuffy bronc. Let the bronc snort, and the judge would run so fast he'd bust through a four-pole corral.

"I wish you were, too, sir."

Judge Mackenzie sighed, then coughed. "My back—right there—" He pressed his right hand against the spot. "You will—er—stay until this is completed, Your Honor?"

"That I will, sir."

The bony face lighted. "That is kind of you."

Mrs. Mackenzie gushered in with a bottle and a spoon. "Time for your medicine, husband."

Judge Bates and Tobacco left.

Outside on the cinder walk, Tobacco grumbled, "That danged four-flusher. He ain't sick. I'd like to jerk off his bony arms an' beat him to death with 'em!"

"Such talk," the judge chided.

"Bates, he's makin' monkeys outa us. Here he sets on his rump, an' me an' you make night-rides an' dodge ambush bullets. He coughs dainty-like into a linen handkerchief. Look what I pack to cough into." He jerked out a dirty red bandanna.

"We got to stay, Tobacco. My oath of office requires it. Besides, we aren't doing too bad, are we?"

Again Tobacco Jones snorted. "What have we done?" He again answered his own question. "You've met another drunk, One-Step Connors, an' his cell-mate, Juanita. We've been shot at. I've bin in a rough fist-fight—"

"Whoa up, partner."

Tobacco stopped talking. He chewed and scowled. He saw a beetle climbing a dried grass stalk. He spat on the beetle and knocked him to the ground.

"Your aim is still accurate," Judge Bates acknowledged.

They went to the doctor's office and took seats, for the medico was out. After ten minutes the doctor returned. He had been to see Judge Mackenzie, he said, and had missed them at the judge's house, for he had also gone to tend to a man who had broken his legs when kicked by a horse.

The judge asked how the slugged guard—the one slugged at the reservoir—was getting along.

The medico said the guard was still on the critical list. He still couldn't talk, though his eyes seemed to be clearing. He had given medical attention to the mule skinner who had been slugged, too, and had put the man to bed in the hotel, where Ma Jacobson would take care of him.

"She's a practical nurse, you know."

Tobacco smiled suddenly. The doctor wondered at the postmaster's sudden mirth. But Judge Lemanuel Bates knew. With Ma taking care of the mule skinner, she would have less time to pester Tobacco.

"How about Judge Mackenzie?" Tobacco demanded. "That man ain't sick. I know he ain't."

The doctor smiled. "He says he has a sore back. There is no doctor in the world that can prove a man hasn't a sore back. I even had one myself when they got me into the war. I got it pushing a cannon around. They gave me a medical discharge."

"Was the cannon heavy?" Tobacco asked.

"I don't know. I just laid down beside it, grabbed the small of my back, and started to groan. And no doctor in the army could prove I was not afflicted with a lame back."

Tobacco grinned. "That's Judge Hoss Mackenzie."

The doctor was stiffly professional. "We shall discuss my patient no longer, gentlemen."

The doctor looked at the cut on Tobacco's eye, pronounced it as healing rapidly, and ventured that the postmaster had good blood to heal so quickly.

"Ain't never diluted it with alcyhol."

Judge Bates grinned at the medico.

The partners went to their hotel room. Trudy had been behind the counter in the lobby. Her mother, the girl said, was upstairs, taking care of the mule skinner. They were both tired.

"Me for a nap," the judge said.

Tobacco chewed reflectively. "Well, I got one good break. Judge, I'm gettin' tired of these surroundings."

Judge Bates lay on his back, seemingly admiring the fly-specked ceiling. He admitted he too yearned for his home in Cowtrail. There seemed to be two alternatives, he reasoned.

"An' them, Bates?"

They could jug three men: Ross Frazier, Cy Montana and Montana's range boss, Shorty Betton. "With them in jail if this trouble didn't stop, we'd know they had no finger in it."

"But their hired hands could carry on."

"That is possible, but not probable."

Tobacco leaned forward, laughing silently. "Man, what if we did that, eh? Man, would ol' Cy hit the ceilin'. An' that Shorty Betton skunk—" The Cowtrail postmaster gingerly fingered his cut eye. "I'd like to get him behin' bars an' forget about him forever an 'a day!"

"We might jail them."

"What's the other plan, Bates?"

This plan, too, was simple. They would follow this one first. Word would get back to Rawhide and railroad officials would send out another wagonload of chuck, They would trail the wagon and see if it were molested.

"Long ride, cold camp in the brush, Bates."

"Might bring some results, though."

Judge Bates had just got his eyes closed when somebody hammered on the door. He asked, "Who's there?" and a voice said, "Sheriff Will Brown."

"Come in."

The sheriff was very apologetic. He hated to dis-

turb their sleep. He knew they were tired. They
had ridden lots of miles at all hours. They were
getting along in years—

"Each day we get further in years," Judge Bates
said sourly. "Now tell us what rides your mind, my
good man."

"The same damn' thing," Brown growled.
"Nothin'."

The judge almost said, "That's only normal,"
but managed to hold himself in time. Further ques-
tioning by the jurist disclosed that both Sheriff
Brown and his deputy had searched for tracks.

"An' by gum, we found some. Two riders had
come off the rimrock an' parked their broncs in the
bresh. We backtrailed, but up there in them hills
the winds had been so rough it had blowed the sand
an' blowed tracks right away."

"Two men, did you say?" the judge queried.

Sheriff Brown nodded. "Two riders." He rubbed
his whiskery jaw. "Maybe the mule skinner was right
when he heard them holler, 'Shorty.' Unless my
'rithmetic is haywire, Cy Montana an' Shorty Betton make two men."

"I doubt that," the judge said. "At their best,
they'd only make about one man and a half."

"No time for joshin'," Brown said seriously.

Brown also said that one of the railroad bosses

had ridden over to the dynamited wagon. He and Brown, it seemed, had some hard words. These hurt Brown more than the fact he had found nothing pointing to the identity of the man—or men— who had burned the freight wagon.

"Them boys got money. They talked to me like I was dirt. They've always talked to me thataway. This gent was no different. Named Straw or Hay or somethin' like that."

The judge told the sheriff not to pay much attention to what Straw said. In his estimation, Straw was just a big blowhard. This cheered Sheriff Brown a little. He said the railroad company was sending out another load of chuck for the dirt camp, and that it should arrive sometime that night.

"I'm trailin' it in," he said.

"Good idea," Judge Bates told him.

Brown stretched. "I'm goin' down the hall an' talk with that mule skinner. Doc tol' me he was up here in room twelve, I believe."

The judge and Tobacco were glad to get shut of the lawman. When the door had closed behind Brown, Tobacco said, "Well, no use us trailin' that wagon, with the law on the job."

Judge Bates laced his chubby hands behind his head and again regarded the dirty ceiling. "All the more reason we should shadow it, friend. Brown is so low in intelligence he might get mixed up an' think he should blast the wagon."

Tobacco lay down again. "I cannot savvy where that dynamite is comin' from, Bates. We've checked the stores here and' none of them has dynamite for sale, even. If we could find out where it come from, we'd have something to work on."

Judge Bates said that they were using dynamite—and lots of it—on the Great Western railroad grade. It would be a simple matter for a man to lift a little of this powder without the railroad missing it.

"Must be where it's comin' from, Bates."

A feminine voice shrilled, "Get outa here, Sheriff Brown. Get out, I tell you, and leave my patient alone."

The voice came from down the hall.

Tobacco sat up, grinning. Even Judge Bates' wide face sported a smile.

Sheriff Brown's whining voice said, "Now, Mrs. Jacobson, hol' onto your hosses. I got permission from Doc to talk to your victim."

"My *victim*!"

"Your patient, I mean."

The sounds of a scuffle came to the partners. This ended, and a door slammed so hard it danced the pins in its hinges. Footsteps sounded down the hall and Sheriff Brown's head, hair mussed, came inside.

"Man, what a woman. I tried to get in to see her patient, an' she pushed me out. She's as strong as a yearlin' bull. I pity you, Mr. Jones."

"Pity me? Why?"

Sheriff Brown was almost stuttering. "I don't want to be counted too fresh. But heck, it's common talk aroun' town. They say you aim to hook up with the Widder Jacobson." Brown jerked back his head.

"My God," Tobacco Jones mumbled.

CHAPTER 14

When the sun went down the night became colder. The first part of it was dark—as dark as a midnight-black horse—but then the moon heeled over the badlands. But there was no warmth in the moon.

"I'm cold," Tobacco said.

No answer.

"I'm sleepy," Tobacco said.

No answer.

"I wish I was home in Cowtrail."

"Anything else wrong with you?"

Tobacco Jones scowled. "Yeah, I'm with you, Bates."

"I can slam you in jail," Judge Bates reminded him.

Tobacco chewed slowly. "That might not be a bad idea. Just so you put me in a warm jail an' not the same one One-Step an' Juanita inhabit. An' just so you make it so the Widder Jacobson can't ha'nt me."

"You ask too much of life," the jurist commented.

They were about five miles west of the Rawhide junction, where the wagon road went into the hills. They had seen the loaded wagon leave the camp at deep dusk, and now it was somewhere below them.

They squatted, using sandstones for a windbreak. Sheriff Will Brown was somewhere below the partners, too. They had seen him hide himself in some wild rosebushes along the bottom of a brush-thick gully.

"What a lawman," the judge had marvelled. "Instead of spotting himself up high where he could see everything below him, he hunkers along the trail. But he's still dangerous."

Tobacco admitted the sheriff was trigger-happy. His nerves had bothered him so long he was as jumpy as a drunk with the delirium tremens. Let him hear a sound behind him and he'd turn and empty his pistol. If'n he weren't so frightened he couldn't move a muscle."

"We'll have to get him out of the way."

"An' how do it?"

"Bounce him once or twice and put him to sleep."

Tobacco smiled. "Right enjoyable thought, Your Honor. Then you can try him in court for failin' to do his duty an' can him in his own calaboose, eh?"

"You take it too far, friend."

"Should've done it before dark, though."

The judge allowed that the moon made enough light. They could hear the heavily laden wagon creaking below. Shod hoofs made sounds on the wagon-trail, and the skinner cursed now and then. They had noticed that a guard rode with the skinner tonight.

They left their broncs and went down the slope, Tobacco toting his rifle. The judge did not take his rifle; he took his jug. They pointed toward the boulders above the gully where Sheriff Will Brown had hidden.

They reached these boulders and squatted and took consultation. Brown had not ridden out to follow the wagon. They found his horse, and the judge whispered, "You stay with the horse. You know how a nighthawk makes a noise, like this—" He whistled shrilly.

"Don't sound like no nighthawk to me," Tobacco murmured.

Evidently it sounded all right to Sheriff Brown, for he did not come to investigate.

The judge talked low and hurriedly. Tobacco would stay with Brown's bronc. When Judge Bates had accurately located Sheriff Brown's hideout, he would whistle. "Then you turn the lawman's bronc loose, understand? He'll make noise in the brush, and Brown will hurry to investigate, wondering how he broke loose and he'll try to catch him."

"Then what?"

"That's where I take over."

"Sure hope he don't see you."

"He won't. Time he learned a hard lesson, anyway."

Still toting his jug, Judge Bates went into the brush. About five minutes later, he was standing in the high buckbrush along a trail, and not more than forty feet away, still in the sandstones and buckbrush, was Sheriff Will Brown.

No sooner had the jurist stationed himself than Sheriff Brown started moving toward his horse. Evidently he was ready to mount and swing in behind the wagon for his self-appointed night chore.

The judge gave his nighthawk whistle. But his lips were too dry, and it ended on a sickening note.

This note halted Sheriff Brown. Judge Bates could see him, limned in moonlight, hand on his gun. He was peering into the brush, but evidently he did not see His Honor.

The judge found himself wishing that Tobacco would soon free the sheriff's bronc. Ages seemed to run past him; finally, he heard the horse move, cracking brush. And Sheriff Brown ran forward, hollering, "Whoa, Baldy, whoa. Now how in Hades did that bronc get loose!"

Sheriff Brown ran past Judge Bates.

Finally, there was only silence. Judge Bates broke it with his nighthawk whistle. This time the whistle was more realistic.

"All set," he said.

Tobacco Jones was breaking through brush. When he came up, Judge Bates was tying Sheriff Brown's feet with the sheriff's policeman suspenders. He tied the sheriff's hands with a bandanna found in Brown's pocket.

"What'd you hit him with, Bates?"

"Betsy."

Tobacco grinned. "That ol' jug sure must be tough. You've buttonholed quite a few jaspers with it for a long sleep. Now what'll we do with the carcass?"

"Lay him out on the trail. He'll come to an' holler an' kick. Might holler loud enough to attract a cowpuncher who might be workin' cattle back in the hills come daylight. Or the wagon might find him on its way back."

"If it gets back," Tobacco said pessimistically.

They carried Sheriff Brown out of the brush to the dusty wagon-trail. Tobacco had him by the shoulders and Judge Bates had Brown's boots tucked under one thick arm. Brown sagged quite a bit in the middle.

"He's purty long atween the hocks an' the bit," Tobaeco said.

They dumped Brown, and he landed with his nose in dust. The judge twisted his limp head around and felt for his heart and found a steady beat. Tobacco bit off a chew and grinned.

"You, a judge, an honored personage of the bar—both kinds, too— an' you slug a county servant, one who shares office next to you. Fella, ain't you kinda ashamed, now ain't you."

"Sure am."

They went back to the rimrock and got their horses. They had left their weary mules in the Wild Horse livery-stable. They got the wagon road but, as the judge said, "We can't follow that wagon too close what with that guard on there. He might glimpse us and open up."

Accordingly they cut across the basin and rode about two miles out of the wagon's trail, travelling even with it as it lumbered across the hills. Soon it would cross the divide, and down-trail into Broomtail Basin, it would be faster. The wagon went so slow that they stopped many times in the rocks and waited for it, keeping it always in sight in the moonlight.

Tobacco yawned.

Judge Bates took a stiff drink. He shook his jug and decided he'd need pay One-Step a visit tomorrow, if tomorrow ever came. But he'd had lots of help in lowering the line in Old Betsy.

"There they go," Tobacco mumbled. "They've crossed the Hump an' will make better time now."

From these high rocks they could see the basin below. Shimmering in moonlight, Broomtail Basin seemed tranquil and without a hint of danger. They turned their broncs west again.

Suddenly flame showed from the wagon, about a mile away. At first, Judge Bates thought it had been dynamited, a slow fuse being loaded with the chuck. Then he heard a high whine and a swift ricochet back in the rocks.

"That danged guard must've caught a glimpse of us, Bates. He's took a shot just for luck. He only missed us by about four rods, too."

"Trigger-happy," the judge said.

After that, though, they were more careful, and they stayed further away from the wagon, now on the basin's floor.

No more shots came.

Nevertheless, the partners made sure they were out of rifle range. A coyote slunk along the hills, and the guard shot at him but missed again. The partners watched the coyote lope back into the **foothills.**

The guard, the judge averred, was not taking any chances. Had they run the other wagon through with a guard, nine chances out of ten the driver wouldn't have been overpowered and the load burned.

Dawn was coloring the foothills when the wagon rolled close to the camp by the reservoir that was slowly being rebuilt. It lighted the hills and threw buckbrush and cottonwood trees into cold relief.

Tobacco said, "I'm sure cold, Bates. Looks to me like we done rid on a wild duck chase again. Me, I got a strange feelin', friend."

"Yes?"

"Somebody around here is smarter'n we are."

The jurist allowed this could be true. There was, he claimed always somebody smarter than you were. But the wagon wasn't in camp yet.

"Danged near there."

They sat cold. saddles, there in the hills, and watched the wagon cross the plain, an ant crawling along the winding trail through sagebrush and greasewood. Yard by yard, teams plodding, it came closer to the camp.

Already men stirred in the dirt camp. The camp-tender was graining the teams for the day's labor, pouring measures of oats into each oat bin, there at the long mangers. The sun was up high enough to show the reflection of his shiny bucket.

Smoke came from the cook-tent.

"Well, there's the guard. That wagonload got there all right." Tobacco spat.

The postmaster was correct. The camp-guard was walking out to meet the wagon. Their cold night had been spent in vain. Judge Bates thought of Sheriff Will Brown, lying back there on the road.

By this time Brown would be conscious and probably hollering. Maybe he could manage to get loose of his bonds. Anyway, one thing was certain; Brown would be plenty cold.

He sort of hoped that Brown had freed himself and was now riding toward Wild Horse town. But common sense told him Brown, if he did get free, would follow the wagon, not head into town. For with him being waylaid and knocked out like that, the lawman would figure sure somebody aimed to highjack the wagon, and had knocked him out first to get him out of the way.

"Here comes a rider," Tobacco said.

Judge Bates followed his partner's finger and murmured, Think of the devil, and he's bound to appear. That's Brown, ain't it?"

"Looks like him, to me."

Brown rode as if the devil, pitchfork and hot coals, were on his bronco's tail. Dust spiralled up behind his bronc's hoofs as he roared into the dirt camp.

"You didn't anchor him tight enough," Tobacco grumbled. "But reckon it don't make much no-account nohow, now. But I was aimin' to head into the camp for a hot cup of java."

"If Brown sees us ride in, he might suspect us."

Tobacco nodded. They turned toward Wild Horse, many miles to the south. They were just leaving the foothills when the explosion occurred.

CHAPTER 15

It was a dull, deep roar, seeming to come out of the bowels of the earth. At first, Judge Lemanuel Bates thought it was the rumblings of a hard earthquake. Then he realized that the earth was not moving under his pony.

He shot a glance at the dirt-camp, half expecting to see tents and teams in the air. But the dirt-camp was intact.

"Yonder!" Tobacco screamed the words. "Over there, Bates!"

The jurist jerked his eyes away from the camp. This time Tobacco's forefinger was jabbed toward the basin.

Down there, a few miles away, dirt and debris had mushroomed upward, as though flung from the bosom of the valley by a giant, prankish hand. Now it was settling, but a great bulk of something—evidently a canvas tarp—still floated in the chilly morning air.

"They've blasted up that well Jocky Smith was punching," the judge said slowly. "That is the location, isn't it, Jones?"

"None other," Tobacco growled. "Here we watch the wagon-load, an' some son blows up the well, casin' an' all."

But already the jurist was riding down the slope. Tobacco swung his bronc in behind his partner's horse. They swung through sagebrush, with Tobacco driving his animal hard; finally he pulled up abreast of Judge Bates' laboring cayuse.

"They've heard it at the dirt-camp," the postmaster boomed. "There is riders leavin' there, too."

They could not see the location of the well, for the sagebrush was too high. They had seen nobody ride away from the explosion. But a dry wash flanked the well spot on the west, and a rider could have hugged it and ridden away, hidden by the deepness of the ravine and the sagebrush.

"There she is," Tobacco grunted.

Nobody moved around the well, now a blasted hole. Judge Bates knew that the working men who were drilling the well stayed nights at the dirt-camp. He also knew that Jock Smith had posted a guard at the well each night, for Smith had told him that down in Wild Horse.

The explosion had evidently been shot off down

in the casing. The derrick—what was left of it—was tipped on one side. The bit lay to one side, cable still attached to it, and the steam engine used to raise and lower the bit was also upset.

"They'll never dig that well," Judge Bates said.

With the casing broken, down in the earth, the well had caved in, and it would be easier and cheaper to start all over again.

"Riders comin', Bates."

The two partners stood in the clearing, hands held high as the dirt-men drove in on running broncs. Sheriff Will Brown was with them.

"Bates and Jones, huh?" Jocky Smith curbed his impatient horse. "How come you two got here so fast?" He didn't wait for an answer. "Somebody sure blasted this hole to—" The dirt-boss swore with great feeling and choice cusswords. "I had a guard out. Wonder where he is?"

"Here he is, Jocky," a man said.

Two men came out of the brush carrying the guard, who was limp between them. Somebody dipped a bucket-full of icy water from the barrel and smashed it into the guard's face, and the two men put him on the ground.

"He's been knocked out," a man volunteered.

Sheriff Will Brown was out of saddle. He kept grabbing at his pants to keep them up. Judge Bates told him that he and Tobacco had left Wild Horse early to ride out to the dirt-camp to make sure nothing had happened during the night. They had heard the explosion and hurried over to the well-digging site.

"And how, sir, did you get to the dirt-camp so bright and early?"

Brown explained he had trailed the wagon-load out of Rawhide, riding guard on it. He had escorted it unharmed to the camp, too. "Not a thing happened on the road, either. I was just hoping somebody would try to blast it. I was ready for 'em."

Jocky Smith was sending men out, trying to cut the trail of the man who had dynamited the well.

"Here's some bronc prints in the wash, Jocky," called a man.

Jocky Smith hurried to the wash.

Judge Bates knelt beside the unconscious guard. The man had a mean cut on his scalp. Finally he struggled to sit up, his eyes wild. They held him until his eyes cleared.

"What happened?" he demanded.

The judge told him about the blast. "Now, what happened to you sir?"

The guard had not been slugged. A piece of flying debris had hit him, he said, and his memory had stopped right there. Under the judge's careful verbal prodding, he told his story.

About an hour ago, he'd heard something move, out in the brush. He'd figured maybe it was a range cow or even a cougar, but he wanted to make sure. So he'd slipped into the brush and looked around, fearing somebody was sneaking back to dynamite the casin.

"I run into a heifer and her spring calf back there. I figured then they'd made the noise, but to make sure, I squatted and waited with my rifle. That was about a hour ago, I reckon."

"You mentioned that before," the judge said.

Men stood in a circle and listened. The tracks in the wash had turned out, so Jocky Smith had said, to be the tracks of a range bronc, unshod and drifting along the gully, looking for bunchgrass.

"Well, I squatted there, cold as billy hell, and then the whul thing went up. I glimpsed that timber flyin' up an' I tried to get outa the way when it come down, but I reckon I was too slow."

The judge asked, "Were you ever out of sight of the well, sir?"

The guard hesitated. He held his aching head. "Onct I was," he admitted.

Jocky Smith started to curse him. The judge and Tobacco moved to one side, and Sheriff Will Brown, still grabbing to hold up his pants, said, "Some hellion has snuck in, planted powder with a long fuse, then pulled out."

"Might be."

"Might be?" Again Sheriff Will Brown grabbed his slipping trousers. "What else could it be, Your Honor?"

The judge kept a straight face. "What happened to your belt, sir? I noticed your pants keep sliding down."

Brown's ruddy face momentarily flushed. "Never wear a belt," he explained. "Wear suspenders. They busted, an' I tried to patch them, an' that made 'em worse, so I throwed 'em away. I'm gettin' me a rope to use for a hitch, onct I get back to the dirt-camp."

Judge Bates allowed he and Tobacco would mosey on back to town, seeing Sheriff Brown was now on the job. This pleased the lawman no little. The partners got their broncs and rode toward town. A man had headed back to the dirt camp for a rig to carry the injured guard in for medical attention.

"Ma Jacobson oughta be off me for good," Tobacco said. "She'll have two sick men to nurse now, I reckon. Bates, who do you figure set off that powder back yonder. We never seen no rider head out, did we!"

"He might have ridden away up that coulee."

Tobacco pointed out that had there been a rider

on the valley floor, they'd possibly have seen him when they were on the high hills. Judge Bates nodded, his heavy face serious.

"A man could have slipped down from that dirt-camp, Tobacco, and lured the guard away, as he said he'd gone into the brush. Then this fellow could've dropped that powder with a slow fuse, and then drifted back—on foot through the brush—to the camp again."

"But them men are working for the railroad, not against it."

"Might be that Cy Montana or Ross Frazier planted spies in the camp. That's an old trick, you know. Fight from the inside and be unsuspected."

"You might have hit a nail then, Bates."

"There's Shorty Betton again," Tobacco said suddenly.

The Cross H man was riding up a gully, about a half-mile away. Judge Bates found himself wondering if, after all, this short Montana rider wasn't tied up in this. He hollered, "Wait a minute, fellow."

"Too far away to hear, Bates."

Judge Bates pulled his rifle out of boot. He found sights and sent a bullet high over Betton. Betton turned around.

"Stay where you are, Betton."

Betton was frowning when they rode up. "What the blazes you mean, men, throwin' lead at me?"

The judge told him he was going to jail. Betton could hardly believe him. "You juggin' me—because that guard last night said a gent named Shorty—? You can't do it. I demand my rights as a citizen."

"Get along," the judge said.

Tobacco got Betton's rifle and short-gun. They made the short cowpuncher ride ahead. Betton kept repeating. "Wait until Cy Montana hears of this. Just you wait. . . ."

Evidently he had great faith in Montana.

"What's the charge ag'in me?" Betton wanted to know.

"Haven't figured it out yet," Judge Bates said.

Betton's face twisted, his lips went hard. "God, what a plague came into this county when the railroad started through, an' when you two grasshoppers come in. Take months of wind after you're gone to blow the stink away!"

"That'll be nice," the judge agreed.

Two miles out of Wild Horse, they met big Ross Frazier, who stared at Shorty Betton, disarmed and riding ahead of the partners.

"What you goin' do with him, Your Honor?"

"Hang him. Get in line, Frazier. You're goin' to the gallows too. Surrender your rifle and gun."

Ross Frazier studied the judge. "That's a odd joke."

"No joke about it, friend." Judge Bates' short-gun was on the Bar S owner. "Mr. Jones, take Mr. Frazier's weapons."

Frazier's hands automatically went up, palms out. Judge Bates watched the cowman's surprise turn into anger.

"You'll never get by with this, Bates. I'll sue you for false arrest. I'll ship in the best lawyer in Omaha and spend every cent I own to whip you."

"That sounds interesting."

Soon Ross Frazier was riding abreast with Shorty Betton. Tobacco scowled and asked softly, "Could that big jassax throw a suit against us, Bates?"

"He might. He'd never win, though."

Townspeople stared at them as they rode into Wild Horse burg. They came out of business-houses and watched and made conjectures. Judge Bates made the prisoners dismount and march into jail.

One-Step and Juanita were playing chess in the bull-pen. They had a flask on the table between them. Judge Bates made Ross Frazier go into one cell and put Shorty Betton in another.

"What's the charge?" the jailer asked.

"I'll write it out," the judge said.

One-Step leaned back in his chair. "Bates, how come you do this to me and Juanita? Here we were enjoying the solitude and homeliness of this little cottage, and you take in these two unshaven, hulking brutes to spoil our homelife."

"They may not be in long."

"I won't be here long!" Frazier snorted.

The judge beckoned One-Step to one side and the prisoner went down into the cellar and filled the judge's jug. One-Step stopped, arms akimbo, and studied the two jailed cowmen.

"You should've picked out somebody with some brains, Judge. I can't carry on any intellectual conversation with this pair. They're of such low intelligence I'll bet neither has a vocabulary of six hundred words. While they are with me, I shall make a test of their possible intelligence rating."

"Do that," the judge said.

Outside, the judge met one of Will Brown's deputies. He told the deputy to head for the Cross H and tell Cy Montana to come into town. "Tell him Shorty Betton is in jail and I have to talk to Cy."

"Sure thing, Your Honor."

Within two hours, Cy Montana was in the same cell with Shorty Betton, and they sat on their bunks, glaring at Ross Frazier, who likewise sat on his bunk, glaring back at the Cross H men.

"Look like three lovesick bobcats," One-Step said disgustedly.

CHAPTER 16

Three things of interest happened that same day. First, the guard died.

He never recovered full consciousness after his beating at the reservoir. The medico reported his death first to Judge Bates and Tobacco Jones, who were in their room in the Wild Horse House, dozing a little after their cold night ride.

Toward the last, the man's eyes had brightened, so the doctor said. He opened his mouth, trying to say something, but the words were jumbled and incoherent. He tried hard to speak, but the words made no sense, and he had lain back and been silent.

"A murder charge to be filed against persons—or a person—unknown," Judge Bates said. "I shall make it out and we shall do our best to find his murderer, Doctor."

The doctor supposed the railroad company would pay for the man's medical care and burial expenses.

Tobacco snorted. "Them big-wigs won't shell out, Medico. Know where an' how they bury a man who got kilt on the job? They lay his carcass in the fill an' drag dirt over him with mules an' fresnos."

"Is that right, Your Honor?"

Judge Bates nodded. "They lose a mule and they holler, sir. They lose a working man and no tears are shed. You see, they have to buy a mule, and some mother right now is raising a working man for them, for just a few dollars a week."

"That isn't just to the county, Your Honor, to pay for his burial."

"The county won't pay for this, sir. I assure you of that. If those railroad officials won't shell out, I'll file a suit against the company a yard long, and stay on this bench the rest of my life, or until I collect. Be assured on that point, Doctor."

The doctor reported on the other two slugged men—the driver of the wagon-load of chuck that had been dynamited, and the guard at the well that had been blown up. They were progressing nicely, both still in bed. "Mrs. Jacobson is nursing them back to health. She gives them too much attention, I think."

"She can't give them too much." Tobacco was emphatic on that point.

The doctor understood; he smiled.

Sheriff Will Brown came in within the hour. He roported the death of the guard, and wondered what to do. Judge Bates told him he was swearing out a John Doe murder charge, and would some day, he hoped, know John Doe's real name.

"Ross Frazier an' Cy Montana got into a fight. They fought through the bars. Frazier knocked Montana down an' Shorty Betton hung one on Frazier, spillin' him. You shouldn't've put them in adjoinin' cells, Your Honor."

"Let them fight."

"You have to take full responsibility for juggin' them three. I washes my hands of the whul affair, Your Honor."

"Don't let your shadow bite you," Tobacco said, smiling.

"'T' ain't I'm afeerd," Sheriff Brown hurried to explain. "I just don't want no suit slapped against me for false arrest. I got a woman an' kids lookin' to me for their eats, men."

Judge Bates told him he had nothing to fear; he himself would shoulder full responsibility for jailing Betton, Montana, and Frazier. Thus assured, Sheriff Will Brown left, face not so glum as when he had entered.

They heard his boots go down the hall and start the descent into the lobby.

Tobacco said, "See he had on new red suspenders, Judge." The lanky postmoster leaned back in his easy-chair. "I too figger you made a mistake by jailin' them hellions so clost together."

"I figure One-Step will smooth that out."

This didn't make good sense to the postmaster, but he let it ride at that. For some reason, the judge seemed to have great faith in One-Step Connors. Tobacco almost remarked that, as usual since coming into Broomtail Basin, they were still cueing the same eight-ball into the same side-pocket.

With the death of the guard, a seriousness had really colored the situation, here on this Wyoming high basin. This reflected in Judge Lemanuel Bates' serious face and showed in the studious thought of Tobacco Jones' eyes.

Now, more than ever, Tobacco knew his partner would be a tenacious bulldog. He would circle this melee, find the right man, and rush in to fasten his teeth. And hades help the man who had murdered that guard.

One of Brown's deputies, and it seemed he had two of them, was the next visitor. Both the jurist and postmaster were dozing by that time.

"And what do you desire, sir?" Judge Bates spoke sharply.

The deputy knuckled his hat's brim nervously.

"Sorry to disturb you men, but the boss told me to come up an' see you. The boss an' his other deputy just left town, you see, an' I'm supposed to hightail after them, jus' as soon as I deliver this message."

"What is your message?"

Words tumbled from the deputy. While Jocky Smith and his men had been working on the reservoir fill with their teams and dump-wagons, somebody had burned down a tent at the camp.

"Maybe the cook had an accident an' it caught fire," Tobacco ventured.

The guard shook his head. "No, tent was off alone, I understand. Off a few rods from the rest. The cook was alone in camp. This tent just caught fire. Jocky sent a man in to tell us an' asked if you two would ride out to the camp an' look around for evidence pointin' to whoever had set it."

Judge Bates promptly vetoed this suggestion. He said, "We've been out to that camp so many times you'd figure we run the danged outfit. Jocky got an idea as to who had set it?"

"One man claims he saw a gent sneakin' into the brush. Said the gent looked like Ross Frazier. But it couldn't be Frazier; he's in the clink. But it might've been one of the Bar S hands. One gent out there—Froggy White's his handle— looks a heap like Frazier."

"We're not riding out," the judge stated.

The deputy crammed on his hand. "Again, sorry disturbed you two men. Well, gotta be gettin' along, I reckon." He slammed the door and almost ran down the hall. They heard him boot his way across the lobby, and then the outer door slammed.

Sharp heels came down the hallway. Ma Jacobson poked in her head. She wore a white cap and had on a white uniform that did not hide her conspicuous bulges a single bit.

"Which one of you went downstairs just now?"

The judge played ignorant. They had both been downstairs this morning, he said. To whom was she talking?

"You know full well, Judge Bates, what I mean. Somebody just left here, slammed the door, stomped down the stairs, an' woke up one of my patients."

"Oh," the judge said, "that was a friend."

"You two seem to have a lot of noisy friends. They seem to forget we have two sick men up here."

"Where's Trudy?" Tobacco asked innocently.

Ma Jacobson eyed him speculatively. "You seem to be awful interested in my little girl, Mr. Jones. It will do you not a bit of good. You are old enough to be her grandfather, and never forget that."

"My josh, I never onct thought of that."

The judge was smiling.

Ma Jacobson studied them each, finally catching on to their humor. A wide smile crossed her face. "But be more silent in the future, please?"

The judge assured her they would be, but they were not accountable for guests. Ma Jacobson said the next noisy guest would account to her personally.

"Goodbye, honey," Tobacco said.

She winked at him and closed the door.

Judge Bates smiled widely. "You call her that again, partner, and she'll forget those two injured guards in a hurry."

"My Lord," Tobacco said. "The word slipped out by accident. I was thinkin' of Trudy, I reckon."

Judge Bates leaned back, heavy head against the head rest of his chair, hands laced across his belly, eyes closed.

Tobacco growled, "Bates, we can't set here, an' do nothin'!"

Judge Bates did not open his eyes. "Talk, Tobacco."

"Well . . . first, the reservoir got blasted. Then we gets jailed—"

"Jump that part, please."

Tobacco smiled. He peeled tinfoil off a fresh plug of eating-tobacco. "Well . . . we got shot at. That wagon was blasted. Then the well got blowed up."

"So far, so good."

"Up to now, we've sorta blamed it either on Montana or Ross Frazier. We jug them, an' a tent gets burned down. Now we know for sure it ain't them two cowmen. But it could be one of their riders, acting under their orders."

"That's so. But sum it all down."

"Whatduhyou mean?"

"Get to the core of it. The essence. The primary fact. The motivation behind this whole trouble."

Tobacco chewed laboriously. "Me, I figger it comes down to this. Somebody aroun' here don't want this railroad comin' through Broomtail Basin. They want it to run northwest through Sagebrush Flats an' then acrost the Rockies on Bridger Pass."

"Why would they want it through Sagebrush Flats?"

"Well, I dunno, for sure."

"Make a guess, pard."

"This reason, I'd say. They could make money if it ran through Sagebrush Flats. If it runs through Broomtail, this party loses money."

"Would either Montana or Ross Frazier make dinero, if the railroad ran through Sagebrush Flats?"

"No, they'd make no money. But they'd keep the rails from crossin' their graze." Tobacco stopped chewing. "Maybe one of them owns Sagebrush Flats, eh?"

The judge doubted that. Doubted it strongly. For if either Montana or Frazier owned Sagebrush Flats, the owner would have come out openly and offered to dicker with the railroad at low terms, just to keep rails out of Broomtail Basin.

"That's right, Tobacco conceded.

Tobacco spat out the open window. Maybe the tobacco juice landed on somebody in the street, but if it had he didn't care. He was silent for about five minutes. Judge Bates started to snore a little. Tobacco's hand shook his arm.

"Yes, Jones?"

"I figger I savvy now, Bates. Somebody here on this grass owns Broomtail Basin. They're workin' from inside to make the railroad disgusted so they'll drive rails into Sagebrush Flat."

"That is my opinion too, sir."

"I don't like this Brown button," Tobacco said reflectively. "I still don't think a man could be as dumb as he puts on. You don't reckon he owns Sagebrush on the quiet, an' is playin' a lawman role an' doin' dirty work?"

"I doubt that. I really believe firmly he is not faking. I believe, earnestly believe, he is of too low intelligence."

"We gotta find out who owns Sagebrush Flats, Bates."

"That is why I am resting. I have a long ride ahead of me, sir, to the wire at Diamond Willow. You too have a long ride ahead of you."

"Where am I going?"

"Sagebrush Flats."

"But that's fifty mile, Bates. That's a long ride."

"But it has to be taken, sir."

The judge outlined his scheme. Tobacco would go to Sagebrush Flats, inquire around, find who owned that country. Then he would report back to Wild Horse. Meanwhile, he himself would ride to Diamond Willow, there to send telegrams to the federal land office down in Cheyenne.

"When do we pull out?"

"When it's dark. We want nobody to trail us."

That settled, they both dozed off. Their next visitor was One-Step Connors. "Jailer sent me down to the store to get a box of raisins for him, Your Honor. His wife, it seems, is concocting a cake for his birthday. I accused him of being about ninety, and he got ired. He informed me, in certain terms, that he was only eighty-seven. I thought I'd drop in on you old fogies."

"Thanks," Tobacco mumbled.

The judge and One-Step had a drink. One-Step

was rather deep in friendship already with John
Barleycorn.

"There is one thing I want of you, Mr. Connors.
Ply all three of those cowmen with whiskey, sit
back, and let the whiskey run their tongues. Listen
to everything they say."

"They can't say much, Your Honor. Both of
them has smitten the other on the mouth, and their
lips are swollen badly."

"Whiskey will loosen them."

One-Step said he hated to waste the whiskey on
the likes of Shorty Betton, Cy Montana, and Ross
Frazier. They might get wise he was brewing in
the jail and get him thrown out of jail. The judge
assured him he had the jail to live in the rest of his
life, and he would see to that. There was only one
catch: Each month he was to send to Cowtail a jug
of whiskey.

"Do you contemplete leaving, Your Honor?"

"Not for a few days."

"This might be a mean and ignoble thing to utter,
Your Honor, but from the bottom of my heart—
if I still possess such an organ—I have been hoping
for the demise of Judge Hostetler Mackenzie, in
hopes a man of your sterling qualities would then
inherit the deceased's bench."

Tobacco groaned.

The judge and One-Step drank again, and they heard the prisoner's uncertain gait navigate down the hall, fumblingly find the stairs, and weave across the lobby into Wild Horse's sleepy main street.

"Now for some shuteye," Tobacco grunted.

Ten minutes later, a knock sounded on the door. Judge Bates opened one eye and growled, "Come in."

The railroad official named Straw entered.

"What's on your mind, Mr. Hay?" the judge asked.

"Straw's the name—not Hay." Evidently Mr. Straw did not like the judge's sharp tone. He evidently did not like to be addressed in the same haughty tone he used on his subordinates. "Have you heard about that well being blown up and the tent being burned?"

The judge assured him he had.

"You're district judge now, Mr. Bates. I, speaking for the railroad, demand instant—yes, instant—action against this culprit or these culprits, whoever or wherever they may be."

"We don't know who they are, Mr. Hay, or where they are."

This time Straw overlooked the slur against his name. "Then why don't you and your sheriff find out who they are and where they are?"

Straw's voice was too loud. Judge Bates heard the door to room twelve open and he knew Ma Jacobson was on her way. He got lazily to his feet. Ma Jacobson reached the door.

"There's a lady behind you, sir," the judge said.

Straw turned. Judge Bates buried one hand in the seat of Straw's expensive trousers and heard cloth rip. His other hand came up and fastened not too gently on Straw's neck.

He lifted the man bodily, with Straw kicking and threshing and hollering. Ma Jacobson jumped back.

"With your permission, madam?"

"Kindly," Ma grunted.

Judge Bates carried the man to the head of the stairs. One heave, and Straw went sailing, hitting the steps with his wide rump. He bounced down into the lobby. The judge followed.

"Now get out, for good."

Straw said, "You'll pay for this," and doubled his fists. The judge started for him, and Straw turned and ran out. He got his horse and hurriedly left town. Judge Bates, puffing, climbed the stairs to where Ma Jacobson and Tobacco stood, both of them smiling.

"You beat me to it, pard."

The judge sucked in his breath. "Not as young as I once was," he apologized. "I'm sorry for this, madam. But I take it you have no love for these railroad officials, either."

"Not a bit, judge. But my patients——"

Tobacco went back to their room. Judge Bates put his arm around Ma's ample waist. Tobacco, head out the door, watched.

Ma said, "Now, Judge. . . ."

Tobacco winked.

CHAPTER 17

The railway depot-agent was about sixty, wiry and thin. He stared up at Judge Bates, his eyes belligerent. He slipped the ear-phone off a head shaped like a muskmelon.

"Whatduhyuh want?"

Judge Bates put his jug on the counter. "Take a drink, friend?"

"Like fun I will. You're prob'ly one of these railroad dicks. You want me to drink so you can can me an' I won't get my pension ten years from now."

"Ten years from now, with your cranky disposition, you won't even be on top the sod, friend."

The short man slipped out of his chair. "Who do you think you are, anyway, to come in here—" He looked down at the telegram the judge was writing. When he saw the signature, "Judge Lemanuel Bates," his anger changed to a wide frown of enlightenment.

"Judge Bates, huh? Man, I've heered a lot about you. Lemme shake your hand for straightin' up young Nero Bucklin an' cleanin' up that crooked legal outfit up in Post Hole Basin some time back. I knowed young Nero when he was just a button, right afore you an' your partner adopted him."

"Well, I swah."

They shook hands. "Pinken is the name, Jedge." The agent glanced around cautiously. "Don't see nobody on the platform, does you?"

"Nobody there."

Pinken drank. He drank as though his life depended on it. "That," he finally said, "is sure fine whiskey."

"Brewed in my own jail," Judge Bates said.

Pinken laughed. "Brewed in jail, eh? That's a good one, Judge Bates. Say, don't register at the hotel; it's just a flophouse. I got a shack on the edge of town. I'd sure be tickled to have you as my guest."

The judge told him he didn't expect to be in the burg long. He thanked Pinken and set about working on another bit of the telegram. Pinken kept saying, "Well, bless my socks, Judge Lemanuel Bates, in the flesh. Judge, if'n it weren't for honest, good-hearted men like you on the bench, the big-wigs would have us poor folks all the time in their clutches— It's only honest men like you—"

"Send this off, please."

"Sure thing, Your Honor."

Pinken read aloud as he tapped his key.

Diamond Willow, Territory of Wyoming.

Pinken glanced up. "You goin' to date this, Your Honor?"

"The date is irrelevant."

Pinken read further.

Michael Nicholas O'Reilly,
Federal Land Office,
Cheyenne, Wyoming.

Friend Irishman,
    Who owns most of the land in Sagebrush Flats, County of Stirrup, Territory of Wyoming? (Wyoming is the territory you are land agent over!)
    Return answer pronto!

                              Judge Lem Bates

Pinken leaned back. "That's it, Your Honor."

By this time, Judge Bates was behind the desk, sitting in the small office with its smells of stale paper and cigar-smoke. Pinken was turned in his swivel chair, and now and then they took a swig out of the jug, placing it in a small shelf, where it would be hidden if anybody came in.

Pinken kept up a line of conversation. Now and then he turned and took some train orders.

Thirty minutes later, a return wire came:

Judge Whiskey Bates,
Diamond Willow, Wyoming.

Dear Jug-Toter,
    Sagebrush Flats ownership changed one month ago today. Now owned by one Jeremiah Boyson, Attorney at Law, Gates Building, Kansas City, Missouri.
    Next time wire a drink.

                                        O'Reilly.

The judge scowled, "Take another wire."

Pinken rapped it out while the judge dictated.

Irish,
    Who owned Sagebrush Flats prior to trans-fer of title to said attorney? Buy yourself a drink instead of mooching one!

                                        Bates.

Again, another wait. Again, garrulous talk from Pinken. Again, the key, dot, dot, dash, dot.

Pinken took down the message.

Dear Judge,
    Cannot reveal name of seller. Against federal law. Sorry. Thanks for the drink.

                                        O'Reilly.

Judge Bates scowled. "That two-bit politician. Take another message, friend."

Irish,
  Federal judge asks that you break federal law. Loosen in the saddle, Irish. Send name of former owner. Otherwise, no drink next time we meet.

                                        Bates.

Again, Pinken's slim finger on the key. Again, another wait, more talk. Again, a return telegram.

Bates, Sorry, no can do.

                                    O'Reilly.

Judge Lemanuel Bates smashed his hand down on the arm of his chair. "Take this, Mr. Perkins!" The depot-agent was frowning in puzzlement.

You Irish peasant,
  Federal judge demands you break federal law. Otherwise federal judge will break federal land agent's jaw.
  Come out, friend, or there'll be a new agent on your high-paid job.
  And two drinks, when and if we meet.

                                        Bates.

Finally the return came.

You Bench Warmer,

Federal law broken. Former owner was James Summers, address, Sagebrush Flats, Territory of Wyoming.

This title transfer always did seem phoney to me. Will look forward to those drinks and will not taste whiskey until I get them.

O'Reilly.

Judge Lemanuel Bates re-read the telegram and smiled. "He won't *taste* whiskey, Pinkens. I mind he never has tasted it; he drinks it too fast to get any taste out of it."

"I don't savvy all this," the agent ventured.

"Me, I don't savvy it myself."

Pinken got off shift inside of an hour. He was feeling pretty foxy with so much whiskey in him, but the judge was his usual self. He had decided to spend the night in town, for his mule was tired, and he wasn't too fresh himself.

Pinken made Bates stay with him.

That night, in bed, Judge Bates put his hands behind his head, and regarded a ceiling he could not see because of darkness. A gent named James Summers had recently transferred title of Sagebrush Flats to a lawyer in Kansas City named Jeremiah Boyson.

He did not know James Summers. He had heard

a little about Lawyer Jeremiah Boyson, though, and
that little had not been refreshing.

But maybe Tobacco Jones, up in Sagebrush Flats
by this time, would fine out something. From all in-
dications, his ride to this town had been worthless.
Still, it might tie in with something Tobacco would
unearth up north.

He went to sleep, thinking of Tobacco, who had
reached Sagebrush Flats that night, his mule plodding and tired. There was a trading-post in about
the middle of the long, narrow piece of worthless
land that went under the name of Sagebrush Flats.
A sod building, consisting of about six rooms.

He had eaten supper there. The post was run by
a fat, easygoing trader, who had a fat, easygoing
squaw to wife. The store was crowded with furs,
bridles, bits, an occasional saddle or two. Steel traps
hung from hooks on the walls. The air had the odor
of prunes and the other commodities that gave flavor
to a frontier trading post.

"Ain't seen a man for some days," the trader said.

The Cowtrail postmaster had been in the act of
lowering his head to consume a hunk of pemmican
impaled on the bent tines of a tin fork. He regarded
the trader for a moment.

"No men around here, huh?"

"Just see a buck Cheyenne now and then. Every

onct in a while a gent drifts through, loaded down
with hardware an' kinda cagey. Me, I never ask
them no questions. Most of my trade is with the
Injuns."

"Heard tell back yonder there was a cow outfit
in here. I was lookin' for a job ridin', too."

"Mule ain't no good for hazin' stock."

But Tobacco Jones was not there to engage in
conversation anent the good and bad qualities of
mules as cow-ponies. "That cow outfit pull out?"

"So I reckon. Run by a man named Jim Summers,
it were. He hit some hard feed periods an' they cut
his cow herd down—lots of them starved. We've
had about ten years of no rain in this section."

"So Summers pulled out, huh?"

"Well, he's still got some cows, back in the brush.
He run the Box 8 iron. About two months ago—
mebbe longer—him an' his riders drifted out. He
had four men punchin' fer him, too."

"Ranch deserted, now."

"They's an old fellow—half-breed—who camps
there, just keepin' eye on things, so the bucks don't
cart everything away."

"That puts me outa a job," Tobacco said. "Guess
I'll just drift through an' go up north. Somebody
tol' me this fellow owned this basin, too."

"That right," the squaw said.

The old trader said, "Get back into your kitchen, woman! Don't go botherin' men whilst they is consumin' vittles!" He threw a tin cup at her.

Evidently the squaw was a good dodger, or else he was a poor thrower. Anyway, the cup missed. She waddled back into the kitchen.

"Yeah, Jim Summers owned this basin. Bought it up as marginal land, or somethin' like that. Reckon he paid all of fifty dollars for the whole shebang." He stowed away a piece of bread, folding it into his mouth accordion-fashion. "But Summers sure got stuck."

Evidently the old man did not know about the Great Western railroad building into Rawhide.

"Been some fellers goin' through here lately with a buggy, stranger. Seen 'em down on the flats the other day. They was lookin' through some kind of a spy-glass, 'peared to me. I rid down there hell-for-horseshoes, but they wouldn't tell me what they was doin'."

"What do you figger they was doin'?"

The grizzled head shook, the jowls wobbled. "Me, I look for Injun trouble. I figger them hombres was army men. They had on some kinda uniforms, too—they was wide acrost the beam in the pants, just like army clothes, an' they wasn't no legs on 'em, they was so pinched in. Funny thing, too. They tell me the navy pants ain't got no beam but is all legs. Looks to me like . . ."

Tobacco let the man ramble. He had no interest in either the apparel of the army or navy. Evidently the trader had encountered some surveyors for the Great Western Railroad, and they had refused to tell him their business on Sagebrush Flats. He paid for his meal and said, "Reckon I'll drift, hombre."

Eyes regarded him from behind rolls of fat. "You don't look like a rider on the dodge, fella."

Tobacco smiled. "I ain't."

"They all tell me that, fella."

The rest had put a little life in the mule. He came upon the Box 8 outfit in the dark. A log house set on a flat, and when he came around the corner of a corral a harsh voice said, "Who rides there?"

Tobacco pulled rein. "A stranger," he said.

"Stand where you are an' forget your guns."

This was a tough outfit . . . a guard out.

The guard came through the darkness. Tobacco saw his rifle. The man stopped about ten feet away. "State your business."

"I'm ridin' through. Lookin' for a job punchin' cows. Is there a law ag'in that, fella?"

"We ain't hirin' no punchers."

Tobacco pointed out that his mule was tired. He hinted that common range decency should insure a chance to flop at the ranch and rest his mount. The man studied him.

"All right, come in."

They took the mule into the barn. "Ain't got much feed. No grass much aroun' here. Cut some buckbrush hay down along the gulch. Your mule'll have to eat that. Nobody but a damn' fool would ride a mule, nohow."

"When I left the last place, I grabbed the closest piece of four-legged flesh. It happened to be this mule, but he got me outa town."

"You sound all right."

They went into the house. By this time the man had lost his vigilance. He lit a candle, and the feeble light showed bare walls, rough with mortar in the cracks of the logs.

The furniture—such as it was—was made of native willow, hammered together with wooden pegs. A door led to what Tobacco guessed would be sleeping quarters. The man was short and heavy-set, and his high cheekbones and coffee-colored skin showed his half-breed blood.

"Hungry?"

"Et back at the post. Trader there said there might be a ridin' job for me here. Said I was to see Jim Summers."

"Jim is gone. Him an' the four boys went with

hosses a month or so ago, maybe longer. Don't ask me where he has gone, either."

Tobacco grinned.

"You got a bottle?"

"Out on my saddle."

Tobacco had bought a bottle back at the trading-post.

"I'll go get it," Tobacco said.

"No, you set there. I'll get it."

The half-breed left. Tobacco, sure he was gone, darted into the hall. Three rooms were ahead of him, doors closed. He went into the first and lit a match. He doubted if the 'breed would see the flare through a window, for the rooms were on the back of the house.

Dirty riding-gear, piled in a heap; an old suitcase, opened. Bedding ruffled and disorderly. A washstand, a chair. That was all.

He figured the 'breed slept here.

He went into the next room, lit another match. It was in about the same disorder as the first. He jerked the drawers open on a bureau; they were empty. But time was running against him, and the half-breed should be back from the barn.

He glanced at the third door, but knew he would not have time to search that room. He hurried back to the living room, hoping the 'breed had not returned. He beat the man by a few seconds.

The half-breed's dark eyes lighted at sight of the full pint. "Heck, you ain't busted the seal yet." He held up the bottle to the light. "Ol' Crow, eh?" His dirty fingernail cut through the seal,

"Have a drink, stranger."

Tobacco told him no. He had had too much to drink lately, and he had a hangover. The 'breed chuckled and raised the bottle.

"Only thing to do with a hangover, son, is to foundation another drunk on top of it. Take a snort?"

Tobacco shook his head.

The 'breed got a little talkative, but not much. Tobacco got him talking about Jim Summers. Summers, he learned, was a big man, who invariably wore dirty clothes. "He's always filthy. Dirtier'n even me. But this is a womanless camp."

Tobacco realized he was learning absolutely nothing. He didn't like the 'breed's company, either. He was afraid that firewater would bring out the Indian in him and he'd want to fight.

But, here he erred. For the guard got happy and then sleepy. Around midnight he said, "You take that second room. My room is the first. I sleep light, stranger, remember that."

"Don't need to worry about me, friend."

Tobacco did not undress. He sat gingerly on the edge of the dirty bed. But first, he searched the room again. He found nothing. He didn't, in fact, know what he had expected to find.

His ride up, he thought, had been useless.

Finally he heard the guard snoring.

He waited for half an hour. Down at the corral, a bronc neighed. When he was certain the guard was sound asleep, he tiptoed into the next room, carrying his boots. He shut the door and lit a match.

This room, for a change, was fairly clean. The bed was made up, but a film of dust across it told him the covers had lain undisturbed for sometime. A hairbrush and comb laid on the dresser.

He opened the drawers. Shirts, some dirty, some clean, in the first. His match burned out and he stood silent, listening. Only the sound of the wind in the eaves.

He lit another match. He opened another drawer.

More clothing, nothing else. Another match, and another drawer—the bottom drawer. Some papers in here—letters, old newspapers. Down in the bottom was a photograph.

His match went out, he listened again. Only the wind. He opened the portrait's folder and lit another match.

A man and a woman, evidently a wedding picture.

The woman was middle-aged, evidently older than the man. He looked at the man's face closely.

His match burned his fingers.

He dropped it, almost swearing. Then, carrying his boots and the picture, he tiptoed back to his room, but the door closed with a small noise. Hurriedly he put the picture under the bedding.

He heard the 'breed stir, heard him come into the hall. The man entered his room. "You walkin' aroun'?"

"Had to go outside. A man with my kidneys has to do that often."

The 'breed stood, half-drunk, watching him. "You get in bed an' stay there." He turned to leave.

He was only a few feet away. Tobacco's gun and gun-belt hung over the bedpillow. The gun rose and the 'breed grunted, slipping down on his face.

The postmaster jammed on his boots, stepped over the guard, and got his mule. He turned loose all the saddle-horses, hazing them ahead of him, leaving the guard on foot. He carried the picture under his coat.

He headed for Wild Horse, many miles away. About ten miles from the Box 8, he went down, lit a match, and studied the portrait again, looking hard at the man. It had been taken about five years before, the date on the back said. Of course, the man was dressed up.

He remembered that the guard had said Summers had once had a wife. But she left him within a few months after their marriage. The woman was evidently Summers' wife. The man, he figured, was Summers.

He rode on, getting his mule to a lope.

CHAPTER 18

When Judge Lemanuel Bates returned to Wild Horse town, both he and his mule were dog-tired. He racked the mule in the livery-barn, noticing that Tobacco's mule was not in a stall.

That meant his partner was still out of town.

Momentary fear pulled at the judge. But he stifled this under the reassuring thought that Tobacco had had the longer of the two rides. He went to the hotel. Ma Jacobson had her head on the desk in the lobby. Trudy stood beside the fireplace, and she only nodded when he came in. Usually she greeted him warmly.

Mrs. Jacobson looked up, eyes red.

"What's the matter, Minnie?"

Ma Jacobson lowered her head. Sobs shook her wide shoulders. She had no answer.

"I'm goin' to get married," Trudy said. "I just told her."

"My girl is leaving me," Ma sobbed.

Judge Bates looked at Trudy. "This is sort of sudden, girl. I haven't even proposed to you yet."

"I'm not marryin' you. I'm marryin' Sol Winters."

The jurist went to his room and washed and shaved. He had enough troubles without listening to Ma Jacobson's woes.

He went to the jail. Sheriff Will Brown sat in his chair, a deputy seated on the floor.

"This ol' Ma Jacobson has been tryin to get me to run Sol Winters outa town, Bates. I tol' her that the law didn't care who her girl hooked up with. Where you an' Jones been? We figured mebbe you'd pulled out for good."

"We always return."

Sheriff Brown sighed. "This jail has been in a mess, Bates. When them cowmen got done fightin', they got drunk on One-Step's whiskey, an' now they're singin' songs, arms wrapped around t'other through the bars."

"I can't figger out where Connors gets that brew," the deputy said.

The judge went back into the bull-pen. Juanita slept on the floor, mouth open, snoring, and apparently dead drunk. Shorty Betton slept on the bunk, and Ross Frazier and Cy Montana sat on the floor, the bars between them, playing cards. Both bore the marks of their fights.

One-Step sat on his bunk, his jail-door open. Mulligan, cooking on the stove, sent out a fragrant aroma.

Montana asked, "When we gonna get outa here?"

"You seem to be doing all right," the judge said. He beckoned One-Step into the back room. "What do you know, friend?"

"Not an iota, Your Honor. I plied them with whiskey and subtle questions. The drunker they got the more they disclaimed being engaged in this nefarious conduct taking place on this soil. And by chariot, I believe they are both innocent. But get them out of here, please. They break up the home the county is supporting for myself and Juanita."

"Everything has backpopped," the judge murmured.

One-Step filled his jug and the judge left. Again Montana and Frazier wanted to know when they would be freed. The judge ignored them.

Sheriff Brown said, "I figger we'll have to turn Frazier an' Montana an' Betton loose pronto, Bates."

"Hold your horses."

The judge spent a listless day. Ma Jacobson bawled continuously. The doctor told him he had dismissed both of Ma's patients and they'd left town. The judge figured this had hit her harder than her daughter's announcement of her engagement.

He ate supper at the home of Judge Mackenzie. The jurist, by his own admission, had suffered a relapse. Yet, in the midst of his pain, he put question after question to Judge Bates.

"How close is this to a solution? Have you any clues?"

"Not a clue."

Judge Mackenzie winced. His back was worse. His wife helped him from the room. She came back and gushered out words that the jurist hardly heard. The judge was glad to leave. He met Lawyer Myers on the street.

"Where have you been, Your Honor?"

"Out looking for clues, Mr. Myers."

Myers stood under a street lamp. It flickered shadows across his face. "This is indeed a riddle, sir."

And how much, thought the judge, do you really know?

He slept, but his sleep was uncertain. The thought of Tobacco kept preying on his mind. But, around midnight, Tobacco came. He was dusty and tired. "My mule bent his ankle aroun' a rock. Lamed him.

That held me down."

"What did you find out?"

"This." The postmaster gave him the portrait. "That gent there is James Summers. He owns Sagebrush Flats. Hades, I've had a long ride. And found out nothin', 'cept that picture."

"That," said the judge firmly, "was enough."

He told about the fruits of his ride to Diamond Willow. "For some reason, Summers recently transferred the title of Sagebrush Flats to one attorney at law Jeremiah Boyson, of Kansas City, Missouri. I have found out that Lawyer Boyson is dealing with the railroad officials to sell Sagebrush Flats."

Tobacco nodded.

"Get the reason for the transfer?"

"Sure. Jim Summers doesn't want to deal directly; the railroad will get wise to who he is, and why he's in Broomtail Basin. This Boyson shyster is the front for Summers. Together, if they can get the railroad up Sagebrush Flats, they can make a sum of dinero."

"That's the sum and substance, partner."

"Well, we know that much. When Summers left Sagebrush Flats, he took four of his riders—his whole crew—with him. Mind we saw four riders heading away from that dynamited reservoir, the night we rid in. Them four was Summers' men."

"This clears Montana and Frazier, too."

"They might sue you for false arrest."

The judge told how Montana and Frazier were friends now. "They finally got together, talked over their troubles, and finally admitted each was a damn fool, so they buried the hatchet—aided by One-Step Connors' fine brew. When they hear this, they will be on our side, partner."

"I hope so."

"I know so. They have been under pressure for some months. Our information will alleviate that pressure. They will be happy to help us, not angry."

"I still hope so."

"Turn in and get some sleep. I am riding to the railhead at Rawhide. I am going to talk with the official there."

"That won't do you no good, Bates."

The judge got a fresh horse and headed toward Rawhide. About a mile out of town he said, "Tobacco's right," and he turned into the western hills. Dusk found him high in the timbered reaches.

A cold wind sang through pine and spruce. Once he saw a rider in the distance and he hid, watching the man. He lost him in a canyon below. He left his bronc there and went down into the canyon on foot.

Here it was very dark. He squatted, waiting. Finally, after going on a few rods, he could look around a ledge of rock. He caught a glimpse of a small fire. It took him two hours to work up to it.

The hideout was perfect. Surrounded by igneous boulders, four men squatted around the small fire, one cooking something in a skillet. A bronc got the jurist scent and snorted beyond the rocks.

"What was that?"

A boot kicked out the fire.

Judge Bates squatted, short-gun up. He was about forty feet from the men. Only the wind was heard. About ten minutes went by. The horse never snorted again.

"Maybe he sniffed a bobcat," a man said.

"Must've been that. Get the fire goin' again."

By this time, Judge Lemanuel Bates was retreating. He got his bronc and rode back to Wild Horse. Dawn found him riding into the town.

He went to their room. Tobacco still snored. The jurist did not awaken him; he went to the jail. He carried the portrait. His hammering awakened the sleepy jailer, who let him in and then climbed back between his soogans.

The jurist snagged the jailer's ring of keys and went into the bull-pen. Juanita slept on the floor, snoring softly, a bottle beside him. One-Step sat up and said, "Bates, what'd you mean, sir, awakening me at this hour?"

"Crawl into bed, friend, and remain silent."

One-Step watched him owlishly. John Barleycorn was sitting on his lap.

The judge unlocked Ross Frazier's cell. The clang awakened the rancher, who sat up and rubbed his eyes.

"Lettin' us out, Bates?"

"Sure thing."

By this time, Shorty Betton and Cy Montana were awake. They slept with their clothes on, even to spurs. They stood in the cell and watched. "That means we get out too, Your Honor?" Montana asked.

Judge Bates nodded.

He got the three men in the bull-pen and had them squat in a circle. Facing them, he told about his ride into Diamond Willow and its results, told about Tobacco Jones' long trek into Sagebrush Flats.

He told about the night-ride he'd just finished, and the four riders back there in the rough country.

"Where does this tie us in?" Cy Montana wanted to know.

The judge did not answer that right off. "You

men are friends now. I put you in jail for two reasons: one, to keep you out of our way; two, to see if you wouldn't patch up a friendship wrecked over a danged silly calf and a mistake."

Ross Frazier showed a crooked grin. "We've done made up. Your Honor. I'm glad you jugged us."

"Much as I hate to say it," Cy Montana grunted, "it was the best for us, Your Honor."

Shorty Betton smiled. One-Step watched, eyes wide. Juanita kept on snoring softly.

The judge impressed them with the fact that, if they banded and raised the price of the railroad's grade too high, the Great Western would go up through Sagebrush Flats, he figured.

"We'll do that," Frazier said.

"You say this Summers gent is down here on Broomtail, makin' all this trouble, eh? Well, he can have the railroad through Sagebrush Flats, like he wants. We don't care where it runs, just so it doesn't cross Broomtail Basin. We don't care what becomes of Summers, Judge Bates."

"He hasn't harmed us," Frazier said.

Judge Bates saw the logic in their remarks. "A few days ago, a man died here in town. Died despite the doctor's medical attention. That man had been slugged over the head. He never regained consciousness. He died silently."

They listened.

"That man has a little girl back in St. Louis. By now, she knows her father is dead, murdered because of greed and a man's lust for money. A week ago, she played with her school chums in the school yard; she talked of her daddy and she hoped her daddy would send for her, so she could come to Wild Horse and have a pony."

"Dammit," Cy Montana growled.

Ross Frazier was silent, listening. So was Shorty Betton.

"Now that same little girl is crying. Now this guard, as a friend, didn't mean anything to us. But he was a man with a man's responsibilities. He broke the laws that you and I have made and which I enforce. He might not have slugged that guard, but one of his four men did, and he is their boss. I demand you help me bring him to justice."

"I'm with you, Your Honor."

"My gun is yours, Judge Bates."

Shorty Betton said, "I'm in this, till the finish, Your Honor."

Judge Bates cleared his throat. "Thanks, my good friends. Now my plan is this. One of you ride out and keep guard on that dirt-camp. That leaves four of us—my partner, two of you, and myself—to watch those four men out in the badlands."

"But who is this James Summers?" Ross Frazier wanted to know.

Judge Bates took the portrait from under his coat. It passed from hand to hand, and faces grew grim with surprise. At last it came to Shorty Betton.

"That's—that's Jocky Smith," the cowboy said.

CHAPTER 19

So Shorty Betton rode out to watch the dirt-camp, out at the reservoir, and Judge Lemanuel Bates and Tobacco Jones and Ross Frazier and Cy Montana took to the hills, watching the hide-away camp.

They did not ride out in a body. Perhaps Jocky Smith might have had a spy in Wild Horse and this spy—or perchance Jocky Smith himself—might have seen them ride away and therefore become suspicious and trail them.

They did not take Sheriff Will Brown.

"He'd just get in the way," Tobacco said.

That summed up their regard for the lawman. First, Ross Frazier left, seemingly heading for his Bar S iron; twenty minutes later, Shorty Betton and Cy Montana rode out of Wild Horse, presumably going for the big Cross H.

Judge Bates and Tobacco rode south. On leaving town Lawyer Del Myers, standing on the sidewalk, asked, "Where you heading, sirs?" and the judge said they were leaving, for good.

"That will put Judge Mackenzie in a bad light, even if I must say it, Your Honor."

"Not half as bad as he left me. Term of court is over. Good day, sir."

He knew that soon would word go around that Judge Bates, for the first time in his judicial career, had faced a problem too immense for him and was back-tracking. And at this a smile broke the jurist's gloomy countenance.

"Let 'em talk," Tobacco grumbled.

"We'll be back," the jurist promised.

Tobacco, always the more pessimistic, said sourly, "Maybe . . . Bates. Them hellions ain't goin' surrender peacefully. They'll fit it out, I reckon."

"Be more cheerful, friend."

They joined forces with Montana and Frazier at their designated meeting spot, out in the hills. Each man packed chuck and extra ammunition secured in Wild Horse before he had left that cow-town.

They made camp back in the crags. Here the wind seemed relentless, trying in vain endeavor to blow away the rocks. Gnarled trees bent under its strong push, but big boulders broke it from the camp.

They were about three miles from the camp of Jocky Smith's riders, and they were higher above them. They dared not light a fire for fear the thin smoke would betray their presence and their position. They had canned beans and bread and they opened cans with jack-knives.

They took turns watching the camp. There in the rocks, a man always watched, marking the movements of the unsuspecting men below them. A night went by, then a day, and another day.

"By this time," Montana said, "that reservoir should be almost banked up again, I'd say."

"By this time," Ross Frazier said, "it should be ripe for another explosion."

Cy Montana rubbed his unshaven jaw. They were a tough-looking bunch—whiskery, unwashed, dirty. And cold from the night and its chill. Warm during days when they lay in the rocks away from the wind with the sun washing over them.

Tobacco said, "I've lived in better hotels."

There was no laughter. The statement should have held mirth; strangely, it didn't. Ross Frazier said. "Here comes His Honor."

Judge Bates dismounted. "They're still there. All four of them."

Frazier went for his bronc. "My shift," he said.

The judge was restless. Tobacco squatted, chewing fine-cut, and watched his partner. He knew what was bothering the judge. Judge Bates wanted to get

back to Cowtrail. He wanted to slide into the old
schedule: strolls to his office for naps, talks with
Sheriff Whiting and other old cronies, a pinochle
game in the Bucket of Blood, a good bath and clean
clothes and the comfort of his home.

"That Judge Mackenzie," the jurist said quietly.
"Curse him for me, too."

Down there in Wild Horse, Judge Hostetler
Mackenzie was probably walking around the house,
his wife on guard at a window to see if anybody was
coming up the walk. And the minute a person started
in the gate, back Judge Mackenzie would go to
his easy-chair or his bed.

"I ought to twist his carcass around, gentlemen,
until he can nibble at his heels. I should put a kink
in his back so big he could sit on his chest."

"Robinson Crusoe did that," Tobacco said. "He
got on the beach, then sat on his chest."

"When Shakespeare wrote that," Cy Montana
said, "he meant Crusoe's trunk, Tobacco."

Tobacco saw the joke had completely missed Montana. He winked at the judge. "Shakespeare . . . he
gets blamed for everything."

"Who wrote it then?" the judge demanded.

Tobacco scowled. "Daniel Webster."

He was serious. The judge dropped the conversation right there.

And still, another day slid by. Another night.

They could sit there and watch the riders and the rigs down on Broomtail Basin. Far in the distance they could see the dust left by the teams and fresnos as they pulled soil into the reservoir's fill.

"Chuck's runnin' low," Ross Frazier said.

Cy Montana was on guard at the hide-out camp. The judge rubbed his jaw. "I feel like Santa Claus. What I wouldn't give for a shave and haircut and a bath and clean clothes."

Tobacco smiled. "I'd even like to see Ma Jacobson. Wonder if the ol' heifer is through bawlin' over Trudy." He grew reflective. "I'd sure like to be this Sol Winters button."

"She's got a temper," Frazier warned. "I wonder where my wife thinks I am. I'll bet she thinks I jumped jail an' flew the coop. Cy's woman an' girl will be worried too. Nice girl, Cy has."

"Nice they ain't no skirts worried about us," Tobacco said.

The judge snorted. "Ma's worried over you, friend."

"Bates, lay off me. I'll warn you. I'm tetchy."

Ross Frazier winked at the jurist. Judge Bates leaned back against a rock so the wind wouldn't hit him. The sun was warm here out of the wind. He dozed. He kept dreaming of soft beds, plenty of hot water, and lather and a razor.

Somebody said, "Here comes Shorty Betton."

Judge Bates' eyes jerked open. Ross Frazier had spoken. Tobacco, who had been stretched out, evidently asleep, came to his feet quickly.

"Where, Ross?"

"Yonder, around that rock."

Tobacco peered, hand shading his eyes. "Sure enough, Bates, it's Shorty. His bronc is lathered, too."

"And yonder is another rider," Judge Bates said.

Ross Frazier put his field glasses on a rider down on the floor of Broomtail Basin. He handed them finally to Judge Bates.

"That's Jocky Smith, ain't it?"

The jurist adjusted the glasses. "That's he, sure enough. And he's heading for the gully where his four riders are gathered. Evidently he intends to take them on a raid tonight, or to give them orders."

Shorty Betton's bronc was tired. Lather hung from the port-chains of the bit and lather rimmed the edges of the heavy Navajo saddle-blanket. He dismounted and they squatted around him.

"Where's Cy?"

"Down watching the camp," the judge said.

Tobacco said, "He's seen you come in, Shorty. Here he comes now."

Montana rode in and went down and hunkered in the circle. "I saw Shorty come in. Saw a rider down below too. I put my glasses on him. He's Jocky Smith."

Tobacco said, "The time is ahead."

They were all stern-faced. They were all tense. They were all wondering how many of them would be alive within the next hour.

Judge Bates talked slowly. Shorty and Cy would come in from the west. Tobacco and Ross Frazier would go down the sides of the cut, hiding behind rocks and buckbrush as they advanced.

"That leaves the bottom of the gully open," Shorty said.

Judge Bates said he would take that. He wanted them to give him an additional five minutes to get below the men. They would now get their broncs and ride ahead, leave their cayuses in the rocks, and then go on foot.

"I'll probably, by rights, be the last one in the gully," the jurist said. "We want this thing air-tight. When I'm ready, I'll holler, 'Broomtail Basin,' and then we'll close in. Everything clear?"

Ross Frazier nodded.

"I savvy," Shorty said.

Cy Montana nodded.

"Clear with me," Tobacco said.

Judge Bates said, "Join all hands together, in front of us."

Five pair of hands came out into the middle of the circle. They folded in, one over the other, and five men bowed their heads. Judge Bates gave a short prayer, his voice heavy.

He prayed that they would all come out alive. He made it short and purposeful, and he prayed for a little girl, now on a train coming from St. Louis, Missouri.

Hands came back, became fists. Hands held rifles and short-guns. They went for their broncs. Tobacco put his arm around Judge Bates. He had pressure in his arm.

"Be careful, Judge."

Judge Lemanuel Bates had difficulty in swallowing.

CHAPTER 20

Hidden by buckbrush, moving from boulder to boulder, a man sneaked down the face of a declivity, carrying a rifle and packing a Colt .45. He was a squat man, heavy with middle-age, and his hand, gripping the rifle, had short, stubby fingers. By the time he reached the floor of the gully, he was breathing heavily from exertion and tension. He paused there, screened by buckbrush, and caught his breath.

Somewhere, up ahead of him, he could hear men talking; their voices were low and distant, and their words did not stand out—they ran together and were not recognizable.

He moved his leonine head to one side, the silver-buckle on his hat's jaw-straps rubbing his thick throat. He looked at his watch and calculated the time since he had left the rimrock camp.

Now was the time.

He leaned his Winchester .30-30 carefully against

a nearby rock, making sure it was within quick reach. He spread his legs wide, boots deep in the sand and shale; at this point the canyon was about fifteen feet wide. To get past him a man would have to ride him down or knock him out of the way with a bullet.

He put back his head, wet his lips.

"Broomtail Basin!"

The two words sounded loud in the narrow defile. They tossed from rock to rock, seeming to fill the air. And their results were hurried and bombastic.

From each side of the cut came the words, *"Broomtail Basin!"*

Those words had come from Tobacco Jones and Cowman Ross Frazier, who had come in from the sides.

"Broomtail Basin!"

That would be Cy Montana and his range-boss, Shorty Betton, coming in from behind the hide-away camp.

Up ahead, there sounded men moving, men darting, men running. And over it all came Jocky Smith's words, "Who's up there? Who's back of us, an' who's behin' us?"

"Judge Lemanuel Bates, down here in the gully. And my men have you surrounded. Give up and walk out with your hands up high, you five hellions!"

"That's the deal," Tobacco's voice.

"We got you skunks," Cy Montana.

A man hollered, "Fight out of it, men, or it means jail for us!" That would be Jocky Smith.

. A rifle spoke; lead ricocheted from rock. Short-guns joined in. But Judge Bates stood silent, always in reach of his rifle, and now his pistol was cradled in his chubby hand.

He could not see the men, because of the toe of the rock, jutting out into the gully. He heard horses rearing and the neigh of a frightened bronc came to him. Up ahead, hoofs ground into gravel.

He knew that this wouldn't last long. With such a closely tied trap, it couldn't last long.

"Two of 'em is gettin' away!" That was Tobacco Jones' holler. "They're headin down the gully Bates is down there—alone—"

Judge Bates spread his legs wider, glanced at his rifle. Now two men, riding low on their bronc's necks, swept around the jut of rock, roaring toward him. One was Jocky Smith.

The other man saw the judge, whipped a shot at him, and the judge heard its high whine before it splattered rock. He swung his pistol on the man but just then the rider's bronc stumbled over a rotted log. The bronc went down, his rider sliding ahead, losing his gun.

Jocky Smith sent shot at him. He was low on his horse, riding Indian fashion, and Judge Bates, crouched a little glimpsed sand geyser ahead of him. He did not have time accurately to place his shot.

He saw the tip of Jocky Smith's left shoulder, showing above the bronc's mane, and he shot for this. He missed. He shot again, the horse bearing down on him. Then did Jocky Smith leave saddle.

He sprawled out, right boot catching momentarily in stirrup, but the boot jerked free, and Jocky Smith hit the soil. Judge Bates jumped hurriedly to one side and let the wild-eyed horse thunder by and go down the canyon.

Smith had dropped his short-gun. He rolled over with a sickening crash, got to his knees. He tried to creep for the gun, about ten feet away. He could use only his right hand.

Judge Bates said, "Stop moving."

The other raider sat down, watching, his hands high. Plainly he was out of the fight. Jocky Smith kept creeping toward his gun. Judge Bates placed a bullet in front of him. It kicked sand and dust back against Jocky Smith's face and chest.

Smith stopped, lay on his belly. "You're the boss, Bates," he said wickedly.

Two days later Judge Bates sentenced the five

Box 8 men.

People came for miles to listen to their trials. Dirt-men at the railroad camp and the reservoir came in rigs to watch. Even the railroad big-wigs were there. Judge Hostetler Mackenzie and his wife came, the judge using a cane. Once Tobacco Jones noticed the judge forgot to lean on the cane.

Attorney Del Myers was to defend the five raiders. He had protested, claiming, on his rights as county attorney, he should prosecute the five. But Judge Bates said he needed no prosecutor for the county. He had all the evidence he wanted. There was no other attorney in town and the prisoners had to have an attorney.

Myers had grudgingly promised.

Judge Lemanuel Bates waited until the courthouse was full. Then, always a man for drama, he entered from his anteroom, garbed in his black robe. He took his seat, intoned that court was in order, and rapped with his gavel.

"We have, fellow voters and citizens, before us five men who are charged with disturbing the community peace, with wilful destruction of community property, with turning against and firing upon your fellow citizens, designated and sworn in as lawful deputies by this judge and this court."

People listened; the courtroom was still. Jocky

Smith, left arm in a sling, sat with his men, all of whom were more or less roughed up, one with a broken arm. They were a tough-looking bunch, but the steam had been knocked out of them.

The judge glanced at Tobacco Jones, who sat with Cy Montana and Shorty Betton and big Ross Frazier. Montana had a bandage around his head and Frazier had his left leg bound up tightly.

He looked beyond his partner to where Ma Jacobson sat, with Trudy and her intended husband beside her. He ran his gaze over the assembled dirtmen and the railroad officials.

"God, in His merciful way, has commissioned me to prosecute these men, and to pronounce sentence on them. Up to a few hours ago, each had intended to plead innocent of these charges, but now, their attorney tells me, they have changed their minds, and wish to plead guilty."

Attorney Del Myers said, "That is correct, Your Honor."

"Therefore, with these pleas before me, I have only one recourse, and that is to sentence these men. Bailiff, lead forth Bob Bartlett."

Bartlett was a thin, nervous man of about forty. He stood before the bench, hands clasping and unclasping.

"Mr. Robert Bartlett?"

"I'm him, Your Honor."

Judge Bates glanced at the paper before him. He tolled off the charges against the man.

"I am guilty of each, Your Honor."

Judge Bates sentenced him to five years at the territorial penitentiary. Before him came Mike O'Shane, a heavy-set Irishman. He also drew five years. And so did Will MacAdams and Joe Trotter.

"The next prisoner, bailiff."

The bailiff led forward Jocky Smith and said, "Stand here, prisoner." The bailiff returned to his chair.

Judge Bates let the silence grow. Jocky Smith looked at him and then looked down at the floor. The courtroom was very quiet.

"Your name sir?"

"James Summers."

Judge Bates cleared his throat.

He read the charges to which Summers had confessed. They contained all the charges the others had admitted, and to these was added one word: *Murder*.

"You confess, prisoner, to having your riders blow up the reservoir?"

"I do."

"You confess, also, to slugging the guard—out at the reservoir—and this led to this guard's death?"

"I do . . . Your Honor."

"You confess that you ordered two of your men to blow up the wagon carrying supplies to your workers, who thought all the time you were their friend and protector?"

"Lynch him," a man said in the audience.

Judge Bates pounded with his gavel. He looked at the crowd. "I am the man who deals out justice, audience. One more word like that and I will clear this court. That is understood, I hope."

Silence was his answer.

"You commissioned one of your raiders to call the other by the name of 'Shorty', thereby seeking to lay the blame on one Shorty Betton?"

Summers nodded.

"Speak up, prisoner. Yes or no."

"Yes, Your Honor."

"You have other confessions here on this list. You admit sneaking back into your office in town—the office maintained by the railroad—and setting dynamite in it, with a slow fuse, and blowing it up, making it look like the work of either Cy Montana or Ross Frazier.

"You confess other nefarious deeds. You sneaked out, placed a slow fuse and dynamite into the well-casing, after slugging the guard. Then you hurried back to your camp, and you were there when the explosion occurred.

"You burned a tent in your camp, endeavoring to put the blame on either Montana or Mr. Frazier.

"You confess to sneaking ahead of myself and my partner, Mr. Tobacco Jones, and placing an ambush shot over our heads to attempt to scare us out of Broomtail Basin. You transferred the title of your land in Sagebrush Flats to one attorney at law Jeremiah Boyson so he could deal openly with Great Western officials while you pilfered and wrecked ruin in order to make the railroad go through land you wanted to sell, land that proved worthless to you. Do you plead guilty to all those charges?"

"I do, Your Honor." Summers' voice was low.

Judge Bates looked out over the crowd. Pity for the beaten man went through him, and then he remembered a little girl who had recently reached Wild Horse from St. Louis; a little girl who had sobbed in his office and whom he had comforted.

He glanced at his watch on his bench. "By now, federal authorities are closing in on Attorney Boyson. By now, perchance, your hold on Sagebrush Flats is being sold to the Great Western railroad. I have so ordered it, for I found in this exchange of title a clause that violated the Federal Homestead Act.

"The Great Western Railway is going north

through Sagebrush Flats. The money received for payment for what used to be your lands, prisoner, is to be put into a St. Louis bank, there to establish a trust fund for one Miss Lucille Brenner, whose father died, by your own admission, under the barrel of your gun."

The crowd listened.

Again Judge Lemanuel Bates cleared his throat. "By order of Territorial statutes, murder—murder in the first degree—is, in the Territory of Wyoming, punishable by hanging."

Summers' face was pale. Attorney Myers moved forward to help him stand. Summers got his strength, pushed the attorney back. Myers returned to his seat.

"My office requires I so sentence you, prisoner. But"—Judge Lem Bates held up a pudgy hand—"I am, as you know, never one to stick to the strict interpretation of the law of the land. I have never reconciled my theory of punishment with that of capital punishment, as demanded by the Territory in your case.

"I firmly believe that capital punishment is wrong. It is a barbarous, uncivilized method of punishment. The victim is put out of his misery, and I believe he should live and suffer behind bars forever. He should be made to remember his crime and seek some atone-ment during his life and ask his God and his Conscience for forgiveness. This he cannot, of course, do, if he is dead.

"Therefore, in the light of these conclusions, I openly violate Territorial statutes, prisoner. I sentence you to life imprisonment at the Territorial Penitentiary. I specifically state in my sentence that you may never come up before the prison board for pardon or parole."

Color returned to James Summers' face.

"Have you any statement, prisoner?"

"I have . . . none."

"Immediately after this court is recessed, I hereby commission Sheriff Will Brown, aided and abetted by his deputies, to start for the railroad at Diamond Willow, there to take the train and transport these prisoners to the Territorial Penitentiary. Sheriff Brown, escort the prisoners to their cells."

The court stood up, silent, as the prisoners passed by to go out the side door. The courtroom occupants also stood up.

The last prisoner filed through. Judge Bates pounded with his gavel. "Court is dismissed."

The courtroom came to life. Judge Hostetler Mackenzie, forgetting his cane in his excitement, came forward and grasped the judge's right hand.

"A wonderful verdict, Your Honor. This verdict will go down in the history of law annals—it will be repeated and looked up to and admired——"

Judge Bates lifted his left hand and pushed hard against Judge Mackenzie's thin face. The blow sent the judge reeling back, and he fell over a chair. A man bent to help Judge Mackenzie, and Judge Bates said, "Don't pick up the four-flusher. Now he has reason to use a cane."

Mackenzie hollered something about bringing suit. Judge Bates turned. "I'll have you off this bench," he said angrily. "Already I've started proceedings at the Governor's office. You'll never sit on another bench again in Wyoming, sir."

The judge went into his chambers and doffed his robe. Tobacco and Mr. Straw came in. Straw shook hands, openly apologetic; he and the judge drank.

"I'll see that a fair price is paid for Sagebrush Flats, Your Honor. I'll see that every cent goes to the little girl."

"I'll be watching you, sir."

Straw didn't like that. He said good-day and walked out.

An hour later, the partners left Wild Horse. People stood on the sidewalk and cheered as they rode out on their mules. Cy Montana and Ross Frazier and Shorty Betton rode ahead of them, giving them a guard of honor.

Ma Jacobson ran out, and they stopped. The

judge kissed her. Trudy had followed with her future husband. Tobacco shifted his chew and looked at the young man.

"How about it, fella?"

Tobacco kissed Trudy. Her lips clung to his; she'd had practice. He said, "Oh, my; oh, my."

"My turn, daughter."

Tobacco almost winced, but the judge's wink stopped the gesture. He bent down and kissed Ma on the lips. They clung, too, but not like Trudy's.

"Oh, my." Only one "Oh, my," though.

They reached the end of the street. Frazier and Montana and Shorty shook hands with them and rode back. They were opposite the jail.

"Now for home an' Cowtrail," Tobacco said.

Somebody said, "So long, gents."

Juanita had his head out a window in Sheriff Brown's office.

"There's One-Step," Tobacco said.

One-Step Connors had his head out another window. He blew them a kiss. "*Bonjour,*" he said.

THE END

TRAIL TO GUNSMOKE

One

Doc Buckley Malone was working in his laboratory in Buckbrush, Wyoming Territory, that night in late March of 1878 when somebody hammered on his door.

"Open up quick, Doc!"

The tall young veterinarian immediately recognized the voice of Running Horse, his fourteen-year-old Cheyenne Indian apprentice.

"Hold your horses, boy! I'm coming!"

Doc Buck glanced at the wall clock. Already five minutes to twelve! Time sure whooped by when a man worked at something interesting.

He'd been dissecting a tick. He still didn't know if the tick was off margaropus or boophilus genus but he did know its bite caused Texas fever in cattle.

Other ticks crawled listlessly around the insides of a sealed Mason jar on his lab table.

Running Horse rattled the iron latch loudly and Doc Buck then remembered he had locked the door from inside for privacy.

"Just a minute, boy!"

He jerked the door open. Running Horse almost fell into the room with its strong smell of medicines and chemicals.

"Your new drippin' vat, Doc Buck—the one jus' finished today—"

Doc Buck grabbed the boy's shoulders. "What about the vat?"

"Somebody blew it up! Jus' a little while ago, too!"

"Who told you this?"

"Vivie Wilson. She jus' come into town! Ridin' hell for leather, lookin' for Jones!"

Milt Jones was the local lawman, a deputy sheriff out of the sheriff's office in Bulltown, the county seat, thirty-two miles north of the new railroad.

"Vivie Wilson?" Doc Buck asked.

"She said the explosion could be heard at their ranch. Her an' Bill rode over right away to investigate."

Bill Wilson was Vivie's brother, three years older than she at twenty-one. Big Hank Wilson, the father of Bill and Vivie, had died of pneumonia last winter, and Bill now ramrodded huge Rafter V, the biggest cow outfit in Buckbrush Basin.

That the Wilson brother and sister had heard the explosion made logic for Rafter V's home-ranch was three miles north of town on the Buckbrush-Bulltown wagon road—and about a mile from the newly constructed dipping tank.

"And Hatchet John? Did he get hurt?"

"He's hurt, Doc Buck."

"How bad?"

"I don't know. Only reason I know Vivie came in with the news was thet me an' Skinny was playin' dominos in his house an' we heard Vivie ride by hell for lightnin'. We followed her to Jones' house an' listened to her tell Jones, an' thet's all I know."

"What'd Jones do?"

"Him an' Vivie rode north in a few minutes, him whippin' his bronc real fast—fastest I ever seen him move, an' I ran for you."

"Why didn't Jones stop and tell me?"

"Reckon he was in too much of a hurry, but he did send his missus to tell you. She's right behin' me."

"Go to the barn. Saddle James and Pinto. Then lead them here—and make tracks, boy!"

"I sure will, Doc Buck!"

Running Horse wheeled and ran into the chilly night. Mrs. Jones hurried through the open door without knocking, a heavy Sioux shawl around her thick shoulders.

"Running Horse just left, Mrs. Jones. He told me all he knew."

The housewife's wide face showed anxiety. "I'm afraid this country will break open in gunfire, Doctor Buck. Ever since the farmers moved in last year—and reports of more coming. And that new cow outfit—the Diamond in a Diamond—moving last month way south after Rafter V has been the only cow outfit in the Basin since white men came in—"

Doc Buck buckled on his spurs. The woman had hit the nail on the head. Things sure looked gunsmoke in Buckbrush Basin right now.

The vet took his Winchester from the rack.

"And my poor husband. Caught in the middle because he wears a star. And him with a wife and three children."

Doc Buck levered open the rifle's breech. "Vivie say anything about Hatchet Joe?"

"Jus' thet he got hurt, no more."

Doc Buck saw the Winchester's barrel held an unfired cartridge. He put the hammer on safety. "Never said how bad he was hurt?"

"No, she didn't. Poor girl. She was very excited and she had reason to be, for everybody will blame this on Rafter V, you know."

Doc Buck buckled on his heavy .45 and wide gunbelt

227

studded with cartridges. He noticed Mrs. Jones giving the gun-harness and big gun a sudden glance.

Most everybody he met looked twice at the gun and harness for it had belonged to his peace-marshal father, Jack Malone, the famous town-tamer—a marshal who had to keep peace in many a wild trail town.

"How's the baby?" Doc Buck asked.

"Much better. Oh, she coughs some, but that's only naturally after such a bad cold. Your medicine worked, Doctor."

"That's good."

Buckbrush had no medical doctor. Therefore Doc Buck treated humans, also. Tiny Susie Jones had almost slipped into pneumonia. By sheer luck—and God's good help—Doc Buckley Malone had managed to save her life.

Mrs. Jones left. Doc Buck buckled on his chaps, thinking of old Hatchet John Martin, his broken-down ex-cowpuncher friend. He'd met Hatchet John here in Buckbrush right after he'd arrived in town direct from graduation in a New York state college of veterinarian science, and he had two true friends—young Running Horse and Hatchet John Martin.

The stoved-up old puncher had had a bronc go over backwards with him up in Montana Territory a few years ago. While he could still ride he could not ride well enough to hold down a regular cowpunching job. He'd tried being a cook but hated the work and therefore was no success. Upon arriving in Buckbrush Doc Buckley Malone had given the grub-line rider more or less a home and found a few bucks now and then for a beer or two.

In return, Hatchet John Martin hung onto his veterinarian friend with bounds of devotion, Doc Buck's slightest wish being Hatchet John's command,

and between the two had been spun the strong web of friendship.

Within three months, the young Cheyenne, Running Horse, had jumped the Cheyenne reservation, and had joined Doctor Buckley Malone and Hatchet John Martin.

Doctor Buck went out into the star-filled night, pulling his short mackinaw closer around him, for the prairie wind still held a bit of winter's chill—for spring was late in coming this year, the old timers and the cold wind proclaimed.

Running Horse was slow in coming with his pinto and the big lineback buckskin, James. Doc Buck had a hunch the boy had a hard time saddling James. James was more or less a one-man horse, the man being Doc Buck—who had bought the gelding when he'd been a three-year-old from Big Hank Wilson of the Rafter V, right after Doc Buck had hit town. Two years ago come next June.

Doc Buck heard boots approaching. Soon a heavy-set chunky man of about thirty five came out of the night, boots grinding gravel, spurs chiming. "What's the excitement, Doctor Malone?"

Doc Buck told him. The man was Matthew Cotton, who had come into town six months after the veterinarian and had opened a land office. He'd been the one who'd located the claims of the twenty odd nesters Mrs. Jones had mentioned.

"Somebody blew up your new dippin' vat?" Cotton spoke as if he couldn't believe his own words. "Now who in hell would be guilty of that act?"

"You got me," Doc Buck said.

"Well, they sure can't blame it on me an' any farmers," the land-locator said, " 'cause we'd profit by the new tank—it seems to be only our cattle that those damn' ticks are biting."

Doc Buck said, "Time my boy got here with the horses."

"Mind if I ride out with you, Doc?"

"Not a bit."

Matthew Cotton hurried into the night. He had his horse in his barn behind his office halfway down this street which was the north block on Buckbrush's two blocks of street.

Doc Buck kept his horses in the town stable. He started that direction and had gone only a few rods when Running Horse trotted in on his pinto leading a saddled James.

"You're slow," Doc Buck said, jamming his rifle into saddle-boot and swinging up.

"James didn't want me to put leather on him."

James wanted to buck. He always liked to buck a little upon being mounted. Doc Buck didn't want to let the horse pitch. He turned him in a short circle, pulling the buckskin's head up tight, and the horse got out of the idea and straightened out on a dead run, heading for the dip-tank, with Running Horse whipping his short-legged pony for more speed.

They roared down the alley and at Matthew Cotton's barn the land-locater spurred out on his big black, swinging in beside the lunging James, his shod-horse's hoofs throwing more gravel back at Running Horse and the slower Pinto, a fact which made Running Horse curse the land-locator under his breath.

Running Horse didn't like Matthew Cotton. He was sure his boss didn't like the over-bearing land-locator, either.

The trio left the cowtown behind and hit the well-traveled wagon-road north, their hoofs rattling on the dried soil, thus making conversation impossible.

Doctor Buckley Malone was glad there was no talk, for dismay rode his shoulders. He'd put quite a bit of his meager money supply in building the dipping vat.

His stone-mason and carpenter had just finished the vat this afternoon. Paying their final wages had put quite a hole in his small savings. Now the vat lay in dynamited ruins.

First, he'd constructed a big corral. This hadn't cost any more than the labor for posts and poles had been cut free-of-cost from the timber along Doggone Creek. Neither had the rock comprising the tank cost much for it had been dug out and picked up on the neighboring hills. What had cost had been the cement. It had had to be freighted into Bulltown on the new rails and then freighted by wagon the thirty odd miles south to Buckbrush.

The vat and corral had been constructed on his homestead which he'd filed upon soon after coming into Buckbrush Basin. His homestead was independent of those of the farmers who had all filed in a row east and west at the base of the northern hills.

Who the hell had blown up the tank?

And why?

The *why* part was simple. Somebody didn't want the Texas ticks killed off. Somebody didn't want the vat filled with a mixture of creosote and kerosene into which the tick-infested cattle could be pushed and while swimming the length of the vat kill off their parasites.

Logic told him the farmers had not blown up his dipping vat. They stood to gain by dipping their cattle for their stock apparently was the only cattle in Buckbrush Basin with the deadly ticks. So far the Wilson spread had reported no ticks. He'd immediately quarantined the farmers' cattle. Wyoming gave him that power because he was a registered veterinarian.

None of the farmers had any idea where the ticks had come from. Doctor Buck had never heard of Texas fever ticks in Wyoming Territory. The ticks were warm-climate parasites, he'd read.

When trailherds had left the Texas brush-country to head north after the Civil War to Kansas railheads, ticks had accompanied them. Texas cattle had brought ticks into Kansas and later into southern Colorado and Nebraska and Missouri. Farmers in these states had formed shotgun brigades to turn back the Texas tick-infested herds. They'd lost thousands of head of their own cattle because of the longhorn invasion.

Texas cowmen then had learned to run their cattle through vats filled with creosote solution. This killed the ticks. When a cow climbed out after swimming through the greasy liquid her ticks were dead. Only then could a longhorn be moved north.

Huge trailherds then trekked across Colorado into Wyoming. They spread out on Wyoming's hills and plains. Now, with Wyoming free-range well occupied, huge trailherds crossed Wyoming to reach Montana Territory's luscious high-grass range.

And these longhorns had been dipped; therefore, no ticks traveled north with them. This was a puzzle. These local ticks had miraculously appeared out of nowhere. Where had they come from in the last few weeks? What had brought them in?

Pinto's nose appeared on Doc Buck's right. Running Horse finally got out of the shower of gravel and dust. Doc Buck glanced left at Matthew Cotton. Cotton rode a solid saddle, quirt rising and falling.

Suddenly they rode with high cottonwoods on each side. Doc Buckley Malone knew then they were half way. This was Tanner's Grove. Doggone Creek came into Buckbrush River at this point.

Hoofs thundered across the worn planks of Tanner's Bridge. Acting as one, their three broncs swung left, heading for the dipping vat and Doc Buck's homestead, slightly over a mile distant.

Doc Buck realized that Deputy Sheriff Milt Jones and Vivie Wilson had really pounded the trail, for he and his companions had pushed fast horses to their limit and still had not overtaken the lawman and Big Hank Wilson's golden-haired and only daughter. A sour feeling hit the young vet's belly. The whole thing had chanced since pneumonia had killed the old cowman and his arrogant, overlording son had taken over.

Changed completely . . . and not for the better.

Two

Doc Buckley Malone's mind whipped back. . . .

Ten laden wagons. Household goods, cookstoves, all that. Four with a wife and children, six with bachelors.

Big Hank Wilson had happened to be in Buckbrush at that time. He'd spoken to his old friend, Deputy Sheriff Milton Jones. "What the hell is this, Milt?"

"Farmers, Big Hank."

"I'll be a sonofabitch," the big bluff cowman had said. "Nobody but a bare-assed idiot would even think of comin' here to put a plow in the ground."

Townspeople listened in silence.

"Wind blows night an' day. Blow the seed right outa the ground. About ten inches of rain a year an' half comes in snow winter-time—an' good for nothing'—an' the other five inches comes in one cloudburst in the summer an' runs off so fast the gumbo doesn't even have a chance to get wet."

He spoke truth. But he reckoned without irrigation water. For the farmers filed on homesteads fronting the long hills that ran east and west on the north rim of Buckbrush Basin.

They came in early September. Within a month they had their farms fenced with three strands of barbwire strung taut between stout diamond willow posts they'd cut free along Doggone or the river.

And they'd already started building small check dams in the coulees running down the hills on the northern limits of their hundred-and-sixty acres given them gratis by Uncle Sam.

"Winter'll drive 'em out," Big Hank had prophesied. "Cold as all billy-hell—thirty or forty below in them shacks. Man can die from winter in this country jus' as easy as a cow can, you know."

The winter was a hard one. Blizzard after howling blizzard swept Wyoming's plains, but not a farmer or a farmer's family fell victim to pneumonia—although Big Hank Wilson did. Pneumonia killed the cowman.

Night after night, the young vet had sat beside Big Hank's bed, using every medicine and skill he possessed, but he fell short, for one blizzard-ragging night Big Hank Wilson drew his last breath in the bedroom of the big house he'd built ten years before. He'd fought to the end, but in the end as usual death won. He drowned in the fluids of his own body. His only boy, Bill, arrived in time for the funeral but not to see his father alive.

People had not expected the new farmers to attend Big Hank's funeral but they all had, even to silent, watchful children. Big Hank had never lifted a hand against them. But what lay ahead with hot-tempered young Bill Wilson now half-over with his sister of the immense Rafter V?

Young Bill Wilson and his golden-haired sister Vivie had sat with Rafter V cowpunchers on the south side of the building while farmers and families had occupied the north side.

Deputy Sheriff Jones had been openly worried. "Young Bill won't let a word out of him what he'll do—if anything—to the farmers. I've tried to pry words out since he's come, but I ain't got off home-plate, Doctor Buck."

Rumor told Doc Buck that Bill Wilson and his father had quarreled—bitterly, angrily—and then young Bill

235

had gone east to college four years ago.

Doc Buck had learned that from talk with Vivie at a dance early in the winter. "Dad wanted Bill to stay. He said Bill knew enough about ranching now without going to some dude college and learning more."

Doc Buck nodded, listening.

"If Mama had been alive, there'd been no trouble. Mama would have seen to it that both Bill and me had gone to college. Mama was this town's first schoolteacher, you know."

Doc Buck looked down at the lovely little blonde. Vivie came just to his shoulder. Her hair glistened under kerosene lights. *She'd make some man a fine wife*, Doc Buck thought.

"You went to college back east, didn't you, Doc Buck?"

He told her where. "What's your brother's discipline?"

"Discipline? What's that?"

"What is he studying?"

"Something called Agronomy, whatever that is. He made good grades. They even gave him his degree without him waiting for the term to end for he had to leave before his school year was up."

"Agronomy is the study of the use of land."

"I didn't know that. I'm just a dumb cowgirl, no more. Dad used to say I was only good for one thing."

"What was that?"

"Marry some man and raise a bunch of babies." Her hand flew to her mouth. "I shouldn't have said that. I talk too much."

According to Vivie, Bill Wilson and his father had disagreed over how big Rafter V should be run. "One generation against the other," Doc Buck said. "Crabbed old age cannot live with youth, as

236

Shakespeare wrote."

Young Bill wanted to breed the longhorn strain out of Rafter V's immense herds. He had wanted to buy and ship in Hereford or Shorthorn or Black Angus bulls and get shut of the longhorn bulls and breed the cattle up so each steer would carry much more beef.

"They're doing that in Texas," Doc Buck said.

"Poor old cattle. Just living to have their throats cut. I'm sure glad I'm not a cow."

"So am I."

She looked up at him. "You know, I'm afraid of myself around you, Doc Buck."

"You're not nearly as afraid as I am."

They both laughed.

He had danced next with seventeen-year-old Teresa Hernandez whose father and she had four years before crossed Buckbrush Basin with a herd of sheep heading north for Montana Territory. Manuel Hernandez Garcia had liked Buckbrush Basin and the sheep and the other herders had traveled on.

Last year Manuel had decided he'd had enough cold northern winters and had headed south toward his native land, but Teresa had stayed and had opened Buckbrush's only cafe.

Teresa was full-bodied, dark of eyes, dark of hair. She worked hard and had made her cafe a success. She did all the cooking and buying and waiting table herself.

Local young men tried to date her but she turned them all down, and nobody knew the reason why until Teresa had one day told Vivie, "When I marry, I want to stay married. I want a family and a good husband and right now I see no such material at hand."

"Except Doc Buck?"

Teresa had not answered, Vivie later reported.

Teresa had come to the dance chaperoned by the

237

minister's wife. She wore a pink dress with a tight waist and Doc Buck had wondered which was the more beautiful—the blonde or the dark-haired girl.

Doc Buck had found himself eating more often now in Teresa's cafe. He made an excuse: he was growing tired of his own cooking. Now, riding hard through the chilly March night, he grinned at his thoughts.

He'd never asked Teresa to go with him to some social doings because he'd been afraid she'd turn him down as she'd turned down other locals. Someday soon, the right function hit town, he'd ask her. She couldn't do any more than say no.

Vivie had come to that particular dance with Mack Smith who worked with his father in the father's Mercantile Store. Local gossips said that Mack and Vivie made a fine couple.

Doc Buck left such pleasant thoughts and turned to dark thoughts of the present, mostly concerned with Hatchet John Martin.

He'd given Hatchet John definite orders. "If any trouble comes up you head pronto for the buckbrush, understand? None of this junk about you shooting at them after they shot at you—and you hitting them. Sometimes that doesn't work in everyday life."

"How come you say that?"

"Okay, look at my father. After John Wesley Hardin ran Wild Bill Hickcock out of Dodge, my father took over. He put Dodge City out of the 'sin class,' as he called it."

"I saw him once. Down in Cheyenne. He was marshal there. Right afore he got kilt."

"And what killed him? I'll answer that. A drunk squatting hidden behind a water-barrel out on the street in case of fire. Pulled up a shotgun and shot him in two pieces, right above the gunbelt. You ever look twice at my gunbelt?"

"Never have but understand it was your father's."

"The top of the broad belt has a few holes in it. The drunk's shot cut them. But the point is this: don't use a gun unless absolutely forced to. Back down, first."

"Back down? Hell, a man's got pride."

"So my father used to say. And he died with pride on a dusty Wyoming street. A few days later my mother walked into her bedroom and shot herself through the heart. Pride sent her into her coffin, too."

"Okay, but nobody's gonna harm this vat."

"We don't know. Somebody planted Texas ticks in this basin. They planted them for a purpose. Just what the purpose is, we just now don't know—but we aim to find out."

"I'll play cards close, boss."

Of course, the vat had been dynamited. There was no other way outside of black powder to devastate the rock and concrete tank. And dynamite threw objects into the air, in this case rock and chunks of concrete.

What goes up, must come down. . . . And maybe a chunk of some such had landed on a fleeing Hatchet John?

Bent over saddle-fork, Doctor Buck Malone soon discarded this idea, then corrected it to think, *If a hunk of rock or concrete landed on Hatchet John Martin, it would land on him when he was close to the tank he was guarding, not while he was running through the buckbrush. . . . And he'd be on one knee, rifle yammering lead.*

He came back to the ugly present when Running Horse reined Pinto close and hollered, "Lots of lanterns ahead, boss."

Doc Buck looked ahead. Big cottonwood trees hid the lanterns but yellow rays managed to seep through their foliage. He saw shadows scissor their way across the front of the lights.

Suddenly, Matthew Cotton's horse stumbled. The big black went to his knees and for a moment it looked as though he'd plow his head into the ground and go end over end.

Cotton had been a pace ahead of hard-running James. James suddenly veered to the right. Doc Buck glanced down. He saw the outlines of a good-sized boulder. Cotton's black had stumbled over the rock.

Cotton laid back on his reins. His black recovered his lunging stride. They left the boulder behind.

Doctor Buck had ridden over this trail at sundown when he'd left the vat and gone to his laboratory—and this rock had not then been blocking the wagon trail. It had come to this spot since he'd ridden to town.

Dynamite had thrown that rock onto the road.

Running Horse looked over his shoulder. "Looks to me, boss, like half of the town is follerin' us."

"That wouldn't be many," Doc Buck hollered back.

"Buckbrush won't stay like it is very long," Matthew Cotton said loudly. "Not after I get more farmers in. Things'll change then, and for the better."

Doc Buck thought, *I wonder. . .*

"Bill Wilson ain't gonna cause us farmers no trouble," Cotton continued, still almost yelling to be heard above the sound of hammering horse-hoofs. "He ain't no fool. He knows full well he ain't got no legal claim over the range Rafter V has run cattle on these years. That's government land. Uncle Sam's land."

Doc Buck knew that. He also knew that sometimes cowmen apparently weren't aware of the fact or just were too proud to draw back before the invasion of farmers. Or too greedy, too.

For cattle made money for their owner here on range

upon which not a cent in taxes was paid. Most big cow outfits from the Rio Grande to the Montana Milk River were owned by foreign interests—mostly English and Scottish money—who had never seen one of their western cattle, and apparently had had no desire to see such.

Rafter V was one of the few cow-outfits of any size in Wyoming Territory that was owned by an American citizen. Big Hank Wilson had openly stated the day of open range was passing. A far sighted man, he seemingly had known that, with open and free grass gone, the big cow outfit was doomed.

"No use fightin' the farmers," he more than once said. "There's too many of them. When they have enough votes to elect the county and state officials they want, the law will swing over to their side—and then the big cowman runnin' on gover'ment range is doomed."

But how did Big Hank's only son and heir—now operating Rafter V—look at the farmer problem? During his short period as boss of Rafter V Bill Wilson apparently had not mentioned the problem to anybody, including his sister. The entire range—town and basin—were on edge, reading a threat in the young rancher's silence.

"Here we are," Cotton said.

They'd reached the vat site. Kerosene lanterns illuminated the spot. Doc Buck immediately noticed many farmers had come from their homesteads to investigate. Some even had their families with them. Also many Rafter V hands were gathered around, too. The farmers and families occupied the area west of the dynamite-torn tank, the cowboys and Rafter V on the east side.

One hurried glance showed Doc Buck that the corral still stood. That much was on his side.

241

But the vat . . .?

The vat had consisted of a narrow tank about six feet deep—just deep enough to make a cow swim to reach the other end. The cattle would have walked down a ramp, swum about ten feet, then climbed out on another ramp. It was just wide enough to accommodate a big bull. Creosote mix was high priced; therefore the tank was built to conserve mix.

What he saw, made Doctor Buckley Malone's heart fall. Dynamite had blown the tank apart from end to end. The center consisted of rocks and concrete caved in and solid. The ends were shattered. The entering ramp was completely gone. The exit ramp was shattered and crumbled, a mixture of concrete and rock. The vat was a complete ruin. To rebuild it he'd have to remove all the rock and concrete and begin from scratch.

Sick at heart, Doc Buck dismounted, Running Horse and Matthew Cotton following suit.

Buck spoke to the closest nearby Rafter V hand. "Where's Hatchet Joe?"

"Why ask me?" the man said shortly.

Three

The surly reply instantly turned all eyes Doc Buck's direction. Doc Buck realized he'd spoken to the wrong man. The man was named Ron Powers. For three months—young as he was—he'd been Rafter V's ramrod.

Big Hank Wilson's strawboss for years had been old Jake Figgston, who'd come up the trail with Wilson and Rafter V cattle. Last November in a blizzard old Jake had taken a short-cut across Buckbrush River. His horse and he had broken through the ice. The old cowboy had been wet to the skin. By the time he rode into Rafter V's yard he'd been a human icicle, ice from spurs to the top of his bald head. Three days later, pneumonia had killed him—and twenty-eight-year-old Ron Powers had been appointed over older hands as the ranch's range-boss.

Rumor claimed Big Hank, himself crippled and mostly good for nothing, had made young Ron boss because Ron Powers and his son Bill were close friends. Older Rafter V cowpunchers grumbled but said nothing, Doc Buck had heard. He judged the feeling between range boss and his crew at the big ranch was anything but wholesome.

Now Doc Buckley Malone studied Ron Powers, a full two inches shorter but much heavier in shoulders and thighs.

"Not a very civil answer," Dock Buck said.

"Not a very intelligent question," Ron Powers said. "Your man is layin' over there by that tree, horse doctor."

Horse doctor stung. It was laden with scorn. Doc Buck let that ride as he turned and looked at a big cottonwood tree, for the first time seeing Hatchet John Martin, lying on a blanket.

Three people stood close to Hatchet John Martin. One was Vivian Wilson, one was Deputy Milt Jones, and the third was Widow Hanson, who ran a boarding house in Buckbrush. She also had a room or two for a transient since Buckbrush had no hotel. Hatchet John had many times escorted the heavy-set middle-aged woman to school doings and church.

Flickering lamplight showed Hatchet John's thin, whiskery face and glistened on his sunken eyes.

Doc Buck knelt beside the old man. "Don't talk any more than necessary," he said. "Where do you hurt?

"My back. Just on my belt. I guess a rock—flyin' rock—hit me."

"Can you move your arms?"

"Yes." Hatchet John moved both arms.

Doc Buck hesitated, then said, "Your legs?"

"I can't move them. They're like they're dead. I can't feel a thing below my belt."

Doc Buck noticed two pair of boots moving into his vision, one pair on his right, the other on his left. The pair on his right were new and expensive and the ones on his left were older and run-over and showed wear. He looked up. The owner of the polished boots was young Bill Wilson. Doc Buck looked up, left. The owner of the old boots was Ron Powers.

Doc Buck's attention returned to Hatchet John. "I want to put my hands under your spine where you were hit. I won't hurt you. Just lie still and if possible raise

244

your back a little to let my hand under."

"Okay, Doc."

Farmers stood a distance away, watching. Rafter V cowboys were still in a group, and they also watched. For the moment the dynamited dipping vat was forgotten.

Doc Buck began inserting his hand, palm upward, under Hatchet John's back. Hatchet John tried to lift, but couldn't. Sweat popped out on his whiskery face. Hatchet John's eyes were closed, his lips compressed. Finally he said painfully, "I can't raise up, Doc."

"Don't try any more. I got my hand under you now."

Doc Buck's fingers felt, tested, probed, then withdrew. Doc Buck put his head down, eyes closed. What he'd feared had happened. A couple of Hatchet John's vertebra had been smashed. The old timer would indeed be fortunate if he ever again walked.

Doc Buck opened his eyes. He looked down at the expensive boots. Bill Wilson was their owner.

"What did you find out?" the Rafter V owner asked.

"I'll have to get him undressed and give him a complete examination. I wouldn't want to give a verdict on what little I now know."

"Tough luck."

"Yeah," Doc Buck said. "Tough luck."

The expensive boots moved back. Doc Buck looked at the owner of the old boots.

"What do you want, Powers?"

"Not a goddamned thing," Ron Powers said. "Just walked over with my boss. You don't need to get snotty with me, horse doctor!"

Doc Buckley Malone had had enough—no, he'd had too much. This dynamiting—his old friend doomed possibly for life to a wheel chair—Doc Buck went into hard and fast action. He hit Ron Powers below both

245

knees with a flying tackle, his college football training coming to the fore. And he hit as hard as he'd ever hit a football opponent.

His lunging drive drove Ron Powers backwards. Powers lost his footing, almost fell. Doc Buck released the man's powerful legs. Three Rafter V cowpunchers caught their range boss. Otherwise Powers would have fallen.

By now Doc Buck was on his boots.

Hatchet John said, "Be careful, Doc. He's packin' a gun. He knows how to use it, too."

"Jack Malone was my father," Doc Buck reminded.

Powers had his balance, now. He'd sunk into a gunfighter's crouch. "So it's trouble you want, eh, you pill pusher! Well, I'm the man who can give it to you!"

Doc Buckley Malone also had sunk into a gunslinger's position, body sidewise, fingers taloned over the black grip of his dead father's Colt .45. For one moment, all hell hesitated, ready to break loose in roaring, flaming death.

Then, Bill Wilson moved in. He tackled Ron Powers around the knees, dumping him again. Powers' gun went flying. A cowpuncher picked it up. And Vivie Wilson and Teresa Hernandez had hold of Doc Buck. Vivie pushed against him in the front and Teresa held his forearm, making him keep his gun in leather.

"Doctor Buck, Doctor Buck," the dark-haired girl sobbed. "No, no, no guns, Doctor, please!"

Vivie said, "There's no need for this!"

Doc Buck relaxed. He studied Ron Powers over Vivie's golden hair. Thoughts flicked through his mind. He and Vivie going to the Christmas dance and box social. "Ron asked me to go with him but I'd rather go with you, Doc Buck."

Other times he'd come unknowingly between Vivie

and Ron, who town gossip claimed would some day marry her.

Now Bill Wilson said to Rafter V, "There's no use us hanging around here. These people can get along without us. Back to your bunks, all of you—another day's work, tomorrow."

Ron Powers hesitated. Young Bill Wilson's blue eyes appraised him. Bill and Powers had been friends since early boyhood. "Come along, Ron," Wilson said.

Bill Wilson's voice was low but contained authority. Doc Buck had heard Rafter V punchers say their new owner was a just but a hard-driving boss. Wilson had been born into money and authority. His voice showed those qualities now.

"This guy—" Powers began.

"There's tomorrow," Bill Wilson pointed out. "On your bronc, Ron."

Powers looked at his boss. He then looked at Doc Buck. He said not a word but wheeled on his bootheel and went to a blue roan gelding and swung up and Rafter V whirled broncs.

Dust rose behind the Rafter V horses. Then, the broncs and riders were gone, darkness reaching out and claiming them.

Vivie stepped back. Teresa released Doc Buck's arm. Vivie said sharply, "That was uncalled for, Doctor Buck."

"Oh, was it?"

"Yes, it was."

"That's your opinion, not mine." Doc Buck looked at dark-haired Teresa. "I didn't know you were here."

"I tried to catch you, but my little sorrel wasn't fast enough." She still spoke English with a slight Latin accent.

Vivie looked at Teresa. Teresa looked at Vivie. They

were a contrast. They had one thing in common—both were an inch over five feet, and there similarity ended. Where Vivie was light-skinned and blonde, Teresa was dark and suave with glistening black hair that she usually wore in two long braids. Where Vivie's eyes were deep Wyoming blue the Mexican girl had dark, smoldering eyes—eyes that Doc Buck had found impossible to read.

Suddenly Vivie said, "I'm going home." She looked at the farmers and told the world in general, "Since you people came in the whole basin has gone crazy. I wish to hell you'd stayed where you came from, wherever that is."

A farmer said shortly, "Your ranch is doomed, Miss Wilson. The days of open range are gone . . . and forever."

Doc Buck recognized the speaker as Ed Gaboney. Gaboney had been elected head of the Farmers Organization last Christmas. He was a bony man of about forty, a bachelor, and Doc Buck had many times guessed that underneath Ed Gaboney was tough, and took nothing from nobody.

"That's your opinion, Mr. Gaboney, and not mine. But why should I waste my time arguing trivialities?"

"Absolutely no reason," Ed Gaboney said.

Vivie spoke to Doc Buck, ignoring Teresa Hernandez. "Good night, Buckley. I'm sorry about your tank—and Hatchet John."

"Good night, Vivie."

The farmers and wives and families moved in close now that Rafter V was gone. They made a group of tall people and short people and people in between and Doc Buck sensed a tough resilience in them—a feeling that banded them together, made them one strong unit.

"We all were havin' a little social at my shack," Ed

Gaboney informed. "Seein' it's a Saturday night, we were dancin' an' having a little fun, and then your tank went sky-high."

"Sure made a roar an' a high flame," a matron said.

"The point is this," Ed Gaboney stressed. "Every man an' woman an' big child was in on the party, so none of us could be called as bein' the one to dynamite your vat, Doctor Malone."

"Nobody has accused you," Doc Buck said sharply.

He was still raw from his encounter. The Wyoming night had almost been stabbed by howling lead. He had made an enemy of Ron Powers—a *bigger* enemy of Powers.

A farmer said, "Ed's right, Doc. All of us were at his shack. Damn it, a man can't let a thing like a damn fever tick hold 'im down. What'd you find out about them ticks we picked off Bossy this afternoon."

Doc Buck said, "That can come later. Just now I got to get Hatchet John into town and in bed."

"Doc Buck's right," a matron said.

"How'll we go about it?" Ed Gaboney asked.

Doc Buck looked about at the wreckage. He saw only shattered timbers of short lengths. Again he wondered who had dynamited his tank. All signs pointed toward Rafter V.

He spoke to Farmer Ted Lawson. "Ted, when I built my shack, I had a door left over—it was out of plumb. You'll find it in my coalshed."

"I'm on my way, Doc."

Doc Buck's homestead shack was a quarter mile up-road. Lawson and another farmer ran into the night. Doc Buck knelt beside Hatchet John. He spoke over his shoulder.

"Will one of you please bring me my bag from my saddle?"

249

"Right away, Doc."

Doc Buck always had his little black bag tied to his back saddle-strings, the bag packed with what medicines he had. When he made a town-call he seldom, if ever, went on foot, but always on horseback.

He'd received quite a bit of joking about his walking as little as possible, and he'd given the old Texas answer that a dyed-in-the-wool cowpuncher walked only when forced to—he'd ride his horse from the bunkhouse to the mess shack, if possible.

The bag arrived. He filled a syringe from a bottle. He reached under Hatchet John and Hatchet John winced and when Doc Buck's hand came back the syringe was empty.

"That'll kill your pain," he told his old friend.

Hatchet John Martin said, "I was makin' a patrol in the bresh. I thought I'd heered somethin' an'—"

Doc Buck hurriedly said, "Don't tell me what happened. Nobody but you an' me should hear that. Wait until we're alone."

"Us farmers are interested," Ed Gaboney said.

Others said, "Let him talk, Doc."

Doc Buck shook his head. He restored his syringe to his satchel and threw the empty bottle into the night.

He heard the bottle shatter on stone. He looked at Teresa, who stood beside him. She looked up. Lanternlight showed the seriousness of her dark eyes. He looked at Widow Hanson.

The widow softly sobbed. For the first time Doc Buck realized how close the buxom widow and Hatchet John Martin had been. Mixed with this nice feeling was a feeling of suspense, of something deadly and black ahead.

"Here comes the door," Ed Gaboney said.

Four

They carefully placed the skinny body of Hatchet John Martin on the door. The wounded man lay on his back. A farmer had made a hurried trip to his homestead. When he returned he had two heavy blankets and two low saw-horses. They put the door and its human burden on the saw-horses. Doc Buck covered the man with the blankets. Then four strong men lifted the door and Hatchet John and put him in the back of a farmer's democrat.

Doc Buck rode back with his patient. "Take the bumps easy, Homer," he told the farmer who sat on the seat with the Widow Hanson.

"I'll try, Doc Buck."

Running Horse rode behind on Pinto, leading James. The Widow turned halfway on the seat, watching Hatchet John and occasionally giving him words of encouragement. They reached Buckbrush. Widow Hanson said, "Take him to my place," and once at the woman's two-story house they carried the door and occupant carefully upstairs. "In this room," the Widow said.

Doc Buck and the Widow undressed Hatchet John, who wore long-handled woolen, and the Widow said, "Good heavens, look at those dirty underwear. He needs a good woman to take care of him!"

Doc Buck remembered his own pile of dirty clothes.

251

He'd made up his mind yesterday to wash soon, a chore he hated.

Another chore he loathed was sweeping out and mopping his combined living quarters and office. He wished this disliked chore as much as possible on Running Horse or Hatchet John. Of course, Hatchet John's efforts were out of the question, now. He'd miss the old man's helping hands.

Thanks to heavens, his homestead shack had a dirt floor and didn't need mopping. The reason he'd not floored it was simple. He'd put his money in the dipping vat. He'd had no money to buy two-by-four joists and flooring.

"What man doesn't?" Doc Buck said.

"Doesn't what?" the Widow asked.

"Need a good woman."

"You should talk, Doc Buck. You with two jus' waitin' for you to ask!"

"Two? And who are these waiting damsels, may I ask?"

"You know darned well who they are. Pretty little Vivie for one an' pretty little Teresa for the other."

"Doggone now, how blind can a man be?"

"Jus' as blind as he wants to be. You strip those filthy underwear off this man and I'll go out and look for a nightgown or somethin' to put on his nakedness."

"I took a bath yesterday in Doggone," Hatchet John explained. "I didn't have no clean underwear so I put on my cleanest dirty underwear."

The Widow left.

Doc Buck said, "Tell me what you know."

"First, how about me?"

"Ask your questions."

"Is—is my back—busted?"

"I don't know. Your back has been severely

damaged. Beyond that, I don't know, Hatchet. I'm no medical doctor."

"My legs—they're numb. I cain't move 'em one bit. Will I ever walk again, you think?"

The oldster's voice held a pleading note. His watery eyes searched Doc Buck's face.

"I'll be honest," Doc Buck said. "I don't know, Hatchet. I'll send a rider into Bulltown and ask Doc Cochran to come out."

"Lord God Almighty, I gotta walk again!"

Doc Buck's throat was tight. "Now tell me what happened out there," he asked.

Hatchet John spoke through pain. He had been in the timber watching when two riders had suddenly roared out of the night. "They came from the north. They were on me afore I knowed they was even in the neighborhood."

Doc Buck nodded.

"We had a hard south wind out there. That blew their noise away from me."

"Two riders, eh? Couldn't recognize them? Or their horses?"

Hatchet John shook his head. "Dark night. Only men on horseback to me. They come in fast, then left."

"Did you do any shooting?"

"Damnit, boss, I didn't. I jus' saw thet dynamite flare, throw out sparks—an' I ran like the devil was on my tail with his redhot pitchfork!"

"Then what?"

"I fell over sumthin'. Mebbe a rock or a stick. Anyway, I went skiddin' on my belly. The black powder went boom. Lit up the timber like it was a new day. Bright as all get-out."

"You didn't recognize the two in the bright light?"

"Hell, I weren't lookin' at nothin' but the ground

253

under my face. Had both hands over my head an' my prayin' like hell.''

Doc Buck listened.

"Well, one big rock landed smack-dab on my back. When it rolled off'n me, I was paralyzed. I laid there until Vivie Wilson an' Bill rode down from the ranch house an' I hollered to them an' you know the rest.''

Doc Buck said nothing. He had a vagrant thought: Had this old man recognized the two riders? Was he keeping this knowledge to himself? Did he nurse the thought that someday he'd go against these two with a flaming short-gun or rifle? So once again the veterinarian asked, "You absolutely sure you didn't recognize the two?''

"I said I didn't, remember. I'm no liar. You're rubbin' my fur ag'in grain. I'm sick an' I'm tired. Can you give me somethin'—either a powder or somethin' from your syringe—thet'll put me to sleep?''

The old man was sleeping when Doc Buck went downstairs to where the Widow sat in a formless nightgown drinking coffee.

"You're hungry, Doc. You've had a rough night. Here's black coffee and I'll fry eggs and bacon.''

"No, no. . .''

"Yes, yes.''

The coffee was so strong you couldn't dent it with a spoon, but it was just what he needed, and the eggs and bacon made him realize he'd been so busy he'd not eaten a thing since breakfast at five yesterday morning.

"Will Hatchet John ever walk again?''

"I don't know.''

The Widow's wide face was serious. "He's all I have, Doc.''

Doc Buck looked at her. "You take care of him?''

"Gladly.''

"I'll pay you each week. You set the price and we'll talk it over later when we're both more settled."

"May I say something personal, Doctor Malone."

"Certainly."

"I don't want to sound—well, I think the word is mundane, but you're a valuable man in this town. Before you came we had no doctor of medicine."

"But I'm a doctor of animals."

"We all know that. But before you came I'm sure a number of us had to die because the closest doctor was in Bulltown and if he would come out he invariably came too late."

Doc Buck had had others tell him the same.

"There's been a lot of sick people this winter. I know you've gone hours without sleep or proper nourishment. Hatchet John told me that in the middle of the winter you fell asleep from pure weariness as he drove you in a bobsled from one sick person to the other."

Doc Buck got to his boots. "Thanks for the caffeine and the eggs and hog," he said.

Widow Hanson also rose. "I didn't mean to embarrass you."

"You didn't."

"Before you go, I'll tell you somethin' else. Just about every family in this town owes you money."

Doc Buck grinned. "How true, Mrs. Hanson."

"And you don't make any effort to collect. These people here are good people and they are blessed with children but with little money."

"How true," Doc Buck smiled.

"Put them to work," the Widow said.

Doc Buck looked at her. "I've thought of that, but it would be very unethical, wouldn't it?"

"Pshaw," the heavy-set matron said. "What are you talkin' about? Doctor Cochran has a farm out of

255

Bulltown, along the river. When a man can't pay his doctor bill Doc Cochran lets them pay it by working on his farm. Hauling manure to pastures for fertilizer, things like that.''

"Do you think these people would work out their bills?''

"You could try.''

"I'll think it over. Good night, Mrs. Wilson.''

"Goodnight? Good mornin', you mean. Sun's close to comin' up.''

Doc Buck returned to his laboratory. Running Wolf slept on a mattress on the floor, a twelve-gauge shotgun on his right, a Winchester .30-30 on his left. Doc Buck put another blanket over the boy and kissed him on the forehead and lay on his bed after removing his spurs, a thick Hudson's Bay blanket over his lanky body.

He went to sleep thinking of how close he and Ron Powers had been to matching gunspeed . . . and death. He dreamed of his father, town-taming Jack Malone. The dream was not pleasant.

A ten-gauge shotgun's buckshot had shot Jack Malone in two parts, breaking him completely above the waist. His chest and head and neck lay apart from his rump and legs. The head said, "Your mother's ag'in me learnin' you how to handle a short-gun, son.''

"Mom's against all killing,'' young Buckley Malone said.

"This is a wild country,'' the town tamer said. "The people here—well, maybe half could be called somewhat civilized. They kin read an' write. But the rest of 'em . . .''

The top part and bottom part of Jack Malone moved toward the other and he became once again a complete man.

"Lots of them have killed back east. Those that

haven't have robbed an' looted and been criminals. They went west to escape the law. They're no more than animals—wild animals."

"You've told me that before, Pa."

"Somebody has to hold them in check. . . . That's why there are town-tamers like me an' Wild Bill afore he got kilt an' the Earp boys an' Bat Masterson an' his brother. Come with me to the brush. I'll show you how to crouch, go for your holster, level and fire—an' to hell with your mother."

The two parts—now one—stood up. To the son's surprise, Town Taming Jack Malone was now a whole person, hale and hearty. He and his son started into the deep chaparral of Texas's Red River.

Then, just as they reached the brush, Town Taming Jack Malone's body fell again into two parts, toppling before his only child's startled eyes.

And then, another strange thing happened.

The thick and wide gunbelt with its heavy weight of unfired casings—along with the black .45—left the bottom part of the body. It lifted through space and fastened itself, and its pistol, around the slim waist of Buckley Malone.

The tongue of the belt slipped into the big buckle. It automatically tightened the belt around Buckley Malone's boyish hips. The holster and the .45 slapped against his right thigh.

The tie-down cords went of their own volition around his thigh. They made a hard knot inside his hip. The gun was in place, hung low, ready for action. The belt was in place, too.

Then Buckley Malone fought to get rid of the weapon and the belt. He pushed and tried to unbuckle. When he did get the hasp from the hole in the belt, it jerked from his hands and went back again into position.

He struggled. . . .

Then he heard a boyish voice say, "Dad, Dad, what's the matter, Dad?"

He recognized Running Horse's excited, boyish voice. Only when in stress or disturbed did the young Cheyenne call him Dad.

Doc Buck came back to reality.

Running Horse had his palms flat on Doc Buck's shoulders. Doc Buck breathed deeply, coming back to normal. Sweat coated his forehead. His flannel shirt was damp.

"Whew," he breathed. "I don't want another like that." He glanced at the clock. The hands showed ten minutes to six. He remembered the sick cases he had to check on this morning.

"Time I got to work," he said. "That was what you'd call a nightmare, son."

"You sure woke me up."

Five

Teresa Hernandez opened her cafe at eight. Doc Buck was coming from the Jones home after looking in on the baby, who was getting well. The March wind was very chilly. It came out of the northwest and he hugged his mackinaw closer and decided a cup of hot java would hit the spot, so he came into the cafe a few minutes after the dark-haired girl had opened. He was the only customer. He speared a stool at the corner and Teresa looked out over the swinging doors leading to the kitchen.

"Doctor Malone," she said. "Good morning."

Doc Buck returned the salutation. "How's the hot java, Miss Hernandez?"

Teresa frowned slightly. Doc Buck understood why. He had not called her Teresa.

He'd long had the impression that this Latin beauty was trying hard to fit into an environment strange to her, even to language. She wanted to belong to this environment, to be accepted as a part of it, and therefore she wanted to be Teresa, not Miss Hernandez.

"Not quite as hot as you'd like it, Doctor."

"I'll wait." Doc Malone looked at her. "I'm sorry, Teresa."

"Sorry? Why?"

"For not calling you Teresa and not Miss Hernandez."

She did not answer immediately. She looked out the glistening wide front window and her eyes were soft and for a moment he thought she would weep, but then she looked at him and she smiled softly.

"Sometimes it is a difficult task, Doctor."

Doc Malone knew full well what she meant.

She changed the subject with, "And how is the Jones baby?"

He told her.

"And how is Hatchet John?"

She spoke slowly, wanting each word and sentence correct. Doc Buck knew she kept a well-thumbed English-Spanish and vice-versa dictionary in her small office behind her kitchen and living quarters.

He's awake. Widow Hanson fed him."

"Can he walk?"

Doc Buck shook his head.

"Will he walk again?"

"I don't know. I'm not that much of a medical doctor. I'll get Doctor Cochran out from Bulltown to examine him. He knows much more about the spine than I do."

Teresa Hernandez slowly shook her head, eyes concerned. Doc Buck hoped no other would enter the cafe. This was the first time he'd really got to talk to Teresa. He'd tried before, but always a customer had entered. "Mrs. Hanson has a wheelchair," he said.

Her eyebrows lifted. "I wonder where she got that?"

"She told me she's had it for some time. Before I came she boarded a crippled man who died and left the chair behind."

"That is indeed fortunate." She went into the kitchen and returned with two cups of coffee, both steaming in the chill. She put one before Doc Buck and she put herself on a high stool behind the counter, her coffee cup on the ledge of the cabinet holding dishes and glasses. She said, without warning, "You know how to handle a six-shooter," and it was not a question, but a fact.

Doc Buck stared. "Why did you suddenly ask that?"

"Last night, at the blown-up tank. I saw your father, once, when I was a girl—in Amarillo. Dad punched cattle north of there for the Heart Bar Six and Mama and I lived in Amarillo. That was after we came from Zacatecas, down in Mexico. I was born there."

Doc Buck shook his head. She had known Town Tamer Jack Malone.

"Your father could have killed my uncle. On my mother's side, a no-good named Arnulfo."

"On what do you base that?"

"My uncle was a cow thief. He spent his ill-gotten money in saloons. When he got so much *tequila* he thought himself a gunman. He challenged your father one day when my uncle was drinking."

Doctor Buck listened.

"Later they said my father had reason to draw his gun against my uncle, who was no gunman—but thought he was. Instead, your father hit him over the head with his gun, knocking him down."

Doc Buck was silent.

"He was a good man, your father. He didn't want to kill unless he had to. But in the case of my uncle, he might have just as well killed him."

"Why?"

"A couple of weeks later they hanged him. Charles Goodnight caught my uncle in the act of stealing a Goodnight steer. He was rebranding the steer when caught."

"What happened?"

"Goodnight and his crew hanged my uncle from the

end of a wagon-tongue put up in the air."

"Why do you tell me this, Teresa."

"For one reason. I hope your father taught you how to draw and fire fast and deadly, for after last night I think you'll need that."

Doc Buck looked at her. "Do you worry about me, or do I compliment myself?"

"I worry about all people. I'd like to see all live in peace with plenty to eat and children to love."

Doc Buck pulled in a deep breath. "My father used to say the same. Yes, he taught me how to handle a six-shooter. But what he thought did him no good, for hot steel laid him low—tearing him into two parts on that street in Cheyenne."

"I read about that in Amarillo, and mother and I wept."

At that moment land locator Matthew Cotton entered. The big man wore overshoes, heavy California pants, a woolen Pendleton shirt and a knee-length sheepskin coat, his wide face red from the chilly wind. "Hotcakes and hot java, Teresa, please."

His entrance had broken the moment. Doc Buck dug out his wallet. "How's your man Friday today?" Cotton asked.

Buck told him.

"Whole town's talking," Cotton said. "Mrs. Hanson is shooing them away from her porch. Everybody wants to know how he is."

"I'll put up a notice in the post office," Doc Buck said.

Matthew Cotton grinned. "Biggest thing that's happened in this country since I've been here."

Doc Buck said, "You haven't been here long."

Teresa was in the kitchen making hotcakes. She looked at Doc Buck suddenly, Cotton not catching her

262

glance because she was out of his vision.

Cotton said shortly, "Right you are, Doctor. Any idea who blew up your tank?"

"No more than I have any idea how those Texas ticks suddenly arrived in a cold climate."

Cotton took a stool. Teresa came out with a glass of water and untensils, then returned to her kitchen.

"Maybe a trail herd coming up from Texas brought them in," Cotton said.

"What trail herd?" Doc Buck countered.

"I mind now that I heard about a week ago that a big trail herd passed west of here, prob'ly heading for Montana."

"I heard the same," Doc Buck said, "but it passed miles and miles west of here on the outer edge of Buckbrush Basin, and if it had any contact it was with Rafter V cows, not the farmers' animals."

"No Rafter V cows with ticks?"

"None that I know of," Doc Buck said.

Teresa came from the kitchen with Cotton's hot coffee. "Anything to eat for you, Doc?"

Doc Buck caught the drift. She was, in other words, asking him to leave, for the cafe's air was heavy.

"No, thanks."

Doc Buck left. He went to his lab and was watching the ticks crawl around the Mason jar when somebody knocked on the door. "Come in."

Vivian Wilson entered. She wore levis, riding boots, a flannel shirt and a long, buffalo-hide coat. A muskrat-hide cap covered her blonde hair, the flaps tied down under her chin to protect her ears.

She went to the pot-bellied heater red with Wyoming lignite. "Do you think spring will ever come, Doc Buck?"

"It's already here."

"With this cold wind?"

"Came three days ago. March twenty-first."

"Oh, you—" She noticed the Mason jar. "What are those bugs you have in there?"

"They're the ones causing all this trouble. They're Texas fever ticks, either genus *margaropus* or genus *boophilus*, and both carry the *protozoan babesia Bigemina*, which when introduced into a bovine's blood causes the breakdown of red corpuscles."

"Where, in heaven's name, did you learn all those big words?"

"College, naturally."

"Dad always said I'd make only a good housewife, and he had doubts about that. Of course, he was just joking."

Doc Buck smiled. Maybe Big Hank hadn't been joking, at that. "Big words are part of the veterinarian and medical trade."

"Why, I wonder?"

"Well, medical doctors—yes, and we veterinarians—like to act like we're very, very intelligent. So we learn a bunch of big Latin words. Sometimes we can't even pronounce them correctly but the patient doesn't know that, because he doesn't know how to pronounce them, either. That's because he hasn't the slightest idea what the words mean and many time the guy saying them doesn't, either."

"But cows and animals can't understand."

"You got a point there. But the owner of the sick animal is dazzled by the big words, even though the cow isn't."

"Then the doctor of medicine—and a vet—is to a certain extent a fraud?"

"That's right. But name me a profession that isn't?"

Vivie laughed. "I remember a school teacher we had,

right here in Buckbrush. He couldn't even do simple arithmetic.''

''That's common.''

''What are you going to do with those bugs?''

''I'm dissecting one now. I want to learn what genus he is.''

''What good will that do you?''

Doctor Buckley Malone smiled. ''Now that you speak of it, not much of anything important.''

''Where'd you get the ticks?''

''From Farmer Melstone's Holstein-Friesen milk cow. I picked them off her and put them in the bottle.''

Vivie frowned. ''Where do you think they came from, Doc?''

''I don't know. One day they weren't here and the next they were. No trail herds have gone through close to the farmers' cattle and besides all trail herds going north or to the east now have to be dipped and made tick-free before leaving Texas.''

''Maybe the farmers brought them in?''

Doc Buck shook his head. ''That isn't possible. If they'd have come in with the farmers they'd have made themselves evident long before this. Farmers' cattle would have contacted the Fever and died, long before this.''

''You think somebody imported them?''

''They came in someway.''

''Could they be shipped in—well, say in a little box? Or a bottle?''

''They could have been. But that doesn't make sense, does it? Why try to kill off the farmers' cattle?''

''To get them out of the valley, maybe?''

''That points the finger of suspicion right at your Rafter V,'' Doctor Buckley Malone said. ''No, don't get angry, please. I'm not the only one around here that

265

thinks that. There's that rumor running through the town, Vivie.''

"Those farmers pose no danger to Rafter V. We've got hundreds of square miles to run cattle over. A homestead is only a square half a mile on each side. It'd take thousands of homesteaders with land that small to occupy Rafter V's range.''

"They're coming.''

"I doubt that." She stood very close to him. A sudden pang of loneliness hit him. He looked down at her. She looked up at him. There was something in her blue eyes—something teasing and, at the same time, seemingly inviting. His heart beat steadily.

He put his arm around her. She moved closer. She smelled of a faint perfume and she was healthy and young womanhood. She smiled at him. His head came down, blood hammering his ears. Her lips parted. Her breath was warm and nice. His lips came down and found hers. He should have been aware of Running Horse's voice outside talking to somebody outside and approaching the office.

He should have heard a woman's voice answering Running Horse. He even forgot he'd not locked the door. His blood was wild and Vivie's lips were warm and nothing else mattered.

The door opened. He jerked his head upright. Vivie also looked toward the door. A wide-mouthed Running Horse stood there with a woman.

"You forgot your mittens in my cafe." The woman's voice dripped ice. She lay his mittens on a chair and left. Teresa Hernandez!

Six

Noon of that same day found Deputy Sheriff Milton Jones riding in from the dynamited tank against a cold northwest wind. He swung down stiffly and punched his way into Doc Buck's office without knocking. "Been out to the tank," he said.

Doc Buck had finally catalogued the tick as a genus *margaropus*. His microscope, although weak, identified the protozoa as *babesia gigemina*. He'd been checking his work for surely against one of his college texts when the deputy had bowlegged in.

"Find anything of importance?" Doc Buck asked.

Jones stood close to the hot pot-bellied heater. He put his back to it and took off his fur-lined mittens and rubbed his cold hands together. Once again Doc Buck wondered why people stood with their rumps to a hot stove. Why didn't they ever want to warm their bellies?

"Wind blew hard last night. Wiped out tracks, if there were any—even in that cottonwood grove. Then there's a trace of snow, which don't help none." The deputy smiled. "Sometimes I wish I'd had brains enough to go to college like a guy I know and amount to somethin'." He looked at the ticks circling the inside of the Mason jar. "What's them things?"

Doc Buck told him and went rapidly through the symptoms of Texas fever and such points, getting rather weary of reciting the same lecture.

"Mebbe somebody shipped some ticks in," the deputy said. "Either by mail or carried them in on his person?"

Doc Buck said that he'd asked Richard Edwards, the postmaster, if he thought any such package had come in, but Edwards had told him he wasn't a mail inspector. Doc Buck knew he didn't stand high with Edwards. And the reason was simple.

Augusta Edwards was an only child. She had many freckles, buck teeth, a hook nose, sprung knees—and was twenty three, which was considered to be an old maid here on the frontier where women were scarce as hen's teeth and were married at sixteen. Doc Buck wondered how Teresa and Vivie had remained single so long.

The Edwards had invited Doc Buck to their home many times. Doc Buck knew they wanted to palm Augusta off on him. He was just as determined not to have her. Finally the Edwards husband and wife had apparently decided their efforts were of no avail. They then both began to be suddenly cool to the young veterinarian, and well did Doc Buck know why.

Augusta passed him on the street without a word of greeting, and if unfortunate Augusta had one strong point it was her ability to talk and keep on talking. Indeed, many a Buckbrush resident discreetly called her A Gust of Wind.

And when one Edwards got mad at you the entire clan of three got mad. Thus no cooperation from the postmaster for one Doctor Buckley Malone, Doctor of Veterinarian Science.

"We should call a meetin' of the farmers an' Rafter V an' everybody in town," the sheriff said. "This a community affair—a man almost got dynamited to death—and all should talk it over. Or would there be an open fight?"

"There might be, and there might not be. I've beat you to the punch, though. I've already put a notice up in the Merc and the post office setting such a meeting for two tomorrow afternoon."

"How come you beat me to the idea?"

"I built one dipping vat. It cost me almost all the little money I had. I built it for the benefit of those having cattle that needed dipping, not for myself or my own stock—that is, if I buy any. And with this tick scare in the basin, I'm staying without a cow until the problem is settled."

"You sent Charlie Watson to Bulltown to get Doc Cochran out, they tell me?"

"Charlie pulled out at two last night," Doc Buck informed. "Should be back any time now. He'd change horses in Bulltown an' ride out on a rented horse, he told me."

"His own horse?"

"Doc Cochran can lead it behind his buggy. Then he can take Charlie's rented horse back when he returns."

"Could I talk to Hatchet?"

"Not now. What would you like to know?"

"He know how many men hit the tank?"

Doc Buck considered briefly. From somewhere came the thought that maybe it would be best if he'd tell Hatchet not to reveal how many riders had swept down out of the black night. He didn't know why he had this thought, or what motivated it, but he had it. "He don't know. Dark and he was watching from the brush. Saw the dynamite make a flying arc, then flopped on the ground and held his hands over his head, and a flying boulder landed on his back."

"I see. . . ."

Deputy Sheriff Milton Jones left. Doc Buck grinned wryly. Jones owed him almost fifty dollars in this winter's doctor bills for the Jones family. Doc Buck had even bought some special medicines for the youngest boy last January down in Bulltown. And Jones hadn't mentioned paying him for the medicine or for medical attention.

Running Horse came in. "Been out to the tank. I guess I don't revert back to my ancestors."

Doc Buck thought, *The boy is really learning English.* He and Running Horse had an hour of teaching and learning each day except Saturday and Sunday. The arrival of Running Horse made him again think of Deputy Jones.

Running Horse had jumped his tribe's reservation. That made him an illegal alien in the land his people had recently owned. Deputy Jones, by law, was compelled to pick up and turn over to the federal agents any stray redskins.

The deputy had deliberately overlooked Running Horse. Doc Buck figured he'd done this because of a doctor's influence in a small town. He also made a decision that next time in Bulltown he'd go to the county courthouse and see the county attorney about drawing up adoption-papers on the Cheyenne. With adoption papers in his possession, Running Horse would be free of the law.

"What about your ancestors?" Doc Buck asked.

"Them men writin' them Western stories—well, a redskin can read tracks, accordin' to them, where there are no tracks. I sure can't do the same, Doc Buck. Hey, I'm hungry."

"Let's go to Teresa's."

Running Horse looked at him. "Why not cook here

in the office? I'm mix up some bacon an' eggs."

"I've eaten so much bacon, I'm beginning to grunt like a hog. And I've put so many eggs inside of me I'm beginning to cackle instead of speak."

"Okay, Doc Buck."

Charlie Watson came in while they were in Teresa's. Doc Cochran would come out in two days, he reported. "Lots of sick people," he said. "Colds, new-monia, things like that, Doc Cochran said."

"How much do I owe you?" Doc Buck asked.

The bony man grinned. "You got it reversed, Doc. It's how much do I owe you for those two nights you spent sittin' beside my little Ralph last January when he was right sick an' I was feered to my boots."

"We'll talk it over some day right soon in my office," Dock Buck said.

"Rafter V's pullin' out roundup wagons inside a month or so for calf-gather. When thet's over I'll have a few bucks."

Once again Doc Buckley Malone realized how dependent these people and this town was on the Wilson ranch. Big Hank Wilson had built almost all buildings in Buckbrush. Doc Buck paid the ranch rent on his office and living quarters. Rafter V also owned this building holding Teresa's cafe. Well, enough farmers come in, and that would be changed—and changed completely. For ten long years this town had not progressed but progress was ahead, Doc Buck guessed.

Suddenly it occurred to him that now would be a good place and time to test Widow Hanson's theory.

"Charlie, would you be interested in working out the money you owe me?" Duc Buck had almost said *debt* but had caught his words in time. "I'm going to build a new tank."

"Damn it to thell, I'd be happy to, Doc. Why didn't

271

you bring that up afore? I'm goin' loco with nothin' to do. I've braided three horse-hair cinches, two headstalls, an' six quirts this winter. I've even planted my garden, cold as it is, an' I've hoed the ground so much the danged stuff is dust, not dirt."

"I'll let you know later, Charlie."

Charlie Watson left and Bill Wilson and Ron Powers entered, both wearing knee-length sheepskin coats and angora chaps. As they passed Bill nodded briefly but Powers evidently didn't see Doc Buck and Running Horse. Teresa was very pretty in riding boots, a deerskin split leather riding skirt and a blue silk blouse. When Doc Buck had tried to joke with her she had had little or no response.

"She remembers you kissin' Vivie," Running Horse said.

"A man has a right to kiss whoever he wants."

"I suppose so, if a woman stands still long enough. Me, I ain't kissin' no woman—one my age, anyway."

Doc Buck had to smile.

"Well, the Widow kisses me sometimes. Always on the forehead. Hey, I talked with her in the Merc a while back. Hatchet is in the wheelchair an' learning how to operate it good, she said."

"But you don't kiss Helen Jo Garner?"

Running Horse looked at him over his steak. Helen Jo was as bucktoothed and kneesprung as Augusta Edwards, only a younger model, and in the same year in school with Running Horse.

"You aren't funny, Dad," he said.

They continued eating. *Why is it that somebody else's cooking always tastes better than your own*? Doc Buck thought.

Running Horse's words broke into his thoughts.

"Theresa sure talks to Bill an' Powers, though. Look at her gabbing with them, and she won't say a civil word to you."

"My heart is broken," Doc Buck said.

"That may be because Bill is a rich man," the boy continued. "He must be around a millionaire with all them cattle."

"You think a woman likes a man better if the man has money?"

"Don't joke me, please. Here comes Mr. Melstone. Ain't he the one you got those ticks from?"

"Not from him. From his milk cow, Molly."

"I quit," Running Horse said.

Melstone's ruddy face was red from the cold wind. "Got a awful sick cow, Doc Buck," he said. "Rode in for you. Could you come out to the farmer—after you finish eatin', of course?"

"Describe her, please?" Doc Buck asked.

The farmer had caught some of the cow's urine. "Like you tol' me to do when you got them ticks from Molly. An' her water is a dark red color."

Doc Buck thought, *Texas fever*. The farmer kept on describing. Doc Buck figured the cow a goner. "She seems to be goin' downhill fast, Doc."

The meal finished, Doc Buck paid, and Teresa said shortly, "*Muchas gracias*."

Doc Buck, Running Horse and the farmer went out into the cold wind, Doc Buck saying, "I'll get James from the livery and ride out with you, Mr. Melstone."

"I'll wait here."

Doc Buck didn't tell the farmer that his cow was as good as dead—and might indeed be dead by the time he arrived at the Melstone farm. He and Running Horse began walking up-street to the Town Livery Stable. "I

273

go with you?" the boy asked.

"Naturally. You're my helper, remember?"

"And a future veterinary," the boy proudly said.

Seven

Hard knocking on his door awakened Doc Buck at four the next morning. He then went through the cold darkness with a townsman whose fourteen-year-old daughter suffered from a severe pain in her right side.

Doc Buck immediately diagnosed appendicitis. "Has Joan complained of this pain before?"

"A number of times, Doctor Buck," Joan's anxious mother said, "but we thought it would pass in time."

Running Horse had accompanied the veterinarian. "Go wake up Charlie Watson," Doc Buck told his apprentice. "Joan has to go to Bulltown and under Doctor Cochran's care."

"We don't have much money," the mother said.

"Don't worry about that, Mrs. Cotterman," Doc Buck said. He again spoke to Running Horse. "Has Charlie still got his covered wagon-box on his bobsled?"

"Not now. He transferred it to his spring-wagon a few days ago."

"Good."

Running Horse hurriedly departed. The night hid him. "What do we do next?" Joan's father asked.

"We put Joan on a cot. And then into the spring-wagon. That canvas cover Charlie's got—like a covered wagon—will keep some heat down."

"What else can we do?" the mother asked.

"Pray and have much hope," Doc Buck said.

"Is there nothing else you can do?" the mother asked.

Joan groaned, eyes closed.

"I'll give her some strong sleeping powders. That will keep her asleep until she gets to Doctor Cochran. When she's sleeping she won't feel pain or move much. Yes, you can go with her, Mrs. Cotterman."

The family had no cot. Widow Hanson had one. Soon the spring-wagon with it patient started north.

"I've got some ham and eggs," the Widow said. "An' Hatchet John expects you to pay him a mornin' call, Doc Buck."

Doc Buck looked at Running Horse. More hog and more pin feathers. "Why not?" the young Cheyenne said.

"What's he talkin' about?" Widow Hanson asked.

"I surely don't know," Doc Buck said, "and I doubt if he himself knows, but we'll sure take you up, Widow Hanson."

They'd moved Hatchet John downstairs. He was in the warm kitchen sitting in his wheel-chair.

His face lit up upon seeing Doc Buck. He said he was awaiting Doctor Cochran's visit.

"Doc Cochran will be out tomorrow," Doc Buck said.

Hatchet John's face fell. "Couldn't make it today, eh? Dang it, I want to see if I can ever hoof it ag'in."

"Be patient," Doc Buck said.

Once again he wondered if Hatchet John hadn't recognized the two night-riders who had blasted the dipping vat to a mass of stone and cement. He decided he'd push the matter no further. The wounded man probably was telling the truth.

"Heard you rode out to the Melstone farm yesterday to look at a sick cow?" Widow Hanson asked, cutting ham.

"At a dead cow, you mean," Doc Buck corrected.

He'd performed an autopsy on the dead milk cow for Running Horse's benefit. He'd shown his young assistant how the destruction of red corpuscles had made the bovine spleen very enlarged and turgid and how yellow and unhealthy this lack had made the mucous membranes.

Widow Hanson turned the ham over. A nose-tickling aroma filled the big kitchen, reminding him of his mother's kitchen down on the Texas Panhandle.

Maybe there was something to this being married, at that. He looked at the Widow's wide bovine back and tried to imagine Teresa in their kitchen with Teresa cooking breakfast for him and their children.

This fantasy pleased him. He then brushed Teresa to one side and inserted Vivie in Teresa's place. Vivie looked okay, too. He then wondered which vision had pleased him the more—Vivie's or Teresa's. He couldn't decide the winner. They ran neck to neck.

He brought himself back to the unhappy present, telling himself he wasn't making enough money to support a wife let alone a gaggle of young-uns. And he knew, even as he thought this, that he was fibbing to himself. Some of Buckbrush's families were large. But, despite their size and lack of money, they seemed to progress and grow physically and spiritually. The children worked for the benefit of the family and the mother and father worked for the benefit of their offspring.

Widow Hanson said, "If'n I was one of them sodbusters an' there was ticks killin' my cows I'd personally pick after every tick on them—but first I'd scrub them good with lye soap an' hot water."

"That won't kill them," Doc Buck said.

"Won't eh? Then I'd wash each cow with kerosene. I'd start on her front an' work down an' back an' they'd be no danged ticks on Bossy when this ol' woman got done."

Doc Buck scowled. "Some farmers have done just that but others have done a half-job, which is no better than none. I used to think at first that those farmers were ranch-people who'd come to Wyoming to become farmers but I've changed my mind since knowing them as well as I have become."

"What made you think they'd been aroun' cattle an' such?" the Widow asked, breaking an egg.

"They could ride a horse so well. And some were breaking broncs. But now that I'm around them—and got to know them—I find that they're eastern people who'd never been around a horse before."

Hatchet John laughed. "I knowed a family of Norskies who homesteaded up in Montany Territory on the Powder. Fishermen who'd lost their boats in a North Sea storm. Never been on a hoss until they got on the Powder. An' jus' a short while later they was kickin' out broncs an' ridin' like they'd been born to the saddle."

Doc Buck spoke to the Widow. "The meeting we're holding this afternoon—you wheeling Hatchet over to it?"

"She sure is," Hatchet John hurriedly said.

After eating, the Widow accompanied Doc Buck and Running Horse to the door. Dawn was finally making a small indentation against the eastern sky. Hatchet John remained in the kitchen.

"He gets dark moments," the Widow said softly. "I'm afraid, Doc Buck."

"Weapons?"

"I've got a ten-gauge double-barreled shotgun my husband used to hunt ducks. I got it hid. I also hid his .45. I've moved all the butcher knives and other knives up high in shelves where he can't reach them."

Doc Buck had a serious face. Running Horse studied the back of his right hand. Finally Doc Buck said, "Keep him from weapons, Mrs. Hanson. Do the best you can. We still haven't made a pay arrangement."

"Let's do that when things are more ordinary."

"Okay, but if I forget, remind me, please."

"I'll remember," Running Hosre said.

Doc Buck and Running Horse went to the lab and dwelling quarters. It was now fifteen after six. Charlie Watson and the sick Joan Cotterman would now be quite a few miles on the road to Doctor Cochran. It was too late to go back to bed so Doc Buck said, "There's one angle I've not yet checked."

"What's that?" Running Horse asked.

"The Texans."

Running Horse nodded. "Diamon' in a Diamon'. You know, Dad, a Rafter V could be changed easy to Diamon' in a Diamon'."

Doc Buck nodded. "Right, son. Make the rafter into a diamond by adding a V to its bottom. Then make the V into a diamond by putting a V on top of it. What side and where on a cow is the Diamond inside a Diamond located? Or don't you know?"

"I know. Right ribs."

"Same place a cow packs a Rafter V," Doc Buck said. "But we're talking about something that could happen but hasn't had time to happen because the Texans have been in the Landry Hills only about two weeks.

"Let's ride out to their camp. We got time before the

meeting this afternoon."

"You think maybeso their cows could have brought in these ticks?"

"Could be," Doc Buck said.

"But you told me all trailherds leavin' Texas had to be dipped so the ticks would be killed."

"That's the law, but sometimes it's not paid attention to. Texas is a pretty big area, you know."

"Biggest state in the Union. Learned that in school."

They went to the livery-barn. Soon they rode south on Pinto and James, the tough horses fiddlefooting and pulling at bits. The wind was behind them and both wore heavy sheepskin coats and angora chaps. Within two hours, the coats and chaps were tied behind the cantles of their saddles, for a chinook wind now swept in from the northwest.

The chinook had come without warning, as all chinooks come. Within an hour the mercury rose at least thirty to forty degrees. Already the snow on high ridges was beginning to turn to run-off water.

The further south they rode the more Rafter V cattle they encountered. This was logical. The farmers were on the north rim of Buckbrush Basin. Their cattle were dying of Texas Fever.

Bill Wilson had given range-boss Ron Powers orders to move Rafter V cattle south along the north bank of Buckbrush River and Doggone Creek. Thus the young cowman had built a barrier of empty land between Rafter V herds and the diseased cows of the farmers.

Vivie had told Doc Buck this. "We're taking no chances, Doc," she'd said. "Those ticks can't fly, can they?"

"Not that I know of."

"Where in the hell did they come from?"

"Women shouldn't swear," Doc Buck had joked.

"They shouldn't kiss men who aren't their husbands, either." Thereupon pretty blonde Vivie Wilson had stood on tiptoe and kissed him on the mouth there in his laboratory.

Doc Buck and his assistant rode around groups of Rafter V cattle, the veterinarian studying them with a trained eye. None of the cattle showed a sign of Texas Fever.

That pleased the young veterinarian. Upon graduation from his eastern college he'd taken an oath that to veterinarians was the equal of the Hippocratic Oath sworn to by a doctor of medicine. That oath required him to treat any suffering animal regardless of the animal's owner's status monetarily or socially. The animal—not the owner—was what counted to a veterinarian.

"No signs of blackleg, either," Running Horse said. "You can vaccinate against blackleg. Why can't you make a vaccine against Texas Fever?"

"I don't think it could be done."

"Why not?"

"Blackleg is caused by bacteria, a germ. Texas Fever is caused by an amoeba, a protozoan, a living organism—totally different than bacteria."

Running Horse scowled. "I got to study up on some things a lot more. What book would I find this about amoebas and bacteria?"

Doc Buck told him.

Running Horse looked southwest. "Two riders over there about a mile away. Looks like Bill Wilson's big sorrel stud an' Ron Powers' pinto."

Doc Buck looked. The boy was right.

The two Rafter V men had also discarded their angora *chaparreras* and sheepskin coats. Bill Wilson did all the talking. Ron Powers just sat the Al Furstnow saddle on his big black and gray pinto gelding and glowered. The two were checking Rafter V cattle for signs of Texas Fever, Bill Wilson related, his voice holding anger.

Doc Buck told the young rancher that in his opinion in this cold weather ticks would not travel from one cow to the other but stay with their parent cow until warm weather arrived.

"Warm weather's comin'," Bill Wilson said.

"Cows have to brush one against the other to transfer ticks," Doc Buck pointed out. "And the farmers' cows are under strict quarantine."

"Who quarantined them?"

"I did. My license to practice in the Territory gives me that right."

Ron Powers spoke for the first time. "Your power's bein' violated. Yesterday a farmer's entire bunch—about twenty head—was grazin' outside his south fence on Rafter V range."

Doc Buck looked at the range-boss. "What farmer was that?"

"Thet heavy-set gink who's the head of them bastards. Name's Gaboney, er sumpin' like that."

"You saw Ed Gaboney's stock outside his fence?" Doc Buck asked.

"I tell the truth, veter'nary."

"I was with Rod," Bill Wilson said.

"His cattle getting out is news to me," Doc Buck said. "I'll talk to him. I'll fine him fifty cents a head."

"An' where'll the money go?" Ron Powers asked.

Doc Buck studied the range boss. "Not in my pocket, like you just hinted. It goes into the county fund, if you've got to know." He spoke to Bill Wilson. "How many head were outside? You count them?"

"I didn't."

282

"What'd you do with them?" Doc Buck asked.

"We cut the bastardly farmer's fence with fence-pliers." Ron Powers said savagely. "Then we chased his damn' stock back on his damn' pasture. He come ridin' out hell-fer-leather with a rifle but he didn't dare use it. When we left, he was patchin' his fence."

Doc Buck paid the range boss no attention. He spoke to Bill Wilson. "This scare will soon be over. I'll see to that."

"Warm weather's coming," Wilson reminded.

"Just keep your stock with a three mile space between them and the farmers, and you'll get no ticks."

The thought came to Doctor Buckley Malone that Ed Gaboney's cattle had as yet not shown signs of Texas Fever—not a single head. He then remembered that the bachelor-farmer had said he'd washed every head with kerosene with a bit of carbolic acid in it.

"Where the hell did those ticks come from?" Bill Wilson asked.

Doc Buck grinned. "You tell me an' we'll both know."

Ron Powers snarled, "Thet's a smart-alec answer. Jus' about what a man would expect from a cow-college graduate."

"You don't like me, do you?" Doc Buck said shortly.

"Not one damn' bit, cow doctor!"

Doc Buck hesitated. He remembered reading a book where one brother seemingly had been born to hate the other. He'd then thought it impossible that two men—brothers—could instinctively dislike the other. Ever since he and this range boss had met there'd been friction between them. It had started at an insignificant country dance.

Doc Buck had passed a group of Rafter V cowpunchers outside the hall killing a bottle. Ron

Powers had hollered out that he have a drink with the rowdies. Most of the cowpunchers had already been drunk. They'd been looking for trouble. Therefore Doc Buck, new to this range, had politely declined. This had angered Ron Powers. He'd considered this refusal to drink with him an insult. From then on, things had gone from bad to worse, finally culminating on the near gunfight at the dynamited dipping tank.

Now, on this wide prairie, in this warm chinook wind, this hate had arisen again, coiling, vibrant, ugly, deadly.

Doc Buck had his hand on his holstered gun. So did Ron Powers. Then it was that Bill Wilson said, "Seems as if you two are bound to kill one another, or both—so here's as good a spot as any."

"You're wrong, brother Bill!"

The words came from behind Doc Buck, who stiffened at the sharpness in Vivian Wilson's voice.

His hand left his gun's butt. Ron Powers' eyes were narrowed slits as he looked at Vivian who drew her bay even with James. "What you doin' out here, woman?"

"Don't *woman* me, Powers! To you, I'm *Miss Wilson*, savvy. And don't ever forget that I own half of Rafter V and Rafter V pays your wages!"

Bill Wilson smiled. "You speak prematurely, Sis. You won't own half of this spread for about two and a half more years until you get twenty-one."

"Don't get technical with me, big brother!" Vivie was really angry. Doc Buck had never seen her this angry before. He then supplemented this with the thought that never before had he seen her angry. She had spunk, this girl.

Her entrance had broken the aura of kill-madness. Powers had fallen back into silence, only his eyes betraying anger.

Bill Wilson asked, "How come you trail us?"

"I was up in the *mirador* watching you two ride out. Then I caught sight of Doc Buck and the boy riding south, too. I saw you two would be bound to meet. So I saddled Sorrel . . . and here I am."

Doc Buck knew the Rafter V had a *mirador*—a tall three-story tower with a room on top whence could be seen miles and miles of Wyoming Territory. *Mirador* was the Spanish word for *watch-tower*, he knew.

Big Hank Wilson had taken the idea up with him from Texas where every big ranch had constructed a *mirador*, one of the first buildings built.

And each ranch had the tower occupied night and day. On the Texas plains it was built to keep track of Comanche war parties. Here in Wyoming one was built to watch the Sioux and Cheyenne and Blackfoot and Crow and various other tribes when the wars were in progress.

Suddenly Bill Wilson said to Ron Powers, "Let's drift on, friend," and they laid spurs to their cayuses with Bill hollering back, "See you this afternoon at your town meeting, pill pusher."

Then, they dipped into a coulee and fell out of sight. Doc Buck spoke to Vivie. "Thanks for the help."

"You two act like two idiots."

"He forced Dad," Running Horse quickly informed.

"Forget it," Doc Buck said. Then, to Vivie, "We're heading for the Texans' camp."

"Diamond inside a Diamond?"

"You bet," Doc Buck said. "Mind it not a bit if you'd ride with us, *Miss Wilson*."

"Vivie to you, Doc," the girl said. "I'd like to ride along with you."

The three loped south. Doc Buck glanced at the sun. Be about one when they got back in town, if they didn't stay too long at the Texans' camp. They saw one rider

285

heading north. He was about a mile away. He rode a bay horse and headed fast across the prairie. Doc Buck's powerful field-glasses indentified him immediately. Running Horse also carried field-glasses. Vivie had none. Doc Buck handed her his. She looked, adjusting the screw to fit her eyes. Finally, she lowered the glasses.

"What's he doing way out here?" she asked.

"Danged if I'd know," Doc Buck said and spoke to Running Horse, "Who do you think he is?"

Running Horse told him. Vivie repeated the same name. Doc Buck scratched his jaw, which reminded him he'd not had time to shave today.

"Ed Gaboney," he said slowly.

Eight

The meeting was held in the building that served as a schoolhouse, city hall, church and dance-hall. Deputy Mike Jones opened the doors at one-thirty sharp. Already a group of townspeople stood waiting to enter, among them Doctor Buckley Malone and his Indian assistant.

The chinook wind still gently blew. Frozen earth was thawing and releasing water. Word came that the farmers' depleted reservoirs were rapidly filling with run-off water. That stored water meant alfalfa fields would grow green and high in the summer. If you cut the first crop of alfalfa hay early you could possibly grow two more crops this summer if the summer was of usual length.

Each winter Rafter V lost many head to winter-kill. Were the big ranch to buy alfalfa hay from these farmers and feed at least their weakest stock in the winter and pull these through the ranch would save itself a good-sized sum of money—that is, if the price per ton of hay was not too high.

Doc Buck was thinking in this vein as he went to the raised platform and began arranging the desk and chairs. He was also remembering his talk with the Texans a few hours before on the southern rim of Buckbrush Basin.

He had just seen the Texans once in the short time they'd been in the Basin. A few days after trekking in their cattle they'd ridden in a body into Buckbrush. Their visit had not been pleasant. They'd immediately tried to drink the one saloon dry. The lack of girls upstairs had angered them. They'd picked trouble with the townspeople. There'd been fistfights. Deputy Sheriff Jones had had to temporarily deputize Doc Buck and other townsmen to calm down the wild Texans. That maneuver on the part of the deputy sheriff had been a mistake. The Texans wanted such a body to move against them. They had their guns ready.

The Widow Hanson had then taken command. She'd summoned her matrons of the Buckbrush City Ladies Aid. They'd marched in a body to the saloon and demanded the Texans leave town immediately. The Texans had left. Nobody had been killed. Only casualties were a few windows they'd shot to smithereens as they'd bucked their broncs out of town.

Doc Buck had figured that the Texans by this time had built some buildings. He was surprised to see none. The Texans had been ready to drive on for their cattle were all bunched with riders keeping the longhorns in one compact group.

The trail-boss was a bony, bearded man that towered four inches over Doc Buckley Malone's tallness. He had recognized Doc Buck from his one trip into Buckbrush City. "Somethin' on your mind, cow doc?" His voice had been harsh and hurried. "If so, come out with it."

"Why the hurry?"

"Us boys was gonna build a ranch here. Settle down an' run cattle ag'in Rafter V, but we changed our minds. Not enough grass. Not enough space. So we're jus' now readyin' to push on north into Montany Territory."

Doc Buck nodded. Vivie sat a silent saddle, acutely aware of the eyes of the women-hungry cowpunchers. Nobody paid a bit of attention to Running Horse who listened, all ears.

"Sent scouts out. They've all come back. Mussellshell basin, south of the Missouri in Montany. Bluejoint grass to a horse's knees. We're trailin' north to there, commencin' today."

"We got Texas fever on the north rim," Doc Buck pointed out.

The big Texan scowled. "So I heered, doc. An' damn' my buttons—sorry, Miss Wilson—how did them ticks get into this country?"

Doc Buck looked at the distant trailherd. Already Diamond in a Diamond cowhands were stringing out the cattle in trailherd lines, pointing them north. He was, in one sense, glad the big, tough outfit was leaving for sooner or later it and big Rafter V would have met and clashed. Men would have died under snarling lead, their blood coloring red the grass they did not own but over which they'd fought to the deadly end.

"Your herd—"

"What about it?"

"Texas cattle, I take it. You had these cattle dipped before leaving Texas?"

"What ice does it cut with you?"

Doc Buck pulled in air and chose his words carefully. "Texas law requires all cattle leaving or entering Texas to be run through a creosote and kerosene dipping vat to make sure none carries ticks."

"How'd you come to know so much about Texas law?"

Texas cowpunchers had ridden over to listen. They made a tough and taciturn group of cowpunchers and horses, the herd for the moment forgotten. A feeling of apprehension touched Doctor Buckley Malone. He glanced at Running Horse. The young Cheyenne had a solemn face. His glance went to Vivian Wilson. She also had a serious look on her lovely face. Doc Buck momentarily studied the Texans.

His eyes dwelled for a second on a short, red-whiskered man sitting a sorrel gelding. For some reason, his face seemed familiar, and Doc Buck wondered where and when he'd seen the man before. He judged the cowpuncher to be in his middle thirties. He needed a haircut and a shave. Doc Buck looked back at the tough range boss.

"I was raised on the Panhandle," he patiently said. "Could I see your certificate saying these cattle were dipped before leaving Texas, and how many head you had go into the tank?"

"That's my business, and not yours!"

Doc Buckley Malone reached back into his off saddle-bag. He unbuckled the heavy leather flap and came out with a leather folder. He opened the folder and went through the legal papers inside and came out with the right one. "Here are my credentials from the Territory of Wyoming."

He handed the paper to the range boss. The Texan squinted at it and passed it on to the red-headed rider. "You read it, Virgil. My eyes ain't what they should be."

Doc Buck glanced at Vivie. Vivie's lips wore a small smile for a moment. She understood. The range boss didn't know how to read.

"Out loud?" Virgil asked.

"Out loud," the range boss said.

Virgil read rapidly. When he finished the range boss said, "Now translate into English what you read."

Virgil cleared his throat. "This man is a registered

veterinarian in the Territory of Wyoming. As such he has the right to arrest and put in jail anybody who violates one of the Territory's grazing laws or, in other words, laws regarding cattle and the range industry."

"Has he got the right to make me produce my paper showing whether or not this stock has been dipped?"

"He has that right."

"An' if I don't show this?"

"He can take you into town and jail you if his discretion tells him to."

Now, waiting for the hall to fill, Doc Buck looked at Rafter V riders filing in, Bill Wilson in the lead, Ron Powers a pace behind him, and the rest of the crew strung out, spurs chiming, chaps swinging, high-heeled boots hammering the concrete floor.

Then, he remembered yesterday. The range boss had laughed sourly. He'd looked at Running Horse, at Vivian, and then at Doc Buck. And he'd said, "Hell of a lookin' law posse to take a tough ol' bunch of Texans into jail!"

Doc Buck noticed immediately the man's voice had lost its hard edge. He glanced at the short, red-headed man, again wondering where he'd seen him before, if indeed he had. He might be thinking of the day the Texans tried to tree the town of Buckbrush, he decided. That might have been when he'd seen the red-head. He knew the Texans had never again ridden into Buckbrush City.

The range boss spoke to the red-headed buckaroo. "What'd you advise, Virgil?"

"Simple. Let him see the certificate sayin' the herd was dipped."

"Where is it?"

"In my saddlebag."

"Dig it out, eh?" the range-boss said.

291

Doc Buck soon had the certificate in hand. The cattle had been dipped at Dumas, Texas. The dip-notice said six thousand, three hundred and eighty-nine head had gone through the dipping vat.

Doc Buck studied the herd. "How many head you got there?"

"Just what the notice says, minus a few head that went down on the trip north," Virgil assured.

"Why not count 'em?" the range boss' voice dripped sarcasm.

Doc Buck let that ride. He decided to ignore the surly range boss and concentrate his attention on Virgil. "You pick up any cattle along the way?"

"Not a one," Virgil said. "Some strays tried to join us down in Colorado but we cut them all back right pronto."

"All Texas cattle," the range boss said. "Are you satisfied now, horse doctor?"

"Only one thing more," Again Doc Buck spoke to Virgil. "These cattle weren't inspected when they entered Wyoming Territory?"

"Oh, yes, they were," the range boss said.

Virgil gave his nigh saddlebag another search. He came out with another piece of paper which he handed to Doc Buck who handed back the Dipping Credential.

This paper permitted the herd to enter Wyoming Territory and declared it free of contagious diseases and ticks. Doc Buck recognized the signature of the veterinarian who had signed the certificate.

He handed it back. "All legal and above board," he told Virgil.

"Thank you," Virgil said.

The range boss said: "Thank you double, horse doctor." His sarcasm still dripped.

Doc Buck looked at the range boss. "You're free to

move on." He held out his hand. The Texan took it hesitantly. Doc Buck then shook hands with Virgil. "I thank you for your help, sir."

Virgil's grip was sincere. "I like your basin," he said. "I wouldnt mind stayin' here an' becomin' a farmer."

"Lots of good land for the filing fee," Doc Buck said. "And we have a land locator who'll settle you on a homestead. For a fee, of course."

"I heard about him in Branding Iron," Virgil said.

Branding Iron was the first town south on the Powder River Trail. It consisted of a rundown hotel where the stage stopped and a postoffice and general store. At least thirty miles lay between Branding Iron and the south rim of Buckbrush Basin.

"Something good?" Doc Buck asked.

Virgil shook his head. "Not very good. Well, now, I can't say yes or no—maye every land locator has the same clause written in when he settles a homesteader."

Doc Buck frowned. "Clause?"

Virgil grinned, showing tobacco-yellow teeth. "Shucks, what I heered in Branding Iron might be just a pack of nothing, so let's forget it, eh?"

"So long," Doc Buck said.

He and Vivie and Running Horse turned their broncs north again. The day had become real spring with the scent of pine and spruce in the air. Doc Buck noticed a blue and fragile crocus sticking its head through a bit of melting snow. He also noticed that Running Horse was putting his field-glasses back into their leather case.

"Why the glasses, boy?"

Running Horse said, "All them cows back there didn't pack the Diamond in a Diamond iron. Some packed a Circle S on the left ribs."

Doc Buck frowned. "You sure, son?"

Running Horse handed him the field-glasses. "That

brockle-face steer—this side of thet dun longhorn bull—"

The brand showed up clearly scrawled across the steer's right ribs. Doc Buck handed back the glasses. "Now whereabouts is the Circle S located?" the veterinarian wondered.

Vivie shrugged shoulders. "I sure don't know. But I'd judge it to be a rather ordinary iron—a circle with an s in it. Easy to make with a stamp iron."

Doc Buck said, "Those Texans said no other cattle had been added on the trail north. They lied."

They all drew rein. Vivie watched Doc Buck and so did Running Horse. The veterinarian seemed debating a question, face stern.

"I should ride back and call their hand," Doc Buck said.

Vivie shook her head. "Look at it this way, Doc. They're pulling out for good. Once they get out of the Basin it makes no never-mind to you or anybody else, does it?"

"You afraid there'll be trouble?"

"I know there'll be," the girl said.

Running Horse said, "Vivie's right, Dad."

Doc Buck also knew a return trip would bring trouble—and it could be gunsmoke trouble. He remembered the big, rawboned trail boss's open antagonism and sarcasm.

"Okay, you win. Let's ride on."

Vivie rode into Buckbrush City with them to attend the meeting. Once in town, Running Horse went to the lab and dwelling quarters. He had a special buffalo steak he wanted to prepare for dinner.

The town was full of farmers' rigs—buckboards, spring-wagons, democrats, lumber-wagons. The farmers used the hitchrack in front of the barber shop, the Rafter V the saloon's hitchrack. Doc Buck went down in front of the saloon. He'd not mention he'd seen Ed Gaboney riding far south but he would mention Gaboney's breaking quarantine laws.

Gaboney drank with the farmers at their end of the long bar. Doc Buck went straight to the point. "Gaboney, yesterday your cattle were grazing below your south fence. You broke quarantine laws."

Other farmers turned, listening, some with glasses in hands, their eyes hot, inquisitive.

"How'd you know thet?"

Doc Buck waved a hand. "Makes no never-mind how I found out."

"Damn' ol' cow rubbed the latch off the gate," the farmer said. "Opened the wire gate and they all got out onto gover'ment ground." He studied Doc Buck with small, tight eyes. "Rafter V tol' you, I'd guess. Anyway, I wasn't home at thet time—helpin' Ted Lawson repair his corral—but when I come back the cows were aroun' my house an' beside the gate bein' down, my bobwire was cut."

Rafter V was also in the saloon. The farmers were at the south end of the long bar; Rafter V on the north.

Bill Wilson came over, spurs clanging, glass in hand, with Ron Powers following, carrying a whiskey bottle. "I cut that fence," Wilson said. "Powers and I chased your cattle back. And the gate wasn't down, farmer. The gate was closed."

Gaboney eyed Wilson. Silence had held the big saloon. Doc Buck noticed that Gaboney carefully kept his right hand away from the gun on his hip. Finally Gaboney said, "I could call you a liar, Wilson."

"Why don't you?" Bill Wilson taunted.

Sheriff Milton Jones pushed in. "None of that," he said sharply. "One man reach for a gun an' this saloon'll blow itself to hell. There'll be dead farmers an' dead cowboys all over. Talk sensible like men, or shut your goddamned mouths and go back to where you come from."

Ron Powers sarcastically said, "The star-toter's mad, boss."

Bill Wilson smiled slightly. "You're right, Milt. I respect you and I respect the authority you carry." Then, to Powers, "Come on, Ron." Wilson and Powers returned to the bar's north end.

Jones said, "Explain this to me, please, Doc Buck?" Doc Buck did.

Jones spoke to Ed Gaboney. "You broke quarantine. You admitted your cattle were outside your fence. It makes no never-mind how they got there, they were outside of quarantine."

Ed Gaboney said, "Okay, they were—but it wasn't my fault."

"I've seen your pasture," the deputy sheriff said. "You've over-grazed it down to almost bare earth. But that's beside the point. What's the verdict, Doc Buck?"

"Territorial laws say the fine is fifty cents a head per day. They were out there one day and they were counted as they were driven back into your pasture, Gaboney."

"Who counted them?"

"Rafter V," Doc Buck informed.

Gaboney laughed shortly. "You takin' their count?"

"I am. And for this reason. Mr. Wilson said he and Mr. Powers chased back twenty-three head. They were right. I know you have twenty-three head of cattle. I got that in my record book."

"You keep record of how many head of cattle each of us farmers got?"

"That's part of my job."

296

"An' Rafter V? You know how many cows it has, too?"

"Roundup tally last fall on Rafter V is in my office files, too. Territory requires I keep check."

"Well, I'll be a—" Gaboney laughed shortly. "How much per head, Doc?"

"Fifty cents."

"Fifty cents! Holy God, you aim to break a man. That's eleven dollars an' fifty cents, man."

"That's the fine."

"What if I can't pay?"

"I have the legal right to confiscate your livestock, every head including horses, goats, cattle—or what have you," Doc Buck replied.

"Would you do that?" Gaboney snarled.

"I sure would. I'd commission Mr. Jones here, as the local law, to go to your place and remove your stock and drive all into the town corral."

Gaboney looked at Deputy Milt Jones. "Would you do that?"

Jones hesitated, then said, "My badge would require I do so."

"What if you ran into bullets?"

"That would make you a killer—a murderer," the deputy sheriff said. "And local people would hang you—without a trial in county court—to that big cottonwood at the end of the street."

Ed Gaboney's face paled. Evidently he'd heard that across the years Rafter V had hanged three cow-thieves from the cottonwood.

"I ain't got that much money," he said, "but I'll pay what I can, here an' now."

To complete the fine's payment the other farmers chipped in. Doc Buck then turned the money over to

Deputy Sheriff Jones who would put it in the county safe in his office and eventually take it to the county seat at Bulltown. Jones wrote out a receipt on a piece of paper the bartender furnished and handed it to the farmer who folded it and put it in his wallet.

"Case closed," Doc Buck announced, and left.

Now the young veterinarian sat on the platform and watched both Rafter V and then the farmers, each seated as far from the other as possible—the townspeople in between.

Deputy Jones said, "We should arm and deputize some of the local men, Doc. This thing might get out of hand."

Doc Buck shook his head. "Men with rifles standing around would be the worse thing we could do. Widow Hanson said she'd see order was kept."

The deputy smiled. "Her an' her Ladies Aid put the damper on them Texans," he said. "Time I call the meetin' to order, ain't it?"

"That time."

Deputy Jones strode to the podium. Doc Buck looked at the section composed of townspeople. Vivie sat next to Mr. and Mrs. Cotterman. Odd, she wasn't with the Rafter V bunch. The thought then came that Rafter V consisted only of men and she evidently wanted a woman companion for she sat next to Mrs. Cotterman. Doc Buck's eyes caught hers. She smiled.

His eyes traveled on. Teresa and her two braids and her olive-skinned beauty were on the third row next to Mrs. Webster, the town's seamstress. His eyes also met hers. At first her face refused to show emotion but finally she smiled a soft, slow woman-smile.

Doc Buck again looked at Vivie. Vivie had apparently seen the Mexican girl's smile, for Vivie's face was sad and Vivie didn't meet his eyes. Doc Buck smiled.

"Meetin's come to order," Deputy Sheriff Jones intoned, hammering with the butt of wooden pointer.

Nine

Widow Hanson had pushed Hatchet John Martin to the meeting. Some places the pushing had been rough due to the mud. She'd left the wheelchair close to the front and then had retired into the side-room, where the students' wraps were hung, with the other members of her Ladies Aid.

Almost all were stout, heavy-set matrons with families—a determined group of women. Widow Hanson was head of the School Board. The school was short a teacher and she'd received a letter and photo from a young woman in Omaha who'd applied for a local teaching position.

She'd showed the picture to Doc Buck who had seen a pretty red-head with green eyes looking back at him. He'd then read her physical properties. Five-feet-one. Green-gray eyes. Age, twenty. Education: Normal School, Bloomington, Illinois. Qualifications: all classes, grammar school.

Doc Buck had found himself admiring the picture. He especially liked red-heads. Small red-heads, that was. And green-gray eyes always got him. He discovered he looked forward to the arrival of Miss Barbara Case who should hail in any day now to complete the school term.

Now Hatchet John sat his wheel-chair, a bull penned into a branding chute. He pitted himself and with this pity was a solemn, judicious anger. Yesterday he'd thought seriously of committing suicide for he was sure that never again would he straddle a horse or walk with plank-punching cowpunchers boots. He'd almost gone for the Widow's twelve-gauge shotgun. The Widow didn't know that he knew where she'd hid it. She'd put it hidden on the top shelf in her pantry.

Hatchet John wasn't sure he could reach it, either. He didn't know where she'd cached the pistols—his or hers. Anyway, he preferred a shotgun. You put the barrel under your jaw and reached down and pushed on the trigger and they picked your brains off the ceiling around the hole the beebees had made on their way upward.

He soon abandoned the suicide plan. Two men had roared out of the dark and dynamite fuses had made flaring sparks and tons of rock and concrete had gone blasting upward. Those two men had put him in this iron-horse. He'd kill himself after he'd killed the two throwers of dynamite.

Now he sat and glowered and was aware of many eyes covertly glancing his direction. He knew the eyes momentarily studied him not out of sympathy but out of inquisitiveness. He knew that in this town of two hundred or so souls only two of those souls would be actually sympathetic and helpful. Doctor Buckley Malone was one; the other was Widow Hanson.

He looked at the Rafter V men. He wished he was one of them—whole, hale, strong, booted, gun-hung, spurs chiming. Again a pain hit him. It was not a physical pain—for he was filled with that—but a pain caused by memory. Never again would he be like the Rafter V men. He studied Bill Wilson. Wilson was a fortunate bastard, he thought—never had to work to build, taking over after all the hard work had been done. Bill Wilson was no fool. He had a college record, didn't he? Surely he must have known that open range was doomed?

The United States was filling with foreigners. They were coming off the ships by the thousands each day. Where they came from land was precious and belonged only to the extremely wealthy, he'd read. The United States represented freedom to these poor people—and also the ownership of land. The U.S. had millions of acres of free land. These people wanted a bit of that free land. They'd get it, too. And in the getting, the free range cowman was doomed. And what was more, he'd never come back. That was the handwriting on the wall. Clear. Concise. Brief.

Even a college graduate should have that much brains, the crippled old cowpoke reasoned.

He looked for Vivie Wilson. She should have been sitting with her faction—Rafter V—but she sat with the townspeople. She sure was a pretty little girl. His eyes roamed on, landing on dark-haired Teresa Hernandez. She was a lovely girl, also. A feeling of rebellion entered him. Why couldn't he be young—like Doc Buck? Why couldn't he have had money when Doc Buck's age? He swallowed, Adam's apple bouncing.

Deputy Jones called for order. The room became quiet. The deputy talked in a firm, steady voice that carried well.

Hatchet John Martin listened, eyes closed. Jones outlined the peril hanging over Buckbrush Basin. He summed up the tragic end that these perils could bring about. Death, flaming guns. He swore he'd someday discover who had dynamited the dip vat.

"I will someday find out who crippled Hatchet John Martin. And when I do, that person—or those persons—go to jail."

Hatchet John opened his eyes. Necks had craned and

turned and many eyes were on him. He closed his eyes again.

The deputy sheriff disclosed he'd recently sent a wire out of Bulltown to the territorial governor explaining the trouble hanging over Buckbrush Basin. All heads rose to attention on this news. "I sent a long telegram into Bulltown to the depot operator with Charlie Watson when he took Joan Cotterman into Bulltown for medical care," the deputy related. The hall was very, very silent. "I told His Honor, the Governor, that he should look forward to further bulletins from me, and if this trouble goes any further I would want him to send the militia here to keep order."

Hatchet John Martin opened his weary eyes. He looked about and saw only serious, thoughtful faces. The thought of having the militia take over had apparently put a new facet on the problem to all concerned. When and if the soldiers arrived, this trouble would be taken out of the Buckbrush Basin area and become a Territorial problem.

Deputy Sheriff Jones turned the floor over to Doctor Buckley Malone. Doc Buck talked straight to the point. Texas Fever was killing the farmers' cattle. He didn't know where the fever ticks had come from. He was working to find out. He'd quarantined the cattle. Once again he repeated: no farmer's stock could go beyond the limits of the farmer's fences. He mentioned that one farmer had allowed his cattle to stray from the farmer's property. Rafter V had driven the cattle back into their proper area. Next time if and when such happened he, personally, would shoot and kill every head breaking quarantine.

This brought a murmur through the farmers. Finished, Doc Buck asked for questions. The president of the Farmers Organization—bony Ed Gaboney—rose and asked under what permission could a veterinarian kill another man's cattle.

"By permission and order of the Territorial laws," Doc Buck stated. "If interested in reading that part of the code in particular all who wish to do so may stop in my office and I shall show him or her that section."

Gaboney sat down. Bill Wilson got to his feet. Doctor Buckley Malone recognized him. Wilson spoke slowly, carefully selecting words, his voice firm, steady. He ended up his brief speech with, "And, if in the future, I or any other Rufter V man finds farmers' cattle outside their fences, I or the Rafter V men so seeing shall kill those cattle in their tracks."

Ed Gaboney sprang up like a jack-in-the-box. "An' who the hell gives you that permission, Mister Cowman?"

"I give it to myself. Rafter V has ten thousand head of cattle, and if one—even one—gets Texas Fever, my hands and I will ride out and with gunfire eliminate every damned farmer in Buckbrush Basin!"

"And that we mean," Ron Powers said.

Land Locator Matthew Cotton was on his feet, demanding that Doc Buck give him the floor, which the veterinarian did. The big man leaped upon the podium. He strode to the lectern. He hammered with his six-shooter barrel for order. "Gentlemen, gentlemen!" He got no order. Rafter V was on its collective boots. Across the hall the farmers were up, ready for the oncoming fight. The townspeople were penned in the middle. Doc Buck saw many fleeing toward the doors. Vivie and Teresa stayed behind, he noticed.

"We should have collected weepons at the door," Deputy Jones screamed to Doc Buck.

Doc Buck hollered back, "That would have done no

good. They'd only have hidden their arms on their persons!"

Doc Buck looked at Matthew Cotton. The man still screamed for order. Damned fraud parasite, Doc Buck thought. Suddenly he remembered the Texan Virgil and his words. He'd have to go soon to Bulltown. He hadn't told anybody but he had fifty barrels of creosote and twenty-five of kerosene coming into Bulltown by the new rails. The coal by-products had been meant to fill his dip tank. But the tank was no more and he'd have to stall off payment for the barrels someway for they came by c.o.d.

While in Bulltown he'd send a wire to Uncle Fred in Houston, Texas. Uncle Fred was his mother's oldest brother. He'd put the bum on Uncle Fred for five hundred bucks. Uncle Fred was in banking. He'd borrowed from him before while in cow college. His gift upon graduation from Uncle Fred had been a registered letter with a receipt inside cancelling every cent Uncle Fred had advanced during the college years. And Uncle Fred had written one line, "Congrats, neff, and remember me and my address, eh?"

He'd also go over to the county clerk and recorders office and try to make heads or tails out of Virgil's statement about the homesteaders and their filing procedures.

"What the hell am I goin' do?" Deputy Jones hollered. "Right here an' now, Doc Buck, I'm makin' you my deputy!"

"I don't want the dubious honor," the veterinarian hollered back, "but under the circumstances, what other avenue of escape have I? But I'm in your boat, deputy—what the hell can we two do?"

"We go out there an' we get the crap beat outa us."

For the cowboys were heading for the farmers. The

farmers, in return, were heading for Rafter V. They'd meet in conflict in the middle area formerly occupied by the town's citizens.

For this area was now filled with empty benches. Vivie and Teresa had fled to the podium and now were with Doc Buck.

"We got to stop them!" Vivie cried.

Teresa said, and meant it, "Why?"

"What do you mean?"

"They'll fight it out somewhere and some place," Teresa said, "and now is just as good a place and time as any other."

"They got guns!" Vivie said. "They'll kill each other. You've got nobody in there—but I got my only brother!"

Then it was that Widow Hanson and her Ladies Aid entered from their cloak room. They came solemnly out, the buxom Widow in the lead, the other housewives behind her—and each and every one carried but one item, a big long rolling-pin. At that moment, the scene was not comical, but Doc Buck later found himself awaking at night, laughing in his sleep over what next happened.

The moment the women entered the entire scene became a frozen tableau of suspended action. The cowhands stopped in mid-stride, hands glued on holstered guns. The farmers stopped in their tracks, staring at the marching women, mouths open in surprise. "There shall be no conflict," Widow Hanson said.

The women marched into the space separating the two factions. There they stopped, a physical barrier between Rafter V and the farmers.

Doc Buck heard Vivie breathe, "Holy smoke!"

"*Muy bueno*," Teresa said quietly.

Land locator Matthew Cotton had stopped in the

306

middle of a sentence, and he now clamped shut his mouth, staring as if looking at the Pearly Gates for the first time.

Deputy Jones said, "Our problem is solved." And he mopped his sweaty forehead with an old torn blue bandana.

"For a while, at least," Doc Buck assured.

Mrs. Hanson spoke first to Bill Wilson. "Mr. Wilson, you and your cowboys leave first. You go out that side door behind you. There is no use going to the saloon. It is closed and will be closed the rest of the day."

Bill Wilson's good nature came out with, "When did I become *Mr.* Wilson? Seems to me when I was going to grammar school and ate dinner at your house every school day I was just plain Billy Wilson."

"You were then a cute, obedient boy," Widow Hanson said. "Now you're a grown man, just as cute—but not acting like a grown-up at times."

Bill Wilson smiled. "I thank you, Mrs. Hanson."

"If you stop at the barber shop there are five quarts of whiskey there for you and your crew. If you want these, okay—if not, also okay."

"And then?" Bill Wilson asked.

"Rafter V rides out of town."

Ron Powers growled, "Don't let this ol' hag push us aroun', Bill."

Mrs. Hanson spoke to heavy-set Mrs. Kilmer. "Maggie, give that young man the treatment."

"With pleasure."

Mrs. Kilmer strode through the Rafter V men, rolling pin extended, the long handle out. Ron Powers began retreating, walking backwards toward the side door, Mrs. Kilmer jabbing him viciously in the belly. Powers came to the door. He fell backwards and out of sight. Doc Buck heard him land in the mud outside and heard

Powers cursing. Mrs. Kilmer did not go outside. She stopped, rolling pin at the ready, just inside the door.

Matthew Cotton said, "This thing ain't bein' settled. This only makes it worse than ever."

Doc Buck looked at the heavy-jowled man. "You seem to be wanting them to kill each other off?"

Cotton turned hard eyes on the veterinarian. "Sometimes you talk as though you lack somethin' upstairs." Before Doc Buck could answer the land locator had begun crossing the room heading for the front door.

Mrs. Kilmer returned to Widow Hanson. "How about me givin' some of the farmers the Power treatment?"

"You have my permission, Maggie."

Mrs. Kilmer advanced on the farmers, rolling-pin handle protruding, but the farmers were already spilling out the side door, jumping to the ground. Doc Buck could see them land. Ed Gaboney jumped, slid, and skidded out of sight on his rump. Vivian and Teresa saw this. The two woman laughed.

By now, the cowboys were gone.

Mrs. Hanson yelled to the farmers, "Your booze is at the Merc. You have to pay for it, jus' like Rafter V has to pay—if you an' it want the firewater."

"You go to hell, lady."

That came from Ed Gaboney. Although Doc Buck couldn't see the farmer, he recognized Gaboney's voice. Doc Buck started toward the side-door the farmers had used. Vivie caught his right arm; Teresa his left. They held him solidly.

"He insulted a good woman," Doc Buck said.

"Please," Vivie said.

"*Por favor*," Teresa said.

Doc Buck settled back. The girls were right. If he

caught up with Gaboney—they would fight. Well, it would only make things worse. Rafter V might return and there'd be a free-for-all, thus completely destroying the good work done by Widow Hanson and the Ladies Aid.

Widow Hanson said, "Half go after the cowboys. The other half trail the farmers. If either bunch makes a move toward the other use your rollin' pins—an' not just for jabbin' either!"

The women left by the front door. Now only four people remained—Deputy Jones, the two women, and Doc Buck. Jones again wiped his brow. "Think we did any good, Doc?"

"I think so," Dock Buck said. "They at least know how the other side thinks and what it will do if pressed. I think they're both a little bit ascared of the other."

The deputy spoke to Teresa. "What do you think, Miss Hernandez?" Teresa said, "Let us all go to my cafe. Violet Hays is helping me cook. We can have a roll and some coffee."

Doc Buck asked, "And a bit of something in the coffee, Teresa?" Teresa turned her dark eyes on him. Once again Doc Buck saw how limpid and clean and healthy her eyes were. She smiled. Her teeth were even and white.

"With a bit of something if you care, Doctor Malone."

Ten

Early next morning Farmer Ted Lawson called Doc Buck out to his homestead. His youngest boy had taken sick during the night. "Vomits an' unless I'm wrong he's got a high fever, Doc."

Running Horse had ridden out with his teacher and the farmer. Ted Lawson naturally was worried.

"Wife claims up an' down the boy got sick from the cows," the farmer claimed.

Doc Buck didn't smile at such foolish thinking. Teresa had told him that down in Mexico sometimes licensed physicians were driven out of small towns by the witch-doctors and midwives spreading word around that the doctor of medicine killed patients with his bad medicines.

Sometimes he thought these Wyoming people were suspicious and superstitious as the *peons* Teresa had told him about. That theory became a conviction when at the Lawson ranch he saw bright colored strips of cloth hanging from the dewlaps of the twenty-odd head of cattle on the farm. He'd never seen this superstitious habit exhibited before but then he'd not been a practicing veterinarian very long. His college instructors, though, had discussed this display of bright ribbon. They had explained that this came from the Old World and was a superstitious custom dating back many, many centuries. Sometimes a gaily-colored rope was tied to the dewlap. Rope or ribbon, these were

310

called *setons*. Their purpose was to drive the demons out of the cow and make her well and whole again.

Running Horse sidled close and said quietly, "Why do they hang ribbons from the cows?"

"I'll tell you later, son," Doc Buck promised.

"Looks loco to me."

"That it is, son."

While in college his dean had told Doc Buck that when in a sparsely settled section such as this he'd undoubtedly have to treat humans as well as animals, and the good dean had inserted slyly the fact that in his estimation man was also an animal. Thus Doc Buck had acompanied local physicians many times on hospital rounds or on house calls. And when he stepped into the Larson shack he smelled one thing, and one only. Measles.

Mrs. Lawson was tall, angular, and flat-breasted with premature, scraggly gray hair, a worn faded housedress hiding her protruding bones. "The boy got this disease from the cows," she stoutly maintained. "He hangs aroun' them all the time tryin' to make them well."

Doc Buck did not tell her that it was impossible for a human to contract Texas Fever. Were it so, half of Texas would have died off long ago, he thought wryly. "I see," he quietly said.

"We got each cow with a seton on her," the woman explained. "That'll drive away the bad spirits. An' make her well real fast."

She spoke with a shanty southern accent.

"I'm sure they will," Doc Buck assured. He spoke to Lawson. "The boy only has the measles, nothing more."

"Measles?"

"No more than that. I'll leave you a bottle of medicine." He didn't add that the bottle contained only

311

drinking alcohol and some coloring. "That'll bring him out."

"Where would he get the measles?" the mother asked.

Doc Buck shrugged. "Where did your cattle get Texas fever?" He answered.

"Darned if I know," Ted Lawson said.

Doc Buck saw that the woman didn't believe his diagnosis. He certainly wasn't going to impress the fact on her so he and Running Horse and Ted Lawson and the many children went outside.

A cow walked by with a seton hanging. "Women put them on the critters," Lawson said. "I don't reckon it'd do a bit of good but why not try? Man never knows. Did you hear thet finally one of Gaboney's critters got the fever?"

"News to me. How's his rump?"

Lawson laughed. "He sure looked funny slidin' on his rump in the mud. He was mad as a wet hen what had set three weeks on eggs to fin' out she'd hatched ducklin's an' not chickens."

"Lawson's cattle—all twenty odd head—were doomed for the bone-pile." The man's long face was serious. He had a reason to be, Doc Buck reasoned. He'd put most of his money in rocks and cement. Lawson had evidently put the few dollars he had after paying filing fees to Matthew Cotton in livestock and the timber used to build his miserable jacal. Dynamite had put Doc Buck on the financial rocks. An amoeba he couldn't see was breaking this farmer financially.

"Sometimes I think seriously about pullin' out an' leavin' it all behin'," Lawson said.

"Any others thinking that way?" Doc Buck asked.

"Coupla others said the same thet night we held the meetin'—the night your tank blew up."

"Oh," Doc Buck said.

"We decided we'd all try it a while longer, but I have my doubts about the Lawson family." An aura of gloom held the homestead despite the bright and warm sun of spring. Doc Buck and Running Horse were glad to again get in saddle and head west riding along the bottom fences of the farmsteads. Sun and moisture had brought greenery to the alfalfa farms. One farmer yesterday in town had told Doc Buck that his reservoir was full with water running over the spillway.

That farmer had already soaked deep his forty acres of alfalfa. He now had run-off water soaking his grass-field and acreage he would plow and sow into head-crops as soon as the soil dried out.

He reported that when things calmed down—if they ever did—he was going to approach Bill Wilson and see if they couldn't dicker their way into Rafter V buying his surplus hay.

"Feed the rest to my stock," the farmer had said and then added, "That is, if I have any stock left to feed beside my horses."

Doc Buck had said nothing. He'd asked the farmers to burn their dead cattle. That would insure the deaths of the ticks the animals carried. By the time new cows came into the possession of the farmers he hoped to have his dipping-vat finished. And each new cow coming into Buckbrush Basin would go through the vat not once but at least another time. And then it would be carefully inspected to make sure it still had no ticks.

Doc Buck's hope was that no ticks could somehow get on Rafter V cattle. With hot summer just around the corner Texas Fever ticks could live easily on local cattle. Cold winter undoubtedly would kill them—freeze the ticks to death. But by that time, if Fever hit Rafter V's thousands of cattle, there'd be damned few cows left by the time the first hard freeze hit in late fall.

One glance told him Bill Wilson was living up to his promise that many miles would lie between Rafter V cattle and the tick-carrying farmer stock, for you could look south as far as you could see and you'd see only a horse or two, no cattle.

"Tell me why Missus Lawson hung them ribbons from those cows," Running Horse asked.

Doc Buck told him. "Before we had blackleg vaccine they used to hang ribbons on cattle with blackleg, too."

"Seems odd there's no vaccine against the Fever."

"There's a lot I don't know about amoeba and germs," Doc Buck said. "But what are you thinking about?"

"Jenner."

"You been reading about him?"

"Yesterday, in your big book—the one I have a hard time sayin' the name of."

Doc Buck supplied the book's title. It was a tongue-twister, at that. "Tell me what you read so I can check if you've remembered correctly."

"Well, Jenner was an Englishman. He noticed that people who milked cows—especially the milk-maids—got sores on their hands from the teat pullin'."

Doc Buck nodded, eyes on the farmers' fences.

"Well, he took the pus from one of these sores. He was sure they were caused by cow pox, a mild disease."

"Related to what other disease?"

"Smallpox. So he inserted this cow-pox pus into a human, a boy. Then afterwards he took pus from a smallpox—what would you call it?"

"A pustule."

"That's the word. He then injected this into the person he'd put cow-pox pus into. And smallpox didn't affect the person at all. He'd been vaccinated with cow-

314

pox pus an' that made him so he couldn't catch smallpox."

"You remember the year?"

"About a hundred years ago, I remember."

"A landmark in medicine. 1796." Doc Buck shifted weight on his stirrups. "You remember well. What was Jenner's first name?"

"Edward."

"Right you are. You get A on that dissertation."

"What's a dissertation?"

Doc Buck told him.

"Can't the same be done with Texas Fever?"

The subject was getting too deep for Doctor Buckley Malone. The more he studied veterinarian medicine the more he realized what a huge field of study it was.

They came to Ed Gaboney's bottom gate. Running Horse demonstrated to his teacher that he could open and close the wire gate without leaving saddle, the true mark of the experienced cowpuncher.

Gaboney had one cow penned alone at the western corner of his homestead, as far as he could get it from the other cattle which were close to his sod shanty.

He came riding over on an old work-mare. "Somethin' I kin do for you, Doc Buck?"

Doc Buck explained that Lawson had told him that at long last one of Gaboney's cows had ticks.

"Got them yesterday from thet Lang bull," the farmer said. "He lives west of me next, you know. This cow was bullin'. I ain't got no bull. Lang's bull busted through an' rode her an' first thing I noticed she was covered with them damn' ticks. Fred Lang's gonna pay for this cow if she kicks the bucket. His damn' bull is to blame!"

Doc Buck spoke to Running Horse. "Take that small

jar out of your saddlebag and hand it to me, please?"

"Okay, Dad."

"What're you gonna do with a Mason jar?" Ed Gaboney's voice held hardness.

Doc Buck answered. "Pick a dozen or so ticks from this cow. Put them in the Mason jar."

"Why?" the farmer demanded.

Doc Buck studied him. "To take them to my lab. Look them over under my microscope."

"Maybe I won't let you tetch the cow?"

"You're joking, aren't you?"

"Jokin', cowcrap! I'm speakin' true.' I don't like you. You don't cotton to me. We both know that. Mebbeso I ain't doin' you no favors, horse doctor?"

Doc Buck said, "Then I take them without your permission."

Running Horse sat saddle and listened, young face bleak, eyes moving from his teacher to this belligerent farmer.

"Mebbeso I'll stop you?"

Doc Buck shook his head. "You try and I'll not push you, Mr. Gaboney, but I'll ride to town, and ride back with Milt Jones, and he under the law has to guarantee me the liberty of taking the ticks."

"Law pertects you good, eh?"

"No more than it does any other U.S. citizen."

Ed Gaboney's thin face showed indecision. Doctor Buckley Malone realized it was not a bunch of deadly ticks as the bone of contention. The reason the farmer didn't want to give him the ticks was because Gaboney openly hated him.

Gaboney knew that. So did Doc Buck. And so, for that matter, did the young Cheyenne, who now had his right hand resting on the upright polished wooden stalk of his Remington .25-20 rifle, resting in its saddle-boot.

316

Doc Buck looked up at Running Horse. He saw where the young right hand was located and shook his head. "No, boy."

Running Horse withdrew his hand. He laid it carefully over the broad horn of his old Koke saddle.

Suddenly Ed Gaboney said, "Okay, pick to your little heart's desire, sawbones. Only goddamned thing I kin see you're good for. You sure as hell ain't no 'count as a animal doctor."

"You don't say," Doc Buck said.

"If you was such, you'd have these cows well by now."

The farmer turned his mare and loped back to his shack, each stride of the ancient horse bouncing him in his old saddle. He disappeared among the many small buildings and fell out of sight.

"He's mad," Running Horse said.

Doc Buck smiled. "Only dogs get mad, son. People get angry." He sighed and unscrewed the Mason jar's lid. "Seems to me everybody on this grass is angry at something or somebody."

"I know two people hereabouts that's only mad—I mean, angry—at each other, an nobody else."

"Who are they?"

"Vivie an' Teresa."

"Why are they angry at each other?"

"Ain't you got eyes? Both of 'em want you as a husban'. This makes them angry at nobody else but only at each other."

Doc Buck smiled. "They don't know me very well. At heart I'm a scheming, black-livered bastard. So, bossy, so." Soon he had a dozen or so ticks in the bottle. He screwed the lid back on, taking note the small ventilation holes in it were open so the ticks would have air and thus be kept alive. They'd get his full attention

317

later in his lab.

Later they met Fred Lang repairing his bottom fence. Lang was a tall, skinny man of mid-forties who openly boasted he had more children than he had brains. Doc Buck related how Ed Gaboney had accused Lang's bull of rubbing off ticks onto Gaboney's cow.

"Yeah, it happened. The bull's got ticks, but he ain't sick enough to keep from climbin' a cow, it looks like. You put some ticks off'n him in a jar last week, remember, Doc Buck?"

"I remember."

Doc Buck and Running Horse turned their broncs south toward Buckbrush City. The sun was mid-forenoon high, now. The earth was quickly drying. They rode into town at eleven. They racked their horses at the Town Livery Stable and went to their quarters. The Widow Hanson and Hatchet John Martin awaited them in front of the building, for Doc Buck now kept it locked when not on the premises.

"John insisted on coming to visit you," the Widow told Doc Buck. "With so little mud, he's easier to push."

"When the soil dries out, I kin push myself," Hatchet John said.

Doc Buck unlocked the door. Running Horse said he'd cook buffalo steaks all around. Widow Hanson said she'd do the cooking.

Doc Buck said, "Look, you two. We got enough arguments and trouble around here without more."

"We'll both cook," the Widow said.

Running Horse grinned. "I'm goin' learn somethin' about cookin', now." The Widow was considered the town's best cook.

The Widow and Running Horse retired to the kitchen. Hatchet John watched Doc Buck stick a long pin through a tick in the Mason jar. "Where'd those bastards come from?" Hatchet John asked.

Doc Buck told him.

"I was with you when you got some ticks off'n thet bull," Hatchet John said. "Seems to me you're wastin' time, doc."

"Why say that?"

"These ticks will be the same—whatcha call it—oh, yeah, genus as you took from the bull."

"They should be."

Deputy Sheriff Milt Jones came in. "This sun sure is good," the lawman said. "Was out to the tank, still lookin'. Nothin' new, though. You thought of anythin' new, Hatchet John?"

Hatchet John shook his scraggly head. "Dark as the inside of an ol' boot. Nothin' new has come to mind, deputy."

Jones spoke to Doc Buck. "Thet meetin' yesterday. . . . We had so much hell so damn' fast you forget to put it to these people if they'd help you rebuild the tank in payment of the money they owe you, Doc Buck."

"I'm putting up a paper in the Merc," Doc Buck said. "Do it inside the hour. It'll state the facts and have room below for the signatures of those willing to work out their debts."

"Good idea. Gotta git home. Ol' woman'll have the vittles on the table soon. Got to have the boardin' house reach at my shack, so many kids. You grab an' get or you grab an' it's all gone."

The deputy left.

Tantalizing aromas of buffalo steak came from the kitchen. Running Horse and the Widow were laughing and joking. Doc Buck stuck the new tick under his old microscope thinking that when he had more money—if

319

such ever happened—he'd buy one of those new high-powered, high-priced microscopes in the new catalog that had come a few days ago.

Until then, this old cheap one had to do. He carefully adjusted. He carefully studied. Hatchet John Martin watched. Hatchet John saw a hard look creep across his boss's young face.

"Somethin' wrong, Doc Buck?"

"I don't know . . . for sure."

Doc Buck fumbled through papers. He found what he wanted—a sheet with a dead tick glued, bottom down, to the paper.

Below he'd listed the tick's physical properties. He read these out loud, voice low and serious, and then he studied the dead tick carefully before turning his attention to the live one.

"I'm waitin'," Hatchet John said.

Doc Buck scowled. "This tick—the live one—is different than this dead one, which came off the bull."

"Different?"

"Yeah, in size, and in coloring. Yeah, and it has little dots on its back." He looked at the man in the wheel chair. "We took ticks from that bull off all parts of his anatomy, didn't we?"

"Yep, we did. I even took one off his balls." He glanced suddenly toward the kitchen. "Hope she didn't hear."

"The Widow knows what a bull has and his job," Doc Buck said. "This tick didn't come from that bull. I've never seen this genus of tick before."

"Never before?"

"I've tested every tick we've taken from the farmers' cattle," Doc Buck said, "and never before have I seen this kind."

He looked up. The Widow and Running Horse stood

in the doorway. They'd heard the converstaion.

"Then where'd this tick come from?" Hatchet John asked.

"Not from Lang's bull," Doc Buck said.

There was a short, tough silence. Finally the Widow Hanson broke it. "Then you're sayin' that a new type of Fever Tick has been imported into Buckbrush Basin?"

"I sure am," Doc Buck said.

Eleven

Easter Sunday was one week away and the moon was at the point of becoming full. And when Montana has a full moon many times midnight is almost as bright as mid-day.

Doc Buckley Malone checked his notice hanging on the Merc's bulletin-board at noon the next day. Only two men had signed for work, and he frowned in slight discouragement. He told himself that the notice hadn't hung even forty-eight hours. Surely tomorrow this time it would have more signatures.

Doc Cochran was late. He drove into town at sunset that same day in a democrat. He was alone—a weary, middle-aged prairie doctor who rarely encountered a complete night of sleep. And who had many people owing him, as had Doc Buck. Doc Cochran reported that Joan Cotterman was healing rapidly and nicely. She would be dismissed from the hospital within a week or eight days, he told the Cotterman family.

Mrs. Cotterman mentioned the family had little money but her husband would ride for Rafter V during calf-gather next month or in May and they'd do what they could in payment.

Doc Cochran nodded and asked Doc Buck where the wounded man was, and Doc Buck took him to the Widow's house where Hatchet John was in bed on the bottom floor, wheel chair close at hand.

"May I stay?" the Widow asked.

Doc Cochran was a very short, thin man. He turned his eye-glasses on the buxom widow. "Why do you want to stay? You've seen a few naked men in your life, haven't you? Why do you want to look at another?"

Doc Buck grinned behind his hand.

Widow Hanson retreated not an inch. "This patient and I have discussed becoming married. I am taking care of him. I think I am obligated to know how to care for him to the best of my knowledge and I might learn something from you, Doctor."

"Okay with me, Mrs. Hanson."

"I only got a nightgown on," Hatchet John said.

"I'll take it from him," the Widow said.

They got Hatchet John on his belly. The bruised spot was smaller and looked only like a black-and-blue bump, nothing more. Doc Cochran talked to Doc Buck while he examined.

"This Englishman—this Doctor Lister. Have you read about him, Doctor Malone?"

Doc Buck had. Lister was doing research into bacteria. He was following in Pasteur's footsteps.

"When he operates, he washes in strong lye soap for a long time. He uses rubber gloves, carefully sterilized. He has assistants spray the air with carbolic acid."

"To kill bacteria," Doc Buck said.

"He's a great man, a great doctor of medicine, a great surgeon. He makes an insignificant man such as I feel—" The trained fingers touched, examined. "Well, I guess that is what we pay for stationing ourselves on the demographical frontiers, Doctor Malone."

"I'd say you are right, sir."

"Some day we will have a ray—or power—that will allow us to see through flesh and into bone. Then we can tell exactly what ails the flesh, and the bone—but

323

that time, too, is in the far future."

"Until then we have to do the best we can," Doc Buck said.

Doc Cochran straightened, examination finished. He spoke to the Widow. "You can restore his night-dress, if you care to."

Widow Hanson had a washbasin filled with water on the night-stand. Doc Cochran began thoroughly washing his hands. Hatchet John asked shortly, "What's the verdict, doctor?"

Doctor Cochran dried his hands by shaking them, not using a towel. "Many times I have been wrong," he said slowly. "Thus, I'm adverse to giving a positive answer, but in your case I think I shall not be proven in error."

The Widow listened. Doc Malone listened.

"You'll never walk again, sir."

"No, no!" Hatchet John's voice held tears. "No, no, Doctor!"

"I can only diagnose what my fingers, my brain and my experience have taught me. I pray to God above I am in error, but I am afraid I am not."

Hatchet John put his hands over his eyes. "Will I live long?"

Doc Buck studied the man's face. For one moment terrible emotions played across the weather-grooved features. Hatchet John's mouth opened, his wind-cracked lips trembled, and Doc Buck figured he would say something. But he didn't. The terror left his face. His mouth snapped shut. His eyes lost savage luster. And he merely said, "I thank you, Doctor Cochran, for your help and honesty."

Widow Hanson sobbed quietly. She was still sobbing into her apron when she accompanied Doctor Cochran and Doc Buck to the door. Moonlight lay in silent brilliance across the squalid prairie cow town. Beyond town in the buckbrush and greasewood and sagebrush coyotes yipped and sang and occasionally a town cur gave a civilized and lonesome answer.

Widow Hanson had her pocket book. "How much do I owe you, Doctor?"

"Three dollars. But if money's scarce—"

"No, I have a few dollars yet from my husband's insurance. He was a good, thoughtful man."

"Night certainly fell fast," Doc Cochran said. "But it does that this time of the year here on the prairie. Do you like it here?"

"I do. People are poor and pay slowly but they bring beef and food to pay and do the best they can, in most cases."

"This Texas tick epidemic? Tell me about it, please."

Doc Cochran listened in silence as they walked toward Doc Buck's quarters. Finally Doc Buck finished.

"You intend to rebuild your dipping vat?"

Doc Buck nodded. "If and when I have the money. We got to have that vat. It'll not only kill off the ticks but can be used when cattle have skin disease and other parasites."

They came to Doc Buck's quarters. "Come in and have something to eat, please. Spend the night, if you want."

"I'd like to but I haven't time. I'll change teams at the livery barn and start back again."

"I have some business to do in Bulltown," Doc Buck said. "Maybe I could ride back with you?"

"You sure can. I hoped somebody would go back with me. A long, lonesome drive when a man's alone. You can drive and you know what I'll be doing?"

"Sleeping?"

"Right."

They entered the lab. Running Horse had filled a

canteen with hot coffee. He looked out the door. "Moon's bright as day."

Doc Buck looked at Running Horse. "I'm going to Bulltown with Doctor Cochran. I'll be back at least day after tomorrow. When do you leave?"

"In the morning, Dad. I can easy catch that Diamon' in a Diamon' herd. The way I figure it'll still be three more days before it leaves the valley."

"I think you figure right," Doc Buck said. "Now you take care of yourself, boy. Once there were three of us. Now there's only two. And I don't want only one left, savvy."

"I'll take double care."

Doctor Cochran was cutting into a freshly fried veal steak Running Horse had cooked and kept warm for him. "You fried this, young man?"

"I did. Is it—too tough?"

"Just right. You're a good cook."

Running Horse beamed. "Thank you, Doctor Cochran."

Within half an hour, Doc Buck and Doctor Cochran were headed north with a fresh team in the tugs. The owner of Buckbrush City's livery barn also owned a barn in Bulltown.

Thus a man could ride between either town or return on a fresh horse, leaving his jaded mount in one of the owner's barns. Somebody would eventually drive to Bulltown the team Doc Cochran left behind just as somebody would in time return to Buckbrush City with the team the doctor now had in tugs.

"Mind if I hit my bunk, Doc Buck?"

"Go to it, Doctor."

Doctor Cochran had a light mattress in the back of his democrat. He climbed over the back of the leather-covered seat with a blanket he'd had at the foot of the rig behind the dashboard.

He covered himself with this. Doc Buck drove north with his thoughts, occasionally looking at the moonlit prairie around him—and loving every sagebrush, every greasewood, he saw. Ahead two coyotes, phantoms of the range, trotted across the wagon-road, then disappeared in the brush. Doc Buck realized he'd not seen a prairie wolf for some weeks, now. Wolves were getting scarce. Cowmen had rifles out hunting them at so much a head, claiming they killed too many spring calves. He'd seen but one grizzly since coming to Buckbrush Basin. It had been killed a few hours later by Rafter V cowpokes who'd roped it and between five horses had stretched it to death by their catch-ropes.

This endless land that a few years before had belonged to the Sioux and Cheyenne and Crow was rapidly changing. Now barbwire and windmills and irrigation ditches and fenced lanes were coming in and within a short time no longer could a man on horseback cut across country to get where he wanted to go by the shortest route. Soon he'd have to ride in squares around section lines with barbwire, shiny and taut between glistening diamond-willow posts, keeping him penned into strict area, both of the person and of the mind.

The wolf would disappear. The grizzly and other bears—brown and gray or whatever color—would soon also be gone. The antelope and the blacktail deer might exist and live on, but only in frightened, reduced numbers. The coyote would live. He might even prosper. He was like the cottontail rabbit on which he so much fed. He multiplied fast like the rabbit. He was smart, though, where the rabbit was stupid. His intelligence would win through for him, Doc Buck guessed.

The spinning wheels of the democrat ground across

hard soil, hit water puddles, whizzed over sand, occasionally met a bump. The nigh horse did not shy, but the off-horse did. Many times the off-horse shied so diligently he brushed against the tongue, bending it. Finally the nigh horse had enough. He swung his head over and grabbed his companion by the mane and shook, yellow teeth hard and clear in the bright moonlight. But his anger brought no good results. The off-horse still kept shying. Accordingly, Doc Buck held a sterner rein on him than on the other.

The distance was thirty-two miles. When they came to the northern hills the farms of the farmers lay on either side, the wagon-lane a dusty and wide moonlighted snake winding into the northern hills.

None of the farmer's shacks held lights. Therefore Doc Buck was surprised when on entering the hills a man stepped into the trail with a rifle and said, "Who goes there?" Doc Buck pulled the team to a dirt-skidding halt. The man came closer and he recognized Ed Gaboney. "What's wrong with you, Gaboney? This is a public road. You becoming a highway robber?"

"Oh, it's you, eh, Doc Malone?"

"It is. And what in the name of hell are you doing out here in the middle of nowhere at this hour of the night?"

"Keepin' guard, Doc."

"Guard? For what?"

"Rafter V."

Doc Buck studied the farmer. "You farmers now have guards out against the Wilson ranch?"

"We sure do. Ever since thet ruckus in the hall. Thet young Bill Wilson—an' thet damn' Powers—they ain't the kind to forget."

"You think they'd hit in a democrat buggy?"

"Why not? It's been did afore. Had the buggy loaded

down with gunmen an' only one man on the seat a-drivin'. Then when the time come the gundogs jumped out with arms an' all hell broke loose.''

"Where'd you hear about this happening?"

"I didn't hear. I saw it. Down in the Tonty Basin in Arizony Territory. I was sucked into thet war over there when a kid.''

Doc Buck figured the man spoke truth. From what he'd heard and read both in newspapers and magazines Arizona's Tonto Basin had been in a war of some kind for years and years.

"Who you got in the box?" Gaboney demanded.

Doctor Cochran sat up and angrily said, "Me, Doctor Cochran, of Bulltown. Now are you satisfied, farmer?''

Gaboney hurriedly stepped back. "Been treatin' patients in town, eh, Doc Cochran?''

"He has," Doc Buck asked.

"Might I ask who?"

"That's my business and not yours," Doctor Cochran said shortly and then, to Doc Buck, "Drive on, please.''

"With pleasure."

The democrat went forward. Doctor Cochran said, "I've got a .30-.30 rifle. I don't trust that man. This time of the night—I'll keep it on him until a hill comes between him and us, Doctor Malone."

"Good idea."

The hill came and the doctor said, "I'll climb up in front with you. How long did I sleep?''

"Not quite an hour."

"Long sleep for me. Beautiful night, isn't it?"

"Makes a man want to live forever."

Doctor Cochran settled on the seat at Doc Buck's right. "By the way, the injured man—Hatchet John—seemed happy to be alive, even if he is confined

329

to a wheel-chair the rest of his days."

"I noticed that. If I were in his place, I might be tempted to put myself away . . . and for good."

"He seemed very determined about something, Doctor Malone. I am sort of curious, in a slight manner. Have you an idea what he is determined to do, or is determined about—or am I just imagining things?"

"I had that same impression."

"You must know him pretty well. You told me he used to work with you. Hold cows down, rope, things like that, when you went about your medical work."

"I know him fairly well."

"And you have no idea?"

"None."

They rode a distance in silence. Then Doctor Cochran said, "And that farmer back there—hailing us down in the night. I got the impression he wasn't on guard but he was looking for somebody who might be coming in a buggy or democrat or other vehicle."

"I got the same idea," Doc Buck assured.

"Who could he be waiting for?"

"I don't know," Doc Buck said and added, "but I wish I knew the answers to both of our conjectures."

"I think I'll doze off," Doctor Cochran said.

Twelve

Next dawn Running Horse rode out of Buckbrush City on a dun mare belonging to Doc Buck. He did not ride Pinto because the piebald gelding was too showy and easily caught the eye and was too well-known on this range. The little dun blended more into the brushy background. He packed a loaded rifle in his saddle-boot and had a Smith and Wesson .32 strapped to his waist. A thirty-five foot manila catchrope was tied to the fork of his old Koke saddle.

He was sure nobody had seen him leave town. The hour was too early. Still, he took precautions. He would eventually ride northwest. So, accordingly, he left town headed south.

Four miles out of Buckbrush City he turned the dun mare west and within a few miles, sure that no eyes had followed him, he neck-reined the little horse northwest, heading for the point he figured the Diamond in a Diamond herd now occupied in this huge, limitless wilderness of sage and greasewood and alkali flats.

He kept a keen watch ahead, on both sides, and behind. He was nervous and he felt lonesome and small and he wished Doc Buck was with him but by now Doc Buck would be in Bulltown eating breakfast somewhere and getting ready to go about his business—whatever that business entailed.

He rode across the prairie, the sun overhead now and gaining heat. He intended to do some scouting from

Black Butte, an igneous upthrust ahead towering over Buckskin Basin. He had heard that when his Cheyenne tribe fought the white intruders a few years back the Cheyennes always had eyes on Black Butte for from its height the basin below could be easily scanned and searched for paleskin enemies. He would use Black Butte for the same purpose.

He climbed Black Butte at eleven. He had no watch but the sun, and he read it accurately. He climbed easily, which surprised him. He'd figured that the Butte would be tough to climb with its dark-rock upthrusts. But he discovered a trail that went upward on the Butte's eastern side. In some places it was almost covered by buckbrush but once it had apparently been well-traveled but horse-droppings, yellow and flaky, told him that had been some years ago. Finally, he and Chocolate gained the top. Here was a flat, brush covered area about a hundred yards square. Now and then a covey of big boulders were gathered as though thrown there by a enormous, prehistoric hand.

There was no spring or pool of water. Cottontail rabbits, apparently undisturbed for a long time, were so tame they sat upright and watched him, unafraid and inquisitive.

He had two big canteens tied to the skirts of his saddle. He'd drink little and he'd watered Chocolate a few minutes back-trail on Willow Creek, a small stream running southeast into Buckbrush River that now had a little water but during summer became dry. Chocolate wouldn't need water until tomorrow morning. He walked toward the group of cottontails. They then ran into holes dug under the boulders. He knew the rabbits didn't need water. They lived off the water they obtained by eating damp grass. He decided he'd dine on tender cottontail rabbit. He put Chocolate on picket, and then walked to the Butte's western rim.

From here he could see beyond the western edge of Buckbrush Basin, a distance of around fifteen miles, if not more. Below the Butte fell straight up and down, a talus cone of black rock below on the prairie's floor. But the talus cone did not interest the young Cheyenne. What interested him was the cloud of dust raised some five miles to the southwest by the hoofs of cattle headed northwest.

The Diamond in a Diamond cattle had made less trail-progress than he'd figured. They were further south than he had judged they would be. He immediately saw why. Cowpunchers were not driving the cattle. Cowboys loafed in saddle or sat talking in a group as they allowed the cattle to graze their way out of Buckskin Basin.

Running Horse looked northwest. There a deep canyon slashed out of the wilderness and entered Buckbrush Basin. Running through the bottom of that narrow defile was Buckbrush River, he knew. For by that route he had entered Buckskin Basin months ago—a lonesome, frightened boy who had jumped his reservation and had left his mother and father and other relatives behind as he'd sought freedom.

And in Buckskin City he'd been collared by Deputy Sheriff Milton Jones, who would hold him until reservation authorities had been notified, and they would then come and take him back to the reservation. But then Doc Buck . . .

"I'll take care of him," Doc Buck had said. "I'll hold him until the boys in gray come after him." And he'd winked at Deputy Jones who had winked back.

"Not in gray," the deputy said, "but in blue."

And no officer had ever come for him. Running Horse Malone wiped a tear from his eye. He then looked hastily about, hoping nobody had seen the tear, for Cheyennes were supposed never, never to weep—and then he realized he was alone with only Chocolate and a flock of cottontail rabbits.

He put his powerful field-glasses on the herd, but the distance was far. He laid down the glasses. He moved around the boulders until he faced the east. The sun was good. He was glad spring had come. The winter had been long and cold and miserable. Only one bright spot had stood out. That had been school. He'd met a lot of wonderful people there. Don Quixote, for one; yes, and the Count of Monte Cristo. And Edward Jenner, and Louis Pasteur. He shook his head slowly. Doc Buck's text books—they had some long, tongue-torturing words. But Dad was there to help him and explain. . . .

He went to sleep without knowing it. He came awake at around three that afternoon, chilly and shivering for the sun had moved around the boulders, putting him in their chilly shadows. A wind had risen, too. And, at this altitude, the wind was cold, coming in from the higher land which still undoubtedly had a touch of snow on the tallest elevations. He moved into the sun. It held heat. No wonder his ancestors had worshipped the sun god. The sun god made life possible. The white man, he thought, could profit, maybe, if he changed gods?

He looked down at the herd. It had progressed only a mile or two. Beyond the Diamond inside a Diamond herd he saw cowpunchers hazing other cattle south down deeper into Buckbrush Basin.

Those riders would be Wilson Rafter V cowboys moving Rafter V stock out of the vicinity of the Texas cattle. Once again Running Horse put his field-glasses on Diamond inside a Diamond.

A bed-wagon and chuck-wagon moved ahead of the herd, pointing the way. A democrat buggy trailed at the far end of the cattle, well back out of the dust. Running Horse put his field-glasses on the rig. Two bay work-horses were between the tugs. There was only one man on the seat. He was the driver. The Cheyenne centered the glasses on him.

The distance was far but not too far. He recognized the man as Virgil, the go-between for the big ugly Texas foreman. The thought came that Virgil must indeed be a privileged character. He rode high and mighty in the democrat and not astraddle a cow pony.

He moved his glasses in closer. A small herd of about a dozen head lingered in the tail of the herd in a compact bunch. He might have been wrong, but one in the herd looked like the brockle-faced Circle S steer he'd pointed out to Vivie and his dad when they had left the Texans' camp. He studied the other bovines in the group. The distance was too far to make out brands. Seemed odd that a few head of cattle would stay in one herd away from the main herd. Then he had the answer.

He and Doc Buck had remarked a number of times that cattle were like people in one respect—a cow liked to remain with other cattle she'd been raised with. Why, nobody knew but the cow, and she of course couldn't tell. But the herd instinct, as Dad had said, was strong in cattle, and even stronger in horses, for horses had been known to have been driven hundreds of miles from their home range and in time had worked back to their stomping grounds.

Even Vivie Wilson, who knew almost every brand in the Territory, had no idea where the Circle S brand had come from, so surely it must have drifted in from Colorado or even the upper reaches of the Texas Panhandle.

He had a hunch that this small bunch consisted only of Circle S cattle. Somewhere along the long trail north the Texans had either accidentally got Circle S cattle into their herd or had deliberately stolen the Circle S cattle.

Even as the young Cheyenne watched the buggy stopped. The driver came down, tying the reins taut against the brake-handle. To Running Horse's surprise, the driver walked over to the small herd. Running Horse was further surprised when the cattle did not wheel and flee from the man, tails up and kicking dirt behind. The man walked up to the cattle. He went from one head to the other, patting this one, then that. The cattle continued grazing and moving north toward the pass that would lead them out of Buckbrush Basin.

The main part of the herd fell out of sight in a canyon, leaving these few head alone on the level ground. Then it was that Running Horse saw a rider come out of a draw east of the cattle and boldly ride up to the man who returned to the buggy with the rider following him. The rider dismounted at the buggy. The man handed him something and the rider put this in his nigh saddlebag. The two talked for a while and then the newcomer mounted, turned his horse, and rode southeast toward Buckbrush City, hidden by the rise of the land and by distance.

By this time Running Horse had hurried off Black Butte, leaving Chocolate behind. He figured he'd intercept the rider in about a mile. He ran at a long lope, keeping hidden in coulees and draws. Finally he halted, hidden by buckbrush, at the point he figured the rider would emerge. He had left his rifle behind. It would have slowed him down. He had only his pistol and it in holster. He breathed hard. He waited. No rider came. He became convinced he'd run too slowly. The horseman had ridden past this point before he, Running Horse, had arrived.

He was at the point of leaving and climbing to a high elevation where he could see the range when he heard hoofbeats approaching. His ear told him the horse came at a fast trot.

The horse rounded a bend. Running Horse recognized the rider immediately. He held his breath, crouching lower, hoping the buckbrush would hide him, for only fifty feet separated him and this rider. The horse came opposite him. Suddenly, the animal shied, almost sending his rider from leather. Running Horse realized the horse had caught his scent. And the bronc knew no human should be out here in the wilderness.

"What the hell's wrong with you, Smoky?" the rider said angrily.

The rider pulled in. He sat his horse, stirrup-leathers rising and falling to the horse's deep breathing. The horse pricked both ears toward Running Horse's hiding place. Running Horse tried to melt into the ground. The man sat a tall, rangy mount. From his high vantage point he might be able to see him, Running Horse realized with sinking heart.

He had a feeling that if this rider discovered he was in this area he might kill him. He wished now he'd climbed the slant behind him and had hidden in the clump of big granite boulders on the crest of the south hill. The horse snorted again and again. The rider stood on stirrups and his eyes searched the brush. And, to the hiding boy, it seemed that when the man's gaze swept over his hiding place, the man seemed to pause and peer harder.

Overhead a hawk circled. Except for the wind soughing softly in a nearby cottonwood tree, there were no sounds but the harsh breathing of the horse and the horse's snorting. Finally the man settled back in saddle. "There's nothin' in that brush to scare you, horse." He spurred away.

Running Horse began breathing again, but did not stir a muscle until the man and horse fell from sight a quarter-mile away. He got to his boots and worked his way back to the Circle S cattle. He came out on level land and hid himself in the buckbrush about two hundred yards from the small herd.

Hidden, he watched.

The man had killed one of the Circle S cows. He had, in fact, slit the throat of the brockle-faced steer he'd pointed out to Vivie and Doc Buck the time they'd ridden north from the Texans' camp. The man then started out skinning the steer. Virgil looked like a city man who was soft and didn't know stock but he skinned very rapidly and accurately. Why was he skinning the steer? Running Horse didn't know. Only one point stood out. Virgil wanted that steer's hide.

The steer skinned, Virgil rolled the bloody hide into a cylinder, hair in. He then put it in his buggy. He climbed up on the seat and turned the team and started driving cross-country toward the farmers' homesteads miles away.

338

Thirteen

The young Cheyenne returned to the top of Black Butte. Afternoon was changing into dusk. The big herd of Texas cattle had moved a few miles further northwest while he'd been off the butte. The small herd was two miles behind the big herd. Running Horse found himself remembering something Doc Buck had told him. Doc Buck had said he figured the longhorns in the Texans' herd might be carrying fever ticks but the ticks did not make them sick because they were immune to the amoeba the ticks put into the blood-streams of the longhorns. Therefore a longhorn could carry the ticks and the ticks wouldn't hurt him. But he could distribute the ticks to cattle the ticks could very well kill. Running Horse remembered reading in one of Doc Buck's books that some people also could carry a disease and not become sick from that disease. This fact occurred many times in smallpox and diphtheria, he remembered reading.

He had a wry thought. The farmers should have come in with Texas longhorns. Fever ticks would not have affected their stock, then. But longhorns weren't good milk cows. They gave very little milk, Doc Buck had told him—only enough for a calf's sucking, if that much. Holstein-Friesens and Jerseys and Guernseys were good for milk cows, each producing many times in one milking what a longhorn cow would give down. But they definitely were not immune to ticks. Young Running Horse told himself that in many incidents the world seemingly was not constructed correctly for some things should not be allowed to happen on the earth.

Somebody somewhere had erred, he was sure. There were many things about the white men that mystified him. They sure were different than his Cheyenne in thoughts and doings.

But he no longer lived with Cheyennes. He now lived with white men. He was safe as long as he lived with Doc Buck.

Doc Buck was an influential man. He had a college degree. He was a licensed and trained doctor of veterinarian science. Most people—even whites—had trouble pronouncing the word veterinarian. They said veter-narian, not veterinarian. Doc had made him repeat the word time after time until he had pronounced it correctly. He loved Doc Buck. He had a father and mother on the reservation. He had loved them as well as a boy loved his parents but he still loved Doc more, he felt sure. He told himself he'd die for Doc Buck. And he meant it.

He watched two Texans ride back from the main herd to the small herd. By this time Virgil and the buggy and cowhide were out of sight, the hills hiding them from the eyes of the Texans. He could still see the buggy because of his high elevation. He watched the two Texans through his field-glasses. Chocolate cropped on picket behind him. The sun had brought out some new grass. Chocolate was having her first meal in months directly from the earth itself.

She been eating hay—and oats—all winter. Doc Buck fed his stock very well. Hay had been very expensive this last winter. It had been hauled by bobsled from Bulltown in bales.

The Texans apparently did not see the carcass of the slaughtered steer. It lay quite a distance from the herd and was hidden in a clump of brush on the slant of a coulee.

The Texans drew rein and looked at the Circle S cattle. They seemed in no hurry. His field-glasses showed both rolling cigarettes. They were talking to each other. Running Horse wished he'd stayed on the plain until night had come. Had he done so he'd have sneaked close and found out what these cowboys talked about.

But he was on Black Butte, not down by the cattle. One Texan looped a leg over his saddle's horn. Their horses stood hip-humped, resting. Running Horse looked northeast for the buggy. It was out of sight. Darkness was beginning to enfold the high plains. Why had Virgil skinned the steer and taken only the hide? That didn't make sense. When you killed a steer and skinned it you wanted the meat. The hide was of no account. The West was full of millions of hides—domesticated cattle hides and buffalo hides. But Virgil had left the meat behind. . . .

Skinning a cow was not an easy job, Running Horse knew. He had helped Doc Buck butcher quite a few beeves people who owed Doc Buck money had given. They'd hung the dead beef up on a tripod. That made for easier skinning for when a beef was skinned on the ground he had to be rolled over after one side was done to get at the other.

Virgil had skinned rapidly and competently. Plainly, he'd skinned many a beef before, Running Horse reasoned. Was Virgil taking the hide into Buckbrush

City to sell it? If so, he was due for a surprise, for nobody in Buckbrush City bought hides.

The hide-buyer came through in early spring. Besides cow and horse-hides he bought pelts the local people had trapped or shot during the hard winter when fur was prime.

He then remembered Virgil had not pointed the buggy toward Buckbrush City, which was east and slightly south. He'd driven northeast toward the farmers' homesteads. Running Horse looked back at the Texans. He expected them to circle behind the herd and chouse it northwest to join the main herd, which was now completely out of sight in the gathering darkness and distance.

The wind had died down. The wind always blew here on the plains except for a short interval when the sun rose and again when the sun set. Soon it would come up again.

A mosquito buzzed. He slapped, missed. The mosquito season was just beginning. Now how had a mosquito got up this high? Mosquitos were a holy terror here in the summer. People couldn't sit outdoors of an evening to cool off because of the mosquitos. And you didn't have to be close to the river to find mosquitos. They came in buzzing clouds miles from the water. When there was no wind range horses ran madly ahead of them seeking some dark grove of trees into which they could hide. Mosquitos wouldn't enter a dark area. Mosquitos also disliked the smell of manure. He'd seen a horse covered with mosquitos being led into a barn fragrant with manure smell and darkness and the mosquitos peeled off by the hundreds and flew in search of another victim.

Your house could have screen windows and screen doors and care would be taken to enter and leave rapidly

342

so the door would not be open long and that night you'd wake up with not one but a dozen mosquitos making a banquet on your blood. You'd light the kerosene lamp and run each down with the fly swatter and slip off to sleep only to have to soon repeat the angering process.

Finally the Texans below came to life. And, to his surprise, they did not drive the Circle S cattle northwest. They left the few head and galloped over the hill toward the main herd. They fell out of sight. Running Horse untied his catch-rope from the small tree and coiled it and hung it on his saddle-fork. He slipped the curb bit between Chocolate's grass-green teeth and began leading the little horse down the butte.

The descent was steep. Once he slid in shale and skinned his right knee. He remembered Ed Gaboney sliding on his rump in the mud during the ruckus in the hall. He didn't like Gaboney. He didn't know why. Yes, he did know why. Gaboney disregarded him altogether. He'd not even say hello when meeting him on the street. Land locator Matthew Cotton wouldn't speak to him, either. When he met either they ignored him completely. They didn't say it but they might just as well have said, "Go back on your reservation, you goddamned blanket buck."

He chewed on a piece of buffalo-jerky. He'd jerked the buffalo beef himself. One night after school he'd cut a hunk of buffalo meat into strips and had hung them to dry behind the lignite-coal heater. Nights were awful long here in the winter. School let out at three in the afternoon and it was already getting dark at that time around Christmas and in late December and early January. The buffalo meat had dried out and was tough as a manila rope but it had a lot of nourishment. For a moment he had a hungry feeling. He was thinking of the luscious pemmican his mother made each fall.

Buffalo meat and antelope meat and chokecherries and buffalo-berries all ground up and seasoned and crammed into a cleared-out buffalo gut to dry out and be cut in slices . . . Someday, when he was a man and a doctor of animals like Doc Buck, he'd go back to the folks on the reservation and visit. Shucks, he might even practice there, healing their cows and horses and goats and cats and dogs and other animals.

He liked that thought. He'd open a small animal hospital, too—treat the kid's sick cats and dogs and opposums and dehydrated skunks and do it all for free, too. Just like Doc Buck. Nobody knew how many such animals Doc Buck had healed and put on their four paws again.

His mother sure would be proud of him. Doc Buck would come and visit him, of course. Doc Buck would by then be an old, old man. He'd be all of forty-five, or between forty-five and fifty.

Suddenly his boots both slipped out from under him. He did a Gaboney on the loose gravel that had betrayed him. He swallowed the last chunk of the jerky. The piece was rather large. It caught in his throat. He sat and coughed it up. He threw it away, tears in his eyes.

He decided to live in the present, not the past or the future. Doc Buck had sent him on a definite mission. His job was to accomplish what Doc Buck had ordered him to do. Then he would return to Buckbrush City, mission accomplished.

He lay on his belly in the damp earth and drank from a bubbling spring, Chocolate sipping water below him in the small puddles. His inner man watered, he squatted, bridle reins in hand, and waited for the moon to rise, for his oncoming chore needed a bright moon.

A crazy chore, he told himself. But a necessary one, he added. He stretched his right leg to get a kink out of it, wishing he had the papers and material to build a cigaret. Doc Buck didn't smoke. He wasn't against the other smoking, though. Damned fools can rot out their lungs if they want to, he'd many times said. Their lungs. A man has a right to do with what he owns as he sees fit, even if it in the end kills him.

He'd smoked two cigarets. He and Slim and Joe and Jack had made them out of corral dust from the town livery-stable. They'd used the strips of the *Buckbrush City Bugle* for cigaret papers. The first one had tasted terrible. He'd coughed and tears had come to his eyes. He'd made another to show the gang he was all man. That one was worse. Soon all but Jack were rolling, grabbing bellies in pain and vomiting. Jack was used to smoking. That was why he'd not been sick. He sneaked the old man's butts out of the ashtray and smoked them behind the barn.

No, Running Horse would not smoke again. Never. Why not? Because Doc Buck didn't.

It seemed that the moon took forever in rising. Finally it cast its yellow but clear glow over the plains. He glanced up at the yellow disc. The Man in the Moon could be clearly seen. The Man seemed angry. He looked as though he were frowning. Running Horse looked at the palm of his right hand. He could easily make out the life-line. The moon was as bright as it would get.

He did not ride Chocolate. He led the little dun mare. Clumps of brush were dark and ominous. He found his heart beating faster. And the closer he got to the small herd, the harder and more often his heart beat. Many times he dropped to all fours and put an ear to the ground. Cheyennes listened that way, his father had told him. The earth was solid and it carried sound for a long distance. He heard no hoof-sounds. The earth was

345

mute and wide and endless and didn't care.

So, he continued on, coming to the small flat that had held the herd. Chocolate behind him, he peered from the brush—and his heart sank. The clearing was empty. The cattle were gone. Had the Texans returned and chased the Circle S stock northwest and into the Diamond inside a Diamond bunch?

This wasn't logical. He'd surely have heard them yipping the cattle into a trot. Texas cowboys made a lot of noise pushing a herd. They were always *ugging* and *sooing* to the cattle to make them travel faster. Had they driven the cattle away, he'd surely have heard them. No, the cattle had drifted out of their own accord. Or had they bedded down for the night?

Behind him, Chocolate snorted softly. He wheeled, put a hand over the mare's velvety nose, and listened. He heard nothing but the soft sigh of the wind. He looked at his horse. Chocolate's ears were pricked, pointing almost due north. Something she smelled from that direction plainly interested her.

Running Horse looked north. He saw nothing but the plains and clumps of boulders and a few dark splotches of brush. He heard no hoofs. The lack of sound told him the mare worked by scent, not sound.

He left Chocolate there, reins dragging, and went ahead on foot, coming to the lip of the next draw. And there, down in the coulee's flat bottom, he saw the Circle S cattle. They were bedded down, dark spots against the greening soil. Running Horse remembered Virgil walking from cow to cow with the cattle tame and standing still. He decided he would try the same. But he did not walk down now.

He returned to Chocolate. He led her in a half-circle east and came to the lower end of the coulee. He dropped her reins again and took a small Mason jar from his nigh saddlebag. This done, he walked up the coulee toward the cattle, who were watching him and Chocolate. He spoke softly to the cattle. He hoped they'd remain bedded, but his wish was not to be realized—already two spooky old cows stood up, snorting and shaking their wide and wicked horns.

Common reasoning told them his smell was alien and disturbing to them. They were used to Virgil's smell, undoubtedly. Now all the small herd was on its hoofs, watching him and seemingly ready to bolt.

Running Horse's boyish heart sank. Everything that could go wrong had gone wrong this day. His rump was sore from his skidding fall. His knee ached from its skinning.

"So, boss, so." Two more cows snorted. A steer pawed the ground. Then, the cattle broke into a dead run. And, oddly, they ran toward the boy, not away from him.

Running Horse thought, at first, that they were charging him, anxious to puncture his heart and belly with their sharp horns. He leaped back. He leaped too late. The lead cow smashed into him, sending him reeling backwards. Another hit him with his shoulder and knocked him down.

He fell in the herd. He rolled over, covering his face with his arms, and overhead hoofs flashed by, moonlight bright on the ghastly scene. Any moment he expected a thudding hoof to land on him. He didn't expect to escape alive. Doc Buck had sent him on a simple mission. He now lay with cattle thundering over him, a failure. Then, the hoofs ceased.

He pulled down his arms from his face. He staggered to his feet. The cattle were running down the coulee. Chocolate stood where he'd left her. Chocolate tried to graze despite her bit. She seemed not at all interested in the cows.

Anger hit Running Horse. Those goddamned cows were not getting the best of him! He ran to Chocolate. He didn't use a stirrup. He vaulted stampede-fashion into the Koke saddle. He scooped up his reins. He wickedly swung Chocolate, pointing her toward the running cattle. He hit her with his spurs. Chocolate leaped into a run, hoofs digging. Chocolate straightened out, tail extended, ears lying back. Running Horse unbuckled his catch-rope. He tied one end hard-and-fast around the saddlehorn. He built a loop with the other end.

The Circle S cows ran fast but Chocolate ran faster. She pulled into the herd just as the cattle reached the coulee's end. Here was a flatland. The cattle broke from a herd into individual members. Running Horse put Chocolate after a three-year-old steer, the smallest in the group. Chocolate pulled close.

Running Horse stood on stirrups. He swung his loop three times overhead and let it go. The steer had wide horns. The boy's loop landed on the horns but the loop wasn't big enough. It caught the off-horn and the steer shook his head and the loop fell and the steer ran on. Disgusted with himself, while with Chocolate still on the dead run, Running Horse built another loop—a bigger one this time. Again, he whirled the noose, shot it out. This time, it did its work.

It landed over both horns. Running Horse gave the manila a hasty shake, settling it around the base of the horns—and then he snapped back, drawing the loop tight, slack between him and the steer in the lasso. Chocolate knew her business. Chocolate stopped of her own accord and almost sat on her rump, forelegs braced, forehoofs dug into the dirt for anchorage. Chocolate was braced, ready for the strong shock that was due when the lunging steer hit the end of the rope.

Slack shot out of the lasso. The steer smashed into its end. Chocolate almost was jerked on her nose. Nevertheless, the game mare held. The steer went tail over tincup. One minute his rump faced Chocolate and Running Horse; the next, his head and one horn faced the boy and horse—for the steer had broken off his nigh-horn in his fall. He'd smashed down with both horns digging earth. The shock had broken off his nigh-horn at the base.

The catch-rope broke. The steer, getting to his hoofs, whirled, and Running Horse was without a lasso—and without hope. The steer began to run. Suddenly, his knees ran out. He toppled on his nigh-side. He didn't move. The rest of the cattle stampeded on.

Running Horse stared at the fallen steer. He dismounted and ran to the animal carrying the remainder of the lasso. His aim was to tie the steer down before he could get up, for he figured the animal had only fallen in the slippery damp earth. He was wrong. The steer was dead.

Standing there in the bright Wyoming moonlight, the young Cheyenne stared down at the dead animal with the length of catch-rope trailing from his head. He gathered his thoughts. The steer must have broken his neck. He grabbed the horn. The head worked easily. Yes, the steer had broken his neck.

Running Horse took the rope from the horn. He threw it over his saddle. He'd put the small Mason jar in his pants pocket. He took it out and unscrewed the cover and laid himself across the dead steer, fingers searching through the smooth-haired hide.

How in the hell could a human find ticks on a steer in this moonlight, even brilliant as it was? But he had to find ticks. Doc Buck had given him this Mason jar to hold ticks he found.

Doc Buck had said Gaboney's cow had different ticks than those found to date on others of the farmers' livestock. He wanted more ticks to further examine. He'd sent him out to gather some.

And Running Horse was getting some ticks, come hell or high water. He found one crawling desperately to escape. He fastened thumb and forefinger on the small mite. The tick escaped.

The tick had escaped, yes—but he'd discovered one important point. These cattle had ticks. These cattle had brought Texas Fever into Buckbrush Basin. But maybe he'd not grabbed for a Texas Fever tick? Maybe the tick hadn't been one carrying Texas Fever?

Doc Buck said cows carried other forms of ticks. One form lived off the cow's blood and did not inject deadly bacteria into her veins. Another form merely ate cow's hair. But one point stood out, clear and concise—these cattle had not swum through a dipping vat. Had they done that, they'd not have had a tick of any kind.

Fear hit him. With the information he had Doc Buck and Deputy Sheriff Jones had enough evidence to arrest the Texans for transporting ticks into the Territory. Doc Buck and Deputy Jones might make up a posse of local Buckbrush people and ride out to arrest the Texans.

That meant a gunfight. Those tough Texans would never submit to arrest. Their guns would leap from holsters. And Doc Buck might get killed. . . . Many times Doc Buck had said, "A bullet is impartial. It doesn't care who it kills."

His thoughts went to Virgil. Virgil had skinned a steer and rolled the hide into a damp cylinder, hide inside. He now understood. Virgil had killed the steer to get the steer's ticks. With the hair rolled in, the ticks could not escape. Virgil had then loaded the hide into his new buggy and had headed across country for the farmers' homesteads. Plainly, he carried ticks to the farmers. Why? Surely the farmers had enough ticks now? Ticks were killing their livestock. Ticks were driving them off their hard-won homesteads.

Maybe Virgil was taking the tick-covered hide only to one farmer—and one only? One who could possibly be spreading ticks to his neighbors' cattle? But what good would that do that one particular farmer?

Running Horse came back to the present. It then occurred to him that if Virgil took away an entire cowhide he at least could take away a hunk of cowhide, for a hunk of any size would invariably hold ticks.

He'd cut a part of the hide free. He decided on a part on the belly. He remembered Doc Buck saying ticks liked the belly of a cow the best for possibly the hide was thinner there and easier to pierce. His sharp pocket-knife went to work. He had skinned out a piece about two feet square when, to his amazement, he heard voices to the north, coming clearly through the night.

"Where the hell do you suppose them damn' critters went, Jake?"

"They was on this flat when Skirgon an' me saw them last," another voice said.

"Might have drifted down to lower land for water. God damned boss just got a nutty idea they should be in the herd. An' this afternoon he didn't care whether they trailed with the herd or not."

"Let's foller this coulee down."

"Where the hell did Virgil an' thet buggy go?"

"Danged if I know. Virgil's got it over the boss. He can read an' do work numbers an' the boss cain't do neither of them, so Virgil damn him gits special treatment, the lucky stiff."

"Cow tracks leadin' into this coulee. Moon's so

351

bright I kin see them, Jake."

"Let's head down slope."

Sweat popped out on Running Horse's forehead. The two Texans were where he'd seen the cattle this afternoon. He judged the distance away to be around an eighth of a mile, maybe less.

His first inclination was to abandon cutting free the remainder of the hide. He had about eight inches of tough cowhide to cut before the patch would come free. And his pocket-knife was getting dull. It cut much slower now than when he'd started. No, he'd not abandon the piece of hide. His knife slashed down savagely, fighting to free the strip, his ears cocked and listening for the sounds of approaching hoofs.

The knife seemed to cut eternally slowly. The hide seemed thicker than it had been.

He still could hear no hoofs. With one last, desperate swipe, he cut the last of the rawhide loose. The bloody piece of hide hung dangling from his hand. He did not waste time rolling it up at this moment. Leading Chocolate, he hurriedly entered a cut angling in from the north.

It was choked with buckbrush and wild rosebushes. He struggled through this nature-made barrier, leading. Chocolate. Rose spines tore at him, one cutting his cheek. Within a few minutes, he was a hundred yards from the dead steer. He left Chocolate there after hurriedly rolling up the hide and sticking it into a Bemis grain-sack he'd had tied to his saddle-skirts. Ticks might abandon the hide but were penned in the sack. He hurried back toward the dead steer.

He stopped cautiously and lay on his belly and peered through the brush at two riders fifty feet away who sat horses and looked down at the dead steer. He clearly heard their words.

"No coyotes chewed that hunk of hide off'n this steer, Jake. It's cut off in a square an' I sure can't see no teeth marks."

"Too dark to see fang marks," the other said. "But what the hell does a dead steer mean to us?" He answered his own question. "Not a tinker's dam. Our job is to get these damn' Circle S cows back into the herd."

"They been a nuisance and a drawback ever since we stole 'em from thet pasture down in Colorado. Don't know why the boss wanted them then but he'd steal anythin' loose jus' to steal somethin'. Damn' fool's a petty larceny thief at heart."

"Who of us ain't?"

The two turned horses and galloped down the coulee. Running Horse climbed the ridge. Within a few minutes he'd seen the two riders circle the Circle S cattle and point them northwest, hammering them with double-lassos for more speed. Distance and the night absorbed them and their sounds. Only then did the weary Cheyenne boy return to Chocolate and his busted catch-rope.

He was very, very sleepy. He hoped he'd not fall asleep and drop from the saddle. There were quite a few long miles between here and Buckbrush City. He swung into the Koke saddle. Happiness filled him. He had what Doc Buck had sent him out for. He'd not failed Doc Buck. He pointed Chocolate toward Buckbrush City.

Fourteen

The team was fresh. The buggy was new. Doc Buck and Doc Cochran reached Bulltown at daybreak. "Most sleep I've had since God knows when," Doc Cochran said. "Drive down the street to the Bull Horn Cafe. My missus will be pounding her ear and I don't want to wake her up."

Bulltown was six blocks long. The town lay on a rise north of the timber flanking the Bull River. The Buckbrush River ran into the Bull ten miles east of Bulltown. Bulltown was the oldest settlement in this section of Wyoming Territory. It had started as a saloon and red-light district for the Texas trail drivers heading north into Montana Territory and Alberta, Canada. Farmers had started moving in a few years ago. They had turned the wild cow town into a respectable dwelling area. The red-light district was now in the cottonwoods and box elders flanking the river. It got flooded out each spring, a fact certain town stiff-necks bragged about.

They were getting outside hotcakes, bacon and coffee when Mrs. Cochran entered and sat down beside her husband. She wore only a loose-fitting dressing robe and mules on her feet.

"Mrs. Williams was just at the house, Daddy. Billy is sick. Pain in his stomach, she told me. I looked down the street and saw your new democrat so I knew you were here. How are you, Doctor Malone?"

"Just fine, Mrs. Cochran."

"Still without a wife?"

"I've got a couple of prospects," Doc Buck assured. "One has only one ear, though, and the other buckteeth."

"And your little boy?"

"Just fine." Doc Buck crossed his fingers under the table. He hoped and prayed Running Horse was as he had said—just fine. He should have never sent a boy to do a man's job.

"I hear your few farmers are having trouble with their cattle."

"We hope to cure all soon."

The matron looked out the window at her husband's democrat. "Dad's got the prettiest new buggy in town. I expect to see him any time drive down the street with a pretty young thing by his side."

"Already have," Doc Cochran said.

Doc Buck looked at the buggy. For some reason it seemed to remind him vaguely of another democrat buggy. The idea finally crystalized. He now remembered. When he and Vivie and Running Horse had visited the Texans. . . . He'd wondered where he'd seen the man named Virgil before. Now he knew. He'd seen Virgil a time or two in Buckbrush City. Virgil had driven a new democrat buggy, the duplicate of Doc Cochran's.

Doc Cochran and his wife left after getting a promise out of Doc Buck he would have dinner with them at twelve. Doc Buck was sleepy. He had some time to kill. He went to the depot and dozed on a bench. The operator came in at eight. Doc Buck wrote out a brief message to his Texas uncle. "Send it collect, eh?" he told the operator.

"Not collect."

"Why not?"

"If it isn't accepted at the other end, I have to pay—and I've been stuck often enough. You're the horse doctor from Buckbrush City, ain't you?"

"I am."

"You got a bunch of barrels of kerosene an' somethin' else that smells like oil. There on the far end of the loadin' platform. There's a collect charge on 'em."

"How much?"

The man dug into the pile on his desk. He read the sum. Doc Buckley Malone openly winced. "I haven't that much money."

"What'd you aim to do?"

"Can't you put them in your storage room?"

"I can. But you'll have to pay in advance the cost of moving them off the platform into the back room. Then in advance you'll also have to pay at least ten bucks storage fee."

"How much will it come to altogether?"

"I'll have to figure it out. You want to pay for that telegram you want to send to Texas?"

"I'll not send it."

He'd not been much inclined to wire his uncle for money, anyway. His uncle had paid the greater part of his college expenses. He had his degree and a practice now and was therefore supposed to take care of himself financially. Anger ran through his tall length. With this was an irritation. He'd have to get tough with his debtors. He wondered how many—if any more—had signed the paper he'd hung in the Merc.

With this irritation came frustration. People cannot pay their debts if they are not gainfully employed.

Almost all of Buckbrush City's population depended on Rafter V for their roof, board and clothing. Buckbrush needed more farmers. Farmers with healthy cattle.

"I'll be back later," he told the depot operator.

Bulltown was coming awake. Farmers' buggies and spring wagons and lumber wagons were coming into town. He saw one lumber wagon enter the lumberyard. Hands began loading two-by-fours and siding onto the wagon. The feed store was both buying and selling wheat and oats and rye and other local produced head-crops. More than one general store was in operation here, far different than in Buckbrush City.

He went next to the brick court-house. The clerk and recorder was just opening his office. Doc Buck introduced himself and his profession and its location and said he'd like to see the general records holding homestead entries, for this section of the county court-house also handled federal homestead permits.

"You could have read those in Buckbrush City," the clerk informed. "Mr. Matthew Cotton has duplicate records, you know."

"I asked him about that," Doc Buck replied, "and he told me only your office had them. In fact, he was in doubt about that, even, for he said they might be filed only in Cheyenne in the Federal Land Office there."

"I wonder why he told you that."

"I don't know," Doc Buck said. "I'm going to find out when I get back in Buckbrush City, though."

The clerk had homestead entries filed in separate big ledgers. Three ledgers covered entries filed in the Bulltown area and only one contained the few covering the Buckbrush City area. He looked first at Ted Lawson's filing entry. He read it slowly and completely from start to finish. He then read Doug Hays' entry. It read the same as Lawson's. He wondered if he wasn't wasting his time. He closed the book, eyes thoughtful. Virgil's voice kept running through his ears. Virgil had almost came out and said something was phony and wrong about homestead entries filed from the Buckbrush City area.

"Each one of those entries except one carries a codicil," the clerk told him, raising his head from the instrument he was copying in a ledger. "I had to add these later. You'll find them by number in the back of the book."

"Thanks."

He turned to the additional clauses. And, as he read, his brows rose, and when he'd finished reading a handful, he gazed thoughtfully into space, and then remembered the clerk saying all but one were concerned with this additional bit of information. He found that entry to be that of Ed Gaboney. This entry lacked the additional bounds of the codicils.

He returned the ledger to the clerk. "Do ordinary homestead entries contain a codicil like these do?"

"No. That's not ordinary. I understand it was inserted by Mr. Cotton after the entries were first filed."

"Thank you."

"Glad to be of service."

He mulled this over a cup of coffee in the Bulltown Cafe. He asked the waitress if she knew of any store that sold dynamite. She looked at him as though he'd lost his wits and said, "That's not a nice way to commit suicide but I do believe it would be a very convincing way. I'll ask the boss."

The boss was a short, baldheaded Chinaman. "Only the Merc sells dynamite." Doc Buck was surprised at the man's command of English. Chinamen were supposed to talk in a sing-song lingo.

"How do you know?" the waitress asked.

Anger colored the Chinaman's sunken cheeks. "All the time you have a smart question or answer. I'll tell you how I know. I use dynamite to blow out the stumps on my farm down the river, that's why."

The owner of the Mercantile General Store was a short, pot-bellied man. He listened and said, "I used to have but no more."

"Sold out, eh?"

"No, *stole* out—not *sold* out."

"Mind explaining?"

The explanation was short. The man stored his dynamite in a cellar dug out of the side of a bank a mile west of town. Thus if the powder exploded, nobody or nothing in town would be damaged or killed. He'd sold the stock down to the last few sticks. He'd forgotten to place an order back in St. Louis for more. In the meanwhile about a week ago somebody had broken into his cache.

"Sawed off the lock. Cleaned me out completely. Like I said, only a few sticks were left—but they were gone."

"You don't know who stole them?"

"Notified the sheriff, of course. He went out there and played around a while and so far nothing from him."

"Do you keep a record of the people buying dynamite?"

"I do. Territory law, sir. Record always has to be open to the public, too. Don't ask me why. Margaret, bring the dynamite-book for the gentleman, please."

Doc Buck was led to an unused desk and the book was placed before him. Each entry included the name and address of the purchaser and how many sticks of dynamite he bought. The list was rather long. Local

359

farmers blasted out many stumps, the store owner related. Doc Buck took his time. He went down the columns carefully. He found not a name he was acquainted with. Apparently nobody from Buckbrush City had bought a stick of black powder.

He thanked all concerned and left. A glance at the sun told him it was time he reported to the Cochran home for dinner. The meal was a wonderful one. Roast beef, roasted spuds, good home-made whole wheat bread, vegetable soup so clear you could see the bottom of the bowl.

Maybe this marriage deal had something in its favor, at that? He'd never eaten Vivie's cooking. He'd heard she could swing a mean spatula. He had, of course, sampled Teresa's culinary skill. She, too, was no cooking slouch. He then remembered that red-headed little Barbara Case was due any time now in Buckbrush City. He decided then to await her coming. Marriage was a hell of a risky thing. A man shouldn't rush into it, he told himself as he shoveled down a forkful of spuds and gravy.

After the meal Doc Cochran and he retired briefly to the doctor's study for Doc Cochran had some medical tomes he wanted Doc Buck to read up on. "You should get your degree in medicine," the doctor told Dr. Buck.

"I have a degree in medicine."

"Yes, but not human medicine."

Doc Buck smiled. "Animals are enough. They don't complain. I have enough trouble with humans, trying to get them to pay."

"No money, eh?"

"No trade, no jobs."

"Put them to work. I have to do that with some cases. They work off their debts on my farm."

"I've heard about that. I'm starting that upon returning to town."

Mrs. Cochran interrupted. "Wanted at the Harness farm, doctor."

Doc Cochran picked up his satchel. "Duty calls, Buckley. I suppose you'll leave town soon and I won't see you again for some time?"

"Got to make tracks, Doctor."

They shook hands. Doc Cochran climbed into his buggy out on the street, lifted his buggy whip in parting, and his team trotted smartly down the street; the doctor nodding and waving to friends as he and the rig passed.

Doc Buck thanked Mrs. Cochran for the lovely meal and went to the court-house, this time stopping in at the county attorney's office where he said he wanted information about adoption, stating he wanted to make Running Horse his legal son and heir—thus insuring he'd not be taken back to the reservation.

"Would I need the signatures—or consent—of his mother and father?" Doc Buck asked.

"You don't need a thing from his parents. They're redskins and they don't count as human beings—they're numbers in the reservation's record book, nothing more. Just numbers."

"They sure took Custer's number," Doc Buck said dryly.

The middle-aged attorney gave him a discreet glance. Was this young horse doctor a goddamned Injun lover?

"I'll prepare the papers," the attorney said, "and send them out to you on the mail buggy next week. That'll be five bucks, please."

Doc Buck paid. He remembered the bill awaiting him at the depot. He again debated wiring his uncle. Again, he decided against it. He'd just leave the barrels sitting on the railroad's loading platform. Sun nor rain nor hail wouldn't hurt the steel barrels.

"Fill out this information, please, Doctor Malone."

Doc Buck filled and went down the hall to the sheriff's office. He knew the fat politician rather well from trips the sheriff had made to Buckbrush City. They discussed the dynamiting of the dip tank.

"I leave that in Deputy Sheriff Jones' hands," the obese man said wheezingly. "He has that section as his beat. I'm to be called in only in extreme cases, Doctor Malone."

"Such as what, for instance?"

"Murder. Gang fights. Outright killings, such serious crimes."

Anger touched Doc Buck. He kept it hidden behind a straight face. Hatchet John was in a wheel-chair for life. Rafter V and the farmers would have gang-fought—and gang-killed—had it not been for the Widow Hanson and her Ladies Aid.

Texas Fever ticks killed farmers' cattle. And this county official sat wide and broad and belching in his swivel chair doing nothing? Doc Buck got to his boots. "Sorry to have bothered you, Sheriff."

The sheriff didn't rise. To do so would have cost much effort. He sent a slanting, narrow-eyed look up at the tall veterinarian.

"All in Deputy Jones' capable hands," the sheriff repeated.

Doc Buck said, "Good day, sir," and left. He had a sour taste on his tongue. Then came the realization that if the sheriff did journey to Buckbrush Basin and investigate nothing would be accomplished. You can't bring an investigation to a successful conclusion while investigating from the seat of a buggy or spring-wagon as the sheriff would have to do, he being too fat to walk more than a block—if that far.

But he'd filed a complaint in the sheriff's office. He'd at least officially reported the trouble. He made the local law cognizant of Buckbrush Basin's trouble.

He went to the Bulltown Saloon where over a beer and pretzels he checked off items on a mental list. He decided he had everything accomplished except the purchase of groceries and a few other items he could not buy in the Buckbrush City Merc's limited stock. Yes, and a gift or two for Running Horse. What do you buy as a gift for a fourteen-year-old boy? Then came the thought that perhaps there was no more Running Horse. The thought was terrible. What a fool he'd been to bow to the boy's wishes!

But the young Cheyenne had begged and pleaded. And finally, against his better judgment . . . He pushed such black thoughts from his mind. He went to the Bulltown Mercantile where, thank the Lord, he had a charge account. He ordered his groceries from the list he carried and then went to the part where a few books and school supplies were sold.

He knew that Running Horse had read Louisa May Alcott's *Little Women* and he was happy to see a copy of her *Little Men* on the rack. He also purchased a copy of William Henry Seward's trip around the world, for Running Horse loved travel stories, he knew.

Behind him a woman's voice said, "Are you buying books for your son or for yourself, Doctor Malone?"

The voice had a slight Latin accent. His heart beat faster as he turned and looked at Teresa Hernandez.

"Teresa! What a wonderful surprise! What are you doing this far from your cookstove?"

The girl had driven into Bulltown with her team and buggy to buy some supplies she could not get in Buckbrush City. "Things like spices," she said. "You didn't answer my question?"

"Buying for Running Horse."

She looked at his two books. "The boy will love these. He's sat in my cafe and told me all about *Little Women*. I almost know the book by heart even if I've never read it."

"What other book do you advise?"

She selected Longfellow's *Evangeline*. "I've read this both in English and Spanish, and I love it."

"He's already read it."

She restored *Evangeline* to its former nook and selected Longfellow's *Ballads and Other Poems*. She opened it, read a little, then said, "I've never read this before."

Doc Buck looked at the title. "He hasn't this book."

"How are you going home? And when?"

"I'm ready to leave right now. I'll rent a rig at the livery barn, one I can leave in Buckbrush City. Load my groceries and get out."

"I drove down in my buggy. I left before dawn."

Was she inviting him to ride back with her? Doc Buck suddenly thought of Buckbrush City's prying eyes and gossipy tongues. They'd really waggle—those tongues—if he drove into town with Teresa.

"You can drive my rig back, if you wish," Teresa said.

Doc Buck said, "The town will talk, Teresa."

She tossed her dark hair. "Let them gossip. It will limber their tongues and make them happy. All people where I have been are the same. They all gossip. Our people are only normal. They are good at heart, though—and that is what counts."

"Rightly said," Doc Buck agreed.

She and Doc Buck went toward the town livery stable. Doc Buck was very aware of the envious and admiring glances local men paid the beautiful Latin girl. And, indeed, she was a beauty. Dark-haired, dressed in a dark, form-fitting dress, her small feet encased in polished black half-boots, she was a picture of health.

She'd driven down a team owned by the combined livery-barns of Buckbrush City; therefore, she'd have a new team driving south—one that could be left in Buckbrush City's town barn until some Buckbrush City citizen returned the bay harness horses to Bulltown.

Usually the thirty-two miles between the two towns took Doc Buck somewhat over four hours. This time, for some reason, it took him over five. They pulled into Buckbrush City at seven with darkness creeping across the limitless prairie. When they had gone through the farmer settlement Doc Buck had seen a democrat parked in Ed Gaboney's yard that was, in his eyes, the identical twin of Doctor Cochran's new rig.

Virgil visiting Ed Gaboney? His brows rose. There must be some mistake. The well-spoken Texan had no reason to visit a local farmer. He was sure, then, that the democrat did not belong to Virgil, whatever his last name was. It belonged to Gaboney or some other farmer who'd recently bought the new rig and as yet not driven it into town where other eyes could see its red-and-black painted splendor.

He drove first to Teresa's cafe. There he and she unloaded her supplies. "Almost time to close, Doc Buck," she told him. "You'll unload your things next, I suppose?"

"I shall. And then stable the team."

"When you get done, stop in for something to eat on your way home."

Doc Buck smiled. He saw Deputy Sheriff Milton Jones lounging in front of his office despite the chilly evening wind. The locals in the barber shop stood in yellow dim lamplight openly watching him and Teresa. All the town needed was Widow Hanson on the plank sidewalk. "They're already discussing us," Doc Buck said.

"They'll have more to talk about if you have supper with me. And on the house, Doc Buck."

"I never turn down a free meal."

Doc Buck drove to his laboratory-living quarters. He hoped by now Running Horse had returned, but the building had no lamplight. He unlocked the door, carried in his supplies. The building was chilly. It had not had a fire inside for some time, he reasoned. He lit the Rochester kerosene lamp. Running Horse had left a note on the table giving his time of departure.

He should have been back by now, Doc Buck thought, and the fear in him spread. He looked at the old clock on the wall-bench. He'd give the boy until nine. Then if he hadn't returned he'd go out and look for him.

He started a fire in the pot-bellied heater. Soon the Wyoming lignite would warm the room. Lignite gave up good heat after it once had been thoroughly ignited. Anybody with a pick in Wyoming could get his winter supply of coal just by chipping at a vein of coal pushing out of the side of a hill. Lignite had kept the farmers alive during the past long cold winter.

The fire going, he went outside to the democrat. He drove to the livery, left the rig and team there, then walked to Teresa's cafe, where she had steak and spuds and hot coffee waiting.

Widow Hanson had run the cafe while Teresa had been in Bulltown. The cafe had but one customer, Vivian Wilson. Vivie ate alone in a booth. When Doc Buck passed, she merely nodded, not speaking. Doc Buck grinned. Vivie had seen him and Teresa entering in the democrat. He remembered Teresa seeing him kiss Vivian. Turn about is fair play, is it not?

He and Teresa ate at the counter. "How's Hatchet John, Mrs. Hanson?" Doc Buck asked.

"Pushin' aroun' by hisself now," the Widow replied. "Doin' a good job of it, too."

The Widow returned to her kitchen. Vivian finished eating and came to the counter to pay. Teresa left her stool and got behind the counter. Vivie paid and left without a word. Teresa locked the door and returned to her seat beside Doc Buck. "She's not happy."

"Neither were you," Doc Buck pointed out.

Her dark eyes studied him. "When, might I ask?"

"When you caught me kissing her."

"Oh, pshaw! That didn't hurt me a bit. Should it have?"

Doc Buck realized he was getting into high water. "I guess not," he said and then, to change the subject, "I hope Running Horse is home by now."

"Where did the boy go?"

"Went out camping around Black Butte for a day or so. He wanted to go to Bulltown with me but I said no so I guess he went away to sulk."

"He'll be over it by this time."

Doc Buck finished, thanked her, was let out the door, and he hurried toward his lab, seeing lamplight in the windows as he drew nearer. His heart was happy. He'd killed the lamp when he'd left.

He'd also left the door locked. Only one other had a key—Running Horse. His son had returned. He burst into the room, then stopped. For Running Horse was not in sight, but a wheel-chair was—a chair occupied by none other than Hatchet John Martin.

"You have a key to the door, Hatchet John?"

"Yeah. Don't you remember giving it to me?"

367

Fear tore at Doc Buck. When he answered his voice even in is own ears sounded dim, distant. "I must've forgot," he said. "Seen Running Horse around?"

"No. Should I have?"

Doc Buck breathed deeply. "Sent him out on the range on an errand while I went to Bulltown. He should've been back by now."

"Somebody outside now," Hatchet John said.

Doc Buck hurriedly opened the door. Deputy Sheriff Milton Jones entered. "Saw you an' Miss Hernandez drive into town, Doc Buck. You learn anythin' in Bulltown?"

"Quite a bit. You seen Running Horse around?"

"Haven't seen the boy all day. Jim Park an' I happened to be mentionin' the boy hasn't showed up all day."

Hatchet John cocked his head. "Somebody else in the back, Doc Buck."

Again, the door pulled hurriedly open. This time Running Horse stood in the yellow lamplight. The boy carried a close-woven Bemis grain sack with something in it. "Hello, Dad."

Doc Buck felt ten years younger. He was so happy he gruffly said, "About time you showed up, son. What'd you know?"

"Quite a bit."

Fifteen

Unrest gripped Matthew Cotton. The land locator stood in his darkened office and watched the buckboard carrying Teresa Hernandcz and Doctor Buckley Malone enter Buckbrush City. Doc Buck handled the lines. Teresa sat close to him with a robe over his lap and hers. Again her dark beauty struck the land locator. He envied Doc Buck. He had tried to get friendly with Teresa and had failed miserably. She had been kind and considerate but she'd turned down each and every one of his offers to escort her here or there.

The town said she had her cap set on Doc Buck. So, for that matter, had Vivian Wilson, tongues proclaimed. He'd tried getting Vivie to accompany him to dances and other social events. Vivie also had turned him down. That was logical, though. He was *farmer* and Vivie was *cattle*. His farmers were eating into Rafter V range.

The democrat wheeled by. Matthew Cotton resumed his endless pacing, many thoughts running through his agile, dangerous mind. Anger assailed him momentarily. Things were going too slowly. He was barely inching forward. He wanted progress to be more rapid. By now at least a half-dozen of the farmers should have left the country, wagons loaded with household goods, children on the wagon or riding ponies behind. But none had done so.

Oh, yes, tomorrow . . . tomorrow the Qualeys and the Beemans were deserting their homesteads, the first to leave. He grinned. Within a few days the ledger down in Bulltown would show that Matthew Cotton now owned both the Qualey and Beeman homesteads.

Twenty-three farmers. Each with at least two thousand in their homesteads. Forty-six thousand bucks. And the land they left behind for him . . . five thousand dollars apiece, at the minimum. One hundred and sixty acres, each homestead.

Five thousand U.S. bucks times twenty-three homesteads. . . . He stood, wrapped in thoughts. One hundred and fifteen thousand dollars? He silently multiplied another time. Yes, he'd been right. One hundred and fifteen thousand. He added to that sum forty-six thousand, dropping the three zeros—and came out with one hundred and sixty-one thousand dollars.

Those codicils were the thing. He should have thought of them when first filing the papers for those damn stupid ignorant farmers. Now when each abandoned his homestead by law the homesteads passed into his possession and all he had to do was complete the requirements Uncle Sam demanded of each homesteader. These requirements were few. A house and barn, forty acres under cultivation, good strong barbwire fences. Each farmer had already completed these necessary requirements.

He'd planted one homesteader and managed to get him and his homestead in the middle of the string of homesteads strung out there along the basin's northern hills. This man had then worked from the middle out.

He'd been wondering what would aid him in ousting the nesters from their land. He'd first thought of night riders swooping down with flame and roaring guns, killing and sending fear through the honyonkers' hearts.

He'd been ready to put this into action when out of the clear blue southern sky had come the tick-laden cattle. It had been like a gift from the gods. All you had to do was scatter ticks around and kill off the farmers' livestock. Without cattle, they had to move. Without cattle, they'd not have much income. Without cattle, they didn't have milk for their children. Without cows, there'd be no meat on their tables. Their entire present and future depended upon a lumbering, homely cow.

But the ticks—that plan had proven very, very slow. Night riders would have accomplished the chore much faster. Hired gunmen. Fences cut, stock run off. Rifles and short-guns booming death. Night raids.

Naturally the farmers would have blamed the Wilson Rafter V. And the farmers would have joined forces, got out rifles, pistols, cartridges—and fired back.

Lone farmers shot dead from ambush. Finally the farmers would have ridden openly against Rafter V. And with each empty saddle on the side of the farmers, another free homestead and its alfalfa fields for Matthew Cotton. Not to mention buildings and improvements such as barbwire fences, corrals.

And who would have led the farmers on their deadly midnight raids? Nobody but one Matthew Cotton, land locator.

But when bullets sang, where would Matthew Cotton be? He'd be behind the lines, hidden by darkness. He'd count another homestead his as Rafter V bullets emptied another saddle on a nester plowhorse.

Then, when the battle was over? He'd materialize out of the night, his rifle smoking. He'd compliment his farmers and express mock sadness at the deaths. He'd even give each bereaved wife and family fifty dollars to leave the country on. . . .

Then the ticks had arrived. They'd come in with a

trailherd that had papers showing it had been dipped in Texas. It had had papers to enter Wyoming Territory. But along with those Diamond inside a Diamond cattle had come tick-plagued stock. Stolen stock. Stock stolen on the trail north. Tick-ridden Circle S cattle. . . . Of course, some ticks had naturally jumped to Diamond inside a Diamond stock. But this stock was immune to ticks, and plainly the herd had not gone through a thorough inspection when entering Wyoming.

Territorial officials were just as lazy as all other government officials. They hadn't looked too close. Sign the paper, get rid of them, collect their fees. . . .

He'd been unfortunate in some ways, fortunate in others. His big streak of fortune was cultivating the friendship of Ed Gaboney two years ago down in northwest Texas. Ed Gaboney and a locator had played this game down on the Panhandle, only they'd incurred the hatred of the local cowmen toward the nesters and the hatred of the farmers toward the cowmen. A battle of the plains had followed that had put to shame General Custer's campaign against marauding Comanches. When the last shot had been fired the dead count ran to around thirty head, at least. Nobody could be sure of the actual number of cowboys and farmers killed. Much shooting and burning occurred at night. Actually, local tongues said some farmers inadvertently, in their excitement, shot and killed by accident their own members.

Of course, the killing could have been by design, not accident. The instigators had been careful to develop with the farmers—and the cowboys, too—personal hates. And in battle, who watches to see who kills whom?

Thus he and Ed Gaboney had learned from actual experience. They'd moved this experience north to

Buckbrush Basin, Territory of Wyoming. But before they could put their plan of conflict in action, by sheer chance a man named Virgil had come in with a herd of small Circle S cattle, each carrying all the fever ticks they could carry.

Evidently the Circle S cattle were immune to ticks, also, for none got sick. But the cattle of the farmers was not, and once the ticks got on them they began their slow march to certain death.

The ticks had cost money, though. Virgil was a man who looked out for only one person, Virgil. Now he was supposed to deliver his last batch of ticks. He was taking them in a cowhide by buggy to Ed Gaboney. And Gaboney wouldn't have the two hundred bucks Virgil would demand.

He'd given Gaboney only a hundred bucks. "Jew the bastard down, Gaboney," he'd said. "If he don't take a hundred, tell him to put them—well, you know where. We'll pick ticks off your cows."

"You won't get many. I didn't want my cows killed off, but you said if all the cows of the farmers got ticks an' mine didn't have none—"

"Look bad if your cows didn't have ticks, Ed. Mebbe people would get suspicious an' turn on us."

"That was possible. You did right givin' my stock ticks."

"Poor ol' bull. He didn't hump your cow but he got the blame. Kind of reminds me of a husband raisin' a kid that was sired by his neighbor an' he thinks the kid is his."

"That's a common occurrence."

Now big Matthew Cotton seated himself on the corner of his old desk, still playing with thoughts, searching for possible errors . . . and hoping to find none. He thought of the dynamiting of the new dip tank. He and Gaboney had scouted that area well on foot before riding in with their dynamite fuses dripping fire. They'd located that damned Hatchet John Martin sitting back in the timber forty feet west of the new tank with his rifle over his knees.

From the brush, they'd watched the old man for some time, and finally decided he slept, for he made not a movement. Thus both he and Gaboney figured the coast had been clear for a successful bombing. Gaboney had argued that he and his boss go through the timber to the tank, set their powder in proper positions, then light the fuses and ran back. Matthew Cotton had vetoed this plan.

"We were lucky to get this dynamite. If our hacksaw hadn't been able to cut the dug-out's lock down in Bulltown we'd had no dynamite. Luck has been with us this far," Matthew Cotton had said.

"What's your plan, then?"

"We ride in with short fuses. We set dynamite an' we might not get out fast enough to get blowed to Kingdom Come. You and me know nothin' much about black powder."

"You don't need to repeat that, boss. I'm scairt to wet-pants with powder aroun' me. Go on, eh?"

"We ride in damn' fast. We throw our powder damn' fast. Then we ride out faster'n we rode in, hopin' that none of the flyin' rocks an' concrete don't hit us."

"Your idea's best. But what about ol' Hatchet John? He might get some shots at us."

"That old fool's asleep. By the time he comes to an' in full senses rocks will be flyin' an' you an' me will be a long ways off in the dark night. He'll never know who hit the tank."

They'd roared in, low in saddles. They flung their dynamite. They'd roared away, riding hard. The dynamite had boomed. Flame and roar and rocks and concrete flying and falling no more than twenty feet behind the rumps of their hard-running saddle-broncs. . . . Then had come a shout from old Hatchet John. Maybe he had thrown a bullet or two in their direction but if he had the bullets had missed and had not been heard because of the black-powder's belching roar.

Still, there was doubt. It lingered in land locator Matthew Cotton's thick chest, even now. And that doubt consisted of this: Had the old man seen them and recognized them in the bright-as-daylight flare of the exploding dynamite? He and Gaboney had not been masked. They'd ridden black horses, though—so identification could not be accomplished due to recognition of their plunging saddle-broncs.

They'd reined in panting horses on a hill. They'd hurriedly talked it over, both fearing Hatchet John had recognized one—or both. "Maybe we oughta go back," Gaboney said, "an' kill the old sonofabitch! Sneak through the bresh. Shoot him from the back."

Cotton had cocked his head, listening. "Sounds like somebody hollerin' down there. With pain in his voice."

Gaboney listened, too. "That'll be that ol' bastard. Mebbe some boulder or somethin' hit him."

"Somebody comin' from the Williams', an' fast. We'd better make tracks, and right now!"

Gaboney had taken Cotton's horse on to his farm after Cotton had left saddle on the west side of town. Gaboney had gone on but Cotton had walked to the back of his office where he'd accosted Doc Buck and Running Horse, getting ready to head out to the ruined dip tank.

Cotton had also visited Hatchet John Martin a few

times. Each time he'd brought the oldster a few sacks of Bull Durham tobacco and wheat-straw rolling papers. For Hatchet John wouldn't make a cigaret with the white rice-straw papers each sack of Bull Durham carried. Hatchet John claimed white papers gave a man a cigaret cough, something he didn't have. "White papers give a man too much saliver in his mouth, but brown papers don't.

"A man swaller thet saliver an' it gits in his lungs an' gives him a cigaret cough. With brown papers an' no saliver to speak of a man don't cough his goddamned head off'n his goddamned shoulders!"

On one visit Cotton got the old man discussing the dynamiting. He left with the old man's words, "Never got a glimpse at them night-riders. Figgered there must've been about eight of 'em, too."

Cotton figured he and Gaboney were safe.

Logic also proclaimed that if indeed Hatchet John had recognized the raiders—or their horses—he surely would have reported this information to Deputy Sheriff Milton Jones, would he have not? But you couldn't bank on that assumption. Hatchet John was a secretive cuss who apparently liked to work things out to his own satisfaction, regardless of energy used or time expended.

Both he and Ed Gaboney had little admiration for Deputy Jones. Both agreed as a lawman he lacked much but as a husband he seemed okay for he stud-horsed a new baby into life every year, at least.

Jones got an A plus in studhood.

No, he'd left no openings, no slips, nothing overlooked. And tonight was the night Ed Gaboney would die. . . . He had to get rid of Gaboney. Gaboney knew too much. Gaboney might talk if the pressure was screwed down hard. Gaboney also liked the booze too

376

much. And when he got drunk, he talked too much—a habit drunks had.

He'd make the killing look like it had been done by Rafter V. Only yesterday when nobody had been in the town livery-barn he'd stolen Ron Powers' Winchester rifle from saddle-holster. Powers' rifle would soon be found lying beside Gaboney's corpse.

Upon returning to the barn to return to Rafter V Ron Powers had of course found his rifle missing. The hostler had lain on his filthy bunk dead-drunk to the world. Ron Powers and Bill Wilson had rudely awakened the bewhiskered oldster, who of course did not know who had stolen Powers' rifle, or when it had been taken from his barn.

Powers had picked the oldster up, held him at arm's length, and had whipped him with his quirt, raising big blue welts across the skinny behind. He then dropped the man to the floor and he and Wilson had then reported the theft to Deputy Sheriff Milton Jones.

Jones had immediately clamped the handcuffs on the skinny and dirty wrists of Old Man Montrose, who sometimes cleaned out stalls in the barn at a nickel a stall. Although Old Lady Montrose and her four children swore that their husband and sire hadn't left the hovel for at least three days Jones heaved the old man into the town calaboose where he'd been interrogated long and industriously by Powers, Williams and the deputy, but to no avail.

Old Man Montrose had the habit, all knew, of mistaking somebody else's property for his own. His house and its surrounding area were searched. No rifle was found. Missus Hanson and the Ladies' Aid rose up in anger. Hadn't the Old Man a good alibi? He might be a liar but his wife certainly was not, nor were his almost grown children.

Jones had been compelled to turn Old Man Montrose loose. The old man threatened Jones with false arrest. Jones might lose his job. Ron Powers and Bill Williams rode out to Rafter V, the saddle-holster on Ron Powers' saddle empty—sans Winchester.

Land Locator Matthew Cotton in the barber shop idly mentioned he's seen one of the farmers go north in direction of the livery stable. No, he wasn't naming the farmer; hell, he didn't even know if the man had entered the stable. He'd just been heading that way when the land locator had looked out a window of his office. No more than that. Wished to hell I hadn't mentioned it, now.

But it had been mentioned. Tongues took up the subject. Soon it was spread about that the barber had seen Ted Lawson go into the livery-barn. The barber became the center of all activities. He claimed he'd said no such thing but secretly you could see it pleased him to be the focus of attention. Somebody then said that Ted Lawson had a mad on against Ed Gaboney. Nobody knew what the trouble was, but there was serious trouble between Gaboney and Lawson. "Might even end in a shootin'," the town clerk mysteriously put in.

Matthew Cotton's office had an attic. You punched a small section in one corner upward and if you stood on a chair you could pull yourself up into the darkness. Ron Powers' rifle rested there, waiting.

His thoughts swung over to the man named Virgil. What was Virgil's last name? He didn't know. Maybe he'd never heard. Well, what ice did it cut, anyway? None at all, he reasoned.

Sometimes a man's thoughts run around in circles and seem to get nowhere, and this was one of those times to Matthew Cotton, Cotton told himself. Well, what about Virgil?

378

Virgil was business manager on trail herds for the big Diamond in a Diamond cow-outfit whose home ranch was on the Republican River down in north Texas. Many times he accompanied trail-herds north.

He handled the payroll and was time-keeper. Diamond in a Diamond owners—mostly Scottish and English absentees—had him arrange with various banks enroute north for credit to pay off Diamond in a Diamond cowpunchers during the long trek north. Thus if a cowpuncher quit in the Cheyenne, Wyoming Territory region, he could go to the Stockman's Bank in Cheyenne with an order signed by Virgil. Bank officials would then pay off the cowpuncher in bills, silver or gold—whichever he desired. The same could happen in Oklahoma Territory, Colorado or Montana Territory. Thus Virgil was paymaster all the way north.

Virgil was not amiss at earning a little money on the q.t., also—as witnessed by his sale of the tick-covered hides of the stolen Circle S cattle.

Did Virgil know the use the ticks were put to? Logic told Matthew Cotton the man surely did. All tick-bound hides had been delivered at the Gaboney farm. None had ever as yet come into Buckbrush City.

Time inched slowly past. One by one lights went out in Buckbrush City until only one light remained. That came from the lantern hanging from the ridge-beam extending out of the front of the town livery stable. Sometimes Matthew Cotton sat, sometimes he paced. Finally, he dozed off in his swivel chair. Hammering of the wall-clock striking the hour snapped him awake. It was midnight.

Sonofabitchin' Ed Gaboney.... He imagined Gaboney dead, killed from ambush, the Powers' rifle lying beside his corpse and Deputy Jones picking up the rifle. "Cripes, this is Ron Powers' rifle. He never lost it.

379

He jus' claimed he did so's he'd not be suspected of this killin'."

"He's got rattled, Powers has—an' he's forgot his rifle behind." Those words would come from Matthew Cotton.

He'd give Gaboney until twelve-thirty. . . . What if Virgil hadn't delivered a tick-heavy hide? Surely Gaboney would ride in and tell him, his boss, that Virgil hadn't showed up? Gaboney had that much sense, didn't he? Or did he? Maybe I should eliminate Virgil, too? Silence him for once and for always? Could be done. . . .

For soon Virgil would have delivered the Diamond in a Diamond herd in Montana's Mussellshell Basin. He'd then turn his buggy team south to return to Texas and get another herd to escort north.

He'd probably drive south alone. Texas cowboys usually stayed with a trailherd after the longhorns had reached their final destination. They stuck with the cattle until the cattle were fat enough to trail east to market across Dakota or the stock was sold to some army sutler for meat on some Indian reservation.

When Virgil drove back to Texas he'd undoubtedly take the same trail he'd gone north on. And again, he might be alone. One bullet, from the brush—and no more Virgil. A prairie grave, occupant unknown. Grave site unknown, too, except to the ambusher. Prairie buffalo grass soon covering the grave forever. . . .

He'd admired that red and black buggy. Just like the new one Doc Cochran drove. And those two snappy harness horses . . . he'd paid close attention to their brands. They were both branded Bar over an S on the right shoulder. A man could easily change that brand to a Box Eight with a hot running iron.

And two good high-priced buggy horses, too. And the

380

rig? Put a new coat of paint on it. Just a few hours work. Paint what is now red to black and what is now black to red. And nobody'd ever recognize the democrat. . . .

Twelve thirty finally came. And still no Ed Gaboney. Had something gone wrong? Matthew Cotton decided to ride north to the Gaboney homestead and see just what was what. What if Virgil had wanted more money? He'd followed Ed Gaboney's advice: "The bastard's gettin' paid too much, boss. Next time try him for a hundred bucks, not two hundred." So Gaboney had ridden to his farm with only one hundred, not two.

"We need those ticks. We need to plant more on the Gottshell cows. Yes, and on the cows belonging to Mullins and Seals, too. Them three families are just about ready to pull out. We need to give them a boost on the way."

"That's right, boss."

Matthew Cotton cursed under his breath as he got in to his boots. He buckled on his star-rowel spurs. He took a windbreaker from the coat hook and slid into it. Summer apparently would never come. Yeah, it would come, he thought sourly. Nights so torrid you couldn't sleep. You roll over naked and the sheet goes with you, sweat-glued to your back. And you couldn't sleep outside where it was a bit cooler. If you did, mosquitos would stop noisily in and carry you off. Or the bugs would crawl all over your carcass.

When he had those claims to those abandoned homesteads he'd sell the whole kit and caboddle to whoever offered him enough. Then, he'd head back to Texas. North Texas with its howling wind and blue northers and blizzards was heaven compared to this damned wilderness.

He saddled his black gelding, Midnight. The horse

rebelled against the cinch. He filled his belly with air and held his breath. He wanted his master to tighten the cinch when he was full of air. Then when the cinch was tightened he'd let out his breath and have slack in the cinch. Midnight knew all the angles.

But his master knew them, too. When Midnight had his flanks extended Matthew Cotton's right boot whammed up and smashed Midnight in the ribs and Midnight, in pain and surprise, exhaled. The minute the horse let out his held breath, Cotton pulled the cinch up hard and solid, outwitting Midnight at his own game.

A few minutes later, Matthew Cotton rode north in the bright moonlight. He only had to ride two miles out of Buckbrush City. For at that point he saw and heard a rig going south toward town. Accordingly, he pulled Midnight off trial, sitting the bronc hidden in some cottonwood trees growing east of the wagon road. Soon the fancy buggy and high-stepping team of Virgil flashed by with two men on the seat.

Ed Gaboney drove the team and Virgil sat beside him. The sight of Virgil made Matthew Cotton's lips harden. He didn't want Virgil to be seen again in Buckbrush City. Virgil had been in town too often. He'd settle accounts with him and get him out of town fast.

He did not accost the democrat. Logic prevailed. Ed Gaboney and Virgil naturally would be watchful, tense. A call out of the moonlight might bring gunsmoke in return. The democrat flashed by. He thought he made out something rolled up in the rig's back. It could be a cowhide, he thought.

The rig rocked out of sight. Matthew Cotton swung his horse in a wide, westward circle. He drove his midnight black hard. He didn't want the rig to hear his horse's hoofbeats so he spread his circle wider. He grinned. He'd get to his office before the buggy arrived. He'd be waiting for Gaboney. Yes, and Virgil.

Sixteen

They talked it over in Doctor Buckley Malone's laboratory, ticks crawling around inside a Mason jar. It was Doc Buck who mapped out the strategy. Hatchet John Martin had left when the conference reached the point where he heard Doc Buck say it would be best if he and Deputy Jones accosted Matthew Cotton in Cotton's office.

The maimed cowpuncher had wheeled his wheel-chair away with, "I'll read about it in the next issue of the *Bugle*."

"You don't believe me when I tell what I've learned?" Doc Buck asked.

"Maybe you're right. Maybe you're wrong. But this pain—it's killin' me right now—the Widder'll give me a hot bath."

"Can you make it home alone?" Deputy Jones asked.

Hatchet John studied the deputy. "Did I ever ask you—or anybody else—for any help, anytime or anywhere?"

Jones grinned. "Can't recollect any such."

Hatchet John snorted and wheeled to the door and opened it, moving his chair so the door could swing wide. "Nice you put a wide door on this house," he told Doc Buck. "Widder's doors are so small a man has a hard time navigatin' through them with this wheeled bronc."

384

"How's the night out there?" Doc asked.

"Moonlight awful bright. Well, I'll see two in hell." And the old cowpuncher wheeled into the Wyoming moonlight.

"Frosty ol' gent," Jones said. "Now our plan is this—we pinch Cotton first. Then we ride out an' put the handcuffs on Gaboney. An' if this Virgil gent is on the Gaboney farm, we get him, too."

"Virgil isn't so important right now," Doc Buck said. "We can pick him up later when this thing gets to trial."

Running Horse sat to one side carefully listening. "You mean you think they won't fight you, Dad?"

"I doubt it. Cotton's a smart man. In my judgment, he'll surrender, then hire smart lawyers for a trial."

"And Mr. Gaboney?" the boy asked.

"He might be foolish and try to fight but if his boss surrenders peacefully I think Gaboney will follow Cotton's lead," Doc Buck said.

Deputy Jones nodded. "I think—and hope—you're right, Doc. I wanna live long enough to at least see my oldest boy—dang his ornery buttons—get a diploma out of reform school!"

"I wanna help," Running Horse said.

"You'll help the most by staying out of our way," Doc Buck said.

"I can act as a scout, can't I?"

"Okay. Go down and scout Cotton's office. If he's there, come and tell us—and the same if he isn't there."

Running Horse slid out the door. He came back within ten minutes. "He's in his office. Alone, I think—'cause I don't hear him talk to nobody. Sittin' in the dark, Dad."

"Keep an eye on him," Doc Buck ordered.

Butterflies fluttered in the veterinarian's belly. He didn't like the chore ahead one bit. He thought of letting this rest until the sheriff and a deputy or two came up from the county seat. He then wondered if the lawman would come if summoned. He figured the obese star-toter wouldn't come. Hadn't he already told him in wheezing tones that he'd commissioned Deputy Jones to handle the affairs of Buckbrush City and Buckbrush Basin? There'd be no help from Bulltown.

Doc Buck looked at the clock. Almost twelve-thirty. He was surprised. Time had really run by. He then realized it had been rather late in the night when Running Horse finally showed up.

Within a few minutes Running Horse burst in again. "He's gone to his barn an' is saddlin' his black horse, Midnight. I looked in through a crack in the planks. I dunno where he's headin'."

Jones looked at Doc Buck. Doc Buck said, "Follow him but be sure you don't let him see you, son."

"I'm a Cheyenne, remember."

"You also almost flunked mathematics this last school term, too," Doc Buck reminded him. "Which means you're not as smart as you think you are."

"Thank you." Running Horse disappeared.

"Wonder if he locked his office?" Jones said.

"We'll find out."

As they left, Doc Buck picked up half a steel buggy spring he kept as a wedge under the door so it would not blow shut. They had been sitting talking in the dark so there was no Rochester lamp to blow out.

They went silently down the alley toward Cotton's office. The town was quiet except for an occasional town-dog barking in reply to a coyote's lonely wail.

Doc Buck had a queer thought. Teresa and Vivian would be sleeping, unmindful of this night's troubles.

Vivian, he knew, was staying at the Widow's, saying the Rafter V town-house was too big and lonesome, she being alone in the two story house her father had built. Teresa had a room behind her cafe.

They came to Matthew Cotton's back door. It was locked. Doc Buck then moved forward toward the main street by going through the small space between the office and the next building north. The front door, too, was locked.

"Got to use the buggy spring," he whispered to Jones upon return. "We got to get inside and wait for them."

"You sure he'd gone out to Gaboney's?" the deputy asked.

"Where else would he go?"

"Nowhere else, I guess. Our plan is one wait inside. T'other wait in the shed acrost the alley. When he comes in the one in the shed comes in behin' him and we have him penned in atween the two of us?"

"We don't know what he'll do. We got to play our cards close, Jones. Which do you want—the shed or the office?"

"I'll take the office. You be in the office, an' he'll have a case of breaking an' entry ag'in you. But he can't get that ag'in me because I pack a star.

"Besides, I can claim I was doin' my rounds an' his door was open so I entered to see if he was okay—or if the place had been robbed."

"I'd best spring the front door," Doc Buck said. "He'll probably come in the back door and notice that the door has been sprung. This steel is sure to leave some deep marks in the wood."

"Good idea. I'll enter from the front, too."

Then, both stiffened, hands automatically flashing to

holstered guns. Then Running Horse came out of the shadows.

"He's comin'!"

"Alone?" Doc Buck asked.

"He rode out an' met a democrat. Buggy jus' like the one Doc Cochran drove. Two men on the seat."

"Who are the men?"

"Moonlight showed them clear. Virgil an' Gaboney."

Doc Buck said, "You go back to the lab. You wait there an' don't put your nose out the door, understan'? Make tracks, son."

"But, Dad—"

"Do as I say, and right now."

Running Horse moved into the shadows and was gone. Doc Buck and Jones hurriedly went to the main street.

The front door was made of heavy oak. It fit tightly. The spring bent, and Doc Buck put his weight against it, grunting and pushing. Jones helped. The door did not give.

And time was running out, Doc Buck realized.

"No use," Jones panted. "Break a panel. I'll reach in, unlock it. Damn it, did I hear horsehoofs toward the north?"

"You sure did."

Doc Buck smashed the steel into a panel. The heavy wood held, the steel bouncing. He hit again, harder.

The wood splintered.

Two more blows had hammered out a hole big enough to admit Jones' hand. Jones reached in, found the key, unlocked. The door opened. Jones slid inside saying, "I'll say I saw the panel broke when I made my midnight rounds. He won't know otherwise."

"That's right."

"I'll leave the door open."

But Doc Buck was already gone, moving back toward the alley between the two buildings. He halted a foot or so from stepping into the moonlight, listening to the voices in the alley.

"Whoa, boys, whoa."

That would be Gaboney, talking to the team. Next came the voice of Matthew Cotton.

"Goddamn' idiots, both of you. Draggin' that hide into town. Why didn't you leave it at the farm?"

"I wanted to," Gaboney said, "but he didn't. Claimed you'd doubt his word about gettin' thet hide an' he wanted the hide along for evidence."

"Give me my hundred more," another voice said. "Then me an' my buggy'll get the hell out."

That sounded like Virgil's voice, but Doc Buck wasn't sure. He'd heard Virgil's voice only for a brief time.

"But first you'll take this hide back to the farm?" Matthew Cotton's voice.

"Hell, no. I've had enough of this deal. I get my hundred, don't I?"

"What if I don't give it to you?"

"I got plans. And none would be favorable to you."

Doc Buck heard Gaboney say, "Pay him an' we got shut of him. This is the last hide, remember?"

A silence and then Cotton said, "Come into the office. Pack the damn' hide in. I'll hide it until we get it back to the farm. Here, wait until I unlock the door."

Doc Buck heard the door swing open on noisy hinges. He waited a few seconds and then left his hiding place and went to the back door and entered silently behind the trio. He'd been correct. Cotton, Gaboney and Virgil. Moonlight streaming through the front windows outlined the trio clearly. Gaboney carried the hide wrapped in canvas.

Suddenly, the trio stopped. And Doc Buck heard Cotton say, "How come you're in my office, Jones?"

"I'm waitin' for that cow-hide carryin' them fever ticks," Deputy Jones said.

Jones' voice quavered. Doc Buck noticed that Gaboney had moved out a pace or two to Matthew Cotton's right. Virgil had instantly lain on the floor, face down. Virgil took no chances.

"What hide?" Cotton asked.

Gaboney said nothing.

"The one you got wrapped in that canvas," Doc Buck said.

Gaboney whirled, dropping the hide. For one second Doc Buck thought the farmer would go for his gun, and Doc Buck sank into the gunfighter's crouch his father had taught him, hand on his holstered weapon.

Gaboney saw this crouch, steadied, then said, "He sneaked in behin' us, Matt!"

Cotton snarled, "I got ears an' eyes!" and he spoke to Deputy Jones: "State the case against us, if you got one!"

Relief flooded the veterinarian. These men were not going to fight. They'd settle all in court in a civilized way.

But still, he remained in a crouch, hand on gun-butt.

"I arrest you three in the name of the law," Deputy Jones intoned, following the rule-book. "You're hereby accused of putting Texas Fever ticks in among local cattle to cause the owners to leave so you could then legally get their homesteads, Cotton."

"A long sentence," Cotton said. "You got the evidence?"

"That cowhide, for one thing," the deputy said. "Other evidence, gained by Doc Buck's activities."

Gaboney said, "They've got—"

He didn't finish his sentence. Matthew Cotton's sharp voice said, "You keep your big mouth shut, Gaboney! I'm doin' the talkin' here. They got nothin' substantial against us. Be careful and under no circumstances put your hand on your gun."

"No hands on guns." The mocking voice came from the plank sidewalk just outside the big open door. "Then you aim to die without firin' a shot, you night-ridin' bastards?"

All stared out the front door, even Doc Buck and Deputy Jones. Virgil even raised his head and looked. A wheel-chair stood just outside the door. And in that wheel-chair was Hatchet John Martin. And in the old cowpuncher's scrawny grip was a double-barreled twelve-gauge shotgun, the deadliest weapon Doc Buck had ever seen.

He'd seen just such a weapon in roaring, bucking action. Down in Abilene, Kansas. His father, Jack Malone, had handled it.

Where had Hatchet John got the shotgun? The Widow Hanson had said she'd hidden the deadly weapon in a place he did not know about and which was far beyond his reach.

"Hatchet John—" Doc Buck cried.
"This is my affair, an' none of yours. Jones, move a
"This is my affair, an' none of yours. Jones, moved a little to the right, please. I'd hate to plant a buckshot or two in your fat ass!"

Jones leaped two feet to his left.

"Right good action," the broken-down wheel-chair bound cowpuncher said. Then, to Cotton and Gaboney, "I recognized you two thet night you blew up thet dip tank an' the boulder busted my back. I bin waitin' for a chance like this. An' finally it come!"

"You'll have to prove that in court," Matthew

391

Cotton said.

"This ain't gettin' to but one court," the wheel-chair cowpuncher said. "An' it's a Shotgun Court."

"You'd kill us in cold blood?" Gaboney's voice held tremors.

"I sure would," Hatchet John said, "an' with pleasure. You never give me a chance—so I'm givin' you none. Drag for your guns, you two bushwhackin' bastards!"

Gaboney was the one who broke. He pulled his short-gun. He never got to fire. The shotgun's off-barrel blasted out lead and flame. The roar was terrible in the closed quarters. Gaboney was alive one second, dead the next. The blast separated his body in two parts just as Town Tamer Jack Malone's one shot had done to the Texas tough down in Abilene, Kansas. Cotton's gun leaped up.

Matthew Cotton got in three shots. Doc Buck was surprised at the big man's gun-speed and accuracy. Heavy legs spread wide, face torn by hate, the big land locator shot to kill—and kill he did.

All three slugs hit Hatchet John. They drove his wheel-chair backwards. The wheel-chair skidded across planks. It began falling to the left. Hatchet John let go with his second barrel.

The buckshot blast caught Matthew Cotton in the throat. It tore his head from his shoulders. The head hit the floor while the rest of Cotton was going down.

The head rolled to one side, tongue sticking out. It hit Virgil on the shoulder.

Virgil looked up. He stared into the dead eyes of the bloody head. He screamed and leaped to his feet. He ran blindly out the back door. Doc Buck let him go. He could be arrested later. Doc Buck pouched his unfired gun. He ran to where the wheel-chair lay with its

392

unmoving human cargo. Deputy Sheriff Jones was behind him.

"Holy God," the deputy said.

Buckbrush City was coming to life. Doors slammed. Dogs broke out in wild barking. Voices shouted, asked questions—and advanced on the land locator's office.

Hatchet John Martin lay on his belly. Blood showed on the dust below him. Doc Buck rolled the old man over. He saw immediately that blood had drained from the old man's face. Three bullets had pounded through his scrawny chest.

Doc Buck got to his boots. He heard somebody sobbing and glanced at the Widow Hanson, nose in her handkerchief, a white nightgown loose on her big figure. "I had that terrible shotgun hidden—up so high I thought he'd never get it, let alone find it. How did he find out where it was? How did he get it down?"

"Nobody'll ever know," Doc Buck said.

He was recovering his mental balance. He was glad he'd not had to use his gun. He heard a scatteration of horse hoofs and buggy wheels back in the alley. Virgil was making his getaway.

"I'll go get him," Deupty Jones said.

Jones ran for his horse. Buck was aware of Teresa standing on his left, Vivian Wilson on his right, but his mind right now was not on the two lovely girls.

He'd collect money owed him. He'd push hard. He'd get enough to bail out his creosote and kerosene. He'd get debts worked off on building a new dip tank. Creosote, kerosene and the dip tank would free Buckbrush Basin forever from animal parasites. Of course, there'd still be arrogant, insulting Ron Powers but logic told the vet each man living·sometimes in his life had to tolerate a Ron Powers.

He looked down on Vivian Wilson's blonde hair. He

glanced at Teresa's two dark braids. He then remembered Barbara Case. She was due any day now.

OMER ZANE GREY

Classic Tales of action and adventure set in the Old West! Characters created by Zane Grey live again in exciting books written by his son, Romer.

THE OTHER SIDE OF THE CANYON. Laramie Nelson was a seasoned Indian fighter, cowhand, and shootist, and above all a loner. Although he was one of the most feared gunmen in the Old West, his word of honor was as good as his sharpshooting.

__2886-7 $2.95

THE LAWLESS LAND. Back on the trail, Laramie Nelson confronted an outlaw chief, performed a top-secret mission for President Grant, and tangled with a gang of blockaders aiming to start a range war.

__2945-6 $2.95

KING OF THE RANGE. The Texas Rangers needed somebody who could ride all night through a blizzard, who could track like an Indian, and who could administer justice from the barrel of a Colt .44 — they needed Buck Duane.

__2530-2 $3.50